Lost Ecko

A MIRROR WALKER NOVEL

A. C. Mooney

ISBN: 979-8-9907439-2-2
Imprint: Independently published

Also by A. C. Mooney

The Mirror Walker Series

Mirror's Ecko (Book 1)

Ecko In The Dark (Book 2)

Lost Ecko (Book 3)

Coming soon

Cursed Ecko (Book 4)

This third novel in the Mirror Walker series includes many firsts for me. It is the first book that I am publishing all on my own, from start to finish. (Wish me luck. I'll need it!) Writing the books, I have found, is the easy part. Everything that comes after is infinitely more difficult. I bumbled my way through the publication of book one and book two, and many things that I intended to include got left out.

This story, this wild, amazing adventure, has lived inside me for many, many years. I know the characters. I know how they think, how they feel. They are very, very real to me. When I write, it all plays out like a movie as I type out each scene. I can see each character. I can clearly hear their voices. I hear the music playing in the background, songs that perfectly fit the scenes. I intended to include those songs at the end of each book, my own personal playlist for each chapter. Books one and two did not get their playlists. Oops. Again, all I can say in my defense is, becoming a published author is *hard*.

Lost Ecko is the first in the series to include the playlist. (Who knows? Perhaps I will eventually add the playlists for *Mirror's Ecko* and *Ecko in the Dark* on my website.) It also includes my very first dedication, even though I had carefully planned one for each of the previous books.

So, while the message has been altered a bit and is certainly being delivered later than I had planned, the person that I am making my first dedication to remains the same. And that's ok. It fits better here anyway.

For my sister, who from day one, has been my most dedicated and staunch supporter. Thank you for everything, and I do mean everything. For taking the time to edit out all my numerous mistakes and for making fabulous suggestions. For the all-nighters that you pull in order to read each new book, just as soon as it gets completed. For always expecting it to be in your email the very minute that I type The End. For anxiously awaiting each new book to be published so that you can be the first to buy it.

Thank you for the constant, unwavering support. For believing in me and my story. For perpetually cheering me on. You never let me give up. You never let me quit. You are, and will always be, my very own Lenore's Pearl, one of this world's greatest miracles. IYKYK (And if you don't know, you'll have to read book 4, Cursed Ecko, to figure it out!)

Jennifer, Lost Ecko is for you. I would be lost without you.

Table Of Contents

Scream patch
OBLERIAN
Plains
of the
Damned
Isle of
Despair

Black Forest
Elven Forest
The Field of Screams
and Broken Dreams
Sorrow
Marshes
Tangled
Woods
Dead Forest

Prologue: Ecko

LOST

During her early years in school, probably second or third grade, young Ecko learned that if she ever became lost, perhaps in the woods behind her house or maybe in a forest during a family camping trip, the best thing to do would be to sit down on the ground and wait for someone to come and rescue her. Just sit right down and wait for help to arrive. That was her teacher's best advice. After all, it's what *she* had been taught during her own elementary school years, and so she thought it prudent to pass that brilliant nugget of knowledge along to all her own students.

"Sit down and wait. Do not wander around, looking for a path that will lead you back to your loved ones, lest you further lose yourself. You wouldn't want to wander deeper into whatever unchartered, perhaps hostile, and dangerous terrain you've lost yourself in, would you? Of course not! Sit down, call for help, loudly and often, and just wait to be rescued."

But young Ecko had so many questions. She'd had so many arguments, none of which had her teacher appreciated. "Why would you just sit there and do nothing to help yourself? Just sit and *wait?* For how long? An hour? Two? Ten? A day? Two days? Ten?" She'd then pointed out that she would be dead if she sat still for ten days, waiting for a rescuer to lead her to safety.

The longer she thought on it, the more questions arose. Did she have any survival gear on her person on this failed venture? Did she have food? Water? Proper clothing against the elements? Why hadn't she thoroughly prepared herself for a walk in the woods or a camping trip in a forest?

Why couldn't she just look for her own way out? Why couldn't she leave a trail to show which directions she had traveled in? Perhaps mark the paths that she chose so that if she got turned around, she'd find those marks and know what paths not to take. Why would she be lost in the first place? Why would she be all alone? Where was her family? Where was her group, her people?

Most importantly, and the burning question that her mind repeatedly returned to, what if, just *what if* she meekly sat down and waited… *and no one came?*

Meekly sitting down to wait for a rescue that may or may not *ever* come had made absolutely no sense to young Ecko. It makes even less sense now that she's grown. Now that she's actually, truly lost. Now that there is no one, *no one* to help her. It's exactly like she'd told her teacher all those years ago, no matter how adamant that she'd been that *she* was the grown up so therefore *she* was right. "You're just a child, Ecko. I am older and I have more knowledge and life experience, so stop arguing!"

Young Ecko had stopped arguing, but only because she truly didn't like conflict. She did not want to draw unwanted attention to herself. She tried, even at that tender age, to always, *always* remain invisible. But it still made no sense whatsoever. Period.

Well Teacher, no one is coming to rescue her, no matter how long she sits and waits for some imagined hero. There are no heroes here. Oblerian is a terribly cruel and ugly world, a vampire world, where everything is food for something else. Nearly every single thing that has a life force is predatory. Nearly everything that she has encountered has tried, in one way or another, to unalive her. Shoot, even the deaders don't stay dead here, as proper death etiquette demands. Oh yes, the dead openly roam the land as freely as the living. She *hates* deaders. More than anything, ghosts and spooks and spirits terrify her.

But to be fair to that hapless, clueless teacher, Earth is a far more suitable place for 'waiting to be rescued' than Oblerian is. It's much more accommodating to helpless victims. Earth does not have places like the Sorrow Marshes, a haunted swamp that is ruled by a malevolent spirit. A *conscious* swamp, intent on trapping lost souls. A swamp that is determined to hold and cradle its victims in the endless depths of mud and slime, in its rot and decay and doom. Forever.

This is where we take up Ecko's story. Lost in a dreadfully dismal swamp, the spirit of the Sorrow Marshes persistently tracks and haunts her. It follows along, constantly whispering in her ear, begging her to stay. "Just sit down. You're *so* tired. Sit down and rest, just for a moment."

She knows better. To sit still and just wait are the worst things she could ever do in the Sorrow Marshes. That's how the GloomDooms were created. Poor lost souls who wandered the swamp until they became dispirited and lost all vestiges of hope, they sat down and just never got back up. The swamp rushed in. It *took* them. It grew onto them, grew *into* them, anchoring and binding them to the marsh forevermore.

The roots and moss and lichen and slime cover them, making them look like dead tree stumps submerged in the foul, dank water. They are still alive in there, conscious and aware, but unable to move. They will never leave. They will never be freed from the clutches of the spirit that haunts the Sorrow Marshes.

She refuses to go out like that. She will not succumb to the spirit's influence. She will never 'just sit down and wait' to be rescued. She must save her own self, not to mention her beloved, bratty companion. Boodark the Brave. Boodark the Wounded. Boodark the cursed, wingless pixy that she carries in a crocheted rope basket against her breast. Boodark… her ugly little orc-bat buddy.

Left with no other recourse and with no foreseeable heroes' forthcoming, Ecko trudges on and on through the Sorrow Marshes. She *must* make it out of this terrible swamp, for him, if not for herself. The last words he said to her, before he lost his ability to speak, play on repeat in her mind, spurring her onward. "*I falter.*" Over and over and over, those weakly whispered words that were uttered to prepare her for his upcoming death play on a neverending loop. They haunt her. They slay her. They tear giant holes in her heart as she continuously peeks into his blankets to check on him.

"Stay with me, Boodark," she whispers to him as her teardrops splash down onto his face and mix with his own. "Stay with me. I'll get us out of here. I promise."

Prologue: Samara

Girls Just Want To Have Fun

The taxi driver nervously checks on the situation in his backseat as his foot presses the gas pedal down another notch. He steadily increases his speed even though he's already going well over the legal speed limit.

It should have been just another boring, mundane trip. A simple pick-up at the airport, an estimated seventy-three-minute drive, and an easy drop-off at a public facility. A quick, uncomplicated fare before he called it quits for the night and headed home to his one-bedroom apartment and his little yorkie terrier that's always happy to see him.

He glances back at her… again. He wishes with all his might that she had chosen to wave down a competitor taxicab. He doesn't need the fare this badly, and he would have gladly passed it up if he had known what he was getting himself into when he opened the door and helped the beautiful, young woman into his backseat.

Not that she's really done anything wrong. No, she isn't loud or disruptive or even rude. Nor is her companion, even if the man does seem a bit unhinged, rocking back and forth and unceasingly muttering to himself, as he is. She's a little *too* quiet. She's a little *too* still. A little too… *something*. He can't put into words exactly what is wrong with her or this entire situation, but wrong it is.

There's something dark and ominous about her, as if she has a foul, evil death-cloud clinging to her skin. She sits perfectly motionless, her back ramrod straight, hands clasped demurely in her lap. Her eyes focus on nothing that he can discern. They stare, unblinking at something only she can perceive. But that smile on her face, oh, that smile is *truly* what nightmares are made of. She reminds him of a ghostly monster from a movie, a demon creature that silently stands behind its victim, grinning an impossibly huge grin that stretches its face to unbelievable, creepy proportions.

His heart races in his chest and his breathing grows ragged and labored. It feels like there's not enough oxygen in the vehicle to sustain him, even though he has the air conditioning on full blast and his window is cracked to let in even more air. He takes a quick look at the GPS and barely manages to swallow back a moan of disappointment. They're only halfway to their destination, with thirty minutes still to go before he's free of her and her malevolent influence. He can only pray that whatever holds her attention will continue to hold it until then. If those eyes lift ever so slightly and meet his in the mirror, he very well might just send the car careening off the road and into the nearest light post. God, please have mercy on his soul.

Samara is very much aware that the driver has grown uncomfortable. That may be a slight understatement, though. He's practically trembling with fear, gasping and wheezing through nostrils flared wide… and she hasn't even done anything to him! Humans are so pathetic, so easily controlled and manipulated. And *so* much fun to play with, until they break, that is. They are disappointingly fragile creatures.

While the driver tries his best to get her to her destination as fast as he possibly can… *without* passing out from lack of oxygen, she's having her own minor dilemma. She can't decide who she wants to play with more, the terrified driver or the two men following her. What to do? What to do? There's so much fun to be had, right here in the backseat of this rented automobile!

She spent the first half of the trip with her attention focused on the two men that had diligently (though not nearly as stealthily as they thought) followed her from New York to Texas. Lenny and his paid subordinate, a shockingly wicked and lascivious man by the name of Mr. Chadwick, have decided that they want her, both for their own personal reasons. Lenny, who is a powerful drug lord, wants what all men in power desire… more power. Mr. Chadwick simply wants his every depraved fantasy to become a reality, and he knows that she is the only one that can make that dream come true.

Both men want her, and both men have vowed to not underestimate her and the incredible magic that she welds, but both are ignorant of doing just that. Take this trip, for example. They think that they're merely sneaking along behind her, just waiting for the perfect time to approach her and introduce themselves, offering up whatever promises and enticements they believe will convince her to join them. It never even crosses their minds that she already knows all about them and their ridiculous plans.

What they don't know is that she's been aware of their interest from the start. They know that she has magic, but they don't understand it. They know nothing of her Shadows. They don't realize that she's been with *them* the entire time they've been pursuing *her*. She had sent out a small whisp of her Shadows to invade their minds, and while she frustratingly could not access Lenny's mind, she easily infiltrated Mr. Chadwick's. She had learned everything she needed to know about Lenny and his intentions towards her. What she'd learned about Mr. Chadwick had come as a complete surprise, a deliciously welcome surprise, but unexpected, to say the least. Gentlemanly and proper, with impeccable manners and perfectly groomed on the outside, but filthy and wanton, with wickedly lustful desires on the inside. He was a shocking contradiction, and she couldn't help but be intrigued.

That is how she has entertained herself thus far, rifling through the delightful Mr. Chadwick's mind. And the things she's learned from his memories! Oh, she can't *wait* to make his acquaintance! She'll listen to Lenny's proposal, of course, but it's his dirty manservant that she truly wishes to get to know.

She drags her attention from the pleasurable pastime of raiding Mr. Chadwick's mind, lest she get too excited and overly worked up. She's on a mission, after all, one that she has put off for far too long, and she will not be distracted or swayed from her course. She had promised herself long ago that she would get revenge on her nauseatingly 'good' twin sister, the prim and proper Princess Ecko. She had vowed to destroy everything that Ecko held dear, and she's *almost* made good on that promise.

First, she murdered Ecko's entire family, right in front of her. Oh, the joy she derived from that! Then she switched places with her by using Ecko's own mirror magic against her! She had patiently waited for the perfect opportunity, and when her dumb sister (who has no business welding such immense power) accidentally opened up a mirror, guess who was right there waiting for such a blunder to occur. Right! The one and only Samara, that's who! It was a struggle, but she'd eventually managed to overpower her sister. She pulled Ecko through the looking glass to *her* world and effortlessly stepped through it to her dear sister's world. Now, Ecko is trapped on Oblerian, an ugly, harsh, and dying world while she gets to live a life of luxury and plentiful on Earth.

That in itself should be punishment enough. But it's not. She will not stop until everyone that Ecko loves has been taken from her. It was the one thing she dreamed about on all those long Pitches, those endless nights of suffering while it had been *her* trapped in a miserable existence on Oblerian. Fantasies of Ecko's downfall, of her absolute misery were what kept her going, even whilst her father tried his best to beat and torture obedience and mindless loyalty into her. It's what fueled her rage and strengthened her power. She will not be denied her vengeance.

Thoughts of her troublesome sister are interrupted as the car pulls into a crowded parking lot and comes to a rough, almost screeching stop in front of a very large, dismally ugly building. The driver, very close to hyperventilating, croaks out a hasty, "Here we are, ma'am!"

He does not get out to open her door and she grins when she sees his white-knuckled grip on the steering wheel. Aww, just look at him! He's so cute, trembling in fear before her like she's some sort of dark, vengeful god. She *could* stay and play, just for a little while… but no. As tempting as that is, she has other priorities to see to. Business first, pleasure after. She'll have all the time in the world to play her games and have her fun.

"Come along, Robert," she says to her nearly catatonic companion as she opens the door and climbs out. "Let's let this nice man be on his way."

She can't resist one tiny bit of fun though. She just can't. She leans into the driver's open window and allows her Shadows to rise up and fill her eyes until they become obsidian voids, blackas-pitch portals to Hell. "Do you need money?" she asks with feigned, exaggerated innocence.

"No!" the driver shouts as his own eyes just about bug right out of his head. "Oh, no ma'am! It's on the house!" Then, never taking his eyes off hers, he stomps on the gas pedal. The car lurches forward to the tune of tires squealing and his cries of, "Oh God! Please, deliver me from all evil!"

Samara throws her head back and howls out her laughter as she turns and approaches the building. It's time, at long last, to put the finishing touches on her revenge against her sister. It's time to hunt the old ones down and be done with it.

Regal Falls Psychiatric Ward for Troubled Teens holds the answers that she seeks. She's sure of it. There are only two people left in the entire world that Ecko loves, two old, decrepit geezers that surely don't have many years left in them anyway. She could just wait it out. They'll die long before her sister ever finds a way to return for them… *if* she ever manages it. The only way for Ecko to return is through a mirror, and there are no mirrors left on Oblerian.

But no. She won't do that. She won't wait for a natural death to claim her sister's loved ones. Where's the fun in that? She'll finish out this last Ecko-related mission and be done with her twin for good. Then she'll move on to more pleasurable pursuits… like visiting Mr. Chadwick's bedroom, with his hidden closet full of secret toys. She can't wait to play with him. It'll be her reward to herself when she sees this mission through, a treat of pleasure and pain and fun and games.

After all, isn't that what the song says? Girls just want to have fun.

Prologue: The Lokskell and Krispin

All According to the Plan

The Lokskell, the dark Shadow Lord who is more of a vengeful god than his daughter, Samara will *ever* be, paces the floor of his chamber as his spies check in. Not that he cares about *her*. He cares naught of the wayward girl-child that managed to escape his clutches by fleeing to a distant world called Earth. He cares nothing of what she's doing with the powers that she had inherited from him, nor what she will eventually become when she reaches her full potential. She is of no concern to him. She's out of his reach, and good riddance to her and her insufferable defiance. His main objective lies with her twin anyway. It always has. It's why he had created them.

Ecko is the one that he wants, the daughter that he needs. While Samara had inherited his own dark Shadow magic, Ecko had inherited her mother's mirror magic. Irredarrian magic. It was filthy Irredarrian magic that had trapped him here in Sheol castle a thousand years ago, and it'll be Irredarrian magic that will release him.

Ecko's mother had been the cosmos's only living Wandelaar, a powerful being with the ability to travel through the mirrors. He had not been successful in taking the magic from Laelynn, no matter how badly he hurt her. And hurt her he certainly had. He tortured her for years, trying in vain to force her to give up her magic to him. Oh, how he tried! But she was a stubborn, willful woman and she had clung to her powers like her life depended on it. Willful bitch.

Consequently, Laelynn had passed those headstrong and defiant traits on to their daughters…to *both* of them. Irredarrians are powerful and fiercely proud. They do not break easily, but they *can* break. He should know.

Samara does not possess an ounce of Irredarrian magic. She is no use to him. But Ecko, oh, now Ecko holds a tremendous amount of magic. Not only did she inherit her mother's full Wandelaar power, but it seems that she had also, somehow been blessed (or cursed, depending on who you asked) with a substantial amount of… something else.

There's something *more* to her. Something unheard of, that he just can't figure out, something with unparalleled perimeters and unknown origins. Something wild and magnificent, perhaps even omnipotent. It is beyond anything he has ever encountered, and it mystifies him. It draws and compels him, even as the formidable and turbulent nature of it warns him to tread carefully with her. Perhaps he'll be able to figure it all out when he finally meets her. Perhaps he'll be able to unravel the great mystery of her when she stands before him, face to face, at long last.

But oh, how he covets that power! Not to mention that this daughter is his only hope of escaping the imprisonment that her ancestor had cursed him to.

The Vika Vakooja, a roach-beetle spy bug crawls from a crack in the ceiling, quickly scuttling down the wall, across the floor, and up the nearest table leg. Its spikey, little legs click-clack as it darts across the stone tabletop until it comes to a stop beside his wine goblet. And then it waits.

He wastes no time. He sends a bit of his Shadows into the bug's mind, quickly reading every scrap of information that the Vika Vakooja collective has gathered on his elusive daughter, watching the entire collection in the form of memory pictures. The bugs don't think or communicate with spoken words. They only relay back what they have seen.

The images show his daughter wandering in the Sorrow Marshes, lost and confused, but still stubbornly fighting to escape the spirit of the swamp's influence. Such fire! Such determination! She should have given up by now. She should have succumbed to the sadness. Not many survive it.

The scene disappears and is replaced with the images of the blue creature that tracks her. Krispin was Samara's lover, and he is determined to get her back. But unbeknownst to him, he is tracking the wrong sister. He thinks that he's closing in on his lover, but he'll soon be meeting Ecko instead. His rage will be absolute when he catches up to her and realizes that his mate is gone for good.

The images disappear, indicating that the spy bug has no more news to share. He reiterates his orders for the Vika Vakooja collective to continue its reconnaissance at all costs, promising dire warnings of unending and agonizing pain should they fail him. Then he pulls his Shadows from the Vika's mind and sends it on its way.

He leans back in his chair and raises his eyes to the ceiling as he contemplates the possible outcomes of the rapidly approaching confrontation. Smug satisfaction tugs the corners of his lips into a smile. His plan to trick the blue creature into capturing Ecko has thus far worked in his favor, but the true test has not yet unfolded.

Krispin is a cold-blooded creature, reptilian in nature. But his obsession with Samara is an all-consuming, hot-blooded, driving need. Above all else, he is a man in love, with all the raging testosterone that goes along with that debilitating affliction. His body burns with white-hot lust for his mate. His heart yearns to own and protect what he has claimed as his own, and he has a head full of rage towards anyone who dares look in her direction.

A frown slowly wipes the grin off his face as he realizes that Krispin's desire for Samara, that same driving force that has him mistakenly pursuing Ecko for miles across the harsh Oblerian terrain, could very well be the defining factor in seeing all of his well-laid plans foiled. Krispin will be enraged beyond all reasonable comprehension when he finally catches up to his target and realizes that he's been chasing Ecko and not his beloved

Samara. When he learns that his lover has left him, that she has fled to Ecko's Earth… he will undoubtedly lash out.

This is where things may get tricky. If all goes according to his plan, Krispin will merely bloody his daughter up a bit and then take her prisoner. Hopefully, he'll want to figure out a way to use her to get Samara back, perhaps use her as a trade for his lover. If that's the case, he'll carry her back to his home until he can figure out what his next move is.

But he'll be walking right into a trap. There are no less than thirty of the Lokskell's best henchmen waiting to waylay him. They have orders to seize the prize, dispose of the troublesome Krispin, (for good this time) and then deliver her straight into her father's patiently waiting, open arms.

That is the ideal outcome, but it will only happen if Krispin doesn't let the rage rule his actions. If he is beyond all rational thought, he'll blindly and foolishly attack, reacting purely on instinct with punishing fury to guide him. He'll want to beat the Samara imposter to brutal, bloody death, perhaps tear her apart with his bare hands. Brute strength he has aplenty, and his anger will make him even more lethal.

The Lokskell can only hope that his desire to win his lover back will outweigh his need to punish the one responsible for her disappearance. He is not a dumb creature. He is actually quite intelligent and crafty, but he possesses no magic whatsoever, and he is utterly ruled by his passion for Samara.

Ecko, on the other hand, is incredibly powerful, but her magic seems erratic and unstable. If she had any control over it, Krispin would be no match for her. Her inexperience and her lack of training will give the blue creature a fighting chance, but what will he do with that chance? Will he think it through and come to the realization that the sister is the only way to get Samara back, or will he squander that opportunity by allowing his anger to consume him?

Perhaps Ecko's magic will even prevail. She's managed to survive thus far, and Oblerian is not an easy world to endure.

Maybe she'll even take Krispin out of the equation entirely. She is no killer; she's much too innocent and pure of heart for that. But she is new to magic, and the sheer amount of power she's been given is unprecedented. She's overwhelmed by it, untrained and ill prepared, with no one to teach and guide her. She's like a babe, clumsy and accident prone, stumbling in and out of one disaster after another. Gods only know how she's managed to keep herself alive for as long as she has.

The Lokskell pushes away from the table with a grunt of irritation. He can't continue to sit there worrying over what could happen. There's just no way to predict how it will all play out. All he can do is hope that his plan unfolds perfectly, with Krispin taking Ecko as hostage.

No matter what the outcome may be though, the odds do not seem to be in Krispin's favor. If his rage drives him to slaughter his daughter, he will slice that blue bastard into a thousand pieces and scatter the fragments to every corner of that land. If he (unwittingly) delivers Ecko to him, well, he'll *still* kill him, but not nearly as brutally… and that's only if his daughter's erratic magic doesn't do the deed for him.

The sound of the door slamming behind him reverberates though the halls of his castle as his long-legged stride eats up the distance between his study and the women's quarters. He can think of no better way to distract himself than by paying a visit to his lovely ladies. He'll while away the hours in their beds until his spies return with an update on his daughter.

The guards immediately step aside as he approaches, and he snarls through his teeth as he realizes that he has unconsciously and mechanically headed straight to *her* door. He shouldn't even be in this section of the castle. His intention had been to go to the west wing, where the rest of his ladies reside. He keeps *her* separated from the others, her chambers guarded day and night by his henchmen.

He wants her like no other. He *always* wants her, but he shouldn't. It enrages him, the wanting. The craving. She is nothing more than a prisoner, same as all the others. Beautiful, yes, but they are *all* beautiful. He should not desire her so. But time and time again, it's *her* that he seeks out.

He whirls around and storms back down the hall, and the guards automatically move back into position in front of her door. He has no patience for her today. In fact, he has no patience for any of them now. He's furious, his head full of brutal, murderous inclinations. And while he does not mind bloodying his ladies a bit here and there, he has no desire to take their lives. The state of mind that he suddenly finds himself in promises violence and bloodshed, so he changes course yet again and heads towards the dungeons instead. Oh yes, there will be blood. The rage demands it.

The Roots of Sadness

Ecko

Miserable to the depths of her soul, Ecko wades through the knee-deep sludge, her head bent low with fatigue and her heart heavy with unspeakable sorrows. Boodark's been crying for the past two hours, silent tears in a never-ceasing trickle without a single word of explanation. Indeed, without a single word, period.

He's stopped talking. No matter how much she pleads and begs, her loud-mouth chatterbox little friend remains silent, his words all dried up and withered away. The last words he said play on a loop inside her mind. "I falter." And he is. He *is* faltering. She's losing him. If she doesn't get him out of this abhorrently vile swamp and find help, he will surely perish.

So, on and on she trudges through the thick, clinging mud that wars against every step that she takes. She has made it, finally, to the heart of the Sorrow Marshes. She does not need to be told that this is where most lose their way, their hope, and their lives. The very air is heavy with sadness and hopelessness, and broken, withered dreams dance like ghosts through the trees. There are no signs of life here, nothing to indicate life has ever been here. No buzzing of insect wings, no croaking of frogs, no splashing of creatures diving into the water to escape her trespass into their domain. No tall, rustling grasses, nor reeds, nor pads for frogs to perch upon. The only living things in sight are the trees (Debatable. They have no leaves, no new growth) and the mosses that cling to them and hang down from their bare, spindly branches. It's gloomy here. Sad. Empty. Unwelcoming. Her heart aches with loneliness and burden.

When she stumbles onto a large stone slab, she decides to set up there just long enough to see if Boodark will eat something…at least get him to drink some water. He refuses to open his mouth for the soup, but she manages to get a tiny bit of water into him. Not enough, not nearly enough. She lays back on the stone, just for a minute, and looks up. She's desperate to see something, *anything* other than marsh and mud and trees. She wants to see the sky, even if it *is* grey and bleak as the mud. But the trees have grown so tall that she can no longer see the sky. They blot out the light and drench the world in such dismal depression that even Eeyore would pack his bag and find a cheerier place in the Hundred Acre Wood to build his little stick home.

She sighs miserably and rolls onto her side to stare out at her dreary, depressing surroundings. She's so tired. Maybe she can take a nap… just a small one. Just long enough to catch a second wind. Maybe they could just stay here, set up camp, get some *real* rest, and then get a fresh start in the morning. Maybe….

A loud '*Creeeaaakkk*' sound and a slow, almost imperceptible movement from the corner of her eye puts a stop to thoughts of resting and makes her sit up. A tree stump, covered in a thick layer of dark green moss is *moving,* twisting itself in her direction. *The trees really are coming to life,* she thinks as her heart speeds up with apprehension. But when a pair of bright blue eyes suddenly pop open, she can see that it's a *person*, blackened with mold and filth and covered in patches of lichen and slimy, green algae.

A GloomDoom, it *has* to be. Boodark told her that the swamp was full of them. And *this* one's staring right at *her*! So clearly can she make out the shape of him that she wonders how she hadn't been able to see it before. The roots below him aren't growing *down* into the swamp as tree roots do, but up *out* of the water. They latch onto him and anchor him down, rendering him immobile…. Just another stump in a world full of tree stumps. And now she's wondering just how many of the 'stumps' that she'd passed right by without a second glance had been people… people lost to the Sorrow Marshes.

She stares at the closest one… (*Please* be a tree stump!) So close that she can reach out and touch it, *if* she had the slightest desire to, that is. Which she *doesn't*. It very well could be a person under all those tangled roots, contorted into some painfully twisted position. She leans in, peering intently…. Brown eyes full of tiny black root/veins pop open. A mouth stretches wide in a silent, horrified scream, a blanket of moss covering its tongue and sprouting from the cracks between its teeth.

"Time to go Boodark," she announces as she hastily straps her bag back on and settles his basket back in place. Whether the GloomDooms had intended it or not, they'd probably just saved her from their very same fate because in the moments before they started waking up, she'd wanted nothing more than to just sit there on that rock and give up, at least for the rest of the day. They'd set her mind right back where it needs to be… in terrified, 'get the heck out of here' mode. Because fear is now the only thing stronger than her sorrow. Boodark isn't the only one faltering. She is beginning to lose her hope, succumbing to the whims of the spirit that dwells beneath the Sorrow Marshes.

Fear is the only thing strong enough to drive her now. Fear for Boodark, fear of failing and the two of them becoming permanent residents of the Sorrow Marshes force her to put one foot in front of the other. But they're slow, grudging steps as she continuously checks on Boodark's condition. She knows intuitively that she won't make it out of the swamp if he falters.

She's crying now too. She can't stop it. The tears steadily pour from her eyes and drip down her face. The GloomDooms wake and turn towards her as she plods by, their stiff wooden joints creaking from having lain dormant for so long. She doesn't even look at them anymore. She no longer cares if they sleep or if they wake. She's not sure she would care even if they got up and started following her. She doesn't so much as flinch when she suddenly plunges into mud so deep that it brushes against the bottom of Boodark's basket. What does it matter that it's become so thick that it's like trying to walk through a deep pool of cold molasses? Why should she care how long it takes to complete each step? She's not sure she cares about anything at all.

The way forward is so *hard,* but she refuses to stop, refuses to stand still, even for a moment. She no longer remembers or even cares *why* she must keep going, she just subconsciously knows that she must. And although her steps only move her forward an inch at a time, and inch forward is still forward. It's still moving. She has not stopped, and she has not *yet* given up all vestiges of hope. Not quite yet.

She pushes the shirt swaddling aside to peek in and check on Boodark. She *hates* that unfocused gaze that just stares up at her, stares *through* her without seeing. She loathes his quiet, his stillness, and his tears that just won't stop coming. It's *wrong*. He should be flying beside her right now, laughing at her ignorance and hurling insults, calling her a big dummy. He should be asking if they can stop to eat again, pestering her about what they'll eat when they finally do stop…. *if* she will ever take pity on him and stop trying to starve him. He should be driving her crazy with his endless inquiries about Earth food and foodorators and flowers and elastic and plastic. This cannot be the end of all that. This cannot be the end of Boodark the Great, Boodark the Fearsome, Boodark the Annoying. Boodark…. her piggy little orc-bat friend.

She strokes his hair, sobbing and pleading, both of their faces so wet with tears it seems like there are faucets inside their eyes and someone's left the water running. She doesn't know what to do and she goes into full-on, hysterical panic mode when Boodark's eyes roll back into his head, nothing but the whites visible. And then he's convulsing, his body tensed and jerking with seizures. She snatches him up out of the basket…he's choking! He's choking on his own swollen tongue!

She thrusts her finger in his mouth and dislodges it, pulling it out of his throat to clear his airways. She ignores the teeth that cut her finger to the bone as she holds his tongue down so that he doesn't swallow or bite it. She sobs from the torment of watching her friend die in her arms. Because that's what's happening, isn't it? He's faltering right before her eyes and she's just standing there allowing it to happen. She rages inside at being useless and powerless to help him. He won't stop convulsing, his poor body tensed with one spasm after another.

"What do I do? What do I *do*!" she whisper/yells. She's helpless and desperate and she feels absolutely *crazed* inside. Her magic flares to sudden, intense life and her hands tingle for one brief moment as the world around her plunges into a Pitch of her own making… a Pitch that she can see clearly in. It's not true Pitch, it's merely the magic affecting her eyes, making it look as if the world's gone dark.

She blinks at the trees around her, trying to figure out what her magic is up to this time. She has about half a second before the 'weird' kicks in to wonder what her eyes look like with this new aspect of her magic. And then she couldn't care less about what they look like; all she cares about is what they're doing. She throws her arms out for balance as her eyes begin to oscillate. It feels like her pupils are quivering, vibrating at high speed. Everything is dancing, shivering in place. The trees, the GloomDooms, each strand of moss, they tremble and quiver as if the entire world is some sort of snow globe and God is shaking it to wildly rattle the contents.

She glances back down to the little bundle in her arms and he's the only thing that's not trembling and vibrating. He's gone oh, so still and silent. Is he…???

And *now* she starts screaming. She's screaming and screaming and just *screaming*. She throws her head back and all that pent-up anguish and fear and rage bursts out of her mouth and pours up into the air in a black cloud of desperation. It's as dark as anything that Samara has ever produced, but it's an entirely different kind of magic. It may share the same primary color of her twin's foul smoke, but that's the *only* similarity they share. It doesn't look (or *feel*) like Samara's icky, sludgy black Shadows, but more like the hazy wisps associated with auras. It's a pretty thing, deepest black but swirling with purple and blue and red wisps and dotted with tiny, silver mirror sparkles. It flows up out of her and quickly spreads as far as she can see, blanketing the swamp in a starry, Northern lights kind of atmosphere. It's a nebula inside a dark, vast galaxy, full of glittering stars and black holes, swirling with cosmic dust and burning gases of all colors.

This black smoke bears no evil taint, no ill will. What it *is*, though, is all insistence and forceful determination, born of desperation and dire need. Its sole purpose is to fill that need, repair the damage, fill the void inside of her from whence it came from. It's powerful and unpredictable and wild as the wind.

'Beware! Danger!' The words ghost through her, leaving chills of premonition in their wake. No, it's not a bad magic, but it *could* be. It could very easily be twisted into a force of evil because of the sheer will of its nature…. because it will do whatever needs to be done to fix what broke inside of her, repair and eradicate whatever damage and desperation had brought about its birth. No matter the cost, it will find a way. It will not be denied. And *that* could be a very, very bad thing. Although its intent isn't evil, the resulting effects could very well be destructive and detrimental to all that stand in its way.

She shivers and pushes those thoughts… the 'what if's' and 'what could happens' into a mental box and slams the lid shut. She's not evil or bad, therefore neither will her magic be. Period.

Her attention gets pulled away from the brilliance of the galaxy that now illuminates the Sorrow Marshes when her right hand begins to tingle. *'But why just my right hand'*, she wonders as she lifts it up, fully expecting it to be engulfed in familiar blue energy. But that's not the case this time. There's no snapping electric force dancing over her skin, blue or otherwise. Instead, her hand is brilliantly lit up from within, radiating a bright light that shines right through her skin. She watches as the glow begins to lift, to rise up from the bottom of her hand and gather in her fingers, just like the 'lava' rising to the top in a lava lamp. The light bubbles upwards, drawing itself up from the bottom of her hand to gather higher and higher, pooling in her fingers.

She holds her hand up and out, away from her face as her fingertips grow brighter and brighter. Her wayward brain chooses this moment to remind her of that old movie called E.T, the one about the strange little alien that just wants to go back home. He had a light in one of his fingers too.

A sharp, almost hysterical giggle bursts from her lips when she realizes that she *is* the strange extraterrestrial that just wants to get back home. But then she forgets all about E.T as the glow drifts up out of her fingertips to form a brilliant silvery ball of light that floats just out of reach.

"Oohhhh," she breathes in wonder as it hovers for just a moment before her eyes. Then it zooms away… *fast*, zigzagging through the trees, lighting up and illuminating a path through the swamp. Her vibrating pupils zero in on that path and her vision tunnels, following the trail that the sphere of light creates. It's almost as though she's following right behind it, like she's being *dragged* along with it.

She's seeing everything in fast forward as they hurl forward… past countless trees and GloomDooms and a *massively*, long slithery thing that disappears beneath the water the very instant that her eyes spot it. Past a huge, birdlike animal with legs so long that it must stand *at least* as tall as she does, and a patch of swamp where a thousand bald, pink and grey-skinned creatures writhe against one another.

She follows in the wake as the ball of light shoots right up out of the swamp and plunges down into another forest, different from the Black Forest that she'd left behind. And then they slam into a tree. A huge, mammoth tree… the freaking Goliath of the Giant tree tribe. A tree as tall as a high-rise building and easily as wide as the length of two school buses put together, end to end. Then they're *inside* the tree and the tree is a *house*, with an old*ish* woman standing at a table, busily mixing a concoction in a large wooden bowl. Her head lifts and she stares right into that tunnel, down the path that the silver light has made… all the way to where she stands in the swamp until their eyes meet. Ecko can see her clearly, every detail of her, right down to the color of her eyes.

The old*ish* woman smiles. "Hello dear. I've been waiting for you." And then she takes in the tears on Ecko's face and the wild, desperate magic in her eyes. The smile dies away as her own eyes lower to the bundle in Ecko's arms. "Bring him. Quick as you can, bring him to me!"

The silver ball of light suddenly pops and goes dark, just like a burst light bulb. And it takes its magic with it. The lighted path recedes, *rewinds*. It moves backwards, *fast*, retracing its trajectory and shrinking as it goes until it snaps back *into* her and returns her vision to normal. Normal all but for the vibrating, that is, but even that seems to be slowing.

She cries out as a huge gust of circling wind comes out of nowhere. She hastily grabs onto the closest thing to her… which just so happens to be a GloomDoom. Its wild mane of hair, tangled with moss and ivy vines, flies up to surround them all as she presses herself up against it, protecting Boodark's little body as best she can between them.

The whirlwind sucks her black 'galaxy' magic up, spinning it round and round until it becomes a massive and terrifying tornado, a funnel that looks like it sucked up the Aurora Borealis night skies with its stars and swirling, colored lights. The funnel draws in every last trace of her black galaxy cloud and then it begins to move away from her, following the exact path that the ball of light had taken. It roars forward with a sound loud as a freight train and it spews the galaxy cloud back out as it goes. She watches, wide-eyed, as the starlit, black haze settles back down like a blanket over the path. It hovers three feet above the water like Aladdin's magic carpet, only this carpet is in stretch limo form because it's a *long* carpet that extends as far as she can see.

It mimics the path that the silver light had taken, winding and twisting through the trees and disappearing out of sight. The twister appears to be laying down a path made of her 'galaxy smoke' that she can follow, a path that will lead her directly out of the swamp! All she'll have to do is follow the black smoke road!

But for now, she clings to that GloomDoom for all she's worth as the wind tugs at her, roaring and bellowing like an angry giant. She holds onto it until the twister's gone, until it's out of sight and the sound of it is fading off into the distance. Just when she thinks the magic is spent and it's safe to let go, the ground begins to rumble. Not vibrate, not tremble, but rumble…violently.

"Earthquake!" she shouts and then (nonsensically) corrects herself and changes it to "VampireLandquake!" because she's not *on* Earth, is she? Her mind can take the dumbest turns… in the worst possible moments.

She hugs that GloomDoom like it's a long-lost friend as the ground bucks and shakes and quakes. Mud and swamp water slosh up and splatter in every direction, and her heart thuds with fear as the trees moan and groan…*and then they begin to move*! The trees are uprooting themselves! All those long, winding roots are pulling themselves right out from under the layers of mud and sand and swamp slime. The sound of them lifting up out of the muck is even louder than the tornado had been … all *roaring* creaks and groans, and deep, unsettling rumbles. She wants to hold her ears to block out the noise, but that would require her letting go of the GloomDoom and trying to stand on the wildly bucking ground without anything to hold onto to keep her upright and on her feet. If she lets go, she will surely fall and get swallowed up in the mud. And so, she continues to hold on even though the GloomDoom has opened its startled eyes and its shocked mouth only five inches from her own face. She leans back, putting as much distance between her face and *its* face as she can while still holding onto it.

If it wants to bite her nose off, it will probably succeed because her attention is (mostly) on what the trees are doing.

And what they're doing is nothing short of amazing… absolutely freaking terrifying, but amazing, nonetheless. The thousands, *tens* of thousands of roots are coming together to build a path, a walkway in the form of a bridge. They finish pulling themselves out of their dirt homes, homes that they'd never felt the need to leave before, and then lift up into the air and stretch themselves right through the hazy smoke path. The thickest ones reach and stretch towards one another and when they meet, they twine together and interlock. And then the long, thin ones join them. They wrap around each other, snaking in and out and around the larger ones. Thick vines descend from the tops of the trees, slinking down out of the branches like snakes. They knot themselves into the mix, adding additional support from above. Rhizomes and rootstalks slither in, helping to fill in the bare, empty spaces.

They all come together, working collectively until there's a bridge made entirely of roots and vines, suspended three feet above the swamp waters…. a long, winding root bridge that stretches throughout the remainder of the Sorrow Marshes… *for miles*. The magic smoke carpet settles down onto the new bridge, painting it with all the beauty of a nebulous galaxy. A brand new, magical root-bridge now stands where there hadn't been one just twenty minutes earlier. It may not guarantee safe passage through the swamp, but it will certainly provide an easier way through it. Her magic had not *instantly* solved all her problems, but it had improved her situation immensely. Ludo from Labyrinth could call the rocks, but apparently, she can call the roots.

The world quickly returns to normal at this point. Her eyes finally stop their wild vibrating and the darkness that had descended over her vision lifts, allowing her to see the Pale in its usual weak and muted light. The disruptions diminish, the turmoil finally subsides until the Sorrow Marshes is still and silent once more.

She turns and looks into the GloomDoom's wide, staring eyes and immediately shudders in revulsion. She can't help it. They really are horrifying and so traumatic that it actually hurts her heart to look at them.

"I beg your pardon," she murmurs because hey, manners matter even to (mostly) petrified tree stump people. She steps back away from it and looks down at Boodark and thank you, sweet baby Jesus, he's breathing! Small, shallow gasps, but breath means life. She kisses his beautiful, ugly, leathery face and realizes that they're both *still* crying. Her wild, unpredictable magic had provided a safer, faster way to travel, but it did not heal her friend. And it did *not* put a stop to the spirit of the Sorrow Marshes influence, because *still* it whispers in her mind. *'Sit a while. Rest. Be at peace here…Yesss, my love. Come to me. Join us.'* She shivers and sniffles through her tears. "Not today, Satan" she whispers in defiance. "Not today."

And then she hears…*things* behind her. Buzzy, humming, breezy sounds. *Wing* sounds… many, many wing sounds, like a plague of locusts descending to surround her. She clutches Boodark protectively to her chest; she can't bear to lay him back in his basket just yet, and she slowly, warily turns around to face whatever she's gotten herself into now.

Fairies. There are fairies *everywhere*. So many, so very many… a plague of fae instead of the locusts she'd been imagining. As much as she hates bugs and adores the fae, this scenario is so much more unsettling than if she had turned around to find mere insects. The fae are so unpredictable and wild, so potentially volatile… so *other* and alien in their ways and their beliefs. There's no way for her to know how to act or what to do. So, she does nothing, nothing but hug Boodark close and wait for whatever comes next. She knows without a single doubt that she's in peril and that she's very much at their mercy. There are too many of them for her to even attempt any sort of defense against an attack, if that is what they choose to do.

So, she merely watches them, studying them as she waits for them to reveal their purpose for surrounding her. Because she *is* surrounded. She couldn't run now if she wanted to. They hover in the air, hide behind tree branches, and peek through clusters of dangling mosses. They perch upon the fungus 'shelves' that climb up the trees and they hide inside tree knots. There's a cluster of lotus-type pods, massive ones the size of dinner plates, and each little hole has a tiny fairy head poking out of it. Everywhere she turns, there's some sort of fairy leaning closer to get a look at her. Several of them flutter in the air around her. Bold and audacious, *they* clearly don't care if she sees them. But the majority of them are trying to hide from her. They're trying to do so from positions where they can see her, but not be seen themselves. *All* of them are studying her just as intently as she's watching them.

Maybe they're waiting to see what *she's* going to do. Which is nothing. She's gonna do absolutely *nothing* because she doesn't want to provoke them. And also, because she's fascinated and thoroughly captivated, even while she's terrified. She's spent her entire life believing in the wee folk without ever once having laid eyes on them. Now they're right in front of her and she's overwhelmed, completely dazzled and humbled by their presence.

There are so many different *kinds* too, so many different clans! They're obviously all dark fae, but each clan is unique in their appearances. Some are as itty bitty as bumblebees, some as large as barbie dolls, with every size in between. The small group directly in front of her look like tiny bonsai trees. They're all shades of browns and greys with lines and deep grooves etched into their skin like wood grain, and knotty shoulder blades, elbows, and knees. Their hair is all wild, tangled tresses that resemble moss and leaves and twigs. Their faces appear to be hidden behind masks made of lacy tree fungus and lichen, beautiful, woody masks. It's not until one of the braver, more curious females flutters close to her own face that she realizes they're not masks at all. They're extra, external features that cover their delicate bone structure. Built-in masks, if you will.

There are RootFairies with long twiggy bodies, their scraggly hair made of stringy roots and tiny leaves. PoisonIvyFairies with their skin and hair colored to match the lethal, poisonous plant.

They have the longest, thickest green eyelashes, huge leaf-like wings, and they wear clothes made of ivy leaves. Delicate vines wrap around their wrists and ankles and climb up their limbs like intricate, decorative jewelry.

Then there's a small group of fairies that are *immensely* terrifying to look at. They have long bony fingers and tattered, crimson-red wings. Their faces are pale, and their large, black eyes are rimmed in blood red. None of that is too alarming, but oh, their *mouths*! Their mouths are stretched wide, *much* wider than they should be. They grin when they see her staring at them, those wide nightmare smiles full of sharp, jagged teeth. BloodFairies…they *have* to be. Boodark told her about these and the awful things they like to do. She mentally vows to keep her distance from *this* particular clan.

She shudders and quickly turns away, and her eyes land on a *very* large group of MushroomFairies. She takes note of how many different clans of shroom fairies there are. So many! And right at the front of the group… "Sephyr," she cries with a smile of glad welcome. "Sephyr of the Irukandji Mushroom clan, I'm so happy to see you again!"

Sephyr dips her head in a brief bow of greeting. "And you, Change-Bringer," she says with just the slightest trace of humor in her dark eyes. Ecko's own eyes guiltily dart to the swamp's new root bridge and then quickly return, brimming with sheepish embarrassment.

"I didn't *mean* to… It just happened!"

Sephyr grins. "Sephyr say true. Change follow where Ecko lead."

There's nothing she can say to that. She has no legitimate grounds for argument, seeing as how she'd just drastically altered the swamp.

"How did you find me?" she asks instead of attempting to defend herself.

The little mushroom fairy laughs. "*All* find you. Light shines *much* bright." Sephyr lands on a nearby tree branch to rest her fluttery little wings and then continues. "Sephyr follow. Sephyr watch. Speak true, Sephyr no think see you succumb to the Sorrows…. Also, your call *much* loud. Impossible ignore it."

Seeing Ecko and Sephyr greet one another like old friends, the wee folk as a whole appear to grow braver. Either that or they just get more curious and wish to move in closer to… whatever this is that's going on. Many of them are disguised as insects and plants, meant to blend in with their surroundings… clever little swamp dwellers. They brilliantly impersonate beetles, moths, stick-bugs, leaf-bugs and spiders. Some even wear discarded shells as clothing and hats to better mimic their buggy counterparts.

The SpiderFairies are 100% convincing in their arachnid display, so convincing that she doesn't even realize that they *are* fairies at first. They leave their hiding spots and descend down the trees, perfectly replicating creepy crawly spiders. Keeping a cautious eye on them, Ecko shivers with renewed revulsion… until they stand up on their own two feet and begin walking towards her along a low-hanging branch. Only then does she realize that they're fairies… fairies crawling about, wearing molted, discarded spider skins!

With the SpiderFairies completely exposed and out in the open, a swarm of fae, a veritable *army* of fairies disguised as insects and crawly, slithery things appear. They crawl out of every crack and crevice, creep from every nook and cranny and fissure. Wingless fae come out of hiding too, riding upon the backs of large beetles, dragonflies, spittler spidders, and strange hopping bugs that look like a mix between a grasshopper and a cricket.

And then she notices for the first time all the glowing eyes of the fae that remain hidden deep in the darkest recesses. They're concealed in the shadows, in the hollows of stumps and fallen logs where it's dark and moist. They're buried deep in tangles of tree roots, in the spaces directly above where the roots plunge into the water, where it's devoid of all light.

A group of fuzzy, furry ones with giant moth wings flutter in and settle upon the new bridge's support roots. They stare at her with huge, light-seeking eyes. They look so velvety soft and ….

"What do you want?" a voice beside her suddenly, *rudely* demands. She jerks her head around to look at the speaker, and for one heart-stopping moment she believes that it was the GloomDoom she'd been so up close and personal with just moments ago. But slight movements from the GloomDoom's lumpy, misshapen {shoulder?) draw her attention, and she realizes that it was a small, brown RootFairy that had spoken. An intimidating male, (as intimidating as a four-inch male can be) he is all knots and lumps and bumps, colored like tree bark. Nodules and bulging tumors protrude from his back, giving him a distinctly ginger-root appearance. Long, thin black roots stick up in every direction from his head, creating a wild mane of black root-hair. He looks angry, like *seriously* mad. Like he wishes he could make the swamp rise up and swallow her down into its depths, never to be seen again.

She just blinks at him like a scared owl while she stands there trying to figure out what she'll do if he decides to attack. He frowns even more ferociously than he already had been as he turns to Sephyr. "Is it dumb?" he asks. "You *said* it could be reasoned with but me thinks that you spoke untrue. It appears feebleminded to me."

Sephyr nods sadly, agreeing with his assessment. "She slow-witted, say true, but can yet function, *can* see reason. Much effort though."

Ecko bites back the smart aleck retort that's dancing on the tip of her tongue. Why does everyone on this world think she's dumb? And *must* they be so rude? She's standing right here where she can obviously hear every word of their discourteous conversation.

The RootFairy-man turns back and tries again, speaking slowly and dramatically enunciating his words. He uses hand gestures and pointing fingers as visual aids to help make her understand him better. "What. Is it. That you. Want?"

That does it. She's had all she can stands, and she can't stands no more. She's *not* simple minded. "I am not dumb!" she snaps and is instantly gratified when his eyes fly open wide. "I just don't understand why you're asking me what I want. I don't want anything…except to find my way out of this infernal swamp. *You* came to *me*, not the other way around. What is it that *you* want?"

If his eyes get any wider, his eyeballs will fall right out of the sockets. Surely, they will. "What mean you, you want nothing? You call. We come. We are free; we obey none. No ground stomper ever before has commanded the AkarFairies, but now we have no choice! We are *forced* to answer your call." His little nostrils flare and his tree-trunk chest heaves in anger. "Now say true, Change Bringer. Why call us to you? What. You. Want?"

Her mouth drops open in disbelief. "B,b,but I didn't call you! I don't even *know* you!" she stammers.

The RootFairy-man frowns in suspicion then points to the bridge. "Your magic called to the roots, forced them to make a path for you. Every fae clan in all of the Sorrow Marshes heard that call. *All* felt your need, but those of us with ties to the roots felt the pull… much, *much* strong. None could resist the need to come to you." He turns and gestures to the very large, very *angry* fairy mob behind him. "*We* are the RootFolk, the AkarFairies of the Sorrow Marshes. Every Root clan is here to answer your call."

She almost laughs at the absurdity of *her* commanding an army of fairies to help her, but thankfully she gulps the snickers back just in time. This is very serious, she realizes, and he is *not* someone that she wants to offend with an untimely fit of hilarity. "I'm sorry," she says instead. "I'm new to magic and I don't have much control over it yet. Things just sort of happen when I get overwhelmed. Truly, I don't want anything from you, and I certainly would never try to compel you or force you to help me. I free you from whatever holds you here."

The RootFairies whisper amongst themselves for a moment. They aren't smiling, but their angry scowls have disappeared. RootFairy-man bends his head down in the slightest bow and calls out, "We are released. We leave now, but we will remember that you could have made us slaves, and yet you chose not to."

The Root clans all quickly disappear, as if they're afraid that she may change her mind. RootFairy-man remains behind, watching her intently until all of his people are safely away. Then he nods his head in that regal, barely-there bow one more time and tells her, "You are *not* as dumb as you appear." And then he turns and follows his clan as fast as his wings will carry him. She realizes that in the fae way of things, he'd just given her as much of a 'thank you' as he could.

Several of the other clans follow suit. They flutter away with wary, backwards glances and crawl back into crevices, slipping back into the shadows. Sephyr stays behind, along with many of the mushroom clans. She waves a hand in a 'come forward' gesture and the crowd parts to allow a passageway for…

"My shoes!" Ecko cries out as she watches her lost sneakers fly through the air towards her, each one carried by a team of six Mushroom Darklings. She laughs with pure delight as the fae UPS delivers their packages to her. "Thank y…. aaahh!" She catches herself in the nick of time and her voice trails off when she realizes the blunder she nearly made. The fae don't like the words 'Thank you'. "Yeah, uum. I mean, I really appreciate this. I was sure they were lost forever," she says instead.

Sephyr grins and puffs her little chest out as she brags, "Sephyr find. Sephyr convince Irukandji clan carry!" Then she points to Ecko's hand. "You bleed," she adds.

She'd forgotten all about the wound. Boodark's health had declined until he'd had a seizure, (*I falter*) and he'd nearly choked on his own swollen tongue. His sharp little teeth had cut all the way down to bone when she stuck her finger in his mouth to dislodge it and open his airways back up. But of course, as soon as the fairy points it out, it starts throbbing mercilessly. She glances down at the finger that's *still* steadily dripping blood but immediately dismisses it. She knows that it needs to be dealt with, but she doesn't want to take the time to mess with it. "Yes, I know, but I don't really have time to bandage it. I have to find help for Boodark."

Sephyr's eyes drop to the bundle clutched to her chest. "What ails cantankerous one?"

She hugs him closer, protecting him as best as she can as she explains. "The Madar-gens stole his wings. I think he's gotten an infection. He told me that he was faltering and then he stopped talking. He went into convulsions, and I thought he was dying. I panicked, and that's when my magic came out and *that* happened." She points at the bridge and continues. "I really didn't mean to call the AkarFairies. I didn't even mean to call the tree roots."

Sephyr nods, "Say true; you a menace, Change Bringer."

Ecko solemnly nods back. What else can she do? She knows the Darkling's right… that she 'speaks true.'

The little fairy sighs heavily, as if the weight of the world lies upon her teeny tiny shoulders. "Come, Change Bringer. Follow." She starts to fly away, *in the opposite direction of the root bridge*, but turns back when Ecko does *not* follow.

"I can't follow you! I have to get out of the Sorrow Marshes… and the root bridge leads out. I have to get him some help. I don't think he'll make it much longer and I can't lose him. I just can't!" she wails with tears streaming once again.

Sephyr's face softens the slightest bit. "You no make it out before Pitch." She glances up at the sky and frowns. "Spidder Frost come at Pitchfall. Must hide. Must in shelter. Sephyr take you shelter." Then she gestures to Boodark. "Darkling help him." She points to Ecko's injured hand. "Darkling help finger. Stop the bleed. Come, Change Bringer. *Follow.*"

Wait…Spidder Frost? Oh *heck* no. She doesn't know what a Spidder Frost is, but it has the word *spidder* in it and that's what Boodark had called the flying spiders. And that means it's a big fat nope for her. Nope, nope, nope. She follows, grudgingly tromping back into the thick, deep mud.

"Are you sure you can help Boodark? I'll risk whatever a spidder frost is if you're not sure you can help him."

The rest of the fairies that had stayed behind fall in with them, fluttering alongside her as she struggles through the muck.

"Sephyr help," she assures her again. "Need bitterbark. Need cinderoot. Cinderoot easy. Enokitake clan provide. Bitterbark much hard. Much difficult. ThornHopper clans live in bitterbark trees. Much unfriendly. *No* allies with mushroom clans. *Change Bringer* convince. Threaten you must."

She frowns but nods her head in compliance. She doesn't want to make enemies, but she'll do whatever it takes to save her batty little friend. To distract herself from stressing over an unpleasant fight with ThornHopper fairies (whatever those are) she decides to stress over something far more distressing. "Umm Sephyr? Exactly what *is* this Spidder Frost?"

The little fairy pauses and waits for her to catch up to her.

"The Great Hatching! All spidder egg for this cycle hatch on this Pitch. Spidderlings will spill their webs into air, wind carry spidderlings away to new home. Webs cover swamp in thick, sticky layers. New hatchlings ravenous. Devour *all* in path. *All* must seek shelter this Pitch."

Ecko shutters at the thought of what would have become of her if Sephyr hadn't come along to warn her of the quickly approaching 'Spidder Frost'. She can't even… nope. She's not even going to think about it. "Why are you helping me?" she asks instead. "What made you decide to come back?"

All she says is, "Sephyr repay."

Apparently, she'd felt indebted. She had helped the Darkling, and now she's returning the favor. Works for her. She needs all the help she can get!

Find A Happy Thought

Ecko

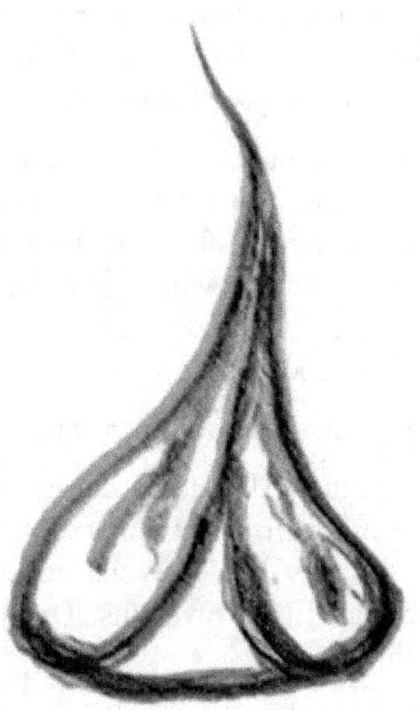

"We arrive," Sephyr calls out.

"Oh, thank you sweet baby Jesus," Ecko mutters under her breath. It's all she can manage through her huffing and puffing gasps. They've only been traveling for forty-five minutes or so, but that's a lifetime when every step feels like she's wading through setting concrete. Her legs and her lungs burn, and her back is a throbbing mass of pain. Oh, the things she would do for a long, hot bath!

She steps up beside her fairy guide and takes a look around. As promised, Sephyr has led her to a shelter, of sorts. It's some kind of bean pod, a *huge* one the size of a small car. It appears to have partially split open and spilled its contents long ago because it's completely dried out and browned with age. It dangles two feet above the ground from a thick, dead vine, swaying gently like a child's swing tied to a tree branch. It's charming, even if it doesn't look like it will be a safe place to hide from spiders. The split in the front is wide open… anything could crawl in while she sleeps!

Sephyr brushes away her concerns when she voices them. "Make barrier. Bar the way. Block spidderlings out," she insists with a careless shrug. *She* may not be worried about a plague of baby spiders crawling into her home and eating her alive, but Ecko certainly is. She opens her mouth to protest but the little mushroom fairy impatiently slashes her hand at her. "No time!" she demands. "Must hurry. Must *fast*! Need bitterbark to save cranky one." She turns aside and gestures to a small group of waiting fairies. "The Enokitake," Sephyr explains. "Say true, say *sad*, they all that remain of their clan."

The Enokitake's are albinos, milk white fairies with puffs of soft, fluffy white hair. Their wings, rimmed and veined in black, and their red eyes are the only other colors they sport. Skinny, long limbed, and standing close together as they are, they very much resemble the clusters of long, white Enokitake mushrooms back on Earth. They're mysterious and ethereal, with dainty, almost fragile features and delicate, gossamer wings, and she can't help but stare in wonder at their beauty.

Sephyr speaks up, snapping her out of her stupefied aww. "Enokitake home where cinderoot grows. Enokitake share."

The seven albino fairies flutter up to her carrying wads of red roots that very much resemble tiny intestines. One after another they drop their offerings into her hands. The last one, the only female in the group, lands onto her open palm. She points to Boodark and whispers, "I see."

Ecko's eyes jerk to Sephyr in alarm, but the Darkling insists. "Trust Nyra."

So that's exactly what she does. What other options does she have? She opens the swaddling so that Nyra can peer in. Boodark is no longer crying. He's staring out at nothing with dull, glazed eyes. She studies him for a moment, then asks Ecko if his skin is cold.

"Yes," she whispers. "He's much cooler than he's supposed to be. Why?"

Nyra and Sephyr nod at one another. "The Algrid-sick," they both say in unison.

"What does that *mean*?" she demands. "What's the Algridsick?"

Nyra quietly explains it to her. "It is the Numbing…a sick that happens *inside*, a sick that festering wounds and rot bring. Not all decay is of the flesh. Some take place in the heart. *His* began with his wounds but then settled into his heart." She sadly shakes her head. "The Sorrows got him. He should never have entered the swamp while he was injured. Heart and body must *both* be whole to survive the Sorrow Marshes."

Surely Boodark knew that, but he never said a word about it. She would *never* have brought him here if she'd known. And that's exactly why he hadn't spoken up. "But…he can be saved, right?" She turns to Sephyr. "You told me that you could help him!"

The Darkling holds up her tiny hands in a placating manner. "Calm, Change Bringer. Think calm! Sephyr no wish for root bridge *here*. Sephyr help him, but not *all* up to Sephyr. Up to him too. Must *wish* to live. *You* must convince him to fight."

She nods and blinks back the tears before they can fall. "I can do that. I *will* do that."

Nyra walks across her hand and lifts up a bundle of the intestine-like roots. "Cinderroot hot on the inside of the belly. It will make blood hot and burn infection out. You mash a whole bundle into paste. Feed him one bundle every hour. He will begin to fight it. *Force* him to swallow. He must. He must consume all. Understand?"

Ecko nods and tells her that she'll follow her instructions to the letter. She will make him eat every bit of it. "I understand, and thank…" Yet again, she barely catches herself in time to swallow her words back. How do you say thank you without saying thank you? They have given her the means to save her friend, the last thing she wants to do is to offend them. "If you ever need anything from me, I will do my very best to repay what you have given to me."

Nyra flashes her a ghost of a smile and then flies up off of her hand to rejoin her clan.

"Cinderroot only *half*," Sephyr reminds her. "Must travel to ThornHopper territory. Get bitterbark. Not far, but must hurry. Pitch comes. Spidder Frost comes. Leave cinderoot in DreamSnare pod." She points to Ecko's backpack. "Can leave big pouch too. Safe here."

Yeah, *that's* not happening. She doesn't want to offend the fairies, but there's absolutely no way she's leaving her stuff behind.

"Oh! Well, I *do* trust you. I know that it's safe if you say it is. But I feel more comfortable with keeping my backpack with me. Besides, I may need it. If the ThornHoppers refuse to help me, maybe I have something they'll take as a trade. I have some food left. Boodark loves granola bars. Maybe they'll like them too."

Thinking about food draws her attention to her painfully empty stomach. She hasn't had anything to eat since the macabre princess party picnic, and that was yesterday. Or was it the day before? She can't even remember, but she does know that many, *many* hours have passed since her last meal… but there's just no time for eating. Every minute that passes is one minute closer to Boodark faltering. Not. Happening. "Lead on, Sephyr. Let's go pay a visit to the ThornHoppers."

But Sephyr shakes her head and points at her wounded finger. "First. See to wound."

She doesn't want to take the time to mess with it and she opens her mouth to argue that it's not important and that she'll clean and bandage it *after* Boodark is taken care of. But Sephyr holds up her tiny hand to stop the argument.

"Be shame *you* get same sickness cantankerous one has. Who care for him then?"

Well, when she puts it like that… While she cleans it (biting her lip to hold her whimpers of pain in) Sephyr grinds some 'swamp ingredients' into a poultice. That's the answer that she receives when she asks what the black blob of *yuck* that the little fairy's busy mixing into the dry, herb-like ingredients. It looks suspiciously similar to the bird poop that Sephyr had been stuck in when they first met. She's pretty sure that's *exactly* what it is but all Sephyr will say about it is, "*Not* StillCrane poop. Worry you no, Change Bringer. Heal wound. Come. Is ready."

She holds her finger up and shivers in revulsion at the sight, feel, and smell as Sephyr smears her foul concoction in a thick layer over the wound. It's absolutely noxious and she gags the entire time it's being applied.

"Wrap it," the bossy little thing demands, and she's quick to follow orders…. anything to mask the unpleasantness of it. Hopefully out of sight really does mean out of mind. Once it's all wrapped up, she insists, "Now be honest. It *was* bird poop, wasn't it?"

Sephyr looks her dead in the eye as she answers. "Sephyr no lie. Sephyr speak true. No bird poop."

Thank goodness, is all she can think. Maybe she can finally stop gagging. But then the little fairy grins mischievously. "Is mudviper poop!"

Nope. Still gagging, and it's even worse than before. Somehow having snake poop smeared on her finger is even nastier than bird poop. She stares at her upraised finger in horror, seriously debating if she really needs that digit. Maybe she could just cut it off…

"Come, Change Bringer. Get ingredients save cantankerous one."

They set out for ThornHopper territory and Ecko asks if Boodark will have to have that vile poultice put onto his wounds.

"No. Not work him," Sephyr calls back. "Mud-viper poop only for ones who disturb swamp. Wake GloomDooms, make bridges, command Akar clans…" And then the little imp flutters so far ahead that her tiny tittering laughter can no longer be heard. Wow, way to avoid an argument. Ecko snorts and yells after her. "Come back here, you naughty little thing!"

"See you not the bridge she create…*with her mind*? Wish you she create another…*here*? Wish you she uproot bitterbark trees and thorn shrubs? Perhaps melt you to trees, turn you to real thorns upon the branches?"

Silence.

"Perhaps she wake more GloomDooms from slumbers. Command them to eat all who refuse to help."

Well, *that's* a little harsh, Ecko thinks but she continues to hold her tongue. While they made their way to the ThornHopper's territory, the two of them had discussed tactics. As agreed, she has kept her mouth shut while the little mushroom fairy does all the talking. So far, it's been a one-sided conversation though.

Sephyr had started out by asking that they all put their feud on hold, calling for a brief truce. She promised that they'd come in peace to respectfully request aid, explaining that a life hangs in the balance. For several minutes, she's been polite and diplomatic and all she's received in return is silence and more silence.

"What say you, Lazuell?" Sephyr calls with just the slightest hint of annoyance in her voice. She's getting angry.

Ecko's not mad, but she *is* getting anxious. This is taking too long. Sephyr has assured her that the ThornHoppers are present and that they're listening. She's assured her that there are *scores* of them listening, but she has yet to see a single one for herself. She squints her eyes at the strange, yellow trees in the distance and then down lower at the scraggly, black shrubs below them. Sephyr hadn't wanted to enter the ThornHopper territory without permission, so they'd stopped right on the outskirts. There's roughly one hundred feet of nothing but mud stretching between them and the 'enemy's' copse of tress, and so she has to strain her eyes to get a glimpse of these new, supposedly hostile, fairies.

The trees (like all the others here) are leafless and bare, but the bark is a sickly yellow color that stands out shockingly against the surrounding dull and drab swamp. The shrubs look just like huge, dead rose bushes, the spindly branches *covered* in wickedly large thorns that she can see clearly, even across the distance. They're a mixture of blacks, greens, yellows, and reds, and there are so many of them that *nothing* could perch upon those prickly limbs without receiving injuries, but time and time again her gaze is drawn to those branches. She keeps catching glimpses of movement from the corners of her eyes, but they cease when she tries to single out exactly where the motions are originating from. Just as soon as her eyes focus on a spot where she's sure there had been movement, something else will move and draw her attention away. She hasn't had any luck in catching them in action. She can't even be certain that the motions she's been witnessing are indeed the ThornHoppers. All she knows for sure is that *something* is moving in those disturbing shrubs.

She's just about to step closer so that she can get a better look when the world begins to grumble its warning that Pitch will be upon them in one hour, and with it will come the creepy crawly spiders. Playtime is over; they are all out of time. The trip from the pod to where they now stand had only taken twenty minutes, so in theory they should make it back in plenty of time to get settled and secured safely inside the shelter. But knowing her luck, things will *not* go the way she wishes them to go. Something will happen to hold her up and then she'll have to fight off swarms of spiders. Nope. They *have* to get this business concluded… *now*. And she's not leaving without what she came here for. One way or another, she'll get the bitterbark that Boodark needs, spiders or no spiders.

"No time!" Sephyr shouts. "What say you, Lazuell? Agree or no? Glad I am to not be you if you deny Change Bringer!"

Ecko has an idea. It's sneaky and not altogether very nice, but desperate times call for desperate measures. And Lord knows that she is a walking, talking mass of desperation…. just ask the tree roots that now form a bridge through the marsh. They'd certainly attest to that, if they could speak, that is.

She unties her camera from her backpack and whispers to Sephyr to not be alarmed. Then she simply walks forward and starts taking pictures of her surroundings, focusing most of her attention on the thorny shrubs. In a world that has only weak, muted light, the camera's flash is brilliant and intense, and it receives the precise reaction that she'd figured it would. A cacophony of small, frightened screams ring out, so many tiny voices joined together that they're deafeningly loud after the silence just moments ago. She nevertheless continues snapping photos, even as her eyes widen in astonishment. The thorns are moving… *fast*, wildly scrambling up and down the main limbs and crawling out across the branches with all the frenzy of crazy ants. As she moves in closer, some of the thorns pick themselves up and try to flee, two *humanoid* legs magically emerging to carry them away. Some thorns sprout wings and fly up into the higher, safer reaches of the yellow trees where the bright light can't follow them. But the majority of them…and oh, this is so bad, and she will surely go to hell for causing it… fall from the branches in a dead faint. They splash down into the swamp water and float atop the mud, the thorns looking just like itty bitty shark fins poking up above the surface.

"Oh no!" she cries out as she rushes to reach them. As she watches, they slowly flip over, going belly up, so to speak. The thorn tips are now under the water, revealing the truth of what lies underneath. They *are* fairies, dark, one-inch-tall fairies with a thorn-like appendage that covers them from the top of their heads to midway down their backs. She's pretty sure that those thorns are strange bug shells that they've acquired and somehow attached to themselves… camouflage and protective gear level 1000. Apparently, they contort and scrunch their bodies up under themselves so that every part of them is hidden behind their thorn shields. Their bodies are also cleverly colored to help them blend into the black shrubs that they live on, dark skin covered in darker blotches. There's absolutely no way that her eyes would have ever seen through their expert camouflage, especially not at a distance.

"I've killed them!" she wails as she stares down at them in horror… just floating there belly up in the mud like dead fish. Just as she bends down to scoop one of them up out of the muck, a voice yells, "Yield! ThornHoppers yield to the Change Bringer! Take bitterbark and GO!"

Sephyr flutters up beside her and declares, "Worry not. They live. Touch them not. Poison in their stings. Come Change

Bringer, permission be granted. We take bitterbark. We go, before Lazuell's mind change!"

But she can't leave things like this. This is terrible! Why does this always happen? Every decision she makes, every 'great idea' she has inevitably ends in disaster. She turns her head towards the shrubs to search for the one that had cried yield. There are several very angry fairies standing upon the branches, and *all* of them are glaring at her.

"I'm sorry! I didn't mean for this to happen. I only wanted to save my friend." Apparently, they don't care. They refuse to speak as they continue to mean-mug her. She turns worried eyes to Sephyr. "Will they be ok? Are you *sure* I didn't kill them?"

The little fairy points to the mud. "See true. ThornHoppers awaken."

Sure enough, the thorny fairies are waking up and climbing out of the mud, briskly shaking their heads as if to clear their senses as they crawl back onto the shrubs. Relief courses through her and she almost sobs aloud.

"No time, Change Bringer. Must hurry!"

She's right. They do have to hurry, but she refuses to leave things like this. She reaches into her backpack and takes out a granola bar. She quickly removes it from the package and shows it to the ThornHoppers. "It's food. My friend loves these because they have sweet berries in them. It is a gift to show my gratitude." She takes a small bite to prove that she's not trying to trick them into eating poison. Then she sets the treat on a nearby branch and turns to leave.

"Irukandji!" That same voice from before calls out to Sephyr. "Irukandji must eat also!"

They don't trust that the granola bar is safe for *them*. Sure, it's not poisonous for the ground stomper, but who's to say that fae can eat such strange food? They want assurances, and they're using Sephyr to get them. She's an enemy to their clans; they don't care if *she* dies.

The little mushroom fairy turns her own glare on her. "Say true, is safe?" she hisses in a whisper that only Ecko can hear.

She nods but then quickly glances away in guilt. Can she really 'say true' that granola bars are safe for fairies? No, she cannot. All she knows is that they're safe for orc-bat… creatures. But hey… he *claims* to be a pixy, and while pixies aren't exactly the same as fairies, they *are* fae. Close enough… *please let it be close enough.*

Sephyr clearly doesn't want to do it, but she flutters over to the treat, leans over and takes a big bite (big for a tiny fairy) with her face all scrunched up in distrust, prepared for the worst. But as she chews, she gets a dreamy look in her eyes, and she beams a smile of pure radiance. Then she plops her tiny butt down on the branch and buries her face in the sweet treat.

Everyone watching is startled by her behavior, shocked by the *om nom nom* sounds that she makes as she scarfs. Ecko clears her throat nervously and then murmurs, "Umm, Sephyr? That's for the ThornHoppers…"

And that snaps the ThornHoppers right out of their momentary paralysis. They fly up off the shrubs and encircle the mushroom fairy. She doesn't seem to care that she's surrounded by her enemies. "Cease! *Our* gift, Irukandji! *Ours!*"

A fierce, mean-looking female with red eyes and long black dreadlocks snarls and darts towards Sephyr as if she intends to attack.

"I'll get her!" Ecko shouts. "Don't you dare touch her!"

The ThornHoppers part to let her through and she reaches in, whispering, "Don't bite me Sephyr." She uses her thumb and pointer finger to gently grasp the tiny fairy around her waist, just below her wings, and begins to lift her up. Feeling herself being pulled away, the Darkling panics and throws her arms and legs around the end of the treat. She clings to it as if her life depends on it, and a brief battle of tug o' war ensues.

Ecko giggles at the absurdity of the whole situation as she reaches over with her free hand and breaks off the chunk that Sephyr's clinging to. The tiny Darkling's got it wrapped in her clutches as tightly as a snake coils itself around a mouse.

"I've got her!" she exclaims. She lowers the steadily munching fairy into Boodark's basket, down by his feet. Then she turns to the ThornHoppers who now surely regret making the

Irukandji fairy test their food.

"It's all yours now, but first…where do I find the

bitterbark?"

They look at one another with confusion clearly stamped on their faces. "Change Bringer dumb?" one of the females whispers to the male that she assumes is Lazuell. He nods in agreement and then turns to address her question.

"It on bitterbark trees."

Really? Just…*really?* "Ok," she says with all the patience she can muster. "*Where* are the bitterbark trees?"

Every single ThornHopper lifts a hand and points a finger at the yellow trees.

"Oh." she mutters. Maybe she *is* dumb, just a little bit.

They watch her walk up to one of the trees and stare at it. She turns back and asks, "What part do I…" Lazuell rolls his eyes up at the sky and lets out a long-suffering sigh. "Go help Change Bringer, Azora. Move fast so we *rid* of her fast."

With Azora's help, she gathers the amount of bitterbark that she's told Boodark will need. Then she gathers a handful more…just to be on the safe side. She's tucking the bitterbark into her pocket when Sephyr finally finishes her granola. She can't contain her laughter as the Darkling licks the sticky from her hands and then flops backwards to lean against the side of the basket. Her little belly is so full that it actually pooks out a little bit. She breathes a sigh of pure contentment as she rubs her hands over it.

"Alright Miss Piggy. I have the bitterbark. You need to get up and lead the way back to the pod. I think we have just enough time to make it back before Pitch."

Sephyr's eyes fly open wide. "Sephyr forget! Sweet food *much* distract! Must hurry, Change Bringer. No time to waste! That way," she exclaims as she points out the direction they need to take.

Ecko snorts. It's not *her* that's been wasting time, but she doesn't argue. She just heads out as fast as the swamp will allow her to. Thankfully the route between the pod and the

ThornHopper's territory had been relatively easy to traverse. The mud is only knee deep and thin as a melting slushie, and they make it back in fifteen minutes instead of the twenty it had taken on their initial trek.

The mushroom clans have all dispersed, probably already tucked into their little nooks and crannies to avoid the upcoming Spidder Frost. But bless their tiny little fae hearts, they'd put up a makeshift curtain/door by draping a thick layer of grass and moss over the opening before they left. She's not sure it will be enough to keep spiders out, but she's going to trust that the fairies know what they're doing. They've survived this long. Surely, they know how to keep one dumb ground stomper and her side kick alive too.

First things first, she hangs Boodark's basket on the pod's vine and digs her flashlights out of her bag. Then she crawls in and thoroughly inspects every inch of the pod's surprisingly comfortable and spacious interior (just in case there were *already* creepy crawlies inside.) After assuring herself that there's nothing already hiding from the Spidder Frost in her shelter, she tosses her bag inside, gently sets Boodark and a now snoring Sephyr in, and then crawls in after them. She wastes no time in closing her mossy door and setting up a couple of flashlights. Then she gently nudges Sephyr with her fingertip. She hates to disturb her because she's just too cute laying there with her tiny mouth wide open and snoring away, but it can't be helped. She's got the ingredients, but she doesn't know what to do with them other than to mash the cinderoot into a paste and feed it to him every hour. She has no clue what to do with the bitterbark.

Sephyr sits up and lazily stretches her arms above her head.

"Soak bitterbark in water," she instructs with a yawn. "Make soft. Mash with cinderoot. Feed him all."

Sounds easy enough, but she knows that the upcoming task of feeding it to him will be anything *but* easy. She's been worrying about how she'll manage to get him to eat not once, but several times tonight. To distract herself, she asks what the bitterbark is for as she gets to soaking and mashing.

"Help spirit," Sephyr explains as she taps herself on the chest. "Push out bitter and sad. Make room for hope. Make room for happy. Cinderoot fight outside rot, bitterbark fight inside rot."

Wow. These Darklings really have things figured out. If this stuff works like Sephyr assures her that it will, maybe she can take some with her when she leaves. It could certainly come in handy on a world that wants nothing more than to destroy her.

It *does* work. After a long, hard night of fighting Boodark, of holding her little friend down and screaming and shouting until her throat became sore and her voice broke, it worked. Finally, *finally* her batty little orc friend seems to be on the mend.

Just as Nyra of the Enokitake mushroom clan had promised, he'd started fighting her after the second feeding. The next three doses were physically difficult to get through. He'd gone from being comatose to a raging Tasmanian devil. She has several new cuts and wounds on her hands and arms to show for it too. He tried everything he could to get her to stop forcing the medicine on him. He fought, kicking and clawing and spitting curses, terrible, hurtful curses at her. When that didn't work, he cried, begged, and pleaded… said it hurt *so* bad.

She was horrified to the depths of her soul when Sephyr confirmed that yes, he *was* feeling excruciating pain. She almost lost it completely and quit at that point, but Sephyr talked her through it.

Doses six through nine were the hardest for *her* to endure. She would gladly have let him tear her hands to shreds if she could have avoided the damage that he'd done to her heart. He gave up on fighting and just cried as if his heart was breaking as he asked her why she was doing this to him. She'd tried over and over again to make him understand that it was medicine and that he would die without it, but he refused to listen. He wouldn't hear her.

She'd sobbed uncontrollably as he begged her to stop killing him. She'd barely been able to speak at that point. "Please, *please* just finish taking it," she'd choked out. "Only three doses left. We can get through three more doses. Just find a happy thought and focus on it. *Fight!*"

And although she really doesn't know much about his family, she realized that she could nevertheless use them as a motivator. What she did know was that he'd done something bad that had resulted in his family's entrapment. She could work with that. And she did. She used every weapon in her limited arsenal to get him through the ordeal and past the danger.

"If you falter now, what chance does your mate have?" she demanded. "What about your babies? Your Secret will stay trapped forever if you don't fight this!"

Boodark had stopped all forms of protest then, dutifully swallowing down every last bit of the dreadful medicine that she shoveled into his mouth. Love is a powerful motivator. As is guilt.

The entire Pitch had been a nightmare, and she wants nothing more than for it to be over with already. Her eyes keep threatening to close as she heats up a packet of soup for Boodark. He'd slept during the down times, when she wasn't busy torturing him. She, however, had gotten precious little rest. There was just too much going on inside the safety of the pod… and also, *outside* of it. She'd been a nervous wreck through this seemingly neverending night and now her mind, body, and soul are crying out, *"Enough!"* She just wants to lay down and sleep, and she has every intention of doing so… just as soon as she gets this food into her friend. She gently rouses him, and he opens his eyes and whisper/begs, "Please, no more medicine."

Her already bruised and battered heart cracks just a tiny bit more.

"Stop mewling, cantankerous one! Need sleep, Sephyr do." The Darkling's curled up atop the blankets, glaring at him in tired and grouchy frustration. She'd managed to get a little bit of sleep here and there, but for the most part, she'd stayed awake to help Ecko get through the trials of the night. The two of them had talked all through the endless Pitch as they'd listened to the spiders drop down onto the top of the pod.

Go back and read that again, just the last part.

They listened to the spiders drop onto the pod. How big does a spider have to be for you to *hear* it thud against the roof like a fallen pinecone …a *meaty* pinecone? She'd asked Sephyr just how big these arachnid monsters were, but she certainly hadn't liked what the vexatious little imp had suggested. She'd pointed her tiny finger at the moss door and taunted, "Peek. See for self."

Uh, no. She would *not* be opening that curtain, not even if the inside of the pod were to catch on fire. She could only imagine the face she'd made at said suggestion because Sephyr had laughed uproariously at her. Then she'd held up her hand, her thumb and pointer finger situated so closely together that the space between them wasn't even visible. "Some tiny. Ground stomper eyes not even see them. Some big as you, Change Bringer."

At that point, all she'd wanted to do was curl up into a shivering ball of denial and forget about the outside world. Maybe she could just live here, in this pod from now on. She could be happy here, she tells herself.

There. Are. Spiders. As. Big. As. A. Person. Out. There.

Sephyr giggled helplessly at the level of horror she obviously felt, and she poked as much fun at her as she could. "Those just Hatchlings. Grow bigger. *Much* bigger." After a while, she decided to take pity, and she'd tried to console her. "Big ones rare. Change Bringer probably never see one."

It was not enough consolation. Not *nearly* enough, and she'd winced with every new thud, every scratching, skittering, scuttling sound of buggy legs scrabbling away. Eventually the number of spider-thuds had lessened, grown farther apart until only the occasional thud-skitter could be heard. Apparently, they'd finally all gone on their buggy ways, scurried off and gone into hiding to avoid the approaching Pale.

'Thank you, sweet baby Jesus' she mutters to, herself now as she gently shakes Boodark awake once more. "It's not medicine! It's food. You need to eat. Think you can eat some soup?"

He cracks his eyes open and nods weakly. She lifts him and props him up with blankets at his back and smiles encouragingly as she begins spooning the tepid broth into his mouth. About halfway through his meager meal, she starts bawling. She can't help it. Her hands tremble so violently, and she's so blinded by tears that she's forced to set the bowl aside for a moment until she can collect herself once more.

"Why cry, Change Bringer? He yet lives. He mend."

She sniffs back her tears and turns her head to see Sephyr peering at her in confusion. "I know. I know he's mending. He's doing so much better. That's why I'm crying. I really thought I was going to lose him. I'm so happy, so relieved that he's getting better. You will never know just how much I appreciate you for coming back. He wouldn't have made it without you. *I* wouldn't have made it without you, not in that Spider frost. We owe you our lives."

Sephyr becomes very serious. "Sephyr repay. Change Bringer and Sephyr even. Equal. No debt you, no debt me. Now we allies… friends."

She smiles softly. "I like that. And since we're friends now, you can call me Ecko."

The little fairy nods and smiles back. "Agree. But *he* still Cantankerous one."

Ecko can't help but giggle when Boodark sticks his tongue out at the Darkling. It's all he can manage in his weakened state, but he's unwilling to let her little insult slip past without *some* sort of retaliation. Oh yes, her little friend is on the mend, she thinks as she picks the spoon back up to finish feeding him the soup.

Boodark looks around at their surroundings as he eats, studying their shelter. "Where are we?" he asks in between bites, and she quickly fills him in with the information that Sephyr had provided during the long hours of the night.

"We're inside a DreamSnare pod! Sephyr's told me all about them. It's a huge, thick mass of vines that produces a single pod. Only one, because the pods grow so large that the vines can only support one. Let me see if I can remember everything she said when I asked her why they're called DreamSnare pods. She said that when they're fully grown, they lay down flat on the ground instead of standing upright like this one is. Once they get into position, they split open, right down the center…like this." She holds her hands out, one atop the other with her palms pressed together, and then opens them up to demonstrate. "I imagine it opens up like a coffin. Do you know what a casket is? I don't know how you bury your dead on this world. …"

Boodark tells her that yes, ground stompers sometimes use coffins to bury their dead, though not always. She nods and continues. "So, the DreamSnare pods split open, and inside is the softest fluff you can imagine. It looks like a soft, cozy bed, and that's how it gets its food! It tempts weary travelers to lay down in the fluff and go to sleep. While the traveler sleeps, the pod closes and traps them inside. And then it devours him … within a few hours! All while he's innocently dreaming his life away. *Literally,* dreaming his life away. When the plant has taken all the nourishment that it can get from him, the pod opens back up and there is nothing left but a skeleton and his empty clothes! The vines creep in to wrap him up and pull him out of the pod. They drag the skeleton away and dump it in the bone pile of its previous victims…hidden away so that the next meal won't see them and be warned that the DreamSnare is a trap. Right Sephyr?"

The fairy nods and then lets out a sleepy yawn. "Correct. *This* DreamSnare die before pod finish growth. Split. Spill all fluff out. Darklings come. Take. Use fluff for beds."

Ecko sets about cooking a package of ramen noodles for her own pitifully insubstantial meal, and then she unwraps one of the last four granola bars. She sets a chunk of it in front of the suddenly wide-awake and *very* elated fairy and breaks the rest of it up into tiny crumbles. She adds hot water to soften it, stirring until it makes an oatmeal-like substance that will make it easier for Boodark to eat. It's quiet in the little shelter as the three of them eat, until Boodark asks how long he's been out of it and what all has happened since he began to falter.

"What's the last thing you remember?"

He scrunches up his face as he thinks back. "The last thing that's clear is when you woke from the Dreaming. After you ate…"

But she stops him right there. "I get it! Please don't say it out loud. Don't remind me. I never want to think of that again!"

He nods in understanding; he doesn't blame her for wanting to forget. Even *he* refuses to eat such vile things as what she'd consumed.

The Darkling gives him an abbreviated rundown of the past events. "Change Bringer command roots. Call all RootFairies come to her. Make bridge go through swamp. GloomDooms awaken. Get ingredients for medicine, hide from Spidder Frost in shelter. Then fight *you* all Pitch until it is now. You miss much, cantankerous one."

Boodark turns to Ecko and asks her to explain everything, in a *proper* language that he can actually understand. "The *Darkling* stinks at tale-telling," he grumbles.

Now it's Sephyr's turn to stick her tongue out at *him*.

'Children. I'm surrounded by children' Ecko thinks as she gives him a rundown (with enough details to satisfy him) of all that had transpired while he'd been so sick and out of his mind.

"See?" Sephyr sasses with a haughty lift of her head.

"Sephyr speak true."

But Boodark ignores her taunt. He's staring at Ecko in amazement, his eyes wide with reverence. "The GloomDooms woke up? They *moved?*"

She squirms uncomfortably under the weight of their eyes.

"Never, in the history of never ever, has a GloomDoom awakened from its slumber. It is unheard of! Once a Gloomer, always and forever a Doomer. And I missed the Spidder Frost?" He wails in despair. "Oh, all those delicious, succulent spidders!" And he has *real* tears in his eyes. He sniffles for a moment or two and then seems to get over his missed gorging opportunity. "Your magic created a bridge that spans across the Sorrow Marshes? A bridge made of roots? I must see it with my own two eyes! Can we go there now? Please, can we go?"

Sephyr hisses at him then, sounding just like an angry cat. "Change Bringer *need* sleep! She awake too long. Long take care of you!"

Boodark sheepishly apologizes. "I'm sorry Ecko. I wasn't thinking clearly. Of course, you need to sleep." He squirms for a moment in embarrassment, looking decidedly shamefaced and uncomfortable.

"It's ok, Boodark. Don't worry about it." She tries to comfort him but Sephyr's tinkling laughter stops her.

"That no why he wiggle about. That no why he shy." Boodark glares at her in disgruntled silence. "Say true, Cantankerous one. Why you wiggle like worm?" His mouth parts in a snarl. "He need relieve himself. Cinderoot hard on belly. Need you carry him out of shelter. Help him relieve himself." She giggles again because all he can do is snarl and growl.

"I won't always be wounded and weak, Darkling. Remember that."

Ecko hesitates at the mossy curtain/door and asks, "Are you *sure?* Just…are you absolutely, one hundred percent certain that when I open up this door, a spider won't dive down onto my head and eat my face off?"

Sephyr heaves a long-suffering sigh and assures her one more time that the Pale has already arrived and that the spiders are all hidden in their lairs. All tucked away in their holes and hollows and sticky, webby beds.

There really is no avoiding this. Boodark has to go and so does she…. urgently. So, she takes a deep breath for courage and approaches the situation like pulling off a band aid. "Just gotta rip it off," she mutters under her breath. And that's what she does. She throws open the curtain and jumps back… just in case, ya know? She doesn't even acknowledge the giggling and snarfling behind her. She doesn't care how much they laugh, as long as a spider doesn't suck her face off.

When nothing rushes into the opening, she tentatively pokes her head out and then gasps in shock. No amount of speculating could have properly prepared her for the reality of just what a Spidder Frost would look like. It is eerily, creepily magnificent. The entire swamp is draped in glimmering, gossamer strands of silk. Entrapped moisture droplets shimmer like jewels and reflect images like millions of tiny mirrors. She knows that no matter how hard she tries, words will never properly describe what she's witnessing, so she grabs her camera before gently lifting Boodark up and carrying him out. Her two miniature friends seem unimpressed by the view, and she really doesn't understand how they're not affected by it. Sure, it's nothing new to them. Sure, they've seen it countless times before. But this is a kind of haunting beauty that she could never take for granted, no matter how many times she witnesses it.

Sephyr chooses a direction and flutters off, so Ecko goes another, waving her arms in front of herself to keep the webs off her face. Boodark reaches up and snatches the thick wad that resultingly accumulates on her arm. And then that nasty little freak stuffs the whole glob into his mouth.

"What? You missed out on eating the spiders so now you have to eat their poop strings? That's just wrong on so many levels," she informs him as he licks up the webs that cling to his face. She sets him down and assures him that she won't go far. "Just yell when you're done." She jabs her finger at him and scowls fiercely. "I mean it, Boodark! Don't try to walk back on your own."

He's already working on getting his pants down. "Yeah, yeah. You may want to leave now," he tells her.

She spins around and flees…just as fast as she can. She gets her own business out of the way and then promptly loses herself for the next several minutes as she comes across one photographable masterpiece after another.

"Coming!" she yells when Boodark calls out to her. She scoops him up and carries him back to find Sephyr sitting on top of the DreamSnare pod, stuffing her face with her own wad of webs, just like a child eating cotton candy at the fair. The Darkling grins a ghastly smile that's full of sticky silk strands as she holds her hand out, offering a tiny blob of webs.

Ecko can't tear her eyes away from that dreadful smile. She fully expects to see an itsy-bitsy teeny-weeny spider crawl out.

"Try, Change Bringer. S'good!" Sephyr insists. The Darkling laughs at the look of revulsion on her face, and with a shrug, pops it into her own mouth to add to the horror that's already in there.

"I'm not eating spider poop. It's just not happening," she says as she fights back the gagging.

Boodark and Sephyr both vehemently deny that what they're eating is excrement.

"It comes out of a spider's butt. It's poop. End of story. I'm going to bed. Nobody wake me up for at *least* six hours. Unless a spider crawls in here…"

She managed to get a whole four hours of sleep before the bickering of those two pesky brats woke her up. And then they had the nerve to call her cranky when she'd kicked off her blanket in a snit and left the shelter without a word. She'd needed a moment to collect herself. She *was* cranky from lack of sleep, and she knew it. She'd stood outside the door and listened to their hushed voices whisper/bickering about anything and everything. After a while, their arguments ceased and there was nothing but blessed silence within the pod. Maybe they'd fallen asleep. If that were the case, she'd just sneak in, crawl back into her blanket, and fall right back into the snooze zone, pick up right where she'd left off. But when she'd turned to do just that, two little faces had been peeping at her through the moss curtain. They'd looked so worried, like maybe they thought that she'd turn them both into frogs for waking her up. She'd felt her shoulders slump in defeat. No more sleepy time for her.

"If we leave now, will we be able to make it to the end of the Sorrow Marshes before Pitch falls?" she asks, and she glances up at the sky as if it holds the answers that she seeks. But there are no answers to be found there. It's the same unchanging sky that she sees every single time she consults it.

"Sephyr know not," the Darkling replies. "Move slow you do, like sleeper-slug. But maybe move faster with new bridge. But unknown still. Where goes bridge? What territories it stretch through? Enemy or ally lands?" She shrugs again, apologetically. "Much unknowns."

She scrunches up her face as she mentally debates the situation. She asks Boodark how he feels about getting back on the road, so to speak. He just shrugs and cheekily tells her, "I go where you go." He says it with absolute seriousness, but then he snorts with laughter. "Get it? I go where you go? You carry me in a basket. Of course, I go where you go!"

Sephyr shakes her head and mumbles, "Cretin."

Ecko just grins as she goes back inside the pod to gather her things… she totally gets his wonky humor, even if the Darkling doesn't appreciate it. She's decided to go ahead and restart the journey. With half a day remaining and no sleep anywhere in her horoscope, it only makes sense to do so. She knows she can't just sit here and listen to the two hardheads snip at one another.

'*Stay. Rest. Don't leave us.*' The whisperings in her mind only serve to strengthen her resolve to get going. The sooner she gets them out of the swamp, the sooner the spirit of the Sorrow Marshes will lose its hold on her…and on Boodark. She can see it in his eyes. The spirit still has a firm grip on him, just as it does on her. They'd both made a tremendous come-back, but the spirit never lets up, never ceases its cajoling. It never sleeps. It steadily chips away at them, spreading its filth just like a cancer.

"Yeah. It's time to go," she announces to no one in particular. She makes the two brats (still steadily arguing) stay outside while she gives herself a much-needed sponge bath. She feels disgusting and only slightly less so after her unsatisfactory bathing experience, but she *is* amazed at how much the wound on her finger has healed. Mud-viper poop must have some seriously magical healing properties because it seems to have sped up the whole process by several days. She wonders if they could put it on Boodark's poor shredded back…

"Mud-viper poop only heal. No regrow," Sephyr tells her just a few minutes later as the two of them inspect Boodark's wound. It doesn't look nearly as bad as it did yesterday. At least the angry red swelling and oozing infection is gone. "Can apply here. And here. On skin only. No on bulbs. Sephyr go get."

She flies off and Boodark mumbles, "Thank the

EverLands! She's finally gone. Now, how does it *really* look? Tell me what the bulbs look like…Better yet, use your viewer. Then you can show them to me."

She snaps a couple photos, saying, "It looks good. The tendon/tentacle things have grown longer, the bulbs have doubled in size. They're green and healthy looking, but…" She holds the camera where he can see and scrolls through the photos. "The one that started off smaller than the rest …well, it's turned blue." Boodark is clearly worried, and he grunts at each photo. "I do not know what it means. I've never heard of this happening before. Wings don't change colors."

She bites her lip in consternation. "But it *is* alive. You can see that it's just as healthy as the green ones. It's just blue for some weird reason…."

Sephyr flutters back in with her hands full of foul black gunk. "Hold Sephyr up, Change Bringer. Sephyr apply so you no have to touch."

The cheeky little thing snickers away as she quickly follows orders, holding her hand out for the Darkling to stand on. Hey, she doesn't mind being laughed at if it saves her from playing in poop. She *would* have done it though. For Boodark, she would have done it, but she's eternally grateful that she doesn't have to!

When Sephyr's done with her disgusting chore, she lifts off and flies outside to wash the yuck off her hands. Ecko carefully bandages him back up and then she washes his face and brushes his hair. Once he's been seen to and her belongings are all packed up, all that's left to do is say goodbye to her little Darkling friend. And to somehow express her undying gratitude without using the words 'thank you'.

She's greeted by a swarm of fairies when she steps out of the safe haven of the DreamSnare pod. Some of them are smiling, but most of these Darkling have serious, impassive expressions on their faces. She would be worried, but Sephyr's ear to ear grin reassures her. Slightly.

"Mushroom clans bring gifts for Change Bringer!" she exclaims with evident excitement. "Much important, much sacred gifts!"

She glances down to where her tiny friend is pointing.

Lying on an old tree stump (a *true* tree stump…not the GloomDoom variety) is a very strange assortment of 'gifts'. Some she recognizes, others are a mystery. Some look innocent enough, while others…not so much.

Sephyr points them out and explains what they are and what they're for. There are bundles of cinderoot for 'fighting off sads' and whistlewasp wax for if she ever needs to plug her ears to block out sound. Ecko coughs into her hand to hide her mirth as the cheeky fairy stares pointedly at Boodark.

There's a blob of golden colored tree resin to chew on, presumably like bubblegum to 'settle bellyaches.' A large blob of mud-viper poo, plopped onto a brown leaf. Three piles of mushrooms: crimson ones for staying awake, indigo blues for sleep aid, and honey yellows ones. "Fly fast. Make Darkling wings go fast. Make Change Bringer foots stomp fast. Minutes *only*," Sephyr explains in her choppy, broken English. Apparently, the yellow mushrooms make you run (or fly, depending on your species) super-fast in a brief burst… just like the SuperStar bonus in the Super Mario Brothers games. The golden star gave the good guys superspeed for 10 seconds. It also gave them invincibility, which would have *really* come in handy on this vampiric world. (Not that she's complaining. Superspeed to help her escape her enemies? Heck yeah!)

There's a Hagstone that had once belonged to a witch but was lost when she became a GloomDoom. "Hagstone for looksee," Sephyr explains. "See things eyes no see." And then there are five different snail shells, all with the holes sealed up with wax.

She can tell that these are the 'sacred' gifts because Sephyr's voice is filled with reverence when she explains them. She starts with the largest one, a green, blue, and yellow colored shell that's shaped just like a unicorn horn and is as tall as Sephyr is. "Seeds from Home-Pods inside. Dead long time. Sorrow Marshes kill. Big important, Change Bringer. Big, *big* important. Keep safe for Irukandji clan."

The one that she points to next is similar in shape but broader and shorter, more like an ice cream cone, and it's silver colored with golden swirls. "Tears of last Raylee. Much potent. One drop, erase one memory. Consume all, forget *all*." Next is a short, round shell. Noxious green with black spikes, Ecko doesn't even have to be told that it contains poison. "Baneberry juice. One drop paralyze for hours. Five drops instant dead."

Ecko shivers as she stares at the next, deceptively beautiful snail shell, her eyes filled with dread. Small and dainty, the pink and purple shell holds one single giggle from a MerryFairy. Not enough laugh in it to kill anyone, but just enough to make the recipient laugh like a loony toon. For hours. Apparently, there are fairies out there that can make people laugh hysterically until they eventually die of it. They *literally* laugh themselves to death. What a terrible, twisted way to die. How long would that take? How painful would it be? She is shocked and offended to her core to learn that this world has taken something as beautiful as laughter and twisted it into something so ugly.

Sephyr nods at her astonishment and says, "MerryFairies Light court. Not all Lightling's good. Beauty not always mean good. *Never* trust."

The last shell is obsidian black with a glossy sheen, as if it's been polished. "Banshee cry inside." Sephyr whispers as if it's a terrible secret. "*All* hate banshee-kind. Crush shell. Let cry out.

Scare away enemy. *Only* when no other choice! And must plug ears…*all* ears with whistlewasp wax first or banshee haunt *you* too." She points to Ecko's ears and then Boodark's and snaps, "Never forget. Plug *all* ally ears!"

Once again, Ecko is stumped and at a loss for words that express her gratitude without saying the actual thank you's that she's used to saying. Honestly, some of these 'gifts' are terrible, and she *really* doesn't want anything to do with them. But she knows better than to turn them down. To refuse a fae's gifts is as offensive as telling them thank you…maybe even more so. She needs to stall so that she can think up a proper appreciation speech. So, she plants a wide, nervous smile on her face as she takes out both halves of the water bottle that she'd cut down to make into a bathtub for Sephyr and then carefully packs the gifts into them. She tries not to grimace as she sets the bottle halves back into her bag, a shirt wrapped around them to protect them from being jostled about. That's *all* she needs is to accidentally let a banshee cry loose on herself.

She settles her bag onto her back and then loops Boodark's beddy-bye basket around her neck (for the first time ever, he's sitting up and looking out instead of lying face down inside of it!) Finally, with nothing left to do, she turns her attention to the Darkling crowd and nervously clears her throat. "I will always be grateful for the kindness that the Mushroom clans of the Sorrow Marshes have shown me. You gave me safe haven, provided me with the means to save my friend, and now you present me with gifts, things that you hold sacred and dear. One day, my magic will not control me. I will control *it*, and I will do my very best to see that the seeds you have entrusted me with grow again. I will try to give you back your Home-pods. In the meantime, know that you have found a new ally. If you ever have need of me, I will do what I can to fill that need."

Every Darkling present gives her a bow, and she returns the gesture with her own clumsy little curtsy. "Benod te sumt. Fare thee well, Change Bringer," they call as they turn and disappear back into the mists of the swamp. All but Sephyr and a mystery male, that is. They're standing very close to one another atop the DreamSnare pod, eyes closed and foreheads pressed together. She watches as they draw apart… and she sees that the male is holding the tiniest fairy baby between them. It coos and giggles and stretches its minuscule baby arms up at Sephyr, begging to be held. The Darkling's face softens as she scoops her up and covers the tiny face with kisses. She hugs her close and turns to Ecko. "Sephyr mate, Bracken. Sephyr newling, Leella."

Bracken nods his head at Ecko but doesn't speak to her. Instead, he looks down at his mate and asks, "You sure?"

Sephyr closes her eyes briefly and then nods. "Must," is all she replies. She kisses her baby one last time and then hands her back to her mate. Then she kisses him so intensely that Ecko blushes and turns away so as not to intrude on their moment. When she turns back, she sees that Sephyr's watching her family flutter away with tears in her eyes. But she refuses to let them fall as she straightens her spine, turns back around, and declares, "Sephyr fly with Change Bringer to Sorrow Marshes edge. May need Sephyr help."

Immediately, her brow creases in a frown as she argues, "No Sephyr. Boodark and I will be just fine. You should stay here, with your family. They need you… Your clan needs you."

But the stubborn little Darkling refuses to be swayed. She lifts her chin and obstinately sticks to her plan. "Feel it here," she insists as she places her hand over her heart. "*Must* Sephyr go."

Boodark snorts and then shouts, "Perfect! Just perfect! See? *This* is what happens when you take in strays. *They stay!* We'll *never* get rid of her now." He scrunches his face up into a terrible scowl and snarls, "Stay here, Darkling. I don't want to deal with you any longer."

Sephyr raises her chin up higher. "No up to Cantankerous One. Up to Change Bringer."

He jabs a finger/claw at her. "You mean Ecko. That's her name. It's up to *Ecko*."

She just nods and agrees. "Yes. Up to *Ecko*."

Boodark grunts and slumps down in the basket. "Great! That's just *great*! That means you're coming. Ecko, better known as The Big Dummy, has a soft, squishy heart. She'd never tell you that you're not welcome. So, I have to do it for her. You're not welcome!"

Ecko laughs and then makes a show of glancing around all innocent-like at her surroundings before she tells him, "Well, I mean… this *is* her swamp. Who am I to tell her where she can and can't go?"

The little drama king throws his hands up in the air in frustration. "Perfect! Isn't this just *perfect*?"

And then her heart melts in her chest when her grouchy little friend scoots over a little and grumbles, "Might as well sit down and rest your wings, Darkling. There's no way such puny little things can keep up for very long."

As she turns and heads towards her root bridge with her two tiny companions in the basket around her neck, Boodark voices something that she's also been wondering. "I don't understand. Why would the Darklings bring you gifts? You didn't do anything for them to want to repay you."

She tries to play it cool by saying, "Well duh. It's because I'm awesome and they want me for a friend and ally, of course."

Sephyr sputters… cough, cough. "Clans want hurry you away. Scared you bring change. Scared you make bridge in mushroom territory."

Boodark howls with laughter as Ecko sticks her nose up in the air with a haughty, "Close enough."

Welcome to the Looney Bin. You'll Fit Right In.

Samara

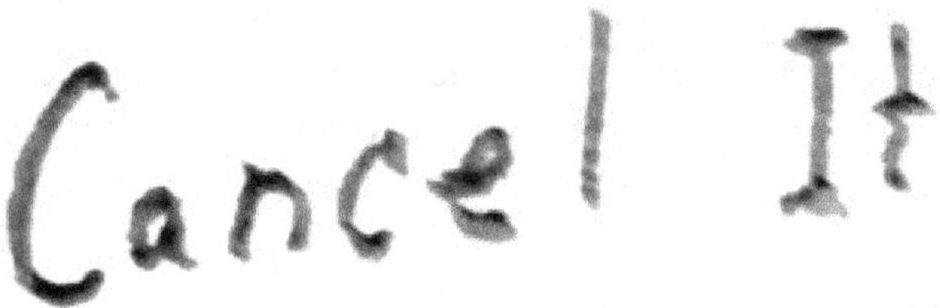

"I'm going to ask you one last time, and then I won't be asking anymore, and you won't have a tongue left to tell it to me anyway. I'm so tempted to rip it from your arrogant head even now." The receptionist pulls her shoulders back and sits up straighter as she denies Samara's request… again.

"I've already told you, ma'am. I can't give you the patient's information, even if the individual is no longer with us. If you want that material, you'll need to go through the proper channels. Come back with a court order. Otherwise, I can't help you, no matter how many threats you throw at me. Now, I'm going to have to ask you to leave the premises immediately. Security has already been alerted, and they're on their way."

Samara grins up at the man beside her. "Oh goodie! She wants to play rough. What fun we're all about to have! What do you say, Robert? What shall we begin with?"

His eyes never even focus as he nods and mumbles,

"Cancel it."

After a moment's reflection, Samara nods firmly. "You are correct as always, my brain-dead companion. This is no time for fun and games. Cancelation coming right up!"

The desk-bitch rolls her eyes and reaches for the phone, but then several things happen in such quick succession that her mind can't keep up with the current events. All she knows is pain and confusion as Robert reaches, lightning-fast across the desk and grabs her face, squeezing so hard that her mouth is forced open under the pressure of his fingers. Samara holds her hand up and makes a vertical fist, squeezes it tight, and then yanks it back towards herself. The secretary feels something that she can't see reach into her mouth and grab hold of her tongue. There's a sharp tug and then there's nothing but excruciating pain amid an explosive rush of hot blood as her tongue muscle separates from her head and thuds down onto her keyboard with a wet plop. She lets out a gurgle/scream and cups her hands up under her chin, for some odd reason trying her best to catch the blood as it pours from her. Perhaps she thinks that if she catches it, she'll be able to put it back.

Humans are strange, Samara thinks as she giggles and picks up the severed appendage. She turns away with it held out in front of her just as two men dressed in security uniforms round the corner. "It's ok!" Samara assures them before they can even say a word, indeed before they can even process the scene. She waves the tongue in the air and cheerfully calls out, "It's all ok! I have clearance! Here… catch!" And then she underhand tosses it to the taller of the two guards. "There's my warrant," she crows, and then howls with laughter as he emits a high pitched, girly scream and hurls it to the floor.

The other guard panics. He draws his gun and points it at her, but he watches the tongue as it flops twice… in his direction. Her Shadows get him before he can pull the trigger. But then he *does* pull the trigger, and he blows an extra breathe-hole right into his partner's face… his partner who never even knew that the gun had been turned towards him. He'd been too engrossed in scrubbing his hands against his shirt to rid himself of the feel of a tongue that he had, on many occasions, enjoyed upon his body… when it had still been attached to the pretty, young secretary. He silently drops to the ground, his sightless eyes staring, even in death, at the bloodied, severed mouth muscle.

The shooter guard re-holsters his gun and then drops to his knees on the floor beside his fallen comrade. The tongue-less secretary, eyes wild with pain and an overwhelming fear moves out from behind her desk. She walks over and picks her tongue up off the floor, whimpering all the while. The shooter guard opens his mouth and Miss Snooty Secretary proceeds to do her utmost best at shoving her own tongue down his throat. They fall to the floor with her sitting atop his heaving chest as she shoves it down with all of her strength.

"Look Robert! She's giving him the tongue! Get it?" Samara laughs gleefully before she turns away and leaves them to it as she heads deeper into the hospital to find someone that would rather speak than lose their tongue. Someone that will help her find the person that she *really* needs to speak to. She spots a man wearing one of those hideous outfits that everyone in these caregiving places always seem to favor. What are they called again? Something to do with washing…Oh yes. A scrub. That's what they're called. Again, humans are strange things.

She sends just enough Shadow into the man wearing the scrub to hurry things along. She's on a time limit. The coppers will be on their way soon, if they're not already in route.

The scrubbed orderly escorts her to an office with a closed door. "She's inside? You're sure?" He nods and replies, "She should be in there at this time of day."

Samara waves him off. "Very good… now go away," she commands and then turns to Robert. "You wait out here for me. I won't be long." Then she turns the handle and lets herself into the room, softly closing the door behind her. The woman inside raises her head and frowns sternly at the rude, no-knock entrance into her private domain, but then her features relax, and a genuine smile lights up her face. "Adrina! How are you?" Her smile falters just a bit at the look in her former patient's eyes, the unfamiliar hardness and cruelty that lurk there. "Adrina? Ecko? What is it? What's wrong?"

Samara lowers herself onto one of the guest chairs that are positioned opposite the doctor, with the desk situated between them. She leans back and slowly crosses her legs. "Wrong sister, Doc. I'm Samara."

The older woman looks truly baffled for a moment as she tries to work it all out in her mind. What had gone wrong? What had caused this relapse? *More* than a relapse…had her former patient suffered a complete mental breakdown? Perhaps created an alter ego?

"Everything's alright, Ecko. Talk to me. Tell me what's happened." She speaks slowly, calmingly in her best, soothing doctor's voice. But her chin wobbles and her hands tremble at the pure malice that she feels radiating off of the other woman. Ecko had been many things, confused, delusional, wounded, and lost, but she'd *never* harbored hatred in her heart. She'd always been good and kind, and for her to change to such an extreme extent is almost unfathomable. It's like she's a completely different person. Or… oh, dear God, could this truly be THE Samara? The one that Ecko had always insisted was real? The girl who lived in the mirror and looked exactly like her? But… *how?* How would that even be possible? She's never been so confused and unsure of herself as she is right now, at this moment. Had she made a huge mistake?

Had she diagnosed Ecko all wrong?

"B, b, but you *can't* be Ecko's sister! She's dead! Her entire family perished in a house fire. And besides… her sister looked nothing like her… like *you*. The two of you could be twins!"

Samara steeples her fingers together and nonchalantly confirms the good doctor's fears. "We *are* twins. Everything my sister ever told you was true. I did kill her family, and if I could have done so, I would have eaten them too. With barbeque sauce. I mean, they *did* cook in a house fire, isn't that what you said?"

She laughs at the look of horror on Dr Bradburn's face. Humans are so easily spooked, so readily offended. "Oh yes, I'm sure that every word she spoke to you was true. Ecko's the oh, so good twin. She would *never* have done anything but speak the truth. Never lie, cheat, or steal, that's our Ecko. The girl doesn't even know how to curse. And she would never, *ever* do anything to hurt another living creature." She pauses for dramatic effect as she gives the doctor her most serious 'fuck with me in the slightest way and I'll gut you like a fish and feed you your own entrails' expression. "I can assure you, Dr Bradburn, I'm not that kind of girl. We may look alike, but we're nothing alike on the inside. Nothing stands between me and the things that I desire."

The doctor nods slowly. "I can see that," she calmly assures as her fingers cleverly and subtly move to press the button under her desk that will quietly let out an alert that help is needed. She lets out a tiny breath of relief when the action goes unnoticed. Help will arrive within a matter of minutes. She just has to stall until then. "Tell me, Samara. What is it that you want from me? What can I help you with?"

The angry young woman grins and leans forward. "I'm so glad you asked! I thought you'd be more difficult than this. Some of your employees have been so rude! It's quite refreshing to find someone so willing to be helpful!"

The older woman smiles reassuringly. "Well, I'm a doctor. That's what I do. I've committed my life to helping people. Now, what is it I can help *you* with?" She quickly glances at her clock to see that a whole minute has passed since she pressed the panic button.

"Why, I just want to find my long-lost sister, that's all. I finally managed to track her down here, to this head shrinker place… which, may I add, I've found *very* disappointing. I haven't seen a single shrunken head yet! Now, I know that my sister is no longer here, so I'm going to need you to look up her home address for me. Actually, on further thought, I'm going to need you to just give me her whole file… every bit of information you have on her. *That's* what I need from you, *Dr Bradburn*, and before you tell me that's classified documentation and you can't share it with me, just know that the last one to say those words to me was your front desk greeter-meeter lady. She no longer has a tongue to tell me no with… or anything else for that matter."

Dr Bradburn nervously clears her throat. "Ahem, yes. Well, seeing as though you *are* her only living relative, and she's no longer a patient… I suppose I can make an exception, just this once." She stands up and unlocks the file cabinet with a key that she takes from her pocket.

"Wise decision," Samara murmurs in approval.

The doctor smiles weakly as she pulls the top drawer open and begins to slowly rifle through the files, even though she knows darn good and well that Ecko's information is three drawers down, filed under the R's for Roberts, Adrina Ecko. She's doing all she can to stall for time until… *that!* The door bursts open, and staff members come barreling into the room.

Before Samara has time to react, she finds herself jabbed in the arm with a needle. They inject some sort of drug into her, a cold, liquid heat that burns through her veins and spreads throughout her body like wildfire. Suddenly, her body's light as a feather and she's floating up, up, up, right up through the roof and into the sky. And she's flying… flying high, fast, and free, giggling like a child as she soars past the clouds… for all of sixty seconds. And then, just as fast as she rose up, her Shadows yank her right back down. She crashes back into herself, *hard*, and now she's pissed.

"Ouch," she snaps as she turns to face the three orderlies who, by the way, are shocked speechless when they realize that she's not a drooling, half-comatose vegetable.

Samara raises her hand up in a fist, focusing all her will on Idiot #1, the man with the empty syringe in his hand. "What the hell?" he wheezes as he feels his heart seize up. She doesn't let up until his heart is crushed inside his rib cage… broken beyond all repair, and he crashes to the floor.

Idiot #2 makes his move while she's distracted with #1, slamming another syringe full of liquid fire into her. He pulls back, his entire body suddenly quaking in fear.

"Hand it to me. Now," she calmly commands, showing no emotion whatsoever. He passes the empty syringe to her with trembling hands and then begins to whimper when she raises her fist up at *him*. She mentalizes that his head fits perfectly in the palm of her hand as she squeezes tight, as she had just done to Idiot #1's heart. The visual effects of her squish power being utilized on the *outside* of a body are much more dramatic than when they're used on the inside organs. And much, much messier.

Idiot #2's head compresses and caves in on itself until it can take the pressure of her invisible fist no longer. With a sudden, loud *pop!* and then a squelching sound, it bursts apart like an overripe melon, spraying crimson blood, grey globs of brain matter, and pink-tinted bone shard shrapnel in every direction. The entire room and everyone in it gets an up-close and personal look at Idiot #2's last thoughts.

Samara turns to Idiot #3 and he stares back at her, his eyes huge and glaringly white in a face covered in red/pink/grey goop. He's not nearly as stupid as his idiot-mates were. He throws his hands up in the air and then makes a run for it. She lets him go; she even giggles as she watches him slip and slide through the blood and the brains and the gore.

"Are we done with all the nonsense now?" she asks and Dr Bradburn nods, her eyes wild with shock. "Good. You have ten seconds to get me that file. Nine. Eight…"

The good doctor probably never moved so fast in all her adult life. The file is in Samara's hand before she can even count down to three. Samara takes the folder and shoves it down the back of her jeans, tucking her shirt in over it to hold it in place. "Look at who's being so helpful all of a sudden!" she taunts. "I bet you wish you would have cooperated and just done as I'd asked in the first place, right? Well, I have one more thing that I need from you… and this is your bonus round. Life or death decision-making time.

I need you to show me a way out of here. A secret way, so that I can avoid the police that I know are coming in through the front doors."

The traumatized woman just stands there, blinking dumbly at her.

"Now, doctor!" she shouts, and Dr Bradburn nearly jumps out of her own skin. "If you think that you can stall me until help arrives, let me assure you that you won't survive round two."

She vehemently shakes her head in denial, "No! I'm not, I swear!" she cries as she stares down at the mess covering the floor.

"Oh, you're a *doctor* for fuck's sake. You *can't* be bothered by a little bit of blood! Move your ass *Doctor,* before I make you clean every bit of this mess up with your tongue."

Dr Bradburn bursts into tears and wails, "Oh God! Please have mercy on us poor sinners!" as she gingerly steps over the bodies of the men that had given their lives to help her. She tiptoes through the mess, trying desperately to not step in… anything. Samara follows her, gleefully stomping her feet into the carnage, causing chunks and gunk and funk to spew and spray up… all over the good doctor.

"What?" she demands when the doc pauses to stare incredulously at her. "You're already covered in it. Stop wasting my time and I'll stop fucking with you. It's as simple as that. I want out of here just as much as you want me gone. Now let's go!"

Robert's still standing in the hall, right where she'd left him. "Cancel it," he murmurs, his eyes vacant and unfocused. "Look Doc, I brought you a new patient. Stay, Robert." Samara commands as he tries to follow her. She pulls her Shadows from his mind, and he immediately collapses to the floor, wraps his arms around himself, and begins to rock back and forth. "Cancel it. Cancel it. Cancel it," he repeats in a nonstop, increasingly loud loop.

They leave him to it and make their way down one hallway after another until they come to a side door. Dr Bradburn keeps her lips pressed tightly together as she swipes her badge in the card slot. As it beeps and the door swings open, the doctor steps back and prays to a God that she hadn't spoken to since she'd been a young woman. She prays, *fervently*, because if everything she'd learned on this day was true, then not everything could be explained by science, as she's told herself repeatedly since her college days. And she prays... *begs* Him for forgiveness for the things she'd done to Ecko, for not helping her when she'd most needed the help.

She watches Samara poke her head out of the doorway and look around, searching for cops or perhaps just getting her bearings. Who could tell what goes on in a mind that twisted, a mind that depraved? Whatever Samara sees out there must convince her that all is well because she steps out, calling over her shoulder, "Thanks Doc, you've been a big help. I'll give Ecko your regards when I catch up to her. Oh, and pray that you never meet me again. Second encounters with me tend to never go well for some reason."

Dr Bradburn slams the door shut just as soon as Samara clears the doorway and then she sinks to the floor, sobbing in relief but also with a deep, heartfelt despair.

The Horrible Wonders of the Sorrow Marshes

Ecko

The root bridge is even more brilliant than she remembered, and an hour of walking its length hasn't muted her fascination in the slightest. It really is nothing short of amazing, and the fact that it hadn't been here before yesterday is completely unfathomable. It honestly looks like it's been here for ages, like it's *always* been a part of the Sorrow Marshes.

As far as she can tell, the entire structure is pure randomness bordering on brilliant engineering chaos. There's nothing consistent about its makeup, no rhythm or uniformity whatsoever. (Other than the obvious fact that roots and vines were the main materials used in the making of it) It winds amongst the trees, curving and weaving around everything in its path. It randomly bypasses some of the obstacles and then cleverly uses others as supports and braces to reinforce its basic structure.

And it's never the same height or width. At some points, the bridge floor lies just above the swamp, almost even with the murky water. Five minutes down the line and it's suspended two feet above it. Sometimes it's wide enough that a loving couple could easily hold hands and walk side by side (*if* there were actually any weirdo lovebirds that find walking through a disgusting swamp romantic) Other areas are so narrow that she has to carefully line up her footsteps to fall one behind the other, toe to heel. There'd been one incommodious spot that was just barely the width of her foot. That tight section had been the exact length of forty-three Ecko-sized, heel to toe steps. It had felt to her like walking a tightrope, but immediately after stepping off of said tightrope, it had widened enough that she would have been able to lie on the floor sideways across the width of it, had she chosen to do so.

The bridge floor is painted with the colors of her magic, Aurora Borealis lights swirling in a midnight black sky. There are even flecks of glitter tossed into that night sky/floor, sparkling like stars in a spectacular, far away galaxy. She cups her hands around her eyes to block out her peripheral vision and looks straight down at the ground as she walks. The effect makes her feel as if she's flying through the night sky. She lowers her hands as she experiences a sudden, sharp pang of nostalgia. She misses Earth's nighttime skies. Oblerian skies are empty, day and night, devoid of clouds and stars and all the miracles of the heavens.

It's inconceivable that it was *her* magic that had wrought this wondrous phenomenon. But (there's *always* a but) as beautiful and awe-inspiring and convenient as she finds this new path, she's also very much conflicted about it. Had it *truly* been a good thing, a gift, as it appears to have been? Or does it have hidden, negative consequences that she has yet to discover? Whether it had been a positive change or a negative one just isn't clear to her yet, and she guesses that only time will reveal the truth of it. Certainly, it's making *her* trek through the swamp about a thousand times easier than it had previously been. No more wading through mud and muck and slime and sludge …Yay!

But she can't dismiss the nagging, bothersome concerns. She's so worried that there'll be unforeseen repercussions for her interference, for her *intrusion* in the spirit's slimy domain. She knows that she's made it easier for other travelers, possibly even saved future lives. With a bridge to lead them out, surely there will be less people lost to the Sorrows. Which means there will be fewer people turning into Gloom Dooms. (And won't that anger the spirit?) But who *else* will now have safe(er) passage through the marshes? Who else will use the bridge to travel through the swamp, now that she's made it easier to traverse? Has she opened up a (red?) door, giving all manner of predators and monsters and bugaboos easier access to innocent victims?

And what of all the *little* lives, the wee creatures and the fae that live in the trees and the roots that she had rearranged? How many homes had she inadvertently destroyed when the trees moved their roots for her? Surely, *they* don't think a bridge was such a good thing. With a weary sigh at all the numerous uncertainties in her life, she pushes her worries into their proper, respective compartments and tries to empty her mind as she turns her attention to the scenery.

Sephyr has fallen asleep, lulled into dreamland by the gentle swaying of the basket as they travel along the bridge. She's snoring, and it's legit the cutest thing that she has ever heard. She sounds just like Cri-Kee, the little cricket from the Walt Disney movie, Mulan. Boodark covertly peeks up at her to ensure that she's not watching him and then he gently covers the Darkling with a bit of his t-shirt blanket, tucking her in, all safe and soft and warm. She pretends not to see, but her 'Boodark love meter' just rose up yet another notch. She nonchalantly continues taking photos as if her heart hadn't just been reduced to a melted puddle of warm goo inside her chest. Ugly and crotchety he may be, but the little batgremgoyle's got a heart made of solid gold.

"It was super sweet of you, letting Sephyr ride in your basket. I thought you were mad at her for tagging along?"

Boodark shrugs with exaggerated indifference. "What can

I say? I didn't want her to come but she's here, so I'll deal with it. I don't sweat the petty stuff, and I *never* pet the sweaty stuff."

Thoroughly grossed out, she stops walking and stares down at him. "That's disgusting, Boodark."

He grins wickedly, his eyes shining with delight at her outrage. "What?" he asks with feigned innocence. "It's sound advice! I *live* by that creed. Sweaty 'bits' is at the top of my list of unfavorite things, right up there with getting newling poo on my hands when I'm forced to change their nappies. I haven't decided which one I hate more."

She really can't argue with his logic, but there's just some things that could (and should) go unspoken. She doesn't need or want to hear about them. Period.

"One day, I'll have to write down this infamous list of unfavorite things of yours… Maybe I'll write a book all about the things you loathe. I'll call it Boodark's List of Unfavorite Things: A document of sage advice from Boodark the Wise. It'll be a guide of nasties to avoid while traveling through a vampire world. I could fill the pages with all of your random quirks and endless complaints."

The fact that she's being sarcastic is completely lost on him. She can see by the excited twinkle in his eyes that he thinks she's serious… and he's in love with the idea!

"Really? When can you start? You really should begin as soon as possible. It will surely take a long time; I have *so many* unfavorite things!"

She chokes out a sound somewhere between a snort and a laugh (a snaugh, or maybe a slort?) "Sure Boodark. I'll get started on it asap…. just as soon as I save the world."

A real snort, albeit a tiny one, drifts up out of the beddybye basket. Sephyr kicks the blanket off and sits up, stretching and yawning. "Stupid cretin. Change Bringer…*Ecko* no serious. Know you not mockery? Call *you* Big Dummy!"

Boodark looks completely crestfallen for about fifteen seconds. Then he rolls his eyes up to glare imploringly at Ecko. "Great, she's awake and already her mouth is busy flapping and spewing insults. This is why I can't be nice to her…. Cretin, she calls me. Big dummy, she says. I'll have you know, I'm a very intelligent creature with a highly evolved intellect. I was smarter as a newling than you are right now!"

Ecko sighs dramatically and mutters, "And just like that, the peaceful, quiet day was shattered by the endless bickering of the world's tiniest, grumpiest antagonists." But she doesn't think they even hear her. They're both too busy trying to out-insult one another.

The terrain slowly begins to change again as they travel deeper into the marsh. The trees are spreading out, putting distance between themselves, allowing for larger stretches of open swamp areas. The water appears to be getting deeper too, with actual *water* below the bridge instead of mud. There are even living things in this section of the Sorrow Marshes, live plants and insects. There must be critters of some kind too, because every so often she hears the splashing of *things* diving into the water to avoid coming into contact with her. They must be expert level hiders and camouflagers too, because she hasn't, as of yet, seen a single creepy crawly, splishy-splashy creature. But there are countless other life forms, and she takes hundreds of photos, recording all the beauties and uglies and oddities and unbelievables that she passes. She wants to show them all to Charlie and Susan when she gets back home, and she thanks her lucky stars that she always keeps several empty memory cards in her camera case. She has no trouble finding all manner of things to fill the cards with.

There are so many different varieties of mushrooms and fungus, which she supposes is only logical. It *is* a swamp, warm and moist and perfect for spore growth and reproduction. She snaps photos of the groups of long, thin mushrooms that look like a dead witch's pale, bony fingers. They poke up through the mud, out of fallen, decaying logs, and decomposing mulch. Then there are the ones that she thinks of as 'people fungi', small humanoid shaped mushrooms complete with head, torso, and even two arms and legs. These are solitary specimens, always alone and half hidden. They peep out from behind fallen limbs and large rocks to watch with their blank, featureless faces as she walks past.

She stops to photograph white, blobby mushrooms with holes that ooze a thick, red liquid that looks suspiciously and eerily like blood. Staring through the lens at them makes her feel sick to her stomach. A vague, unwanted memory of her 'marionette-self' taking a bite out of one has her stomach flip flopping unpleasantly. She shudders in revulsion and hurries on.

A tree that abuts the bridge catches her attention. Not only is it larger than the other trees she's come across since entering the bog, but it also sports patches of itty bitty, white mushrooms. They look just like cartoon bedsheet ghosts, and she finds them incredibly adorable. Wanting to get photos from several different angles, she moves in closer and closer until she's right up on them and only inches separate them from the lens of her camera. She lets out a gasp of delight when they suddenly lift off the tree and float away, as if they really are miniature ghosts! She quickly snaps photos of their floaty retreat until they're out of view.

Minutes later, she comes across a tall, spindly plant with a woody stalk. Pale pink flowers that closely resemble chubby, infant hands hang down on thin, flimsy stems. She can't resist reaching out to touch one, but she instantly regrets doing so when it reaches around and grabs her finger in a grip tighter than any baby could possibly manage. And that's not even the worst of it. Every single evil, devil-baby hand on the plant reaches out and grabs hold of her too!

"Aaiiiyyyy! It's got me!" she squawks as she tugs, frantically trying to break free of their impossibly powerful hold on her. Hoots and howls make her turn her incredulous gaze downwards. The two brattiest brats in Bratsville are rolling all around in the basket, laughing…at her expense! Her pounding heart slows just a bit as she acknowledges that she must not be in any (immediate) danger.

Otherwise, the two crackpots that she's toting around and playing mule to wouldn't be laughing. After a minute, an entire sixty seconds of enduring their ridicule, she nonchalantly informs them, "I have three granola bars left in my backpack. I *had* been planning to share them with my *friends* when we stop to eat, but I don't think I have any of those here. *Friends* wouldn't let friends get snatched by plants that have possessed baby-hand flowers. *Friends* would help their friends, not laugh at them. Guess I'm gonna have to eat the granola bars… all three of them, by myself tonight. If I'm not mistaken there's a berry one left too…"

And just like that, their laughter dries up (like magic) and both of their faces flush with regret. Sephyr immediately flutters over to the base of the plant, draws her little foot back and lets a tiny/mighty kick fly. Amazingly, the hands immediately snap open and release their hold on her. The Darkling hastily puts distance between herself and the clutching, grasping fists of freakdom, lest they snatch her up too.

"Much sorry, Change Bri…Ecko. *Much* sorry."

Boodark nods, all solemn and serious-like, but his mouth is still twitching and spasming. "Me too. I'm sorry." (Sputter, sputter snicker, snicker) He buries himself under his blanket, hiding his face from her while he desperately tries to get his giggles under control.

Sephyr, who doesn't know her quite as well as Boodark the Obnoxious does, can't believe that he's still laughing. Not when there are such dire consequences at stake.

"Relax Darkling," he tells her when he finally comes back out of hiding. "She would never withhold food. Not ever."

The little fairy's eyes, full of equal parts fear and hope dart up to meet hers. She sighs in resignation and grudgingly confirms his statement as the truth that it is. "I would never," she agrees as she starts walking again. Stupid soft heart.

"Kreeper Krud. No touch. No go near," Sephyr admonishes when she stops to examine the patches of stringy, orange strands that stretch towards the travelers as they pass by.

"Parasite," she adds, and that's *all* she needs to say. Ecko walks right down the center of the bridge to avoid the reaching, hair-thin tentacle limbs as Sephyr explains just what Kreeper Krud is and why she should avoid it at all costs.

"Fungus *and* parasite. Infect host. No *plant* host." And she points to the closest patch of it, growing right there on one of the bridge's support roots. "Kreeper Krud on root die soon if it no find blood host. Need *creature* host. Parasite need blood. Fae, ground stomper, beast, crawlers. Species no matter. Spread fast. Grow on host skin. Grow in host body. Make host live long time. Suffer long time. Much hard kill. Much hard cure."

Ecko shivers and mutters, "It sounds dreadful." But she has no *real* concept of how truly dreadful it is until she actually sees a poor little caterpillar/worm with the Kreeper Krud growing on it like patches of tiny sea anemone tentacles. Her dumb, soft heart immediately starts acting up again. She feels so bad for the little guy.

"Can't I just pull it off him? I have gloves to protect my hands from touching it."

Sephyr and Boodark both vehemently shake their heads, for once in total agreement. "It takes hold easier than you could possibly imagine," Boodark tells her. "Besides, pulling it off won't kill the Kreeper Krud, but it *will* kill the wiggler. The Krud has gone in too deep. The wiggler can't survive without it now."

She snaps a quick photo and moves on before she starts crying… over a worm. More and more patches of Krud appear, and so do more unfortunate victims. She photographs a moth in much the same state as the worm had been in. And then a wasp and a beetle and another worm. And then a whole horde of parasitically infested insects as they all start crawling out of their hiding places.

She feels like every single one of the infected turn and watch as she passes by. She can just imagine their tiny voices begging her for help. Then she really does hear a voice whispering through her mind. The spirit, trying to coax and cajole her to 'Go ahead. Help them. Touch them. They will die if you do not. Will you truly ignore their pain?' She ratchets her chin up a notch and focuses her eyes straight ahead. She can ignore the voices, but there's nothing she can do to harden her heart enough to block out the pain of all those doomed little lives.

"It looks like a big blob of grape jelly," Ecko observes sometime later as she stares down at the gelatinous, purple mass atop the fallen and half decayed tree. Boodark is taking a nap, and she keeps her voice lowered so as not to disturb him. She's amazed and absolutely thrilled at how well he's been doing since their fight for his life, but he still needs rest in order to recover and to heal properly. His loud snores block out the quietly spoken conversation about the gunk that seems to have completely captivated the Darkling.

The large, semi-solid globule looks for all the world like someone (a *giant* someone) had been walking along, splashing through the swamp while eating a colossal sized pb&j sandwich, and a great glob of the grape jelly had oozed out and plopped down onto the log.

"What be grape jelly?" Sephyr asks as she sits down... *right beside it.*

"Jelly is a squishy, sticky spread that's made from sugar and fruit, grapes in this case," she explains as she eyes the blob distrustfully.

"For eating?" Sephyr questions as she mimes putting something into her mouth for added emphasis.

"Yes, it's food. A sweet treat, kids love it. Actually, I believe I still have a packet of jelly in my bag if you want to try it tonight.

Ummm, Sephyr? Should you be that close to it? I think there's something moving in there."

Sephyr's eyes light up just like a child's. "Yes! Sephyr arrive at perfect time!"

They both watch as the blob starts *growing*, swelling up into a boil-like bubble. It expands and bulges and grows and there *are* things moving inside of it, squirming like…

"Umm, I *really* think you should move. Now!" Ecko squawks, but it's too late. The exhilarated fairy jumps to her feet and claps her hands gleefully as it bursts open like a swollen, infected cyst, spilling wiggling worms and magenta-colored jelly chunks.

Sephyr squeals and snatches up one of the smallest worms (small, but still as long as her tiny fairy arms) and shoves it right into her mouth, biting off a very large portion of it. She closes her eyes briefly in apparent appreciation of the (disgusting) delight upon her tongue as she enthusiastically chews. Within a matter of mere seconds, the worm is no more and she's reaching for the next one.

"Come, Ecko. Eat! Wake cantankerous one. Sephyr share. Plenty everyone eat!" the Darkling delightedly crows with her mouth full once more.

Her stomach turns and her head gets a light, fuzzy feeling as she watches Sephyr dunk the last (still squirming) bit of worm into the jelly, like dipping a french fry in ketchup. She pops it into her mouth and nods enthusiastically while she hums in pleasure. "Sweet treat," she agrees as Ecko throws her hand over her mouth and turns aside.

Boodark suddenly sits straight up in his basket, his bat nose twitching as he sniffs the air. "Clabber wigglers?" His quivering nostrils direct his eyes straight to the feasting Darkling and he lets out a tormented moan.

"Let me out, Ecko. Down! Put me down!"

She most certainly will *not* put him down. "Boodark, you can't seriously want…"

His distressed outcry cuts her argument short. "That dirty Darkling is eating it ALL!" he wails as he watches Sephyr slurp a tiny one up like a spaghetti noodle. Eyes full of panic and desperation clearly stamped on his face, Boodark kicks off his blanket and gets to his feet. Before she realizes what he's up to, he dive-bombs face first out of his basket. She barely manages to catch him before he hits the ground.

"What in the world are you thinking? Do you want to hurt yourself worse than you already are?"

But he's not listening. He's wiggling and struggling to break her hold on him. "*Please!*" he yells.

"Fine!" she yells right back. "Go on, be disgusting! But you're not riding in the basket. I don't want your worm breath that close to my face!"

She plunks him down on the log, on the opposite side of Sephyr so that the object of her next nightmare is situated between them. She quickly turns and walks further down the bridge so that she can't see, hear, or smell the horror show. With a disgruntled sigh of annoyance, she plops down onto her own butt to wait it out.

"I'm just gonna sit over here and drink some water," she needlessly informs them. "They don't care," she mumbles under her breath. She doesn't think they'd care if she got up, walked away, and left them behind. Not right now, at least. They would later though. Well, perhaps not Sephyr. She can fly away. But Boodark certainly wouldn't like it. He's not used to being a ground stomper.

An hour later she stops to swap out the memory card in her camera for a new one. The peculiar vegetation of the Sorrow Marshes and the inhabitants that dwell amongst it helped her mind get past the clabber wiggler incident. Her oddly wired (faulty?) brain has done that amazingly convenient trick again and filed the whole event away as just another mildly traumatic experience. Hopefully her mind loses the key to *that* box and she never, *ever* has to revisit the memory again. But she has a sneaking suspicion that from here on out, the memory of Sephyr dipping worms into jelly and then slurping them up like spaghetti will resurface every time she tries to eat a peanut butter and jelly sandwich, and quite possibly whenever she eats spaghetti too.

Her two tiny companions had fallen into a food coma the very moment that she picked them up and settled them back into the beddy-bye basket. She'd even had to pick Sephyr up. The Darkling had eaten so much that she'd fallen over and couldn't get back up. There's no way she would have been able to fly anywhere. Besides, friends don't let friends gorge themselves into a drunken stupor and then let them fly.

The two frenemies are currently curled up together under the blanket, all close and snuggly, snoring away without a care in the world and she can't help but giggle as she glances back down at them. They'll be so mad when they wake up and she shows them the blackmail photos she now has in her possession. Cue evil laugh, Muahaha! Revenge is such sweet satisfaction!

She scrolls through her latest batch of pictures as her march continues onward, ever onward. She soon begins to frown though, and her heart starts skipping every other beat as the slideshow of her progression through the swamp points out what she'd failed to see in person. The Sorrow Marshes has stealthily but steadily been growing darker, and the objects of her photographic attentions have become decidedly more hostile and forbidding to look upon.

She hadn't noticed the Pale growing dimmer because it had been so gradual, and honestly, it's *always* dim and gloomy in this vampire-suck-fest land. But it's true. Photos don't lie. The flora and fauna and the creepies and crawlies in this darkened section of swamp have a new, sinister feel to them, a sense of foreboding and ill-intent in their physical designs. It's almost as if their creator had penned a bit of evilness into their blueprints at the last minute when he'd been designing them. It's subtle at first; that's why she hadn't caught it right away. Now that she's watching it play out like a video on her camera's display screen, the evidence is glaringly apparent.

The swamp grows darker with every photo that she scrolls past, and the creatures get more *wrong*, for lack of a better word. The first critter to show up in this newer, darker section of the Sorrow Marshes had been a water creature. She's reluctant to call it a fish, but it lived in the water so that's close enough. But it wasn't a fish. Period. It was glowing a bright, neon green color; that's how she'd noticed it through the dark, murky water. She had to lean over the side of the bridge to get a closer look (and a better angle for photographing.) When it noticed her attention, it poked its head up out of the water and stared right back at her. It looked like a fat-headed eel *thing*. But it was *furry,* and it had arms.

She only stayed there long enough to take a couple of hastily shot photos because the fish/not fish was very unsettling to look at. It must have gotten mad when she stepped back to leave because it flew up out of the water to scream at her in warning. The mouth opened strangely too, as if it had jaws that moved sideways as well as the traditional up and down ones. The four corners of its mouth lifted *outwards* in all directions. And then the nasty little thing projectile vomited a bright orange and disgustingly vile substance at her, which had thankfully missed her completely.

Shudder of revulsion, aaannnddd scrolling right past and moving on to the next photo. There are pictures of frog-like creatures, grotesquely fat and oddly colored. They're covered in sharp, pointy spikes and they have impossibly long, super-sized legs. She's not so much of a big dummy that she needs to be told to stay away from *these*. She instinctively *knows* that they're poisonous and deadly.

There's a disturbing beaver/rodent type thing with too many eyes and a snail as large as her hand that she's nicknamed Death Slimer. It has a skull for a shell, and it leaves such a tremendous slime trail in its wake that a Darkling could drown in it. *And it has a skull for a shell.* Did she already mention that? The side of the shell spirals in typical snail shell form, with the beginning point at the center colored black as night. The black fades to darkest brown then further lightens as it winds around, each coil lighter than the one before until it ends with the bone white face of the skull. The skull's upper row of teeth (the entire bottom jaw is MIA and unaccounted for) are embedded into the snail's soft and squishy slug body. Death Slimer seems like a reasonable name for such a creature. It probably produces acid slime, too. It certainly wouldn't surprise her.

She stops walking forward and looks up from her camera when she bumps into the edge of the bridge. Thank you, sweet baby Jesus, the roots had created a dummy block on this part of the bridge, or she would be very wet and very sorry right about now. A waist-high wall of thick sturdy roots has strategically grown upwards to create a guardrail… Aka a dummy block for people that don't pay attention to where they're walking. She turns her head to (belatedly) take in her surroundings and to get an understanding of *why* a dummy block had been added to this section when there hadn't been one anywhere else.

She almost dies right there on the spot, her heart threatening to give up the fight as the reason for the path coming to its abrupt end becomes glaringly, horrifyingly evident. Her bridge takes a sharp turn to the right in order to avoid a patch of land about a hundred yards ahead, a small island with a huge mound, a *massive* pile of sharply pointed leaves at the center of it. But there's no tree on that island that could account for that suspicious heap of leaves. No trees or shrubs, indeed no plant life at all. It's just a dirt island with a veritable *mountain* of fallen leaves in shades of green, yellow, gold, and black.

She studies that pile as her brain intently tries to work out the puzzle. Suddenly, there's a slight ripple of movement, a soft disturbance in the lay of the leaves. The stirring builds up speed and the leaves begin to *slide*. Her eyes narrow in on a concentrated section that seems to be lifting upwards instead of shifting sideways. Her breath freezes into a painful lump of ice inside her lungs when two red eyes *the size of dinner plates* blink open and look back at her. (Blink open in a sideways motion, from left to right instead of up and down.) Her startled cry rings out, tearing through the silence like a shotgun blast. The noise seems to agitate it, and the slithering, sliding movements escalate as it uncoils itself into the biggest, most fear-inducing serpent she's ever seen…even in fantasy books and movies. The leaves hadn't been leaves at all. They're scales, thousands upon thousands of pointed, leaf shaped scales, their sharp tips now dripping venom.

The thing of nightmares glares at her for daring to disturb its slumber and she whimpers as her bladder threatens to let go. She stands there frozen in fear as it slowly, inch by inch, pulls its head back into the striking position, drawing a huge breath in as it does so. It doesn't try to strike out though. Instead, it opens up its huge, gaping maw and roars at her. Not hisses. Roars. An enormous, gusting blast of eardrum-threatening sound waves. Just like a tyrannosaurus rex. Its bottom jaw dislocates and juts out into a massive underbite, and she is absolutely horrified to see that it has a mouth full of angler fish teeth. Needle sharp spikes of varying lengths line the entrance into that cavernous oral cavity and strings of saliva fly out from between them with the force of its battle cry. She doesn't take a photo of this swamp dweller… She's far too focused on running. Nope. Bye Felicia.

"Deep Marshes," Sephyr whispers, her voice quivering and full of dread. "Sephyr scared. Sephyr back go. No go Deep Marshes."

Her two companions are finally, *finally* awake. While that doesn't bring her any guarantees of safety, it does at least afford the comfort of knowing that she's not alone. Boodark the 'Oh, so brave' huddles under his blanket, his head completely covered up with just his huge cartoon eyes peeking out. The nervous little fairy flutters so close beside her that the wind coming off her wings stirs her hair.

She never slows her steady pace as she tells her, "I don't like it here either. I can't go back, but you can. I certainly won't blame you if you do. And you should. Go back to your mate, Sephyr. Go back to your daughter. Be safe. There's no need for you to go through this. Besides, how will you get back if you continue on to the edge of the swamp with me? Won't you have to come back through the Deep Marshes on your return trip? All alone?"

Sephyr fervently shakes her head in denial. "Go around.

Never go Deep Marshes. Only lost Darklings go Deep Marshes. Bad here. *Big* bad here."

It's bad everywhere in this funky, freaky swamp Ecko thinks, but she doesn't say it because it *is* big bad here. Bigger badder than any other place she's ever been. It just *feels* terrible. This entire world feels hostile and wrong, but not like this place does. This is…something else entirely. Something *wicked* and wrong. Even time seems drawn out and slowed down in here.

She just wants to go home, or back to the Black Forest, or the never-ending beach with its butt-pinching monstrosities. Anywhere but here. She knows that her magic is leading her out of the Sorrow Marshes, straight to the woman who lives in a tree. Her ball of light, tunnel vision experience showed her that much, but she knows nothing beyond what it revealed. She has no clue how far it is between here and there. She has no idea what dangers may lie in waiting along the path that's been laid out for her. She's not even sure that the woman is friendly. She could very well be an evil witch disguised as a sweet, old*ish* lady. All she knows for sure is that she wants to be anywhere but here in this big, bad *wicked*. But apparently, she must get through *here* to get to *there*.

"Want basket!" Sephyr cries out, her lip quivering in fear. "Want cantankerous one!"

Boodark scooches over to make room and lifts a corner of the blanket up. "Climb in, fraidy-fairy" he tells her, but his voice is trembling too. Everyone in their little group is scared. Even *she* wishes she could climb into the beddy-bye basket and hide. Since that's not an option, all that's left is to continue walking forward. Why, oh why couldn't she have gotten flying magic instead of bubble magic? Perhaps she can bubble herself and float her way out of the swamp. But on second thought, nope. Knowing herself as well as she does, she fully admits that she'd more likely than not, trap herself and her little companions in the bubble for all time.

Or float it right into the open, gaping maw of some giant monster. Ground stomping it is. One foot in front of the other, even if she's so terrified that her legs tremble like Jell-O.

There's a large, oak-like tree up ahead that looks as if it belongs in the scariest scary movie ever filmed. It has a massive, round-top doorway hollowed out at the base of it, so tall and so wide that a car could easily drive through it… if the door was open, that is. Thankfully it's not.

The insides of the tree are lit up with a strange, flameless fire. She had once come across a tree that had been struck by lightning, and it had burned from the inside out. This looks much like that other tree, but it feels very different. She can't help but think that this tree is one of the doorways to Hell. If that's the case, she hopes with all her terrified heart that it's a one-way doorway… an entrance *into* Hell and not an exit out of it. If something were to come out of that fiery doorway…. She never takes her eyes off of it as she tries to creep past, mentally praying that she goes unnoticed by anything that may be looking out.

A slight, pulsing movement high above the doorway catches her attention and her eyes are drawn to it, away from the tree's inner inferno. There are several tree knots, lumpy holes as big as her head that eerily resemble mouths. And they're *moving*, pulsating as though they're breathing, drawing air in and then expelling it right back out. In, out. In, out. In, and then back out in a sudden coughing fit, belching out huge, stinky clouds of smoke like an old man puffing on a pipe. The entire tree trembles and shakes from the force of the choking and coughing until it suddenly sucks a huge draw of air back into those gasping, wooden mouths. That indrawn breath is so powerful that it feels like a vacuum that's trying to suck her and her friends up into its figurative lungs.

A fearsome inner rumbling begins deep in the belly of that air fouling, chain-smoking monster, and she doesn't wait around to find out what *that* means. She takes off like a rocket, like someone just lit her butt on fire. She throws her hands up over the top of the basket to keep her friends from bouncing out as she flees for her life, imagining all the while that the tree is going to belch out the fires of Hell to chase her down and incinerate her to ash.

She runs as long as her lungs allow her to, which unfortunately isn't long enough. She stops and bends forward, hands on her knees as she gasps for breath.

"No stop! Must hurry, Change Bringer. Must feet fly! Must out!" The tiny mushroom fairy is in full hysteria mode, her speech more garbled than ever. Boodark grabs her by the ankle and forces her back into the basket to prevent her panicked flight instinct from leading her to almost certain death.

"I just have to catch my breath Sephyr. I'm going. See? I'm going!" She *is* moving forward, but she can't run anymore. She's too winded and much too tired. She has a sneaking suspicion that the Deep Marshes are sapping her strength, but she doesn't need Sephyr to tell her that this isn't the place to stop and rest. *Nothing* could make her stop for a little siesta in this place. Nothing except what's most likely right up there past that next bend in the bridge, that is. She tries with all her might to ignore the sounds coming from up ahead. The moaning and wailing, the keening cries. There's a ghost up there, howling like dead things do. She's sure of it.

"Woooo!"

Boodark's hugging the quietly sobbing fairy against his chest, but his eyes fly open wide when he hears the eerie, ghostly lamentation. He starts shivering so hard that the beddy-bye basket is actually vibrating against her chest. He looks down at Sephyr and she looks up at him.

"Awoooo!"

Boodark starts crying too, and the two of them wrap their arms around one another so tight that she couldn't have pulled them apart had she tried to.

"WOOOOO!"

"Aaagghhh!" All three of them scream in a completely reflexive response. Dragging the distraught fairy with him,

Boodark the Cowardly Chickenbutt dives under blanket to huddle and shiver and shake under cover where it's safe-*ish.*

"Ooowhhhooo!"

With every step, the cry gets louder and louder. She does NOT want to keep going. She wants to turn around and take her chances with the Hell Tree. She's very much considering it.

Boodark must be reading her mind. "Can't go back," he says, his voice muffled by blanket.

"That's easy for *you* to say. *You* are in there. *You* aren't out here about to meet a ghost! *You* don't have to see it!" she fires back, just a bit peevishly. Oh, how she wishes she had a basket big enough for her to climb into and ride through the creep zone in.

"Elfslugs and earwax!" Boodark curses. "She's right. I can't make her do this alone. Sephyr, stay under the blanket. You'll be safe, I promise."

It must have taken every bit of courage he possesses in his little body to come up out of that security blankie of his. She smiles in appreciation and whispers a quick, "Thank you." There's nothing he can do about the monster around the corner, but at least she doesn't have to face it alone.

They cautiously approach the curve in the bridge and the moaning suddenly stops. Somehow, that's even worse! Where is it? Why did it suddenly go silent? *Did it somehow get behind them?* Ecko now knows *exactly* how the poor cowardly lion in the Wizard of Oz had felt. "I do believe in spooks. I do, I do, I do," she whispers as she whirls around to check for ghosts behind her. "Oh, I do believe in spooks. I do, I do, I do, *I DO!*" she repeats as she spins back.

"So do I!" Boodark whimpers as they round the curve and find… nothing. Nothing but swamp and swamp life, that is. No ghosts in front, no ghosts behind. And no ghosts to the sides.

Nothing but a tree with small clusters of blackened, apple-sized flowers dangling from its branches. And it's right in the middle of the bridge, blocking the way forward. For some reason, the magic that had built the bridge hadn't gone around to avoid this particular obstacle like it had all the others. It had split the bridge in two so that each half of it circles around the tree and then comes back together and rejoins on the opposite side. There's room to get around the tree, but just barely. It'll definitely be a tight fit. Maybe if she turns and shuffles sideways, she'll be able to squeeze by.

Her mind is stuck on trying to figure out the why's of this new perplexing dilemma. She concentrates her full attention on the tree, studiously trying to understand *why* it's in the middle of the bridge when she suddenly makes out what her eyes had missed during her first quick perusal of its branches.

Boodark must have just caught sight of them too. "Umm Ecko?" he squeaks in alarm.

Those black, dead-looking flowers aren't exactly flowers; they're skulls. "They're probably just seed pods," she tells him.

"You're serious?" is his snarky comeback. "*Seed pods* that just so happen to resemble people skulls?"

She nods. "It's a real thing, believe it or not. I've seen something like it before. There's a flower on Earth called a Snapdragon. When the blooms die, the dried seed pods look like tiny, brown, shrunken skulls."

The blanket shifts as Sephyr pokes her head out to look too. "Sephyr no like. Ecko in water go." She uses her pointer and middle fingers as an 'Ecko' puppet to mime jumping off the bridge and into the water. Then she walks 'Ecko the finger puppet' in a curving, circular path across the blanket to show that they should walk a wide circle around the skull tree.

She glances over the side of the bridge to the water below. It's the deep-water variety, not the ankle deep, sludgy stuff. "I'm not jumping into that. I hate water. If I can't see right through it, I want nothing to do with it. Haven't you been paying attention?

Haven't you *seen* the things that live in the waters here? And you want me to get in there *with* those things? Not. Happening."

Sephyr looks pointedly at the tree. "Think you bonehead tree safer?"

Ecko snorts. She's not even gonna bother answering that. *Of course*, it's safer than the water. Water is the BIG scary. "Besides," she reasons, "there's probably leeches in there. That water definitely looks leech-ery to me."

Boodark and Sephyr both laugh at that. "Leeches no live water. Leeches live land!"

She has no idea why that surprises and shocks her, but it does. Immensely. "LandLeeches?" she whispers, and they both solemnly nod their heads at her.

"Well, I'm still not going in there. Just forget it. What are you worried about anyway? You don't have to go around the tree *or* get into the water. You can fly up out of that basket and flutter yourself *over* the water …as far away from the tree as you choose."

The Darkling wiggles her wings experimentally and admits (with the cutest, embarrassed grin) "Oh! Yes. Sephyr fly!" And she does just that, flying herself over the water while sending them a small, self-satisfied grin.

"I hope nothing down there mistakes you for a bug and jumps out of the water to gobble you up!" Ecko calls out with just a hint of spite in her voice. The little Darkling's grin falters and then her wings lift her a few more feet above the waterline, just in case.

Boodark giggles. "That was mean!" he tells her.

Sephyr has her *own* best wishes for Ecko. "Hope skulls not drop from tree. Bite you all up!"

Boodark gulps. "That was mean*er*," he whimpers, and she has to admit that the tiny Darkling has won this round.

The sliver of bridge on the right looks the tiniest bit broader, so that's the path she takes. She's walking all leaned over to the side, trying to keep as much distance between herself and possible incoming paratrooper skulls as she can manage. She's watching them as she inches her way past, watching them closely.

Boodark's eyeballing them too. They both see it, but it still scares the living ___ (fill in the blank) out of them when it happens.

"Wooooo!" One of those tiny skulls opens its mouth up and screams, just *screams* out a howling, hair-raising and heartstopping cry, right beside her face! That one outcry must have been a signal because before the last *ooo* has left it's rounded, withered mouth, the rest of them take up the cry too. Moans, *loud* moans and ghostly wails fill the air and Boodark adds his own terrified screech in before he throws his hands over his ears to block it all out.

Her eyes dart down to the water in panic. It's the only way to escape the keening…

"Down! Must down!" Sephyr shouts right into her ear so that she can be heard over the skully uproar. "Must down! Must on hands! Must on knees!"

Ecko instantly drops down onto her hands and knees, below the branches, and she hustles like a crab scurrying away from a crabber's net. The screaming skulls revolve on their stems to watch her scramble by like bodiless heads hanging from miniature nooses. It only takes seconds to make it safely around the screaming demon deadheads, but those seconds seem to last a small lifetime while she's spending them in a terrified state of… *"Please-don't-fall-on-my-head! Please-don't-eat-me! I-don'twant-to-die!"*

She watches the bridge floor speed by as she crawls as fast as she can, channeling her inner Dori but substituting the word swimming for crawling… "Just keep crawling. Just keep crawling," she sings as she scuttles for her life.

Tittering laughter breaks into her mad mental ramblings. "Change Bringer safe! Stand. Ground stomp now."

She lifts her head up and tentatively takes in her surroundings. Wow, just *wow*. She must have been moving much faster than she'd realized. She's somehow managed to crawl close to twenty-five feet beyond the spot where the bridge halves merged back together. Embarrassed but too proud to show it, she climbs to her feet and brushes the dirt from her hands. "Well! Looks like we both survived going our own separate ways, right Sephyr? Good for us!"

And nothing more gets said about how scared they all just were. They each respectively put the terror of the moment behind them, preferring to leave all that behind with the screaming deadhead tree.

"They're Hooker Lips!" she exclaims just minutes later. "We have those on Earth too, although the ones there are much smaller than these... I think. I've only seen them in National Geographic magazines. They don't grow where I live, or rather, where I used to live. Look at them! They look exactly like women's bright, red lipstick-painted lips. This is so cool! I've actually found something on *this* world that's on my bucket list!"

Boodark and Sephyr glance at one another and shrug.

"What Hook-Her?" Sephyr wants to know.

Her face instantly flames in embarrassment at the thought of explaining *that*. "Oh, just an Earth woman," she says with a dismissive wave of her hand.

"So, you're a Hook-Her?" Boodark asks in all innocence.

"No!" she yells as she glares down at him.

"But you said..."

She cuts him off before he can go any further. "No Boodark. I'm *not* a hooker. Those are not... nice ladies."

She turns back to admire the candy apple-red flowers that are growing out of the water on long, thin stalks, similar to sunflower stems. Thirty seconds pass in silence before he tries again. "Sooo," Boodark begins. "You're a Hooker-Her only when you're being mean to me?"

"No, Boodark! I'm not a hooker. Ever! I've never been, nor will I ever *be* a hooker! Now that's the end of the discussion!"

He turns to Sephyr and loudly whispers "She sounds like a Hook-Her to me! *Not nice!*"

She ignores him and snaps a couple photos to put in the Bucket List album that Dr Bradburn had given her as a

'Congratulations, you're not crazy!' gift. These may not be *Earth's* Hooker Lip flowers, but hey…Does that really even matter? She doesn't think so. They count! She can cross this 'hope to someday see' off of her list.

"Hmmm?" she distractedly murmurs as she focuses her camera on a particularly pouty pair of lips. "Stop whispering, you two," she says as she snaps the photo.

"Pssswwssss." The whispering, nonsensical sounds continue.

"Seriously, you guys. It's rude."

Sephyr flies up in front of the camera's lens, blocking her view and ruining the shot. "Not whisper Sephyr!" she insists as she points from herself to Boodark. "Whisper *them!*" she insists as she turns her accusing, pointing finger to the flowers.

And they are! The stalks are leaning towards one another, and those lush, red lips are moving, whispering soft secrets that, for the life of her, she can't figure out how they'll even *hear*. They're all mouth and no ears, in every sense.

"Spwwweeessssssp." The whispering secret-telling continues.

She can hear them well enough to pick out a word here and there, but nothing is really clear. She leans closer, out over the edge of the bridge so that maybe she can actually understand what they're saying.

"Look at her! Would you just look at her pale lips?" Tittering laughter, then gasps all around. "Are those *petals* on her top?"

"Are those supposed to be *RED?*"

"I would hide my buds in the water if I had petals like *those!*"

Ecko's mouth drops open in shock. "Oh! They're *mean!*"

Sephyr's face turns bright red (as red as those nasty hooker lips) when she hears what they have to say about *her*.

Boodark has to grab her ankle again to hold the little spitfire back. "What's going on?" he shouts in confusion as he realizes that his two female companions are getting angry. Like really, *really* angry.

Ecko answers him, but she never takes her eyes off of the offensive blabbermouths. "What's going on is that those… those… *hussies* are down there talking smack!"

His face crumples into a bewildered frown. "Talking smack? What does that even mean?"

"It means," she practically snarls, "that those big mouths down there are telling lies and spreading rumors… just like those mean, gossipy flowers in Alice in Wonderland's talking garden. Only, those were *beautiful* flowers, not raggedy *weeds* like these old, spent blossoms. Why, I've seen dead, brown grass that looked better than…"

Boodark's panicked cries interrupt her furious tirade. "Run, dummy! *Run!*" He screams as the first spitball lands on the bridge and begins to sizzle a smoking, smoldering hole into the roots. "They're spitting! Oh, those nasty little things are actually *spitting* at us!" Ecko screeches to her equally outraged fairy friend.

"Let go Sephyr, Cantankerous one! *Let GO!* Make pay. Make *regret!*" She's struggling with all her tiny might against Boodark's restraining grip on her.

Suddenly, there's a pair of lips directly in front of them, lifted to the same height as Ecko's face. Several more pissed off and puckered up lips are right behind it, backing it up it like a gang of hood-rats. It takes her a moment to figure out that the *stalks* are growing longer, shooting upwards so that those rumor weeds can reach them with their acid spit projectiles.

"Yeah, it's time to go Ecko. Right now!" Boodark shouts in desperation. He doesn't know how to get them out of this situation.

Apparently, the Hook-Her Lips only affect females. He hasn't heard a single word come out of those mouths, but he can sure see that they're firing acid spit shots at his girls…which means that they're spitting at him too. He dares not let go of the hissing Darkling, nor can he force Ecko to retreat… He suddenly remembers what she'd said to him back at the DreamSnare pod. 'Love is a powerful motivator, as is guilt.'

"What about Charlie? And Susan?" he asks as she angrily dodges wads of acid spit. "Getting melted by a spitball would be such a pathetic way to let them down, wouldn't you say?"

She glances down at his earnest, pleading little face and the fog of anger lifts the tiniest bit. Just enough for her to whirl around and run out of the danger zone.

"Yes!" Boodark pumps his one empty fist up into the air in triumph, the other still desperately clamped onto the furious Darkling's leg. Ecko may be calming down, but not so their little fairy friend. She's steadily spewing Darkling-tongued curses.

"That's it Ecko, snap out of it and get us away from here.

I've got Sephyr!" Boodark crows.

Her head clears and her blood cools with each pounding footfall that she takes away from the Hooker's bridge/street corner.

Boodark's heart almost gives out when she suddenly stops running and spins back around. He's *sure* that she's about to run back to try and finish her fight, even with the unbeatable odds of being outnumbered and *not* possessing acid spit. But all she's doing is lifting up her own fist and screaming out one final threat, ensuring that she gets the last word in.

"You rumor weeds better hope I don't come back here with an electric weed whacker, ya bunch of nasty strumpets!"

"This is it, it *has* to be," she insists. She's spent the last half hour searching for a relatively safe place to make camp.

"Nowhere safe. Must keep go!" Sephyr has spent the entire thirty minutes arguing. She doesn't want to sleep in this part of the swamp. And she doesn't blame her for that, not a bit. But she's seriously about to pass out. She can't go much further. Her head feels light and floaty, and her limbs feel like they've suddenly gone on strike. They're sluggish and slow to obey her brain's commands.

"I can't go on another minute, Sephyr. I need food and I need sleep... *real* sleep. Some of us need more than four hours of down time after they've been awake for days. Pales, I mean. I need more than four hours of sleep after being awake for several *Pales,*" she clarifies as she checks the immediate vicinity for possible dangers.

This section of the bridge is more elevated than the rest of it had been. For whatever reason, it's suspended at least ten feet above the water level. That *should* make it harder for creepies to get at them from below... She looks up into the surrounding tree crowns. Those could be (and probably are) hiding potential threats, but really, where *aren't* there threats? Nowhere is safe. But that doesn't change the fact that she still needs rest. She turns her attention back to the angry Darkling. Sephyr's got her hands on her hips, hovering in the air and glaring at her... looking very much like a dark, emo Tinkerbell.

"No sleep here. Must go. Must out! Must..."

The Pitch rumble interrupts her tirade and Ecko sighs. "Look Sephyr. Even if I wasn't about to fall on my face or stumble off the side of the bridge, Pitch is coming and I'm not traveling in the dark. If you don't like this particular spot, then why don't you fly ahead and see if you can find us a safer one."

Her little eyes pop open in alarm, eyebrows rising so high that they're almost up in her dreadlocks. "Sephyr *no* fly ahead, looksee safe place. Danger! Danger for alone Sephyr!"

Ecko nods. That's just what she thought the obstinate little thing would say. She lowers the beddy-bye basket to the bridge and shrugs off the backpack.

"Then here we stay." She ignores the ranting as she goes about setting up a fort-like shelter with her tarp. ("Bad place. *Never* Sephyr come here. *Never* Darkling come here. Sephyr *hate* here. Danger. Danger *all!*") The best she can do is drape it and tie the tarp to the root and vine dummy block/guardrails. When she's done, she has a crooked and uneven, three sided and roofed shelter. The entryway will just have to stay open. This way, they'll be able to look out at all the nighttime swamp terrors. Perfect. *Not.* She longs for the tent that the FireFairies had burned up.

She finishes tying the last knot and stands up from her squatted position, throwing her arms out for balance as the world sways with a sudden bout of dizziness. Her head swims and her vision blurs and she's then falling, crumpling down in a dead faint. The last thing she sees before lights out is Boodark's terrified eyes as he shouts her name.

It's also the first thing she sees when she awakens. He's all up in her face, shouting for her to wake up and help them. Help them what? Her thoughts are sluggish, as if the brain matter that they must swim through is thick as the Sorrow Marshes mud. Pitch has fallen, but it's not the total blackout that she's grown used to. "Oh, thanks be to the EverLands! *Yes!* Wake up, Ecko. I need you to *wake up!*"

She slowly and carefully sits up to find out what's happening now, and her breath catches at what she discovers. The area around her is lit up with tiny, glowing…. *octopuses?* (Octopi?) She turns in a slow, still-sitting-on-her-butt circle as she tries to take in the brilliance around her. Hundreds, *thousands* of them surround the campsite. They cling to the trees and the sides of the bridge with their black, googly eyes focused on her. She cries out with a childlike wonder as a group of them alight from the closest tree. Their bioluminescent lights glow electric blues, neon greens, and fluorescent pinks as they swim/float through the air using their diminutive tentacles to propel them along.

One of them darts in close to her face and Sephyr immediately drops down out of the air to block it. She draws her little foot back and then swings it forward with all her tiny might. When her foot connects, the bitty, baby octopus lets out the most pitiful, high pitched *Eeep!* sound that she has ever heard. She watches in absolute shock as the poor little thing gets launched out into the night, tumbling head over tentacles.

She turns her disbelieving eyes to the fairy that she *thought* she knew. "How could you?" she whispers. "Oh, how *could* you?" Sephyr doesn't even bother to answer her. She's too busy punting the next one away.

"Stop that!" she cries as she jumps to her feet. "Leave them alone! Poor little guys. They're adorable!" She holds her hand out to an especially bitty one the size of a marble, and it air swims closer to reach her. She's momentarily distracted from its cuteness by Boodark's shouted, "No, Ecko!" She glances down and her mouth drops open in shock when he ninja-slaps one right out of the air and it splashes down into the water below the bridge. Meanwhile, Bitty Butt reaches her and settles onto her wrist, and she immediately lifts her arm up closer to her face so that she can see it better.

"Oohh, hey there little one," she coos in a soft voice so that she doesn't frighten it away. It's translucent *and* bioluminescent, allowing her to see right through it to the irradiant inner workings of its body. Its insides are made up of nothing more than glowing blue lines and splotches and a brilliantly lit blob at its center, which she assumes is its heart... or perhaps its brain. Who can tell?

Bitty Butt opens its mouth up into a wide O and something's *happening* in there. How strange! It seems to have an overly large tongue curled up inside its mouth. She watches in fascination as it sends it out, unrolling, *uncoiling* it as it emerges until it's as stiff and straight as a.... Wait a minute. That tongue looks just like a straw, a *proboscis*, and it has a pointy, jabby dagger at the tip of it. *Just like mosquitos have...* only much, much bigger than a mosquito's.

"OW!" she yells as she figures out, too late, exactly why her companions have become professional punters in this new game called octi-punt. Or should she call it squidball? Focus, Ecko!

That cute little octopus plunges its freakishly long and fat tongue into her wrist, driving at least three quarters of it into her flesh. She's just about to flick it off of her arm when she realizes that it's not a typical insectile proboscis; it's a double decker. It looks like two straws had been glued together, side by side, to make one long suck-tube. And the strangest thing is happening now. It's so strange that she's entirely too fascinated to give it the flick that it deserves for tricking her with its cuteness, for bamboozling her with its deceptively innocent adorableness… for abusing her trust. The octopus isn't sucking up her blood. It's drawing some sort of shining, white light out of her. As it travels up one side of the double decker straw-tongue, blue bioluminescence from inside of *it* travels down through the other side. Like an exchange of bodily fluids. Giving and taking. The blue light goes into her skin, and she can actually see the glow as it flows into her arm. It burns like cold fire, scorching and freezing all at the same time.

Now she flicks it off. She rubs at her wrist as she watches it air swim away in a drunken manner, slow and sluggish and wobbly. The other octopuses hold still as they witness one of their own kind drink and drive… or sip and fly is more like it. They all watch Bitty Butt until his light disappears, swallowed back up into the darkness of the swamp. Then thousands of pairs of googly eyes suddenly turn back and focus on her. Her dumb brain sends her a mental picture of them all tying little napkins around their necks, tiny forks and knives clutched in their tentacles and held at the ready.

"Oh, troll turds! We *need* to do something!" Boodark yells.

"Fight!" Sephyr shouts back as the swarm renews their attack in earnest. They're both steadily knocking away incomers like pros while *she* performs the craziest, most absurd dance of hokey pokey in hokey pokey history. She turns herself around in frenzied circles as she swipes and slashes the air like the world's worst ninja. She gets lucky and actually manages to land a few blows, but several sucky-pusses inevitably get past and find their mark.

She instinctively slaps at the sharp sting on the back of her neck and grimaces at the resulting *squish*. She pulls her hand back and stares down in horror at the crime scene. It looks just like someone had cut open a glow stick, poured the contents onto her hand, and then tossed two googly eyes on top of the mess. It's *horrible*. She wipes her hand on her pants as her friends continue to battle the horde of tiny air octopuses. They go flying in every direction, lighting up the Pitch with their glow, the air resounding with their little *'Eeeps!'*

"What do we do?" she shouts as she punches one away from her face. Nobody answers. They're too busy, and they don't know what to do any more than she does. *'Think Ecko'* she admonishes herself. What does she have at her disposal that could scare them away? Fire! Fire just may do the trick. Most creatures fear flames. She whirls around and digs in her bag for a lighter and her hand brushes against one of her flashlights. Hmmm, maybe she won't need fire. The sucky-pusses are obviously nocturnal. Why else would they glow? Maybe they don't like the light. After all, they hadn't shown up until after Pitchfall.

She snatches the flashlight up, clicks it on, and shines it out into the night. Tiny hisses and screeches and *eeps!* fill the air as they immediately go from attack mode and into escape mode.

"Yes! Oh, yeah! Good thinking, Ecko!" Boodark praises. "Yeah, you *better* run!" he calls after them.

But the sucky-puss horde doesn't go far. They only retreat far enough to escape the light's reach, settling back into the trees. And they wait. They watch.

Boodark holds a flashlight on them while she quickly drapes the extra blanket (the one that *he* uses at night) over the opening to their fort/tent, tucking and tying it into place so that it won't slide off. She tosses her things inside, takes the flashlight back, and then holds the blanket/door aside so that her friends can go in. Then she wedges the flashlight between the roots of the bridge's floor so that the beam points up and out. She crawls in after them and prays that it'll be enough to keep the sucky-pusses at bay…. and that the batteries last.

"Surround Change Bringer *only*." Sephyr explains. They're discussing the octopus swarm as they eat their meager dinner. Her two companions insist that *they* had never been in any danger, that *they* weren't targets.

"Why?" she asks, her mouth stuffed full of stale crackers. She's starving, absolutely, *insanely* ravenous. Too many rationed meals, too much exercise, (physical *and* mental) and not enough sleep are taking a drastic toll on her. She desperately needs real sustenance. And about a month of uninterrupted sleep. And a scalding hot bath. She sighs longingly as she shoves another dry, unappetizing cracker into her mouth.

Sephyr takes a sip of water and answers. "Want Change Bringer light."

Okay, now she's just confused. She glances over to the flashlight that's busy lighting up their shelter. "Nooo. They *didn't* like the light," she argues.

The little fairy shakes her head and points at it. "No that light." Then she points at Ecko. "Changer Bringer light. *Ecko* light. *Inside.*"

She stops stuffing food into her mouth long enough to ask, "*My* light? What do you mean? I don't have a light."

But the Darkling insists that she does. "Change Bringer shine bright. Like Glowstone. *Many* see glow. Want. Want *steal* glow. Want take for self."

She looks down at her hands and then at Boodark. "I glow?"

He shrugs and looks away. "Don't ask me what nonsense she's speaking. I don't see it." Then he changes the subject as if the whole conversation is boring him. "There are more important things to discuss than whether or not you glow. After you decided to take your nap, I retraced your steps a little way back so I could add my own water and mud to the swamp below." He pauses to snicker at the two females making their retching noises. "There's something you should be aware of." He pauses for dramatic effect. "The bridge is disappearing."

She just looks at him for several seconds, waiting to see if he's going to elaborate or maybe even say 'Gotcha! Just kidding!' But he does neither. "What do you mean, *disappearing*?"

He snorts and rolls his eyes. "I *mean* the bridge is no longer back there. It's gone. Vanished. Departed from sight. Faded away to nothing. Dematerialized. *Disappeared!*"

She thinks it over while they finish their meal. "Well, I don't see how it really matters. I wouldn't have gone back anyway. I *can't*. This was always a one-way trip for me."

Sephyr and Boodark both perk up and pay close attention to what she's doing now as she slowly and distractedly unwraps the granola bar that she had set out for their dessert. "Maybe the magic is fading because it was only meant to help *me* get out of the

Sorrow Marshes. I'm not sure if that's a good thing or a greedy one. The bridge could have saved so many innocent lives. Of course, it could very well have saved the not so innocent ones too."

She's thoroughly engrossed in her speculations and hypotheses, unwittingly waving the treat in the air as she talks. Two sets of completely captivated eyes track it.

"Um, Ecko?" Boodark begins but she interrupts him before he can say what's on his mind.

"Anyway, I think we'll be ok… unless it disappears right out from below us. Wouldn't *that* suck? Maybe it's a timed magic, like sand in an hourglass … the magic dissolves and the bridge disappears when the sand runs out."

She looks to her friends to see if they have any insights they'd like to add, and she finally notices what their eyes are glued to. Smiling sheepishly, she apologizes and breaks the granola bar in half and hands it out. They both pounce on it like starving, rabid animals, but Boodark, the sweet boy, tries to hand back the last half inch of his portion. "Take it. I know you're still hungry."

She is, but she refuses to take the treat from him. "I'm more tired than anything else," she insists. "I must not have slept very long when I was passed out earlier."

Sephyr nods. "Minutes," she informs her in between her om nom noms.

Yeah, that's what it felt like. "I'm going to bed. Since your blanket is currently a door, you can crawl in here with me when you're ready for sleep. Oh, and you too, Sephyr. We can all snuggle while…." She's out just like a blown-out candle before she can even finish her sentence.

Sex, Drugs, and Rock & Roll

Samara

Lenny, ever the pragmatic overthinker, has Mr. Chadwick drive around the building, slowly so that they can locate every single way in and out. Obviously, there's the main entrance at the front, a side entrance for employees only, three fire exits, and a loading bay at the rear for supply trucks. Satisfied and confident that he knows exactly which door Samara will emerge from, he has his man park off to the side where they'll be out of the way but still able to see both the main entrance and the employee entrance.

Based on the options, Lenny's willing to bet money that she'll be coming back out of one of these two doors. All he has to do now is wait.

"Would you care for a drink while we wait, Sir?" Mr. Chadwick calls back to him. "I had Charles stock the car with your favorite beverages and a few extra precautions… just in case things don't go as smoothly as we desire."

Lenny opens the built-in refrigerator to find that it is indeed stocked with some of his favorites, and he gratefully pours himself a glass of Glenmorangie single malt scotch. He does some exploring as he sips, savoring the delicious burn of fire that trails down his throat and pools in his belly. "Remind me to give you a raise when we get back home, Mr. Chadwick," he praises.

The chauffeur *almost* smiles when he answers. "Very good, Sir. I'll do that."

Lenny *does* smile. He already pays the older, much larger, always calm, cool, and collected in any given situation gentleman an ungodly amount of money. So far, he's been worth every penny of it.

Take this car, for example. Mr. Chadwick had the presence of mind to reach out to his Texas connections the very instant he learned that the two of them would be in the neighborhood. This car and two others had been prepped, stocked, and delivered to the airport, all with a loaner team of men at his disposal to use as his own personal guard. Lenny had chosen to utilize the Land Rover and had immediately sent the other two… along with the extra men away. He's grateful for the loan of a car, the burner phones, and the guns. He's equally appreciative of the bottle of fine scotch and the Texas sampler pack of top-grade recreational pleasures that Mr. Chadwick's connection had so thoughtfully provided.

But Lenny is a private man, and he never, *ever* mixes business with pleasure. As such, he has two rules… Actually, he has many rules, but only two that are set in stone. His two personal commandments, he calls them. #1 He never lets other people, especially people that he's never met and therefore doesn't trust, in on his business. And #2 He keeps his head free, sharp, and clear of all things narcotic or otherwise mind-altering and mood-enhancing while he handles said business.

That's where most people in his line of work usually go wrong. They trust the wrong people and/or they can't keep their business and their pleasures separate. The only thing he ever allows himself during a job… *any* job, is a drink or two. Nothing more.

Bringing Samara into the fold is his top priority, and perhaps the most lucrative and rewarding business move he'll ever make in his entire illicit career. He can't afford to screw things up with a muddled head or by putting his trust in potential rivals who may want to take what's his. And Samara *is* his; she just doesn't know it. She's *his* discovery, and as such, he'll be keeping her to himself. All he's got to do now is catch her and convince her that she belongs to him… that she *wants* to be used by him to further expand his empire. Easy peasy lemon squeezy… as long as he doesn't piss her off and get himself killed in the process. The girl is a hard-core killer and a *wicked* badass. And she's psychotic to boot.

They'd been parked for no more than twenty minutes when the sound of rapidly approaching sirens draws their attention. "That was fast, even for you, sweet Samara," Lenny murmurs as he sits up in his seat and leans forward to get a better view of the exits.

"Come on, come *on*" he urgently whispers. "Where are you?" He's beginning to worry that he'd made the wrong choice. Just a few minutes ago, he would have bet on his mother's life, God bless her, that Samara would need to make a quick and inconspicuous getaway, and that she would do so through that side door. She could very well come out the front, but he doesn't think so. She's learning, evolving. She still causes chaos and bedlam everywhere she goes, but she's been getting better at avoiding the authority figures, aka the boys in blue. Not that she needs to avoid them, not with those incredible powers that she possesses.

Maybe he'd been wrong though, and she'd head straight for whatever exit was closest to the chaos that she'd created… one of the fire escapes, perhaps. She could already be gone. He could have lost her! Panic fills his head, squeezes his throat shut so that he can't draw a breath…. And then the side door opens, and a red headed, a red *everything,* mess of a woman steps out. Lenny's heart stutters briefly before it picks up its normal rhythm and he regains his ability to breathe.

"Hurry now, Mr. Chadwick. Let's go get our girl."

They pull up alongside her and he puts the window down, leaning over so that she can see him there in the backseat. "Climb in, Samara. We need to get away from here before the boys in blue figure out that you're no longer in the building. We'll go get you cleaned up, and then we'll talk."

Samara takes a moment to glance around as the sirens wail and the tires screech to a stop at the front entrance. Then she opens the door and gets in, leaving blood and bits of… stuff on everything she touches. His man wastes no time in getting them out of there, away from the danger of being discovered and apprehended as accomplices to… whatever *this* is.

"Damn girl, what'd you do in there… make the crazies swallow live grenades and then just stand there in the rain of guts?" He watches her eyes light up at the thought and he can't help but throw his head back and laugh in sheer delight. This is *it!* This is really happening!

"Find us a motel, Mr. Chadwick. Our girl is in serious need of a bath."

Lenny leans back and watches her as she watches him. He notices her fiddling with something in her hand and he frowns in confusion. "Don't tell me you went there, went through all that… *mess* just to get crazy people drugs."

Samara, who'd been quiet up until that point, picks a bit of entrails out of her hair and flicks it at him. "No, *this* was just a distraction, a delightful little discovery. What I went in there for is none of your concern, *Lennard Rollins.*"

The car swerves almost imperceptibly as Mr. Chadwick's eyes meet his employer's in the rear-view mirror. He's silently asking for any new instructions that may be forthcoming at this new development. Lenny calmly pulls the chunk of shredded viscera off his cheek where it had landed and stuck like a sticky, al dente spaghetti noodle.

"On course, Mr. Chadwick. Stay on course. No matter what else may occur, Samara will still need to get cleaned up." He turns his attention back to his guest as he wipes the blood smear from his cheek with his crisply folded, pristine-white handkerchief.

"I see that I wasn't as successful at remaining hidden as I thought I'd been. It's true, I *have* been following you, watching you, studying you." He holds his hands up in supplication as he adds, "Surely you can't fault a man for being cautious where you're concerned. You're certainly not known for your tolerance… especially towards men. But, if you'll be patient just long enough to hear me out, you may find that you like my proposition. I'm certain that we can be *so* good together, Samara… if you give me the chance to prove it."

She's quiet, studying him oh, so intently for so long that he begins to feel like he's a bug under a magnifying glass. It takes every ounce of willpower that he possesses to hold still and not squirm under her scrutiny, even as he fervently prays that she doesn't decide to angle the magnifying glass *just so* in order to fry him with the rays of the sun.

"You've amused me thus far. It's the only reason that you're still breathing. I will go with you to your rented room. I will listen to what you have to say. But first, you will get me more of whatever was in this vial." She shoves the empty syringe at him before she continues. "*Then* I'll decide if I shall let you live."

Lenny nods. "Fair enough, but I've got something much better than *anything* they could have shot you up with in that hospital." He selects one of the baggies of snow-white powder, pours it, cuts it, and pushes it into a thin line as he sends up a quick 'Thank ya kindly' for Texas hospitality. He'll have to remember to send an outrageously expensive and extravagant thank you gift to Mr. Chadwick's connection once this whole business is concluded. *If* he remains amongst the living long enough to do so, that is.

"Here you go, baby. Try this. I promise you won't be disappointed." She eyes it hungrily but warily, refusing to make a move towards it. She doesn't trust him. She doesn't trust anyone. Good girl. Smart.

"You first," she demands. He doesn't even balk at breaking commandment # 2. She needs proof that he's not trying anything nefarious… he'll give her whatever proof she desires. The little white line disappears up his nose and he quickly sets up another one for her. She watches him closely for the next few minutes, just to be sure. Only then does she follow suit and mimic his actions.

Lenny relaxes slightly as the first euphoric giggle escapes her lips. *'Got ya, sweet thing'* he thinks with a self-satisfied smile as they pull up to the sleazy, no questions asked motel.

Samara's never felt so wonderful in all her life. The only thing that even came close was those times she'd been in Krispin's arms… pinned beneath him, pushed up against a wall, or riding atop that divine body of his. But this, oh, *this* is pure bliss, euphoric even. She has the sudden urge to dance or sing or fuck or slay dragons; she's not sure which. Perhaps *all* of those things. In the end she just shuts her eyes and rides it out, just to see where it will lead.

They arrive at their destination, and she allows Lenny to lift her out of the car and carry her into the rented motel room. He lays her down on the bed, blood and all, and she immediately stretches like a cat, basking in the ecstasy that she's experiencing. She rides the high and she must admit that Lenny had been right. This *is* far superior to the stuff that Dr Bradburn's goons had pumped into her. It lasts longer too, but not by much. She's stone cold sober again within ten minutes… but what an amazing ten minutes it had been!

And she wants *more*. Now, right now. But no. She's going to wait until after she's bathed and heard what Lenny has to say. She would pick it from his mind herself if she were able to, but she's already learned that she can't do that. Not with *him*.

She sits up and swings her legs to the floor, bringing a sudden end to the men's quiet conversation. She stands up and slowly peels her disgusting, half stiff, half sticky/soggy clothing off and drops the whole mess to the floor. Ecko's file, the information that she'd searched for and gone through so much trouble to gain, falls unnoticed to the floor and gets buried beneath her soiled clothing.

Unnoticed by *her,* but not by Lenny, that is. His eyes are always on the move, picking up every detail in every situation that he finds himself in. He's trained himself to see what no one else sees, and the instant that folder hits the floor, he determines to get his hands on it and discover just what it is that's so thoroughly caught his girl's attention. And he vows to himself that he'll divert that attention to other things, *pleasurable* things, to distract her from whatever her bloody mission had been about.

Mr. Chadwick, always the gentleman, spins around and stares at the door as soon as he realizes that she's disrobing, but Lenny watches every move she makes… and she in turn, watches his eyes while he stares at her body. There's desire there, lurking back behind his greed. Of course, there's desire. He *is* a lover of females after all, in fine health and at his prime. And she *is* beautiful, with a luscious young body with curves in all the right places. But Lenny doesn't *want* to want her, not in that way. Oh, he's appreciative of her feminine form, but it's not her body that he's after. He wants her for her magic. He wants the power that having her at his side will bring him.

Samara knows all this, not by sending her Shadows into *him* and reading it straight from his mind as she normally would, but from his man's mind. She's learned it all from Mr. Chadwick. *He's* an open book, just like everyone else. He has no shields, no defense against her Shadows. He can't even feel them in there, not if she doesn't want him to feel them. But Lenny is different. Somehow, he's immune to her Shadows. They can't get inside of him, and therefore she can't read his thoughts. Nor can she use his mind against him or control him.

There's only been one other like him, only one who'd also been immune. Krispin. It had driven her bugfuck crazy that she'd never been able to read Krispin's private thoughts, and that she could never control him. Her only consolation had been that she'd never allowed *him* to control *her* either. He'd only taken from her what she'd allowed him to take, and vice versa. They'd had a whole lot of mutually satisfying sex, and that was it. There hadn't been anything more to their relationship. Period. End of story.

Samara determines right now, in this moment, that she will have dominion over Lenny in every way. There are other ways to control a man, even one that thinks he's strong enough to resist her charms. He thinks that he'll be able to use her. He thinks that he'll get her hooked on the dope that he deals in and that she'll be his pet, his little lap monkey… nothing more than a highly entertaining party trick to show off. He thinks he'll be getting a convincer, a punisher, and an executioner all in one subtle and unsuspecting little package. He thinks that he'll use her to convince others to bow to him, to punish those that refuse him, and to execute his sworn enemies.

She may not be able to get inside Lenny's headspace, but there's nothing stopping her from crawling around in Mr. Chadwick's. She learned *everything* from reading Mr. Chadwick's thoughts over the last several days. Oh yes, she'd been aware of them following her. Of course, she had. They'd been foolish to believe otherwise. But she'd been intrigued by Lenny's immunity to her powers, just as she'd been thoroughly amused by his plans for her. She *let* them follow her around. They just hadn't realized it.

Now, Samara saunters up to Lenny, naked hips swaying seductively. She leans in and slowly runs her hands up over his shoulders and grasps the back of his head to pull him down to her level. She kisses him with every bit of the passion that *never* leaves her, no matter how many people she beds. Then she steps back and without breaking eye contact with him, she lets her demands be known.

"When I get out of that bath, I expect clean clothing, food, and drink. And I want dessert… something chocolate. And more of that delightful white powder. Think you boys can handle that?"

Mr. Chadwick never turns his eyes in her direction as he fumbles the door open. "Very good, ma'am. I'll see to it!" he calls as he rushes out the door and slams it closed behind him.

Samara throws her head back and laughs up at Lenny. "I think I make your man nervous. What do you think?" She purrs as she moves in closer. "Do I make him nervous?"

He grins back as he answers, "Undoubtedly."

Her fingers lower and trail over his chest. "And you?" she whispers against his lips. "Do I make you nervous as well?"

Lenny reaches up and places his hand over hers to stop their wandering. "Only so far as I know that you can kill me where I stand and never even raise a finger to do so," he replies as he takes a step back. "Look Samara. I think you misunderstood the meaning of all this. I didn't bring you here for sex. I don't want you in my bed."

He rushes on when he sees the storm clouds gathering in her eyes. "Hear me out! You must understand. You *are* tempting… one of the most desirable women I've ever seen. You have no idea how ummm *hard* it is to keep my hands to myself right now. But you're not an ordinary woman. You're special. You're unique. You. Are. *Spectacular*."

He takes a deep breath and plunges on. "I can have most any woman I choose to see to my pleasures… beautiful but *ordinary* women. You are no ordinary woman and I refuse to treat you as such. You, my dear, are meant for greater things. You are meant to be a *queen*."

She snorts as she glances down at herself, standing there in a cheap motel, her naked body covered in dried, flaking blood and brain matter.

"Pretty words, Lennard Rollins the third. Now tell me the *truth*."

He lifts his chin and stubbornly, bravely sticks to his story. "It is the truth, part of it anyway. You *are* the most spectacular thing I've ever had the pleasure of meeting. But it's not the *only* truth.

Another one is that I have a business proposition that I think, I *hope* you'll be interested in. And one other truth is, and I swear that I say this with all honesty, humility and respect… I've seen the men you take to your bed. I've seen the condition you leave them in, after you're done playing with them. Call me crazy, but I choose to keep my eyeballs and my tongue inside my head, my dick firmly attached to my body, and breath steadily pumping in and out of my lungs. You, my sweet serial killer, are an unpredictable sociopath and I respect and admire the hell out of you. And *that's* the Godhonest truth!"

Samara listens carefully to every word and then she nods. "Very well. We will discuss this 'proposition' when I'm clean. You may want to go over your speech while I bathe. So far, you haven't said a single thing that will win me over."

She turns and heads for the bathroom and he can't help but watch her ass sway as she goes. "But I'm still alive!" he calls out to that delectable, retreating backside. "You haven't killed me yet, so I consider that a win in and of itself!"

She never turns around, but she laughs and acknowledges his point. "How very true. Score one for you, Lennard."

She emerges in a cloud of steam an hour later, clean, naked, and dripping wet. She does have a towel in her hands, but she's not even trying to cover her nakedness. She's using it to dry those dripping red curls of hers before they can frizz up into a snarled puffball.

"I hate these places," she complains. "They never provide enough soap to wash away all the blood. Nor do they leave enough towels."

She plops down onto the bed that's been remade with clean linens. The old, bloody duvet has vanished, along with her ruined clothing. There are several shopping bags of clothes containing everything that she could possibly need to outfit herself for a day or so.

Lenny, who's seated at the small table for two that all motel rooms seem to possess, watches her rifle through the bags. He takes note of everything, the way she rubs her fingers over the silky lingerie, how her eyes light up with pleasure when she sees the flirty green skirt that will show off her legs and bring out the brilliance of her emerald-green eyes.

Her pleasure in the new clothing surprises him, throws him off guard... it's such a *normal* woman's reaction. But then she pushes the stacks of clothing away as if she couldn't care less what Mr. Chadwick had purchased for her.

"I'm starving. Why is there no food? Where is Mr. Chad..." The knocking on the door cuts her off, and she watches as Lenny gets up to peer through the peephole.

"Ah, speak of the devil," he murmurs as he swings the door open wide to let a heavily laden Mr. Chadwick into the room. The man's face is red and beaded with sweat, either from the heavy load that he's carrying or from having to rush around in order to fulfill her demands in the short time frame that she'd given him.

"Sorry Ma'am, sorry Sir. I got back as fast as I could. There are policemen everywhere, searching cars even. I called in the cleaner for the Rover and traded it for a Cadillac... I hope that's acceptable. There was no time to be picky. Would you like me to set your dinner up there on the bed or at the table, Miss?" His face flames red when he sees that she's sitting there all naked-like.

"On the bed. I hope you didn't forget the chocolate," she warns.

"*Oh, no* ma'am. I would never deprive a lady of her chocolate," he tells her in all seriousness.

The two men work together to remove the food from the bags. They open up boxes and cartons and containers, placing it all on the bed within her reach. She immediately digs into a slice of decadent chocolate cheesecake, sighing in utter bliss. She devours that dessert so quickly that Mr. Chadwick's mouth drops open in awe.

"Thank God you didn't forget the chocolate," Lenny mutters. "We'd both be dead."

Samara ignores them both as she selects a rich, dark chocolate mousse. She leans back against the headrest, getting comfortable so that she can take her time with it.

"So, tell me, Lenny. What is it you want from me? Why are we here? Convince me to not rip your throat out with my teeth just as soon as I finish this lovely meal."

Lennard Rollins the third puts on a good spiel, she'll give him that much. He goes on and on about his empire and how he plans to expand it, which directions he wants to branch out in. He wants her by his side, not as a mate but as a business partner… his very own secret weapon. His *deadly* secret weapon. Oh, he paints it all up and wraps it up in a pretty bow, making it seem as if he'll be doing *her* a favor instead of the other way around. But he's not telling her anything she doesn't already know, and he's certainly not saying anything that makes her want to be a pawn in his empirebuilding games.

"And why should I align myself with you? Why align myself with *any* human for that matter? You're all weak, puny, and insignificant… and so easily broken. So far, all you've told me is what I can do for *you*, not what you can do for me. Let me assure you that this is in no way convincing me of anything but taking what I want from you and leaving your corpse to rot in this room. You've been following me for days, watching my every move. Tell me, what *exactly* have you learned about me? Don't be shy, now. Speak up."

Lenny frowns as he thinks about it for a moment, searching for a diplomatic response. "I know that you live for your pleasures. You aren't afraid to take what you want, and you let nothing stand in your way. And that you are a vicious little thing that greatly enjoys violence."

Samara laughs as she licks the chocolate from her spoon. "That's such a pretty way of saying that I'm selfish, greedy, and wanton."

Lenny opens his mouth to argue but she stops him. "I know what I am, Lenny boy, and I make no excuses for it. I *am* a selfish bitch. I care about only one person in this world, and that's me. I am the only one that matters to me, and I will never feel guilty for it. I do what I want, I go where I want, I take what I want, and I fuck who I want. And if a little blood gets spilled in the process, that's even better. As you mentioned, I love the violence. I adore the bloodletting. I cherish the screams."

She leans forward and looks over the food selection, eventually settling on a carton of shrimp fried rice. "So, knowing all that, you *still* haven't offered me any fucking reason to join you. I couldn't care less about this empire that you're building. I don't care about *your* hopes and dreams. I care about what *I* want. I care about *Samara*'s hopes and dreams. So far, all I've heard is what I can do for you, and nothing about what you plan to do for me."

Lenny looks genuinely surprised at her words. "Forgive me, Samara. I thought that was made clear in the beginning. When I said that you were meant to be a queen, I meant every fucking word. I will *make* you a queen. I'll give you anything. Everything. Whatever your dark, little heart desires, I will do my utmost best to see that you get it. I'll see to it that all of your wicked dreams come true. You want houses of your own? Houses with servants that wait on you hand and foot? Closets bigger than this room, all filled with the finest clothes? Cars? Diamonds? Lovers? A parade of men for your bed? You want to hobnob with important, powerful people? I'll introduce you."

He walks over and places a baggie of the white powder on the bed beside her. "You'll have all the cocaine you desire. I noticed how fast it wore off for you earlier. That's not normal, but hey, I deal in blow. That's what I do. It's the foundation of my empire… *our* empire, if you agree. I too, am a selfish, greedy bastard. I know what it's like to come from nothing, to live down at the bottom. I've been cold, hungry, and filthy… *Weak.* Never again. I will *never* feel like that again and I know that you feel the exact same way. I don't know anything about your life, where you come from, or what you've done. But I do know that you've lived at the bottom, just like I have. I know that you suffered at the hands of someone bigger, someone stronger than you were... just like I did."

He leans in real close to her and his words are little more than a whisper, spoken softly but heartfelt and sincere and oh, so cold. "I hope you killed him. Slowly. For days... just like I did. I hope it brought you some semblance of peace, just as it did for me. I know that we can be good together, Samara, if you'll only give us a chance."

Samara gets right to it. "I spent my time in the bath not only cleansing myself, but also thinking your proposition through. Yes, I already knew every point that you were going to try to sell me on, even before today. Magic, remember? My Night Shades are the whole reason you want me. They may not be able to get inside *your* head, but..."

Lenny's eyes pop open in shock. "Wait! What? Your...

Night Shades, you call them? ... you can't use them against me?"

Mr. Chadwick moves so fast, so *unexpectedly,* that Lenny has no chance to protect himself from being slammed up against the wall. He has no way of avoiding the gun that's suddenly pressed to his forehead.

Mr. Chadwick's hand shakes and he grunts, his face turning red as he fights the compulsion that he finds himself under. "I'm sorry, Sir. I can't stop it. I can't fight her," he grits out from between clenched teeth.

Samara leans forward so that she can see around the man's broad back. She wants to look directly into Lenny's eyes as she makes her point. "I didn't say that," she begins. "*Of course,* I can use my Shadows against you. Care to find out what it feels like to have your brains splattered on that wall like bad art? Go ahead. Interrupt me again and you *will.* As I was saying, I may not be able to get into your head, but there are ways and ways around that. I can always get into Mr. Chadwick's mind. In fact, I've been rooting around in there since the moment I discovered your interest in me. And before you even begin to entertain the idea of eliminating dear Mr. Chadwick, let me make this very clear, I forbid it. Mr. Chadwick is not to be reprimanded… in any way. Besides, I can assure you that I'd be able to use *anyone* that you replaced him with."

She takes a long draw of cherry cola straight from the bottle as she waves the man and his gun off. "We're good now, Mr. Chadwick, thank you. You can put that toy away. I've made my point, have I not?"

She raises her bottle up at him in mock salute as he tucks the gun away and steps aside so that his boss can get off the wall. He turns and takes up the vacant spot, putting himself up against the wall, his eyes shut tight against the shame in what he considers as failing his boss.

Samara laughs at his discomfort. "Oh, come now, Mr. Chadwick. Lenny's not mad at you, are you? Tell him, Mr. Bossman. Console him. You've known all along that I can use anyone I choose against you. The two of you have even discussed this exact scenario! There's no room for hurt feelings at this late stage of the game. Everything we're establishing right here and right now is exactly why you've pursued me so diligently. This is what you *wanted.* You *want* my power, but it's no fun when it's directed at you. Is it?"

The men don't say anything, but then again, she wasn't really expecting a reply. She waves a hand at them. "Never mind all that. I have my own demands, my own stipulations to add if we're to do this thing… some of which involve our Mr. Chadwick here. The two of you will just have to make your peace with the fact that I can and will be privy to *everything*. There will be no secrets kept from me. And absolutely no lies. I cannot abide a liar, Lenny. This is the only time I will say it. I promise you right here and right now that you won't enjoy the things I'll do to you if I find that you've told me even the smallest, most inconsequential untruth."

She pauses and considers the two of them for a moment, then she smiles. "Tell you what. I will make you both a promise; and know that I don't make promises unless I plan to keep them. I promise that I will never use my Night Shades to force Mr. Chadwick to do anything, ever again. I'll even call back the little bit that I've left in his head all this time in order to keep track of the two of you."

She grins and winks lasciviously at the man before she turns back to Lenny. "Whew! The stories I could tell you about the secrets I've found in Mr. Chadwick's mind! Oh, nothing like that Lenny, calm yourself. There's absolutely nothing dishonest towards you. He is your man 100% and loyal to a fault. You can trust him. No. These secrets that I'm speaking of would shock you, make you blush right down to your skivvies. Let's just say that I believe Mr. Chadwick and I are a lot more alike than you and I appear to be."

She glances over to where the other man is trying fervently to blend into the wall to avoid the weight of their stares. "And just so you both know, I *will* be sampling that," she adds as her eyes travel the length of his body. "Just as soon as we conclude our business. But where was I?" she asks as she turns her attention back to demands and deals and negotiations. "Oh yes. I was going to withdraw my Shadows from our dear Mr. Chadwick's mind."

She raises her hands up and they all watch as a tiny, barelythere wisp of black fog flows out of him and back into her. He doesn't feel them leave, but he immediately feels better. He hadn't even known that he was feeling… not bad, exactly, but run down and worn out. Languishing. But now, all of a sudden, he feels magnificent. It's almost like he's feeling the sunlight on his skin for the first time in years. He smiles, almost giddy from the rush of exhilaration that he feels.

"Oh, that's not to say that I will never send them back in again. I don't trust anyone. Ever. I *will* be taking a peek inside all of your men's minds… whenever and wherever I choose to do so. But that's *all* I'll do, just as long as you honor your end of the bargain.

I won't turn your men against you, or against each other, unless *you* force me to do so. Are we clear so far?"

Lenny nods and nonchalantly waves his hand at her as he says, "I already knew that you would keep tabs on me and my men. I would expect nothing less. I do appreciate your promise to limit your dealings with them to just mind reading and to not resort to mind control. I promise you, here and now, that I will never lie to you. So, is that it then? Do we have an agreement? You will join me?"

Samara grins and tells him that yes, she will join him, help him to grow his enterprise. Then she adds her last stipulation. "You've said that you do not want me, that you do not wish for a spot in my bed. But you will do it. *That* is the price I demand. You will fuck me, whenever and wherever I demand. Plain old, ordinary, sex… just how you like it. No pain, no bloodletting, no kinks. Just straight up sex."

Lenny frowns as he tries to figure out her angle. "Why?" he demands. "I thought that a platonic business relationship would be better for us, *easier* if we didn't complicate things with sex."

Samara snorts and tells him, "Sex is not complicated. It's two… or more… bodies coming together to fulfill basic, animal needs. That's all. It only gets complicated if you allow emotions into the bed along with the pleasures. So, don't. Just *don't*. I promise you that I will never love you. I will never care that you bed other women. Treat me the same and there's no complications to be had."

He runs his eyes over her body, and she leans back and spreads her legs apart so that he can see what it is that he's bargaining for. He licks his lips as his body grows hard with anticipation. "I mean, I don't have any issue against it, not now that you've promised to leave me in one, unbloodied piece. You *are* deliciously tempting, after all, and it's been no secret that I desire you. Watching you these past several days, I've had to take care of myself more times than I have since I was a horny, young teenager. But… and don't take this wrong… but *why*? Why do you want to force this issue?"

He flinches when her eyes grow cold, *hard* as she answers his questions. "Because I say so. Because I want it. Because I demand it. Because you do not get to use me like you'd planned to. You forget, I know all about the things you've said to Mr. Chadwick in private."

She lifts her hands up and her Shadows pour out and surround him. They trail across his body, lowering down to concentrate on his stiff, swollen cock. "You want to use me. I will use you right back. I won't hurt you if you don't overstep your bounds. Don't try to control me and never, *ever* lie to me. If you do, I will consider our agreement null and void, *and I will fuck you up.* Do you believe me, Lenny?"

He swallows hard as the Shadows swirl around him, gripping his dick tight as a fist. "I do. I am fully aware that I'm only alive right now because you do not wish me otherwise."

Samara climbs out of the bed and stands before him, looking up into his eyes. "And do you agree to *my* terms then?" she asks, and he wastes no time in nodding his head in assent.

"You *know* that I do," he murmurs, his voice husky with desire. His eyes focus on her lips as she sends her small pink tongue out to wet them, and then he sucks in his breath when she leans in and licks *his* lips.

"Then I agree too. I do believe that we will be good for one another, just as you've said."

Lenny stands there, his entire body stiff as she recalls her Night Shades. They immediately quit toying with his body and flow back inside of her. He licks his own lips, tasting her there and wanting more. She turns and saunters back to the bed, pushes all the leftover food to the floor, and then climbs back in.

Lenny's hand flies up to fumble with the buttons on his shirt. He's excited, eager to get to it now that he's no longer got his mind set against bedding her.

"So, are we gonna fuck to seal the deal? Is that it?" He tears his shirt open but then freezes when she laughs and shakes her head.

"Not now Lenny… when *I* say. Our deal is already sealed. We'll fuck when *I* decide. *I'll* become your drug, your own personal addiction. I'll make you want me just as fiercely as I crave your white powder… which I'm going to help myself to right now."

She tosses the baggie to Lenny and tells him to show her one more time just what to do with it. And when she's flying high once more, she turns to Mr. Chadwick with a sexy, sultry smile. "And now I'm going to get to know our Mr. Chadwick a little better." Lenny turns to look at the other man, his eyebrows raised in surprise.

"You ok with this?" he asks, almost incredulously. The man only nods, his eyes never straying from the woman on the bed. Samara grins and answers for him, "Oh, let me assure you, Lenny boy, he wants it. He'll gladly take one for the team."

She holds out her hand to beckon her next lover to her side. "Did you bring the stuff?" she asks. He steps forward and dumps the contents of the bag he'd been concealing onto the bed. Lenny's eyebrows raise even higher at the strange variety of items that spill out. A taser, silk ropes, a spaghetti spoon, some sort of small metal clamps with sharp little teeth, a fuzzy rabbit head mask, an impressive vibrating dildo, three butt plugs of varying sizes, a mouse trap, a pair of handcuffs, a barbie doll, a shock collar, some plastic cock rings, and a rubber chicken, the kind that screams when it's squeezed. "I couldn't get my hands on a butt-lock ma'am… not in the amount of time you allowed me. I, of course, will be better equipped to accommodate you once we're back home… once I have access to my regular connections and my own collection, of course."

Samara turns excited eyes to Lenny. If *his* eyes get any wider, they'll fall right out of his head. "Turn the songs back on the TV … some of that rocker roller music. Then leave, Lenny. Find something to occupy yourself with for the rest of the day." She points to the bulge in his jeans. "Rent your own room and take care of *that*, if you wish. Then procure us all a seat on one of those air flyers… not for today. I'll be busy the rest of this day. Tomorrow. I want to be back in Virginia by tomorrow night. I have a fierce desire to inspect and make good use of Mr. Chadwick's personal collection."

She dismisses Lenny and turns her full attention to the other man. "Why are you still wearing your clothes, Mr. Chadwick? Take them off and let me see what you're made of."

He smiles, just as courteous a smile as ever as he reaches up and begins unbuttoning his shirt. Lenny clicks the television on and channel-surfs until Samara suddenly yells, "Stop! Leave it here. I love this song! It's called 'Evil Boy' by Die Antwoord. Are you familiar with this band, Mr. Chadwick?"

She leans back against the headboard and watches him slowly unzip and then lower his slacks, her eyes widening with excitement when she sees that he's a commando kind of guy.

"Come to me." She grins and crooks her finger at him as she listens to Yo-Landi sing about what a badass chick she is and about all the wicked things she's going to do to the man that she's got tied up in her bed.

Samara tears her eyes away from Mr. Chadwick just long enough to frown at Lenny. "Why are you still here? Leave. Now."

He spins around and marches to the door, but he can't resist turning back, his incredulous eyes returning to the pile of randomness on the bedspread. "B,b,but… what in the actual *fuck* are you two gonna do with a spaghetti spoon?" he exclaims as he reluctantly lets himself out of the room and returns to the front office to book his own room… hopefully the one right next door to this one so that he can try to listen in on the things that'll be going on in there.

"What the *fuck*?" he whispers again as he walks away.

Lost Ecko

It's not until much later… *days* later that Samara pulls her head up out of that delicious white powder long enough to think of anything other than Mr. Chadwick's bed, with his wickedly addictive kinks. When she does finally come up for air and steps away from his bedroom, she immediately remembers the mission she'd been on to find Ecko's old geezers. "The file," she murmurs to herself as she wonders what the fuck had happened to it.

Never Say Goodbye

Ecko

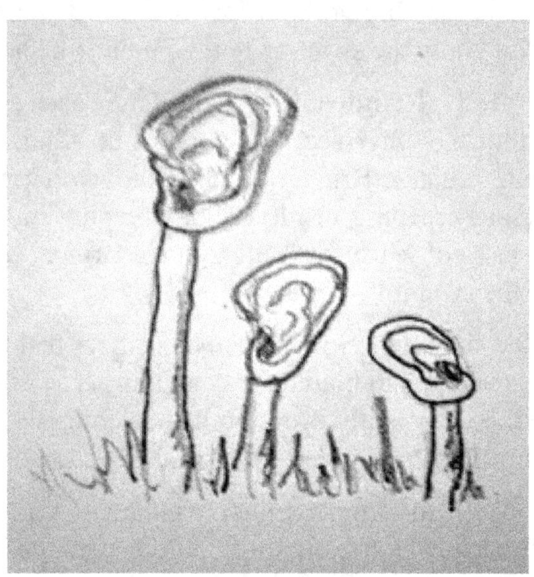

Every time she goes to sleep on this dreadful world, she reawakens to something unpleasant, or worse. She never knows what new horror awaits her when she opens her eyes each Pale. Usually it's something hostile, something that wants nothing more than to unalive her and then possibly eat her. Thankfully, that's not the case this time.

When she opens her eyes, she's greeted by nothing more than a sore body, an empty belly, and the two bickering frenemies. She sighs as she wonders what's got them arguing this time. Not that they need a reason. Those two will argue over anything, it seems.

She lays silent and still for a moment longer, just long enough to learn that they're bickering about *her*. Sephyr wants to wake her up so that they can hurry on their way. Boodark, on the other hand, thinks that they should let her rest as long as possible.

"She needs sleep, Darkling!" he insists. "Did you not see how exhausted she's been? Did you not notice how hungry she is? She needs sleep and she needs food. One of us should stay here to guard her, and the other should go hunt for something to eat. You have wings *and* you know the swamp. You go hunt. I'll stand guard."

"Sephyr see!" The little fairy instantly fires back as she angrily stamps her foot. "Sephyr see all! Sephyr not blind! But Sephyr know what ails Change Bringer. Sephyr know what wrong *Ecko*. Sorrow Marshes creeping inside Ecko. Creeping in like Kreeper Krud! Must fast go! Must fast out! Change Bringer eat and sleep *after* escape the swamp!"

Boodark's shoulders slump when he realizes that the Darkling is right. The swamp is to blame for what ails her. The spirit of the Sorrow Marshes constantly preys on her, relentlessly wearing her down. "You're right," he admits. "I'll wake her up."

"I'm awake," she informs them as she sits up and gingerly stretches her back. She tries not to groan or whimper aloud at all the aches and pains that greet her. It would just make her little friends worry more if she were to show how bad she really feels.

"I'm up," she repeats. "We'll pack up and head right out. I probably slept too long as it is. It's a miracle nothing bad happened. I should have stayed up and kept watch…" She starts folding up the blankets as she continues muttering on about how *anything* could have happened to them during the Pitch.

"*We* did it!" Boodark exclaims. He proudly puffs out his chest as he points first to himself and then to a grinning, nodding Sephyr. "We switched off all through the Pitch. I took the first watch, and when I got tired, I woke Sephyr for her turn. It was no big deal. We got enough rest. Besides, we've both had plenty of sleep while you carried us. What we really need to worry about… is *that*," he insists as he points a claw at the sucky-puss's glowstick poop that's still embedded in her wrist, shining through her skin. "How many of those do you have?"

She rubs at the splotch as if that will miraculously scrub it away. "As far as I can tell… nine. This one on my wrist, two on my left leg and three on my right. I can't exactly see my back side, but I can feel three more spots back there. One on my neck, one on my right shoulder blade, and one in the middle of my back, right on my spine."

They feel so strange, like someone used a hyperemic needle to squirt Icy Hot up under her skin. And they're extremely irritating, like a bee sting but without the pain. "I keep hoping they'll just go away," she tells him. "It's not like I can do anything about them either, unless I want to slice my own skin open and bleed the gunk out… which I *don't*."

She sighs and focuses on folding her blankets and packing up her things. Then she changes the subject because she really just doesn't know *what* to do about sucky-puss poo, and she's got other things to worry about anyway. "I'm sorry we have to skip breakfast, I mean FirstMeal." She doesn't say it, but they'll probably have to skip the MiddlinMeal too. But she'll worry about lunch when lunchtime arrives.

Boodark rolls his eyes. "Stop apologizing, Ecko. And stop worrying. We'll be fine. There *are* things to eat on Oblerian. We *did* manage to survive all this time without you providing our food for us. Now, I'm gonna go make water behind the shelter before you take it down. You may want to do the same, but me first. I *really* have to go!"

They all take their turn 'going' behind the tent and she sees for herself that the bridge has indeed disappeared. Maybe fifty feet remain between her and the place where the bridge has been eaten away by the Nothing. As she stares out at where the bridge *should* have been, she gets the creepiest feeling that something's staring back at her. Something perverted and twisted and depraved.

'Something Wicked this way comes.'

"Time to go," she whispers as she turns away. But she should have paid better attention to that warning. One day, if she lives that long, she'll learn to listen to her intuition.

"Look!" Boodark yells three hours later. He points to something in the distance and starts laughing. Then Sephyr's chiming in, giggling and clapping her hands gleefully.

She looks too, but she doesn't see anything worth cheering over. It's just never-ending swamp and then *more* never-ending swamp. The only difference she can see is that there seems to be more trees crowded in here than there had been since she'd first set foot on the bridge. She grunts in irritation. "What? I don't see anything. Why are you two laughing?"

"Hear Shrooms!" they both shout.

"What the heck are Hear Shrooms, and why are we so excited about them?"

Sephyr lands on her shoulder and reaches out to touch the curve of her ear as explains with her excited little girl voice. "Mushroom look like ear. Eat. Make hear strong."

Boodark gasps and then screeches, "*What?* You can *eat* Hear Shrooms? I didn't know *that*. Are they tasty? I was told long ago that they're poisonous, so I never tried them. And they increase your hearing, you say? Permanently or for a brief time?"

The Darkling shrugs. "Hour. Two. More eat. More long."

Ecko walks until she reaches the Hear Shroom patch that's in all reality, too big to be called a patch. They're everywhere, and they seem to grow in clusters of three, four, or five 'ears' each. They cover the trees, upright and fallen alike, and they blanket every bit of exposed land. And they really *do* look just like human (or whatever passes for humans on this world) ears. Fleshy and cup shaped, they have a tough, gelatinous but elastic texture. They're all different sizes, and every flesh tone from palest white and baby pink to darkest brown and deepest black, with every hue in between. They even have folds and wrinkles and veins to make them appear more realistic.

"Yeah, I'm *so* not eating those. I don't care if they do give super hearing. What do I need super hearing for anyway?"

Boodark peers up at her with the most serious, intent look on his face. Then he slowly leans over to the left and lets out a tiny squeak from his butt.

"Gross, Boodark. Like I really need *those* amplified. I already hear enough of your butt rumbles… too many of them!"

He may be well over three-hundred years old, but he still has the mind of an adolescent boy. She starts walking again, careful to keep to the middle of the bridge so that there's no chance of her brushing up against any of the Hear Shrooms. They *really* give her the heebie jeebies.

"Wait," she says and stops again to glance down at Boodark. "Why were you so excited to see them if you didn't even know what they can do?"

He snorts at her. "Two reasons. But first, I never said I didn't know what they could do. I *know* what they can do, just maybe not *everything* they can do. Set me down here and I'll show you." So, she lifts him out of the basket and gently lowers him to the bridge.

"See that cluster up there?" he asks as he points it out. "Go pick them for me. All three of them please."

She does as she's told, cringing at the rubbery, *warm* feel of them. She tugs at each one and they come loose easily. They don't seem to have a root system, just one short, hollow taproot that anchors them to their designated growing areas.

She carries them to Boodark, but he takes only one. "Give the little one to the Darkling and you keep the bigger one. Now Ecko, you go that way," he gestures to the way forward. "And Sephyr, you go back the way we came. I'll tell you when to stop." When everyone's in their proper positions he tells them to lift the Hear Shrooms up to their own ears. "Not like *that,* Ecko. Put the root part *in* your ear."

Ummm no thank you. "I'm not sticking fungus in my ear, Boodark!" She has to yell to be heard across the distance. "What if it latches in and grows into my brain?"

The little brat stomps his foot in frustration. "Just *do* it! I've done it a hundred times, and nothing's ever grown in my ears," he shouts back. He can hear her rude snort all the way to where he's waiting.

"I've seen inside your ears. There is all manner of nasty things growing in there!"

He looks very offended at that but then he shrugs it off. "But not Hear Shroom fungus!" he calls back. "Trust me!"

She's probably going to regret this but…. She lifts it up and just barely puts the end of the root into the cup of her ear. Sephyr, she sees, has no issues with sticking fungus into her ear. She *is* a Mushroom Fairy, after all. What does she care? She's already got fungus growing out of her head.

Boodark holds his up to his mouth instead of his ear and starts speaking into it. "Well, hello, beautiful ladies! Don't you both look just ravishing on this lovely Pale? Wanna come over to my tree hole later?" His voice is coming through those ears as clear as if he was standing right beside them! It's like speaking into walkie talkies or a tin can telephone, but without the string.

She moves her shroom to her mouth so that she can talk. "This is incredible Boodark!"

Then Sephyr has to do it too. "Sephyr hear Ecko! Sephyr hear cantankerous one!" Her peals of laughter fill their ears (their *real* ears) as they move to meet back up where Boodark's sitting. He grins as Ecko lifts him back into his basket. "That's a neat trick, right Sephyr?"

The Darkling nods and boasts, "Sephyr know new trick. Show to mushroom clans!"

Before they get back to walking, Ecko digs a wet wipe out of her bag and thoroughly scrubs her ears with it. It was indeed a cool trick, *but* the world is a vampire and all that…

Boodark explains that the Hear Shrooms only work with the ears in their own groups. "When you speak into a Hear Shroom, your voice only comes out of the ears from its *own* cluster."

Ecko rolls her eyes at herself with the next thought that pops up into her mind. *'Talk about a case of going in one ear and out the other! Shut up stupid brain!'*

"So, if a group of five ground stompers want to talk to each other, they would have to find a cluster with five ears in it," Boodark continues to expound, completely unaware of her mental dialogue. "You could also use them to spy on someone. Set them up in different rooms inside their home and listen to everything that goes on."

She asks him how he'd learned about the Hear Shrooms and he starts fidgeting, as if he's suddenly uncomfortable. All he'll disclose is that he learned it from a witch.

They walk in silence for several minutes. Well, almost silence. She's *trying* not to hear the sounds of Sephyr eating her Hear Shroom. It's *crunching,* like she's chewing up gristle. She *has* to find something to talk about to drown out that noise. Oh! She almost forgot. "What was the second reason?" she asks Boodark.

"Hu?" Apparently, he'd forgotten too.

"Earlier you said that there were two reasons why you were happy to see the Hear Shrooms. You only told me one."

Sephyr answers for him. "Happy reason!" she says as she points. Her eyes follow the line of the Darkling's finger, and she immediately starts bawling. All out, tears and boogies flowing bawling.

Land. Blessed, solid, un-swampified land.

"Hear Shrooms only grow at the borders, on the edges of the Sorrow Marshes," Boodark adds. Her heart pounds with excitement as she power-walks the short distance. The root bridge ends at the very edge of the mushy ground and gives way to a path that's been painted with the same Northern Lights display as the bridge's floor. It's strange how abruptly one landscape ends, and another begins. Like a line drawn in the sand, they each keep to their own proper boundaries: swamp on one side, terra firma on the other. She stands right on that cusp, tracing the new pathway with her eyes. It almost instantly gets swallowed up in the dark and foreboding forest ahead.

"The Dead Forest awaits," Boodark ominously whispers, and she feels his shiver through the basket. At this very moment she doesn't care why it's called the Dead Forest. All she cares about is that she beat the spirit. Against all odds, she's made it out of the Sorrow Marshes.

She fully expects that first step from marshland to solid ground to be beautiful, magical even, but it is not. She's suddenly overcome with exhaustion, drained of energy to the point where she has no choice but to drop to her knees for an unplanned and completely unwanted intermission.

She kneels upon the ground, head bent low with fatigue. She's desperately trying to hold onto her consciousness and to not pass out again, struggling to keep the world in focus. She doesn't even have enough oomph in her to lift her head. Figures that she would finally get free of the Sorrow Marshes and… wait. Is she *really* free? *Why* is she so tired? Is there such a thing as energy leeches? Maybe that's what those sucky-pusses were after… her energy. She glances down at the spot on her wrist. It's still glowing under her skin.

"Something's wrong. I swear there's something sucking the energy right out of me. I don't know what's happening, but *something's* sapping my strength."

Boodark and Sephyr exchange worried glances. "Surviving the Sorrow Marshes is a grueling ordeal. It can take a lot out of you. Maybe you should lie down for a while, take a nap. Just rest, Ecko. We'll keep watch again," Boodark offers with a sympathetic pat on her arm.

"I don't want to take a nap!" she wails, just like a petulant child. "I shouldn't even *be* tired. I slept for over twenty hours! I want to know what's wrong with me."

Sephyr hovers close to her bowed head. "Look Sephyr," the Darkling orders. Ecko raises her head up and the two of them study one another. Then Sephyr nods and says, "Pale. Black around eyes. Face skinny. When start? Think. Remember. When tired start?"

Boodark looks up at her too, and his eyes well up with tears. "She's right. You *are* pale and you *have* lost weight… a lot of weight. How did I not notice that? I shouldn't have eaten so much of your food! I'm fat! I'm a fat, nasty, ungrateful orc-bat! I'm no better than a Grunter!"

Sephyr drops down and delivers a sharp slap across his face. "No sorry self, Cantankerous one!" Boodark grabs his stinging cheek, nods, and does his best to stop his sniffling.

"What's a Grunter?" It's all she can think to say.

Boodark doesn't answer, so Sephyr does it for him. "Half man, half swine. Nasty. Eat all the foods. Make much mess."

A pig man. Figures. She strokes her little friend's hair to comfort him. "Stop Boodark. Whatever's happening to me isn't your fault. You didn't make me tired, and you didn't eat too much. I don't think it has anything to do with the amount of food I've been eating or even the amount of sleep I get. I think this is something else. Besides, we're in this together, you and me. We take care of each other." He gives her a wobbly half smile and a final sniffle.

Sephyr repeats her question. "When tired start?"

So, she thinks back, trying to remember the last time she'd felt truly healthy and strong. Her mind flashes back to the morning after Boodark had gotten himself drunk on Sprite. The first time, that is. She suddenly recalls that icky, nasty wind that had slammed into her, leaving her with an invisible but foul residue on her skin. And also, on her soul. That's when it all started. That's when she'd begun to weaken and tire easily. It's just steadily gotten worse since then. She explains to her companions what she's remembered, but they don't know what it could possibly mean.

Neither one of them had ever had anything like that happen to them, and they'd never heard of it happening to anyone else.

"You never saw it… whatever it was?" Boodark asks.

"No. I didn't see anything at all. I just felt a cold, filthy wind. It hit me, went *in* me and then back out again. But it left some of its *ick* behind. I just ignored it because I didn't know what else to do. Just like with this glowy poopy stuff. I don't know what to do about it either," she adds as she gestures to her wrist.

She looks up and stares into the Dead Forest for a long moment, then sighs heavily. She sets Boodark and his beddy-bye basket aside, drops her backpack to the ground, and then lays *herself* down, right there on the dirt. "I don't want to do it, but I think you're right, Boodark. I think I *do* need to take a nap before we go in there." She props her head on the backpack so that she doesn't eat dirt in her sleep. "Just for an hour," she murmurs as she drifts off.

She's not asleep, not exactly. It's more like she's lost in a fog. She can hear Boodark and Sephyr talking about her, trying to reason it all out. Trying to decide what to do, discussing what, if anything, could help her.

"Ecko need zingberry," Sephyr says.

"I don't think she'll eat it. She hasn't eaten anything but the food she brought with her. Well, not *willingly*. The Sorrow Marshes had hold of her for a while. She ate a lot of things then, and none of them were good. But she didn't *know* she was doing it; she was stuck in something that she called The Dreaming."

The Darkling stubbornly raises her chin. "Must make. Must zingberry eat. Change Bringer need strength."

"Yes," he murmurs. "She does need strength. It's a good idea… IF we had any zingberries just laying around. And IF she would agree to eat them. We don't and *she* won't, so this conversation is pointless."

"Sephyr be back. Sephyr find zingberry. Cantankerous one convince. Make Change Bringer eat."

"She's a hardhead, I can't make her do anything! Where are you going? Come back here this instant! Don't you go back into that swamp! Don't you *dare!"*

Sephyr's voice fades as she flies away. "Be back!"

"Stupid Darkling!" he shouts after her. Then he's in full tirade mode, cursing and yelling about the hardheaded females in their little group and bemoaning the fact that no one *ever* listens to him. And then no one's listening to him *for real* because sleep has finally, mercifully come to claim her.

"I'll eat it."

Sephyr has made it back with her berries and now her companions are arguing about how to get her to eat it. They're in such a heated discussion over who's idea will work best that they don't even realize that their squabbling has woken her up. The fairy wants to try and slip it into her food. Boodark doesn't want to be dishonest about it.

"I'll eat it," she says again, a little louder so that the malcontents in the back can hear her this time. They rush to her side as she sits up, worry for her heavy on their little faces. "I'm ok, honest. But I *could* use an energy boost. Is that *all* the zingberries do?"

They both nod and then Sephyr adds, "Wake brain. Wake body. One berry, one hour."

It sounds good to her. At least it's a just berry and not some kind of weird alien fungus. "Alright. Let me have it."

Boodark holds up a cluster of them for her to inspect. It looks exactly like a cluster of grapes, but the berries are as small as blueberries. She plucks one from the cluster and suspiciously eyeballs it. It's dark brown, almost like a chocolate chip. She hopes it tastes like chocolate too. But it's hard, *really* hard, like a nut.

"It's hard as a rock! How am I supposed to eat this thing?"

Sephyr holds her hand out. "Sephyr show. Ecko hold out hand. Catch." The fairy takes it and strikes it against the stone that Boodark holds up for her. Then she cracks the zingberry open like an egg, pouring the contents into Ecko's waiting palm.

So much for being relieved that it's not fungus. She almost drops it. It looks just like a blood clot, same color, same consistency, same slimy, jiggly *yuck*. She can feel her face pale at the thought of sticking it into her mouth.

Boodark hurries to reassure her. "I know it looks disgusting, but it doesn't taste that bad. And it will help you. I promise."

The longer she looks at it, the worse it gets so she doesn't stop to think about what she's doing. She quickly tosses it back, just like she had the one (and only) time she'd tried raw oysters with her dad. So. nasty.

It goes down easier than she'd thought it would, but it leaves a bitter aftertaste on her tongue. She shudders and gulps down half a bottle of water. "I don't understand why anyone would willingly eat something so gross," she complains as she shudders with revulsion. But thirty seconds later she knows *exactly* why. She feels amazing, better than she'd felt in a long time. Her companions grin as she jumps to her feet. "This is awesome!" she gushes. "I bet I could run a marathon! I won't, because who in their right mind runs for the fun of it? I don't feel *that* good. But close!"

"I hate this! I don't want to say goodbye. I hate that you have to make your way back home all alone. I wish you could come with us." Ecko's trying not to cry but not even coming close to succeeding. The Darkling had stuck around while she boiled and purified more swamp water and refilled her water bottles. (Still yuck, but necessary). They've stalled as long as they can. It's time for their little threesome to part ways and everyone's sad but trying not to show it.

"Sephyr have mate. Have newling. Must home go," the fairy tells her. "Darkling no say goodbye. *Never* say goodbye. Bad luck. Darkling say, 'Benod te sumt.' Sephyr na lewa. Malkyo lo lang karo, Ikaw hel ey lost ako Sephyr, tak Sephyr ako sa."

With tears in his eyes, Boodark whispers the translation. "She says: Fare thee well. Sephyr must away. Until we meet again, you will be missing from me. And I from you."

Ecko's chin wobbles when her little fairy friend adds, "Sephyr *much* miss Ecko." She hands the Darkling the goodbye gift that she'd whipped up at the last minute. She'd cut open a tea bag, dumped the leaves out, and filled the empty pouch with as much crumbled up granola bar as it would hold. Then she'd tied it shut with a string. Now Sephyr's lips tremble as she takes it and ties the string around her waist. The tea bag looks huge against the little fairy, but Ecko knows that she won't have any trouble carrying it. Darklings are seriously strong, despite their diminutive size. "I'm glad to have known you, Sephyr of the Irukandji Mushroom clan."

Sephyr glances down at Boodark and lifts her chin. "Fare thee well, Cantankerous one. Keep Change Bringer safe."

He nods once, briskly, and then stubbornly lifts his own chin. "It's going to be a lot quieter without *you* around, Darkling."

Ecko and Boodark both watch as Sephyr turns and starts fluttering back to the swamp, her head lowered in sorrow. She stops and hovers in place for a moment and then she suddenly spins around and zooms back… right into Boodark's open and waiting arms. The two of them are bawling, *howling* out their grief.

"Come home Sephyr. Sephyr take care cantankerous one. Feed until wings grow back. Boodark and Sephyr together eat clabber wigglers."

Ecko's heart splinters when the Darkling adds in a whisper, "Sephyr love Boodark." The fairy's tiny shoulders shake from the force of her sobs as he tells her that he loves her too.

She reaches down and lifts Boodark… with the fairy wrapped in *his* arms for a threesome hug.

"Quiet!" Sephyr suddenly hisses right out of nowhere. They instantly quiet their sniffling and crying as they look at her with hurtful expressions on their faces.

"Hear something," she explains as she pulls out of the hugfest and flies over to where the ground path changes to bridge path. Her head cocks to the side as she listens to something that only she can hear. "Something comes," she warns.

"I don't hear anything," Boodark says.

She spins around, a frown on her tiny features. "Sephyr eat Hear Shrooms. Sephyr hear. Something comes!"

And just then something *does* come. Boodark and Ecko scream out in horror as *something,* a snarling blur of blue springs right up from under the bridge and crushes the tiny fairy in its grasp.

Pleasurable Pastimes

The Lokskell

High-pitched chittering and agitated clicking sounds penetrate the blood-lust fog that has consumed his mind and kept him in his dungeons for an indeterminate amount of time. He had funneled all his emotions into one singular entity inside himself, and he'd let it all become fuel for his Rage.

The unwanted lust for a woman that he can never get out of his head joined the frustration of being imprisoned year after year. Fury over all the indignities he'd been forced to suffer merged with the angst over wondering if his plans will play out in his favor. His desire to get Ecko within his grasp coalesced with the fear of yet another failure. All those emotions swirled together and joined as one, and it created a powerful tempest inside him. It became a thundering, churning cyclone that needed, *demanded* an outlet. As much as his body craved release, in his current state of mind, he knew better than to pound into his women with his dick. He knew that he would not stop there, and he had no wish to break his toys. He chose, instead, to pound his fists into his prisoners. Perhaps he'd be able to go to his ladies when his anger was finally spent.

He'd let all those wants and needs and desires and furies loose until there's not a single prisoner left standing, and the blood lay congealing in deep pools on the floor. The sweat pours in rivulets down his body, mixing with the blood until it glimmers like liquid rubies. His chest rises and falls with each gasping breath that he takes. His hand raises to slick blood-drenched hair back out of his face as the rage-fog lifts enough for his mind to understand what the chittering sounds are. His spies have returned.

The bug is well hidden, with nothing but its eyeball antennas poking out of a fissure in the wall. It knows very well not to interrupt his tirades. For it to do so now must mean that it has news of great importance. Still, it knows to proceed with extreme caution.

The Lokskell sends his Shadows into the bug's mind the very second that he locates it. He doesn't wait for the Vika Vakooja to join him. He doesn't even wait for it to scurry down the wall. "Show me," he commands, and the bug hastily produces the information it has come to relay to its master.

It only takes a moment for him to understand that these are no memory pictures. What he sees is happening now, in real-time. There is a Vika Vakooja near enough to his daughter, *right now*, that it is able to send what it's witnessing through the buggy collective, where it's being relayed to him through the mind of *this* Vika.

Krispin has caught up to Ecko and is preparing to launch himself out of his hiding spot. The bulge in the front of his pants makes it glaringly obvious that the blue creature's mind is set on mating, and it only amplifies his own raging desire for sweet release.

"Follow!" he snarls to the bug as he spins around and heads for the women's quarters. He'll kill two fairies with one stone. He'll watch the scene unfold with Krispin and his daughter while he takes his own pleasures… and hopefully when it's done, he'll be that much closer to obtaining his ultimate goals.

Hissing Things, Blue Things, Strange Things, Rude Things

Ecko

"Nooo!" Ecko howls as the creature opens its clawed hand and drops the Darkling to the ground… as if she's nothing more than garbage that he's tossing away. Her eyes slowly lift from Sephyr's still, broken body and zero in on the monster's face. He grins, a slow, wicked leer as his eyes rove up and down her body. Her head is instantly full of pressure, her hands already lit up without her permission, indeed without even her knowledge. She knows not what's happening to her, nor what's going on around her. She doesn't even notice when Boodark dives out of her arms, hits the ground rolling, and rushes to his friend's side. All she can see is this monster's smile, his eyes disgustingly full of lust as they look her over.

"No more running Samara. I told you. You. are. mine!"

And then he's on her before she even sees him move. His body slams into hers and the air whooshes out of her lungs as they fall to the ground. It happens so fast, startling her so badly that even her magic falters. She feels it recede, snapping back to wherever it goes to sleep when it's inactive. She starts kicking and fighting for all she's worth then, and they go rolling across the ground in a jumble of straining limbs and heavy, desperate blows. When they finally come to a stop, she's sprawled on her belly, blood oozing from multiple wounds. He's lying on top of her, the weight of him pressing her down into the dirt. He lewdly rubs himself against her, groaning from the thrill he gets from the act.

"Feels so good to have you back in my arms, right where you belong." He reaches up and yanks her sweaty hair back from the side of her face so that he can see her better. "I like the filth," he growls and then sinks his teeth into her shoulder, so deep that she immediately feels the blood gush. She screams and bucks wildly, desperately trying to throw him off.

He pulls his teeth out of her and jerks back. "You taste wrong," he says. Then he buries his face in her hair and sniffs at her. "You *stink!* You smell all wrong. What have you done?"

She spits the blood and dirt from her mouth. "I'm not…" But she's interrupted by a fearsome and unholy uproar. She lifts her head to see… "No Boodark!" she shouts, but it's too late. Screaming out his fury in a rip-roaring, ear-splitting battle cry that belies his diminutive stature, her brave little friend launches himself right onto the beast's back in a desperate attempt to save her.

She sucks in a full breath as the weight is suddenly lifted off her back and her frantic gaze locks onto her friend. He clings to the beast like a bull rider who knows that if he lets go or falls off, he will most certainly meet his demise. He's got his own claws buried into the blue man's back and his face is scrunched into a fierce scowl. He's yelling, "Get off her! Get off her! Don't you touch her, you filth! Don't you *ever* touch her!"

Boodark has the upper hand for a moment or two because he'd landed right in the middle of the back where the blue man can't reach him. But all the wild bucking and rolling about inevitably dislodges him and he slips down lower. The monster reaches around and snatches him up in a crushing, punishing grip and pulls him from his back, breaking off every claw on Boodark's right hand in order to do so. The five severed dagger-claws stay deeply imbedded in his back as he throws her small friend to the ground and lifts his foot up high. He's going to stomp on him! There's no way her orc-bat will survive that.

"Please!" she screams. "Don't hurt him. Please. I'll do anything you want. Just let him go." She sits up slowly, her hand held out in a calming, beseeching gesture. The blue man growls at her, his chest heaving and his eyes wild as he glares at her. In a cold and calculated movement, he lowers his foot and slowly presses Boodark into the dirt.

"I'm begging you! Don't hurt him," she pleads.

He snarls with barely suppressed rage in response. "My Samara begs for nothing, pleads for no one! Who are you?"

She can't tear her eyes away from the threat of Boodark's little body being crushed. "My name's Ecko." Her breath hitches as she reluctantly adds, "Samara's my sister, my twin."

The monster grunts and pushes his foot down another fraction of an inch, causing Boodark to gasp as he struggles under the weight. "Where is she? What have you done with her? Tell me now, or he becomes nothing more than a stain upon this ground!"

She scrambles to her knees and raises both hands to show that she's cooperating. "Ok! Ok! I'll tell you anything you want to know. I have magic inside of me, but I didn't until my eighteenth birthday. I was overwhelmed when it hit me. I didn't know how to control it, and I accidentally opened up a mirror. Samara was watching me at the exact same time, waiting for that to happen. She switched us. She pulled me here and then she went to my world. And she broke the mirror on her way out so that I couldn't get back home. Please let him up. You're *hurting* him!"

He only grunts as he processes what he's learned. "She's gone?" He looks bewildered and lost and broken for all of five seconds. Then he's pissed. "*You* did this. *You* took her from me!" His nostrils flare and his hands tremble with the intensity of his rage. "You made her life miserable. She spent her entire life searching for you, enduring punishment after punishment for not *being* you! I was going to save her. I was going to fix her."

His voice goes low and menacing then. "You took my love away. You *stole* her from me." Then he lifts his foot and focuses his attention on the tiny body quivering before him. "I will make you suffer, just as I suffer. First, I'll take what you love from you, just as you took my love from me. And then I'm going to make you bleed. For an eternity." With that, the monster brings his foot back down with all the tremendous strength he could muster.

She doesn't feel the magic build. She doesn't feel it gather in her hands and her vision doesn't change. All she feels is a massive headache, a devastating, incapacitating pressure against her skull. She throws her hands atop her head to prevent her brain from exploding as the pressure builds to the breaking point. And then it *does* break, and it feels like a nuclear bomb goes off inside her skull.

And just like that, it's over, suddenly gone as if it had never been, and the relief she feels is *tremendous*. Her head no longer hurts. Her brain has settled back into its proper place and no longer threatens to explode. She has no idea what, but something huge has just happened.

She's lying on the ground with Boodark right up in her face, hovering over her. His eyes are wild, and his lips are moving but she can't hear what he's saying. Has she gone deaf? But no. Sound slowly returns, faint at first, but getting better with each passing second.

"Oh! Thank the EverLands! You're alive!" he exclaims just before he starts sobbing and blowing snot on her.

"Gross, Boodark. Ugh! What in the world happened?" she asks as she sits up and takes in her surroundings. "Oh!" she gasps as she sees the blue monster lying dead in the dirt twenty feet further from where she last remembers him standing. Her brow creases into a frown as she tries to think back, to remember…

"Sephyr!" she suddenly cries out as she recalls what that monster had done to her. She scrambles to her feet and rushes over to where the little Darkling lies in a broken heap upon the ground. The sight of those crumpled and bent wings slays her, just rips her heart open. "Oh no. No, no, no, no," she whispers as the tears flow. The Darkling's eyes flutter at the sound of her voice

"She's alive!" she shouts to Boodark as he rushes to her side. "Sephyr? Can you hear me? What do I do?" She looks to Boodark and begs, "What do I do?" But he doesn't know what to do any more than she does. He starts crying too as their little friend regains consciousness. "We're here, Sephyr. Don't try to move," she croons as the Darkling whimpers and opens her pain-dulled eyes.

"Not dead blue creature. Sephyr hear… (painful gasp) Sephyr hear. Heartbeat." She's using up the little bit of strength that she has left to warn them that the blue man is still alive. "Don't worry about him. What can we do to help *you*? Is there a mushroom that can heal you? Is there a berry that you can eat that will fix what's broken inside of you? Just tell me what to do. Tell me where to go. I'll do whatever it is you need me to do. I'll go back into the Sorrow Marshes if you say there's something that can heal you. *Please* say there's something that can heal you!" she begs.

Sephyr coughs and there's blood on her lips. "No Ecko go back. Hissing clans watch. Come. Help Sephyr. Carry Sephyr home. Ecko convince do no harm. Must say true, Change Bringer mean Hissing clans no harm."

Ecko lifts her head up and looks around. "I don't understand. Hissing clans? I don't see anyone. There's no one here, Sephyr."

She coughs again then whispers "Clans look. Wait. See safe first."

The Darkling insists that these Hissing clans are watching and that they'll help, but *she* must first assure them that it's safe to come out of hiding. She stands up and looks towards the swamp. "Please come out. I swear on my life that I'm a friend to the

Darklings. I mean no harm to the Hissing clans of the Sorrow Marshes."

Silence. The swamp is still and quiet, granting invisibility to those that wish to remain hidden.

"Please, I'm begging you. Help her!"

All of her pleading receives the same results; whoever's out there continues to ignore her. And God help her, now Rage is awake and trying his best to get out and take control. "Sephyr is my friend and she's hurt. She's Darkling-kind, same as you. How can you ignore her need?"

One lone fairy flutters out from behind a blob of moss in the tree branches, and she immediately understands why they're called the Hissing clans. If Medusa were real, if she'd been shrunk down to six inches and had wings glued to her back, this would be her. *This* is a true Darkling, one of those dark fae creatures that seem so alien and cold. Evil almost, but most definitely *other*. She's menacing and fearsome to look upon, and Ecko shivers as they stare at one another, both silently taking the other's measure.

She assumes that *this* is the leader of the Hissing clans. She's wearing a golden crown that has tall, jagged points, and she's got tiny snakes in her hair, weaving themselves in and out of the headpiece. Her face is strangely beautiful, even if she does have a decidedly reptilian appearance. But those snake eyes are terrifying! Huge purple irises dominate most of the eyes and the pupils are those disturbing vertical slits. Her forehead has a thick ridge of bone that protrudes slightly. Her nose is small and sharp, and her lips are dark and thin. She's pale-skinned, but there are dark shadows and smudges at her temples and around her eyes. She even has little circles of scales scattered across her skin.

Ecko's eyes lower to the snakes that are wrapped around the Darkling's body. They move all around her, their slithery little bodies constantly in motion. Hissing. Tasting the air in her direction. She can hear them across the distance, and she can't help but shudder in revulsion. She hates slithery, sneaky snakes.

This Darkling is a freaky little thing, that's for sure. But Sephyr trusts her, and she desperately needs their help… so here goes nothing. "My name is Ecko. I am ally to the Mushroom clans. Sephyr of the Irukandji clans has been injured. She needs help! She has told me that the Hissing clans are also allies with the Mushroom clans. She says that you will aid her and help her get back to her home."

The Darkling opens her mouth and hisses through her fangs. That's it. That's all she does… Like… what's that even supposed to *mean?*

"Please. Will you help her? She has a mate and a daughter, a newling. They need her."

More hisses. She's beginning to wonder if this snake lady can even understand her. "Umm yeah… can you understand me?"

All eyes turn to Sephyr as she starts coughing again.

"Understand Ecko," she whispers. "Deciding. If help or no help."

Boodark leans forward and whisper/yells, "I thought you said they're your allies. Allies help each other!"

Sephyr explains as best she can. "Clan ally with clan. Sephyr no ally with Queen Istral. No friend. *Clan* aid *clan.* May choose aid Sephyr alone or choose no aid Sephyr alone. Up to

Queen Istral."

Ecko frowns as she tries to make sense of her friend's strange speech. "So, your clans are allied, and that means that the clans are required to give aid when the other *entire* clan has need of them.

But the clans don't have to help on a personal level? They don't have to help individual members just because your clans have an agreement?"

Sephyr nods weakly. "Sometimes help alone member of ally clan, sometimes no help. Up to leaders."

Now Ecko understands, and it's up to her to convince them to help her friend. She takes a deep breath that does exactly nothing to settle her nerves and starts walking towards the hissing fairy. She completely ignores Boodark's frantic, "What are you doing? Get back here!"

The rest of the members of the Hissing clan immediately come out of hiding to surround and protect their sneaky snake queen. They hold their spears up threateningly and even the snakes on their bodies lift their heads and focus their full attentions on her. All of them, fairies and snakes alike, are hissing and spitting at her. She refuses to be intimidated, at least outwardly. *Inside* there's a whole lot of crying and quaking and whimpering.

She holds up her hands to show that she means no harm and she stubbornly keeps walking. Very slowly. When she's only a few feet away from them she drops to her knees in the shallow, stagnant swamp water and bows her head. "Queen Istral, if you help my friend, I will be a good ally to the Hissing clans of the Sorrow Marshes. I will promise to come to your aid if you ever have need of me, if I am in a position to do so."

One of the females gets a little excited or angry or… who can tell what a snake fairy is feeling? They're nothing but hisses and menacing glares. But this little fairy is most definitely pissed because she rushes forward and slices her cheek open with her spear, her *poisoned* spear.

She feels it instantly begin to seep into her bloodstream, and now Rage is absolutely livid. She turns her attention to the one who'd just attacked her. Whatever the Darkling sees in her eyes has her obviously rethinking her life choices. Her spear drops from her hands, and she backs up, getting as close to her queen as she possibly can.

She feels like there's someone else inside of her, someone else moving her lips and using her voice to spill words from her mouth. Her voice comes out low, calm, and oh, so steady as she turns her eyes back to the queen and says, "I can be a great ally, or I can be an even greater enemy." She reaches up and swipes the blood from her face, then points at the overly zealous, spear-happy fairy and adds, "That one's a freebie… Meaning, I'll ignore this one slight because I understand *that* one's need to protect her queen. I want no quarrel with the Hissing clans, and I will willingly ally myself with you. But *only* if you help my friend. Think before you speak. And choose wisely. I am the one they call Change Bringer, and I swear that if you let her die when you could have saved her, I will rip this swamp to shreds and build a bridge to aid you on your way to hell. Choose. Every second you waste is one more that Sephyr must suffer."

The queen nods and somehow retracts her fangs so that she can speak without the hisses and lisps. "We ally. We will take the Irukandji home to Mushroom clan territory." She turns to her subjects and brings the fangs back out to play as she hisses out orders, literally hisses them.

She doesn't understand any of it, but they all move to obey. They break up and fly off, and when they come back, they're carrying things from the swamp. Moss, leaves, vines, and a single Hear Shroom that's about as big as her hand. She watches the Hissers as they busy themselves with carrying out their queen's orders. They lay the Hear Shroom on the ground and stuff it with soft tufts of moss. Then they tie the vines onto it to make straps. They're making a travois, a sling that the injured Darkling can lay in as they transport her through the swamp.

The work gets carried out quickly and everyone crowds around Sephyr, with Queen Istral kneeling on the ground at her side.

Ecko and Boodark watch as the queen reaches her hand up to her head and makes a series of hissing and clicking sounds. A tiny blue snake slithers out of the tangled mass on her head and right into her waiting palm. The two concerned friends are just about to *enthusiastically* begin protesting as the queen lowers the snake towards the wounded Darkling. Queen Istral must know exactly what they're thinking, must feel their unease and distrust because she suddenly pauses her actions, tucks her fangs away, and starts explaining. She lovingly strokes the little snake in her hand like it's a pet as she does so. "This is Chimera. She is a Dreaming Viper. Her bite will help. It will send Sephyr to the DreamLands where she will feel no pain as we carry her home."

Ecko nods but Boodark mutters, "It *better* not hurt her."

Queen Istral holds the snake over Sephyr and says, "Now is the time to say your fare thee wells. She'll be asleep within seconds of Chimera's bite."

The queen's breath hisses in as Ecko bends down and whispers in the Darkling tongue. "Benod te sumt, Sephyr of the Irukandji clan. We will meet again, you and I. I feel it here," she says as she places her hand over her heart. "I will find a way to come back and check on you. Somehow, someday. Until then, you

will be missing from me, and I from you."

Boodark barely manages to choke out his, "I love you, pesky Darkling."

Chimera strikes then, plunging its fangs right in Sephyr's chest, and the little fairy lets out a contented sigh and smiles with the relief of drifting away from her pain. Two nearby males lean down and lift her in their arms, and only then does she realize how much bigger these Hissing Darklings are as they gently lay her friend's poor, broken body in the travois. They're almost double Sephyr's size, so they should have no trouble carrying her through the swamp.

Boodark lifts the tea bag full of granola off the ground where it had fallen and places it in the Hear Shroom travois, right beside his sleeping friend where she'll see it when she awakens. Then he turns around with tears in his eyes and begs, "Please tell me she'll be ok. Please."

Queen Istral nods and her hair-snakes hiss. "Broken bones heal. Wings heal. I will wake her and feed her crushed Fouler bones to heal inside wounds…. Stop inside bleeding. She will heal, Changed-one-who-is-not-in-true-form. Hissing clans will take care of ally Sephyr."

Ecko clears the lump in her throat and vows, "I will always remember the favor you have granted me this Pale. I owe you a great debt and I will repay it if I am able to. I meant what I told her. I *will* be back some day. I don't know when, but I know that it's true. When that Pale comes, I hope to meet you again, Queen Istral of the Hissing clans."

The queen turns and hisses at the female that had recklessly sliced Ecko's cheek open. The contrite Darkling flutters forward carrying a blob of something that looks like bright green and yellow snot.

"Naga act hasty, without thought. Naga regret," she lisps around her fangs with her eyes lowered in respect.

She's quick to assure her that all is forgiven. "It's ok Naga. I'm not mad at you." She holds perfectly still while Naga smooths the gunk onto the wound.

"Leave on until Pitch. Draw venom out," she advises and then flies off to rejoin her clanmates.

Ecko and Boodark watch as several Darkling males lift Sephyr's sling by the handles and fly her away, disappearing back into the Sorrow Marshes. Both are worrying if they've done the right thing by letting the Hissing clans take her from them. It feels wrong, watching her leave like that, but what else can they do? It would take far too long for them to bring her home themselves, even if the root bridge still stood. It had disappeared almost completely sometime in the last hour, the last of the roots slipping away unnoticed… back to where they belong. All but for a single root, painted with the colors of her magic to mark the spot where the root bridge had ended and the new path through the Dead Forest began.

And to be honest, the Hissing clans know better how to care for Sephyr. They are Darkling-kind, so they'll know exactly what is needed to properly care for their tiny, wounded friend. Queen Istral had already assured them that she would feed her crushed Fouler bones to stop the internal bleeding, just as soon as she woke up from the Chimera-induced sleeping coma.

Yes. Sephyr is in more capable hands than her own would ever be. Besides, she has no idea what a Fouler is, where to find it, or how to crush its bones.

"I don't know, Boodark! I have (huff) no (huff huff) idea what (puff) happened!" She stops running for a moment and bends over, sucking precious gusts of air into her oxygen-starved lungs. "That's why I need you to tell me everything that you remember, because the last thing *I* remember is that monster preparing to stomp you into the dirt."

She straightens up and looks back the way she'd come, praying that she won't see a blue blur coming for her. She's been running for almost an hour, her panic apparently stronger than her need to breathe. As Sephyr had warned, the blue man was, indeed alive and he'd started to wake up as she stood over him, wondering what in the world she was supposed to do.

At first, she hadn't believed it. He'd certainly looked dead to her. She hadn't been able to see a single shred of proof to support the Darkling's claims. He didn't move a muscle and his chest didn't rise and fall with breath. There was absolutely no way she was going to lean in and listen for a heartbeat to be certain though. But then he *had* moved, just a twitch and she'd turned tail and run like a scared little rabbit. She's done running now though. She's pretty sure she broke that setting. Even the 'sprint' setting is out of order. She hasn't got enough breath or stamina for it. The best she can manage is a steady-paced walk. She chugs half a bottle of water and then offers Boodark some before she sets out again. She can't run anymore, but she also can't stop to rest.

"I don't know what happened either," Boodark tells her. "One minute you were screaming and holding the top of your head down like you were afraid it was about to blow up, and the next minute a big flash of bright white light blasts out of your eyes and slams right into Mr. Blue-balls bully-boy. It was so bright I thought I'd gone blind! It took a few minutes for my vision to come back and even then, I was seeing spots. I sat up and looked around and you were lying on the ground and so was the blue man. But he'd been thrown backwards…*far* backwards by whatever you hit him with. I really thought he was dead. I thought you were too, for a moment." He sniffles as if he's fighting back tears, then he orders, "Don't *ever* scare me like that again."

She lets out an undignified snort. "I don't even know what I did, so how can I stop it from happening again?" She thinks it all over as she walks and then she suddenly starts laughing at what she discovers.

"What could you possibly find funny about *any* of this?" Boodark asks. He watches her closely, like he's afraid that she's gone mad, and it makes her giggle even harder.

"I'm Psyduck!" she howls. Tears of mirth stream down her face and she's forced to stop walking again until she can get herself back under control.

"What's a Psyduck?" he asks in total bewilderment.

Trying to explain Pokémon to someone that's not from her world is a trying experience. Poor Boodark doesn't have a clue as to what she's talking about. And really, how do you explain cartoons and animations to someone who's never seen a movie or television or even a picture book. She finally just tells him that Pokémon are make believe creatures in a make-believe story.

"Psyduck is a psychic duck… a water bird with psychic powers. He's usually unable to think clearly because he always has a headache. He walks around stunned and clueless, constantly trying to soothe the ache in his brain. But when he gets too stressed out, the headache grows stronger. And when it gets too severe, it releases the tension in the form of a strong, psychic ability. A brain wave explodes outwards, blasting everything in its vicinity. When it's over, Pysduck feels better, but he never remembers what happened."

Boodark thinks about it for a minute then disagrees. "I do not think you are a Psyduck. Your headache power didn't hurt *me,* and I was right there in its path. It only hurt the blue man. Besides, you have no feathers, you look nothing like a bird."

Yes, *that's* the reason she's not a Pokémon character. It has nothing to do with the fact that Pokémon aren't real.

"Ugh. This place is as bad as the swamp, in its own way. Why's everything dead?" She mumbles. It's terrible here. Not only are all the plants and trees dead, but so is everything else. They've passed dozens of bone heaps and rotting carcasses. Dead, dehydrated insects crunch under her feet as she walks… thank you, sweet baby *Jesus* for Sephyr finding and returning her shoes. She doesn't even want to *think* about how bad it would be to have to step on them without foot protection. And there's no avoiding them; she's tried. There's far too many, piles and piles of them. Boodark's pouting because she won't stop and let him down to eat them, and she absolutely refuses to scoop them up for him to eat in his basket.

"Get over it, buddy. We don't know if we're being hunted so we're not taking a time-out for you to have a snack. And I'm not touching them so that you can eat on the go. You'll just have to wait."

He sulks for a while and then changes his tactics when he realizes it's getting him nowhere. Now he's all sad, forlorn sighs and fake sniffles and whining. "Oh, I'm *so* hungry," he moans for the twelfth time.

"Shhh! What *is* that?" she suddenly demands over his complaints.

He pokes his head up from his dramatic 'withering away, dying of starvation' pose to see what she sees. "What is what? I don't see anything!" he grumbles.

"Shhh! Don't you *hear* that?" She cocks her head to the side as she listens and Boodark mimics her. Someone's whistling a slow, melancholy tune. She can't tell exactly where it's coming from. The sorrowful melody seems to bounce off the lifeless trees and then reverberates all around the Dead Forest. "What *is* it?" she whispers. Then she begins to panic. She has a terrible suspicion that it's the blue man and that he's not only caught up to her, but he's somehow gotten in front of her. It's possible. He *had* been able to move incredibly fast. Maybe it's someone, *something* even worse than the blue man… With her heart trying to pound its way out of her chest, she spins around in circles, searching every which way for the threat.

"Whistlewasps," Boodark moans, the dread clearly apparent in his voice. "We need to be *very* careful. There's probably a nest somewhere close by, and we do *not* want to disturb it."

She's not convinced. "Seriously? You're telling me that it's *wasps* making that sound?"

He rudely jabs her with an elbow to her ribs. "Yes, Whistlewasps! And we need to keep our voices down. We do *not* want to draw attention to ourselves!"

She grins sheepishly at her previous display of fear and draws in a breath of relief. "Oh, thank goodness it's just bugs!"

Boodark snorts at her. "There's nothing good about Whistlewasps, so don't be thanking any goodness for them. We need to be quiet and move out of their territory. Very. Carefully."

She starts walking again and her scared little friend cringes at the sound of the dry, empty bug shells crunching beneath her feet.

"I'm just so glad that it's bugs and not something worse. It *could* have been the blue man." She shudders as she remembers the lust in his eyes, the feel of him rubbing his hard *thing* against her buttocks. She may be an innocent, but she's not *that* innocent. She knew exactly what he'd been doing, what he'd wanted, and it terrified her as much as it repulsed her. "I hope I *never* see him again. So yes. I'm glad it's just bugs that we have to deal with now!"

A second whistle joins the first, then another and another. Boodark looks up at her, his eyes wide with alarm. "Yeah, just bugs…. with arse daggers! Are you *crazy*? We are in *danger*, girl!"

Arse daggers?

"Oh *no*," he whispers in horror as more and more whistles join the melody. "There's definitely a nest close by and they're obviously aware of our presence. Watch the ground. Be very careful where you step…"

But the warning comes too late. She glances down as her foot kicks something that's half buried beneath a mound of dead bug bodies. The whistling stops as the big, pink ball that she's just disinterred goes rolling over insect shells and carcasses.

"Oh, butt shrooms and troll turds, you've done it now! I *told* you to watch where you were stepping!"

Huge, *massive* green wasps as long as her hands start pouring out of the entrance/exit hole, and their whistling is no longer slow and sad. It's loud and *very* agitated as they move to surround them.

"Run, big dummy! Run!" Boodark screams. She runs, but she does something first. She has no conscious thoughts of doing it, she just does it. She reaches down and snatches up the biggest dead bug she sees and stuffs it right into the nest's hole. *Now* she runs, and not a second too soon because if she thought their whistle song was angry *before*, she was grossly misinformed. It sounds like they're whistling screaming death metal music in her ears now.

"What did you do that for?" Boodark wails. "Now they're *really* mad!"

She doesn't turn back to see if they're chasing her. She doesn't need to. She can *hear* that they're chasing her. Some had stayed behind to help unplug the hole and release their hive-mates, but many of them had elected to hunt her down. "They were already mad! It was a purely instinctual distraction tactic. And it *worked!* They're distracted! Now there's not as many of them after us."

Boodark screams as one of the wasps darts in close to his face, threatening him with its… arse dagger. She slaps it away before it can jab him with its *inch-long stinger!* He screams again, and if the situation weren't so serious, she would laugh. He screams just like a little girl.

"Aaghhh! They're trying to stab me with their butt knives!" He yelps and then buries himself under his blanket.

She never slows her stride as she pulls off her backpack and digs for her can of Off! bug spray. She gets stung/stabbed six times in the process but finally she's got it in her hands. "Stay under the blanket!" she shouts as she slams on the brakes and spins to confront her tormentors. She holds the nozzle down and sprays a cloud of wasp-be-gone all around her.

The unsuspecting butt-knife wielders cough and choke as they plunge into it; they actually cough tiny *ack ack acks* and then back themselves out of the poison cloud. They try to go around and come at her from different angles, but she holds the can up and threatens them with a direct dousing if they try it. Eventually, they decide that she's not worth it and turn back to help the rest of their hive-mates escape their buggy prison. As soon as they're gone, she turns and runs again… just in case they're planning to come back with reinforcements. Better safe than sorry. Things on this vampire world hold *serious* grudges. Just ask Mean-Green Jaida.

"I wish I had taken the time to look around before I ran from the swamp. I could really use a zingberry or three," Ecko complains as her exhaustion causes her to stumble. Again. She'd been in such a panicked rush that she'd not only left the zingberries, but she'd also left one of her precious water bottles behind. She takes out her frustrations on a dead beetle thing, kicking it and sending it tumbling down the path. She watches as it crashes into other bugs and scatters them every which way. Bug bowling. This is what her life has come to. Running from all manner of freaky things, forever feeling drained of energy, and bug bowling. And she *stinks*. Ugh.

She uses her foot to sweep aside the scattered insect carcasses; there's not as many of them in this area as there had been behind her. Most seem to have perished long before they made it this deep into the Dead Forest.

"I can't go any further," she mutters. "I don't care *what's* after me. I have to rest." She sits down in the spot that she'd cleared and uses the opportunity to clean and disinfect the wound on her shoulder from the blue monster's bite.

Boodark, on the other hand, immediately hops out of his basket. Now he's scrambling around picking up the buggy corpses, crunching them like pork rinds. He eats and eats and eats until all that's left in the vicinity is bug crumbs and the occasional disarticulated leg or wing.

With everything in sight devoured, he plops himself onto the ground beside her, closes his eyes, and sighs contentedly. He rubs his belly (even more distended than it normally is) and grins up at her. "Oh, I'm so full! I wonder how many I ate. I lost count after one hundred and sixty-two."

She barely hears him. She keeps nodding off, falling asleep even though she's sitting straight up. Her eyes close and her head slowly lowers until her chin touches her chest. Then she jerks herself awake just to do it all over again. It doesn't help matters when Boodark starts snoring beside her either. It takes every ounce of will she possesses to rouse herself and her lazy friend enough to get up and start walking again. If she ever makes it back home, she's going to sleep for *weeks*.

"Uumm, Ecko?" Boodark interrupts her daydreams of going to sleep and doing some real sleep-dreaming. "I hate to mention this, but there's something big and blue up ahead. Maybe we should figure out what it is before we get any closer."

She drags her head up from its drooped position to see what he's pointing at. She stops walking and stands there in the middle of the path just staring at it until he gets uncomfortable with the situation. "What are we doing? Why are we standing here like a big, dumb target? What's wrong with you?"

She grunts and starts moving again but her wishy-washy little friend isn't happy with that action either. "What are you *doing?* Why are you walking *towards* it? What if it's the blue man up there?" he whisper/shouts.

She shakes her head. "It's not. Whatever's up there is too big to be the blue man. Color's all wrong too. He was more of a blue-grey. That thing is sky blue."

This assessment confuses him. "I think you have that backwards. I would say that *he* looked more like the sky than *that* does."

It takes her sluggish, overtired brain a minute or two to figure out what he's talking about. "Oh, I see what you mean. The sky on Earth isn't like the sky here. It's much bluer than this one is. It changes, but most of the time it's a light blue shade…just like that thing up there. That's why I called it sky blue. On Earth, that color *is* sky blue."

"I see. But why are we still walking towards it when we don't know *what* it is?"

She shrugs even though he's not looking at her. "We won't find out what it is standing still."

He can't argue with that, but he clearly doesn't like it. He burrows beneath the blanket so that only his big cartoon eyes are peeking out.

"I think it's… Is that a DreamSnare?" she asks once she gets a bit closer. He pops his head back out of hiding to check. "Oh," he mumbles sheepishly. "Yes. That *is* a DreamSnare."

He must be really embarrassed because he quickly adds, "I wasn't *scared*, you know. I just wanted to make sure that you were paying attention, that's all."

She's too tired to even tease him, and her fatigue intensifies about a thousand times more when she's standing right in front of the DreamSnare. Sephyr hadn't properly prepared her for the allure of it, the sheer magnitude of enticement that it exudes. She knows from the Darkling's description that the bed of palest blue, fluffy down hides a snarl of deadly vines beneath it, so she keeps her distance. But it's oh, so very hard to resist. She stares at that bed with such longing that Boodark knows without a single doubt that they're in trouble.

"Stop looking at it and keep moving! You *know* what it does. You know that it entices… it's just trying to suck you in!"

She hears him yelling at her to keep moving, to snap out of it and to just look away, but she hears it all as if from a distance. As if her ears are stuffed with cotton (or DreamSnare fluff) his words don't even penetrate. She just wants to go to sleep, longs for the blessed release of sweet, sweet slumber. She's never wanted anything more, so desperately. Her eyes are suddenly so dry and heavy that they refuse to stay open. She *has* to rest them, for just a minute.

"WAKE UP THIS INSTANT!" Boodark shouts as he jabs her in the ribs.

"I'm awake!" she insists. "I'm just resting my eyes." But her words are so slurred that he can't understand them.

"If you lay down on that fluff you will instantly fall into a deep sleep that you will *never* wake from. The pod will close and then those vines will slither in and wrap you up. They'll cradle you, soft and safe and warm, and it'll feel just like a lover's soothing embrace. And there you will stay, comforted by the lie of the DreamSnare until you're nothing but dried up, old bones. You'll never feel a thing. You'll just sleep until it sucks you dead. Is that what you want? To dream your life away?"

She starts shuffling forward. "Yeessss," she whisper/hisses like a mindless zombie begging for brains.

"Noooo!" he howls as he climbs up her chest, his claws tearing holes in her shirt as he scrabbles upwards. When he gets close enough, he reaches up and slaps her right across the face, knocking the sleepy right out of her. She's *instantly* wide awake. Unfortunately, so is Rage.

Such intense fury engulfs her… there is no word in the human vocabulary that's strong enough to describe the sheer magnitude of it. And it builds inside of her like magma rising up in a volcano. She can't contain it. There's no *way* she can keep all that inside of her. It has to go *somewhere*. Her hands tingle but they don't become engulfed in that familiar blue haze. They light up white-hot and streaked with red…. the fiery colors of burning rage.

Boodark gulps and slides down her chest to land with a *plop!* back in his basket, hastily burying himself back under his blanket just as she throws her head back and screams up at the sky. Her hands lift of their own accord as her fury boils over.

White-hot streams of rage-magic burst out of her and blasts into the DreamSnare pod. It doesn't catch fire, but it somehow burns anyway. It burns from the intensity of her fury, a flameless fire that she can *usually* keep safely hidden within herself. She dispassionately watches the cobalt blue vines come out of hiding and thrash about, whipping back and forth like uncontrolled, high pressured water hoses. The DreamSnare emits a high-pitched screech of agony as it blackens and shrivels up into a petrified fossil. It's all over with just as fast as it started, the entire process taking a mere matter of minutes.

The magic quickly recedes, and her head begins to clear. But the magic takes with it the last dregs of strength she had left, leaving her completely drained and weak as a newborn kitten. Her eyes roll up and she crumples to the ground. Strangely, her last thoughts are of a tiny black and brown dog that she used to watch in the mirrors when she'd been a small child.

She awakens (who knows how much later) with a cry on her lips. The memory of what happened floods her mind before the sleep fog even has time to dissipate. Her outcry must startle Boodark because he pops up out of his blanket, nonsensically shouting, "I did no'ting!" Then he catches sight of the ruined DreamSnare, and he slowly turns his terrified eyes up to meet hers. In a horrified voice he whispers, "Remind me to *never* slap you again!"

Her eyes immediately well up with tears. "I didn't mean to," she whimpers. "I don't know what happened. I was just suddenly full of such rage that …" Her breath sucks in on a gasp. "Oh, no. *Rage!* Has he broken out of his cage?" she whispers urgently to herself. She tries to search her mind for him, but the ground begins to shake beneath her and Boodark lets out a scream.

"Aaagghhh! We're dead. Oh, we are so dead! Dead, dead, dead!"

She stares at him as her dumb brain flashes back to a scene from the Disney movie, Anastasia. For just a brief moment, she actually *sees* Bartok, the little bat from the movie instead of *her* little orc-bat. She deliriously whisper-quotes, "They're dead. Dead, dead, dead. *All* the Romanovs are dead."

Boodark stares back at her like she's lost her mind. Perhaps she has. She doesn't feel well, not at all. She smiles weakly, trying to reassure him. "Never mind," she mumbles. "I'm fine. Everything's fine. Don't be afraid."

He groans as he jumps to his feet. "Oh, flipping fly eggs and poop-patty parasites! Come on, come on. Get up! We have to go. We must find shelter! Immediately!" He lets out a frustrated grunt when she continues to sit there. Now *she's* staring at *him* like he's the one that's lost his mind. "Can you not hear the words coming out of my mouth? We. have. To. Go!"

But she's *not* paying much attention to him. Her head is all foggy, almost like she's back in the Dreaming. She knows that she should be concerned that Rage may have escaped her mind prison, but she can't find the energy to care. She honestly feels as bad as she had back in those early days at the hospital, when she'd been so drugged that she hadn't even known her own name…. And hadn't cared to learn it either. Nothing seems to matter much right now either. Boodark's words seem irrelevant and unimportant, of absolutely no interest to her. She absentmindedly starts contemplating what's more urgent, the need to fill her empty belly or her almost overwhelming desire to lay down in the dirt and go back to sleep.

"I think we'll sleep here tonight," she murmurs, her voice dreamy and distracted. "I'll just throw the tarp down and we can sleep right here on the path."

Boodark screeches in frustration. Then he gets up, runs around behind her, and starts shoving her as hard as he can. "What's wrong with you, *now?* Move (grunt) your (groan) giant (ggrrr) butt!"

She shakes her head to clear away the fog and it actually seems to help a bit, just in time for him to *really* put his back into it. He presses his shoulder against her and heaves with all his strength. She twists away from him in irritation, then she searches all around for the threat, because *surely,* he's panicking for a good reason.

There's nothing, not a single danger in sight.

"Stop that!" she snaps. "Why are you freaking out? Nothing's after you. There's nothing here…. Nothing but dead things. So just calm down and help me set up camp. I'm hungry, even if you're not."

Her strange little friend rushes back around to stand in front of her. "I am *to* hungry! I'm *always* hungry! But you don't understand. There's nothing but dead things all around us. We are surrounded by the dead!" He gulps and whimpers all at the same time. *"Dead things tend to get up and walk around in the Dead Forest during the Pitch!"*

Now *that* is the perfect motivational speech, a sure-fire way to clear the fog from one's mind. Simply introduce a deeply profound fear into the situation. It'll wake you right up. The fog instantly gets swept away by her fear of all things deceased. (Zombies and ghosts and vamps, oh my!) She feels her heart drop down into the pit of her stomach and she forgets how to breathe for a minute. "Why didn't you tell me this hours ago?" she scolds as she lurches to her feet. She snatches him up, shoves him into his basket, and gets moving again.

Offended, he snobbishly lifts his nose up and insists, "I *did* try to tell you! You didn't want to hear it. You were too glad to be out of the swamp. And then the blue monster came and we almost lost Sephyr and I almost died, and you almost died. *Everyone* almost died and I just forgot, *ok!* Is that what you want to hear? That this is my fault? Fine! It's my fault. Punish me later… If we're still alive later. Let's just *please* find a shelter before dark. I don't know about you, but I really hate deaders."

Enough said. She also absolutely *loathes* creepy dead things that don't have enough decency to stay dead too.

She hadn't been able to find shelter before Pitchfall, nor had she been able to find one *after* Pitchfall. There hadn't been a single suitable place to hide, and eventually she stopped looking for any sort of safe haven. She just ran… as long and as far as she could. She kept moving, concentrating on putting one foot in front of the other when the coast was clear and then hiding whenever the threats appeared.

And there were threats, indeed there *were* dead things walking. Terrifyingly gruesome dead things. Bone people and decaying creatures. Thankfully though, not *every* dead thing got up and moved around. As far as she could tell, most of them observed proper protocol and stayed properly dead. True dead. It was only a small percentage of them that decided to come back and haunt the forest. But even one was too many for her. Shoot, even some of the dead trees are walking around, their stiff joints and limbs creaking and groaning as they slowly move amongst their less-mobile brethren.

"Kreekers," Boodark whispers after they (somehow) survive their first encounter with an ambulant, woody perennial… aka a walking tree. "Kreekers are terrifying even when they're alive and outside the Dead Forest's borders. They don't stay still. They uproot themselves and then use their roots to drag themselves around in search of food. They're hunters and they eat meat." He glances up at her then and adds, "We're meat, in case you didn't understand that." She only nods. She *does* know that. Everything on this world wants to eat her, or at least kill her. Even *he* had wanted to eat her, once upon a time.

She has only a brief moment to wonder if perhaps the trees she'd seen at the very beginning of her swamp nightmare/adventure had been Kreekers… the ones that crept in and surrounded her. Had any of that even been real? She can't tell any more what was true and what had been imagined. She'd been so very lost and…

"At least there's no spooks," Boodark says, interrupting her unpleasant trip down Memory Lane to steer her straight towards Fear Street. He said it in an attempt to comfort her, but she's not comforted. Not the slightest bit. She hadn't even been worried about ghosts until he brought them up.

"Perfect!" she whisper/shouts at him as she ducks behind a large dead tree (one of the stationary ones) and clicks off her flashlight. The dark settles over her like a heavy blanket made of the blackest Duchess satin, yards and yards of doom clinging to her, threatening to suffocate her under its great, black weight. When she tells Charlie all about this night, she knows in her heart that she will *never* be able to convey the sheer terror she'd felt *every single time* she'd been forced to click off her flashlights and stand oh, so silent and oh, so still in the utter black of the Pitch.

"All clear," Boodark softly calls out as the most recent deader finally, *finally* passes them by. She clicks her light back on with a heartfelt sigh of relief.

"That's just *perfect!*" she immediately continues her spook rant. "You just *had* to go there, didn't you? Now there's definitely gonna be spooks. You jinxed us!"

He gives her huge, startled eyes and trembling lips, almost as if she's struck him a personal blow… but then he must have thought it over and agreed because he falls silent. He also seems to keep a closer eye on their surroundings. Probably waiting for the ghosts to make their appearance!

The next several hours are every bit as hellish as the swamp had been, in their own way. The only good thing about it is… she doesn't remember much more of the night's events than she remembers of her time trapped in the Dreaming. It's all a jumbled blur of being terrified, running through the dark, being terrified, stumbling and trying not to fall on Boodark and squish him, hiding from deaders, and being even *more* terrified.

At some point during the Great Escape of the Deaders in the Dead Forest, she had remembered the gifts that the Mushroom clans had given her, the small clusters of mushrooms, in particular. She had no use for the blue ones, because they would act as a sleeping aid. As much as she desperately needed the rest, there was nowhere safe for her to hide, so sleep was out of the question. But the other ones sure had come in handy. The red ones helped her stay awake and the yellow ones granted her the ability to run superfast.

The hours upon hours of fear, of running and hiding had taken a toll on her. She had quickly depleted the small supply of mushrooms and she's convinced that she feels even worse now without the stimulants. She'd already been drained and exhausted before entering the Dead Forest. Now her condition is critical. She no longer cares about the dark or the deaders or even the spooks. *That's* how far gone she is. She's stumbling like a drunkard, barely clinging to her consciousness. But oh, it's closing in on her, so close. The only thing keeping her upright is the fact that Boodark will be left alone and helpless in this hateful world if she should falter. That and she *really* doesn't want to be eaten by a deader.

"There's a light." The words don't even penetrate the trance she's fallen into, the routine of putting one foot in front of the other, of crawling when she falls to her knees, and of getting back up to walk on just as soon as she can muster the strength to do so.

"I see a light up there," Boodark repeats. He turns his head to look up at her when she still doesn't respond. He knows that she's in bad shape. She's gone silent, just like he had when he'd come so close to faltering. They need help… fast. He can only hope that the light bearer is friendly.

He continues trying to get her attention as she trudges onward, following the path that her magic had laid down for her. He calls her name over and over again, his voice trembling and tears threatening at her continued refusal to acknowledge him. His breath catches as she stumbles and falls to her knees again, and this time *stays* there, kneeling upon the ground. Her head is lowered under the burden of fatigue, and she sways slightly as if a wind is shoving at her from all directions.

"Ecko *please*," he cries. "We're so close, so close now. Look. Please look! If you will just lift your head up and see what I see. I think we've come to the end of your magic path. I think the light ahead is your old woman in the giant tree." He stops to wipe his streaming eyes on his t-shirt blanket. "*Look* Ecko. You kept us both alive throughout the Pitch and brought us to a safe haven… hopefully. I mean, when you told me of your vision, you seemed to think it was a safe place and that the old lady was friendly. I sure hope so anyway. But we'll never find out if you don't *get up.*"

Still no answer.

"AArrggg!" he shouts in frustration. "Cursed Madar-gens. I'll make them pay if it's the last thing I ever do! If I had my wings I could fly ahead and check it out, bring help back for you. I can't do it without my wings. I move too slow on the ground; it would take ages for me to get there and back again. I dare not leave you alone for that long. We go together or not at all."

He sniffles back his tears as he remembers that love is a powerful motivator, and so is guilt. "Get up, Ecko!" he orders in a firm, stern voice. "What would Charlie think if he could see you now? *What would your father think?*"

She goes oh, so still at those harshly uttered words. She doesn't move, never even looks up. "My father's dead," she tells him in a flat monotone voice.

So empty.

"Charlie and Susan are probably dead too."

So emotionless.

Boodark sucks in a sharp breath at her words…elated that she finally acknowledged him, but heartbroken at her desolate tone and the finality in her words.

"Dead does not necessarily mean the end," he tells her. "It does not mean that life has ended permanently, it simply means that life has ended on this plane of existence. Dead means changed, gone on to a different place, a different kind of living. Who's to say your loved ones aren't in some other state of existence right now, watching you, rooting for you… *believing* in you?"

She takes a deep, shuddering breath. "Maybe it's time I join them," she whispers back. "I'm too tired, Boodark. I'm tired of fighting. I don't even remember what I'm fighting for."

He reaches around and hugs as much of her as his small body will allow, his heart breaking for her. "You're fighting for everyone else. For all those who *can't* fight. For all the little ones that are too small to right wrongs, all the innocents trapped on vampire worlds. You're fighting for the helpless ones, the voiceless ones, and the cursed ones. You're fighting for me and my Secret… for my babies. For all the people on Irredarr, where you possibly have a family that you've not yet had the opportunity to meet. For your Earth and all Earthians, the peoples of your heart. For all the worlds that are threatened by the evil influence of the Lokskell. And whether or not you realize it yet, you're fighting for *you.* You have hopes and dreams, and there are still things that you want to do, things that you want to see. You want *life,* and all it has to offer. You are *not* a quitter. You're a fighter, the bravest, truest one I have ever met. I've seen you survive so much. Indeed, *we* have survived so much together. I refuse to believe that *this* is it…that *this* is as far as we go. I refuse to believe that it was all for nothing. We have *not* endured everything this world has thrown at us just to sit right here and let it win!"

She swivels her head just enough for her eyes to meet his as she acknowledges the truth in his words. So many others are depending on her, so many innocents have lost their lives to her father, to her sister… to evil. And every day more of them die.

Boodark's words are like a puff of wind on a dying ember. It rekindles the tiniest spark in her heart, stokes the coals and feeds it the fuel it needs to burn hotter. It's just enough to get her back on her feet again.

"*Yessss!*" he shouts as he victoriously punches the air. She takes one unsteady step and then follows it with another. And another and another until her wobbly, uneven gait strengthens and speeds up. Her eyes focus on the light up ahead, holding it in her sights like it's a visual lifeline as it gets closer and brighter with each step that she takes.

And then she's there, standing before the towering, gargantuan tree. She shines her flashlight up the length of it in a futile attempt at discerning just how tall it really is. Up and up and up, it extends far higher than her little light can possibly touch. But everywhere it *does* reach reveals fruits of some sort. Strange fruits that look remarkably like plump, round grapes. But they're not hanging down in clusters in typical grape fashion. They're growing right out of the bark of the trunk and branches, looking for all the world like someone just glued them all on there. They're much larger than grapes too, more the size of plums, and they're so purple that they actually appear black.

"Oh!" she cries out in excitement. "It's a Jaboticaba tree! I've always wanted to see one and taste its fruit." She rushes forward and plucks one from the trunk, marveling at how big and heavy it feels in her hand. She brings it up closer to her face, studying the strangely curved, double ridges right across the center. "I hope it's not poisonous. Do you think it's safe to…Eeecckk!" she squeals as her hand reflexively opens and drops the fruit to the ground.

"*What?*" Boodark shouts. "What happened?"

She shines her light down, searching the ground for wherever it had rolled to. Surely, she'd been mistaken and hadn't seen what she *thought* she'd seen. Surely, it had to have been a trick of the light, the shadows from her little light bouncing off the darkness around her. There's no way it had been … but it was.

The light finally locates what it's searching for and Boodark lets out a screech almost identical to the one she'd just emitted. It's an eyeball. It's a freaking-fracking eyeball, and she'd had it *in her hand!* She'd thought about tasting it!

The purple/black peel is more of a skin to cover over the actual eyeball, and those weird double ridges across its center seem to be its top and bottom eyelids. With the light shining on it now, they slide closed and then back open as it blinks up at them from the dirt.

"Oh, I know! I know what this is!" Boodark exclaims. "It's the SeeAll tree! It's one of the seven magic EverRealms! Supposedly, it's the hardest one to find, too. I *never* dreamed I'd get to see it."

"Some magic," she scoffs. "It's not very hidden. And how do you hide a million-foot tree anyway?"

She shines her light back on the tree and just about has a heart attack when every single fruit that the light touches slides open and peers back at her. Even Boodark, in all his obvious excitement over finding this magical SeeAll tree is taken aback by the thousands upon thousands of eyeballs staring down at them. He recoils and shrinks himself down as small as possible, like that will really help him to go unseen by the eyeball masses.

"Ha! Hahaha!"

They simultaneously let out piercing, little girl screams as a raucous cackle scares the bejesus out of them both. Hand trembling violently, she points her flashlight up into the tree's branches, looking for a mouth fruit to go along with the voice. (Hey, it's a logical assumption that if a tree has eyeball fruits that can see, then it could very well have mouth fruits that can laugh and speak. She'd *never* understood how those clusters of moving eyeballs in the movie Labyrinth had made all those sounds if they didn't have mouths to make sounds *with*.)

Her light doesn't locate any mouth fruits, but it does reveal the old*ish* woman from her vision instead. She's perched on the branches directly above them, her dangling legs only inches away from touching the top of Ecko's head.

"How'd she get there? *No way* she's been there the whole time!" Boodark urgently whispers. The wily woman drops to the ground and briskly dusts off her hands. "You *can* eat them; I do it all the time. So do my Na-Loofs," she informs them. Then she shuffles away and opens a cleverly hidden door. Light pours out from the interior, where not even a hint of it showed through when the door had been closed.

Boodark's mouth drops open. Hers too, probably. She can't help but study the design of it. It's small and round, just like a Hobbit door, the circular shape helping it to blend right into the surrounding swirls and ridges of bark. The doorknob is disguised as one of the many eyeball fruits scattered across its surface. She *never* would have known a door was there if the woman hadn't opened it and was now making her way inside.

"You can stay outside and sample them if you wish, but I've made tea and cookies if you'd rather come inside and forgo the SeeAll eyeball consumption experience. Up to you!" She lets out one last cackle as she disappears inside the tree.

Boodark and Ecko glance warily at one another. "We going in?" he asks.

She turns back and peers out into the darkness then down at the magic-made path beneath her feet. "I guess we are. We've come all this way, after all. And we can't go back." She shudders at just the thought of it.

The eyeball fruits roll around and follow her movements, keeping a close eye (snort!) on her as she steps over the threshold. "Besides, she said she has cookies."

She stands there in the doorway and moves her own eyes over *everything,* searching for hidden threats and possible escape routes. She's stepped into a huge, open room… the ceiling much higher than in a typical house. It's sparsely furnished with only a large, stone slab table and crude chairs made from thick tree branches taking up the entire center of the room. She notices that there's also a room off the back wall, just beyond the table, and another one in the far-left corner. She can only guess at what's inside those rooms because they're both hidden from view behind closed doors.

'Probably sleeping areas', she thinks and then dismisses them as her attention moves on. Just like she'd seen through her weird tunnel vision experience, there's a small, open kitchen area to the right, and that's where the old*ish* woman is busy puttering around. There's a massive fireplace for cooking, with cast-iron skillets and pots neatly hanging from hooks above it. The roaring fire in the hearth is what provides the main light source, filling the room with a soft, pleasant glow, and the braided hemp/fiber rug on the floor before it adds to the overall charm.

Just beyond the fireplace, curving along the entire rightside wall is a counter that's crowded with jars and wooden bowls and spoons. There's even a sink area, a large basin for washing although there doesn't appear to be any sort of water faucet to supply it with water. The island in the middle of the kitchen area holds a tray piled high with cookies, jars (of jam?) and three little wooden teacups.

"Don't just stand there, child. Shut the door and come help me with this tray." The abruptness of the woman's demand startles her, and she automatically spins around to do as she's told. As she's pulling the door closed, she notices the spiral staircase in the frontleft corner of the room that climbs up and disappears through a hole in the ceiling. Completely suspended by vine/ropes, it looks like someone took a rope bridge, lifted it up, and twirled it into a spiral to create a ladder. But the steps aren't made from traditional wooden planks. They're actually huge chunks of bracket fungus

(also known as shelf fungus, but *she's* always called them fairy ladders because of the way they climb up the trees.) She has always been fascinated with fungus, and she's taken thousands of photos of many different varieties, but she's *never* seen anything like these. Not only are they much larger than any fungus she's used to seeing, but their age-rings are brilliantly colored in shades of blue instead of the customary Earthy tones. Royal, cobalt, periwinkle, steel blue, and blue-tinted silver rings form a spectacular pattern across the surface of each shelf/step. Her fingers twitch as the urge to capture their beauty in photos has her automatically reaching for her camera.

"Cookies, tea, and introductions first!" the woman calls out. "Tour after!"

So, she pivots back around and rushes to gather up the tray. "Yes, ma'am!" she gushes in a slightly embarrassed voice. She carefully carries the tray but stops just short of the table to stare at the three cat… *things* that are now sitting atop the surface. Boodark takes one look at them and hisses loudly before burrowing deep under his blanket.

They're strange, she'll give him that. They're certainly not like Earth cats, that's for sure. The one closest to her is something straight out of a fairytale. It *looks* like a cat, but at the same time it looks like something that belongs in the water… like some sort of mermaid/cat hybrid. Its face and the shape of its body is feline, and it has short, stumpy legs like the munchkin breeds have, but everything else about it seems aquatic.

Its long tail is covered in bushy, hair-like bristles, like the fins on a Betta fish. Its extra-long neck, circled with raised ridges, lends it a seahorse-type appearance. Pointy ears stick straight back on its head instead of extending in the typical upright direction. Long whiskers and more of the fin bristles flow backwards from its head in a billowing, fishy mane. It even has what looks like gills at the base of its ears, right along the lines of its cheekbones. The fact that its scales are blue and flecked with purple highlights only adds to the overall mythical sea creature appearance.

She reluctantly turns her attention to the 'cat' sitting just behind it. *This* one looks like a perfectly normal, fluffy white kitty… as long as she ignores the large set of feathery wings poking out of its back and the long griffin's tail that it's currently licking. As if it can feel her watching, it stops bathing itself to return her stare, and she sucks her breath in on a startled gasp.

The black eyes that regard her look like galaxies, full of stars, glittering dust, and swirls of rainbow-colored gases. They look *exactly* like the galaxy smoke that her magic had produced back in the Sorrow Marshes before it had settled onto the root bridge-path. She would have willingly lost herself and stared into those bottomless orbs all night if the third cat had just kept its insulting mouth shut.

"I fear that we are all doomed. If this sad, clueless creature is *truly* the new Wandelaar, I say we search for alternate ways to save our *own* selves," it sneers in a deep, condescending voice as it crinkles its nose at her.

This cat looks just like a demon, a sanctimonious, judgy one, at that. If Satan had a pet cat, this is just what she imagines it would look like. Silky fur as black as night and a pair of long, thin devil horns atop its head lend it a decidedly devilish demeanor …sharp, sticky-stabby horns that she immediately vows to steer clear of.

Stamped in the center of its forehead, filling in the space between horns and eyes is a silver, crescent moon beset with blue stars around it. The hellcat stares back at her with solid orange eyes as it curls not one, but two tails around itself. Those twin tails are long and sleek, the silky tufts at the tips twitching as if it's vexed by her intrusion into its domain.

She drags her eyes away from the overly intimidating creature (although she feels like she really should keep an eye on it, lest it try to suck her soul out and drag it down into the fiery depths of hell) as the woman scuttles around her to shoo the three of them away. "Shoo! Off with you now. I *told* you to stay out of sight until she's more at ease. You never listen!"

The winged cat and the mer-cat instantly obey, but the big mouth one lingers behind long enough to throw a few more verbal punches.

"And *you*!" The woman jabs her finger at the Satanspawned black one that refuses to budge (the one that she mentally nicknames Beelzebub) "*You* keep your opinions to yourself!"

His eyes narrow as he hunkers down in that catty way that cats do when they're vexed about something. "Just look at her," he snips. "A puny, pathetic creature such as herself should *not* be in charge of the fates of the worlds! Plus, she stinks."

That's it, that's *it!* She marches forward and plunks the tray down on the table so fast that the rude cat creature is forced to dart out of the way. He hisses at her from the far side of the table, but she just lifts her chin up and blinks back sudden, useless tears.

"I'm sorry I'm not up to your standards," she tells him. "*You* try wandering lost in a swamp for days and days and see how clean and fresh *you* smell!"

He turns his head away as if he's bored with the conversation. Then he idly murmurs, "One *could* give oneself a lick-bath. *If* one had cleanliness in mind, that is." He stands up and nonchalantly gives himself a full-bodied stretch before adding, "Cleanliness in close to Godliness… if you ask me. But that's just my *opinion.* What do *I* know though? I'm just the truth-speaker, that's all."

The woman snatches a cookie from the tray and launches it at him, but he darts off the table before it can strike.

"*Doomed,*" he repeats his dire warning before lifting both tails high and strutting away.

"Hmpff," the woman snorts. "Opinion giver is what you *should* be called, and a rude one at that!" She sends Ecko a soft smile and apologizes for the behavior of the 'unbearable beast'. "Please ignore him. He doesn't get out much and I fear his manners are sorely beginning to suffer from his prolonged isolation. Please, sit. Let your little friend know that it's safe to come out. Those naughty Kreeleerians are gone now."

She reaches down and pokes at the lump under the t-shirt blanket. "You hear that, Chickenbutt? It's safe to come out."

All she gets in return is a muffled, 'Wah wa wah wah wah' sound.

"I can't understand a word you're saying, Boodark. Come out," she tells him as she peels the blanket back. He immediately tries to pull it back and a tiny tug of war ensues. She decides to try a different approach. She takes the appeal to a more powerful court… his stomach. "She has cookies. I think they even have bits of fruit or berries in them. But I guess we'll just have to eat them without you, since you refuse to come out."

There's a slight rustling under the blanket and then a small, declawed hand emerges. It opens and closes in the universal 'give it to me, put it in my hand' signal.

"Nope. I'm not giving you anything until you come out. It would be rude to our host if you hide in there and eat all her cookies. I refuse to encourage bad behavior."

She knows he won't be able to resist. She busies herself so that she doesn't start laughing as he pokes his nose up over the edge of the basket in order to get a whiff of the promised treats. She takes her backpack off and sets it across the seat of a chair, creating a makeshift booster seat for him to sit on that will allow him to reach the table. She sets him on it and hangs his basket on the back of his chair. Then she awkwardly stands behind her own chair wishing that she could excuse herself and go wash up. Beelzebub the devil cat was rude and unwelcoming, but he was right. She's dirty and she *does* stink.

The old*ish* woman smiles again and tells her not to pay any attention to him and that there will be plenty of time for her to wash up after she gets some food in her belly. "Go ahead child. Sit. Eat." So, she nods shyly and fills a plate for Boodark and pours him some tea before sitting down and serving herself. Her little friend immediately begins shoveling the food in, all the while uttering his customary Murunng mrung mmrruunngg foodpleasure sounds.

"Boodark! Politely!" she admonishes in a reproachful voice… that he promptly ignores.

"Oh, don't scold him. It does my heart good to know that my simple fare can bring such joy. Do let him be, child, and let us make our introductions. My name is Athtandakapootha

Delainnianth Carpathilla" She holds up her hand and quickly adds, "Don't try to remember it, don't even try to pronounce it. I, myself was almost full grown before I could pronounce it properly. And learning to spell it? Forget about it! Please, call me Tanda."

Ecko samples a cookie and wishes with all her heart that she could be like her little bat buddy and shovel them into her mouth whole. She manages to restrain herself though…barely. "And my name is Adrin…"

Boodark grunts loudly, frantically shaking his head.

"Stop it, Boodark. I'm sure we can trust her. She *is* from Irredarr, after all." She turns back to the woman and says, "Aren't you." It's a question, but it's not *really* a question because she already knows that it is so. And it's confirmed when the woman's eyes dim just a bit, and she nods sadly in agreement.

"That I am, although I have not seen my home world in many, many years. You feel it, do you not? The pulse, the heartbeat… the connection that we Irredarrians all share?"

She nibbles on another cookie as she thinks about it, considering how much she should share. Should she blindly trust this woman? She decides to be as honest as she can be without revealing *everything*. "Yes, I feel it. I felt it the moment I entered the Dead Forest. I wasn't sure what it meant until now though." The old*ish* woman smiles such a beatific smile then; it transforms her face and has Ecko rethinking her true age. She's old, a crone almost. But confusingly, she's *not* old too. Right now, she appears to be around Susan and Charlie's age, but at other times she appears older. Much, much older. And still, other times she looks like she could be her father's age.

She shakes her head to stop her thoughts. She's confusing her own self. "My name is Adrina Ecko Zyanya, but everyone just calls me Ecko. And this is my friend, Boodark."

He snorts out a rude noise. "Big mistake, giving her your full name," he grumbles, spraying crumbs out of his mouth. "Maybe you *can* trust her, but what about those hideous hairballs? Think you can trust *them*?"

Well, darn. She hadn't thought of *that*. Beelzebub hadn't even tried to hide his dislike of her.

"The Kreeleerians are loyal," Tanda informs them. Boodark merely grunts and gets back to devouring cookies so fast that he probably could have won a cookie eating contest against the cookie monster.

"Tell me *everything*. How did you get here? Where are you traveling to? What are you searching for? Do you know anything of your mother? Your father? Have you seen our world? Have you been to Irredarr?" The questions pour out of her as if she'd been waiting years to ask them, and she probably had been.

She decides to go back to the very beginning…back to her first memory of seeing the OtherWorlds in the mirror when she'd been a small child. She opens her mouth, but the words never get the chance to leave her tongue because suddenly her head feels all woozy and the room is spinning around her. She drops her head into her hands and tries to breathe through the nauseating vertigo.

"Poison!" Boodark shrieks as he spits the cookies from his mouth in a disgusting spray of crumbs, half chewed chunks, and saliva. "Ack! She's poisoned us. I *told* you not to trust her!" He scrubs at his tongue, trying to remove every single soggy crumb, never mind that he's already snarfed down ten cookies to her two. If it were poison, he would have fallen ill long before she had.

"It's not poison. I just don't feel so good right now." She pushes her plate back and lays her head down, the coolness of the stone tabletop a balm against her hot, flushed skin. She watches silently, miserably, as Beelzebub lithely jumps back onto the table and Tanda leans in so that he's able to whisper into her ear.

The woman sighs in resignation as she turns back to peer at the afflicted girl. She sends her a small, gentle smile, rife with worry and regret as she agrees with whatever the hellcat had to say. "Yes, I suspected as much, but I had to be certain. I suppose we'll need to take care of that right away."

The demon cat lays down and curls up as if he's making himself comfortable for what's to come. Ecko could almost swear that he was smiling smugly at her across the expanse of the table.

Tanda holds her left hand out and uses her right pointer finger to trace something onto her palm. Unbelievably, a rune of some kind appears as if her finger is a magic sharpie pen. The symbol lights up briefly, the lines of it moving and rearranging themselves into a small circle. Somehow that two-dimensional, flat circle inflates into a marble-sized, 3-dimensional bubble that floats up off her hand. Tanda cups both hands together around the mini bubble, lifts it up to her lips, and begins to whisper to it.

Ecko lifts her head up off the table and exchanges a worried glance with Boodark. His look says 'She's crazy. We should run now' while hers is worried, but also intrigued. After all, she herself had made a magic bubble and it had turned out to be a fairy prison. Was she about to be imprisoned also? She honestly doesn't feel threatened (as of yet), but she lifts Boodark onto her lap and wraps her free hand around her backpack straps, just in case they have to make a run for it. It never hurts to be prepared.

The two of them watch as the more Tanda whispers to the bubble, the bigger it grows. Her words seem to be the air that inflates it! Soon they can see what's actually going on *inside* the sphere. Tiny, silver runic letters float around inside of it, all scrambled up like a metallic alphabet soup. Apparently done with saying what she'd needed to say, Tanda lifts her head up and looks right into Ecko's eyes as she calls out her name…her *full* name.

Boodark was right. There *is* magic in knowing one's full name.

"Adrina Ecko Zyanya," Tanda says in a loud, clear voice and the bubble immediately lifts up and begins to float towards them. "Be not afraid, child. I wish no ill will upon you. Catch it."

Ecko trusts her, perhaps unreasonably, perhaps foolishly, but even so, she does as she's told. Or tries to, anyway. She holds her own hand out, palm up as the bubble drifts right into it. It touches down briefly and then floats back up a bit, hovering perhaps three inches above her outstretched hand.

A hole appears in the bottom of the bubble, in the exact spot that had made contact with her skin. She gasps in awe as the runeletters begin to spill out. They pour themselves right onto her palm, forming words and sentences that she can read perfectly. They're as familiar to her as if she'd learned the runic alphabet and had been reading rune-words her entire life.

The message begins without any preamble, straight to the point. *'You have one of the Lokskell's Slivers attached to you.'* The words on her palm flare brightly and then burn up, one letter at a time after she reads it. She feels no pain whatsoever, no heat even as the words burn away. When the entire sentence is reduced to glittery ash, the next line of the message pours itself out of the bubble, the scrambled alphabet soup magically settling into the message that Tanda wants to tell her.

'It is the reason you've been so weakened. It's somehow feeding off of you in a way that I've never seen before. It's draining your power, tainting the magic inside of you... gorging itself on your magic so that it can grow and spread inside you. I can remove it, but it will be painful... extremely painful. Say nothing. It hears all. There is no telling what damage it will cause you if it realizes that you are now aware of its presence. If you wish it gone and agree to accept my help, simply stand up, remove your shirt, and move over to the fireplace. Then brace yourself child and know that I am truly sorry for the pain you are about to suffer at my hands. Just know that this is necessary and that I would find another way if such a thing were possible.'

The last of the message burns away and the empty bubble bursts, raining tiny shards of rainbow-hued glitter onto her empty palm. She raises her eyes to Tanda's and nods. Then she hugs Boodark and sets him back onto his own chair.

"Everything's going to be fine, Boodark," she says. "Just stay right here for me."

He tries to protest as she gets up and walks to the fireplace, pulling her shirt over her head as she goes. She pays him no mind. She can't explain anyway, not without letting the *thing* attached to her hear it. And she knows without a doubt that what she'd just learned is true. A Sliver, Tanda called it. Just the name of it puts ice shards in her soul and makes her skin crawl. She takes a couple of deep, fortifying breaths and then turns back around to face Tanda. She pulls her shoulders back, lifts her chin, and waits for whatever is to come.

Tanda lifts her hands again as she walks towards her, and a ball of fire appears on her palms. A strange fire unlike any she's ever seen before, the pure white flames blaze with a soothing, comforting light.

"*Soul Fire,*" Ecko whispers, somehow knowing exactly what it's called. The old*ish* woman nods as she gets closer, then winces in sympathy as she presses her hands against Ecko's chest. The flames that are anything *but* soothing disappear beneath her skin, and she begins to scream.

She burns on the inside for a long, long time and unfortunately, she feels every second of it. All of a sudden, she can see it, can see *inside* of herself to the parasite that's been living off of her life force. It had gained entrance to her body when that cold, foul wind blew through her. The Sliver is the *ick* that got left behind! It attached itself to the middle of her back, up high so that it remained out of her sight and out of reach. It had latched on, burrowed inside, and spread like an ink spill throughout her body. Her insides are now riddled with the icky, black veins but they're mostly concentrated around a blazing, white ball of light at her core. Her soul? Her magic?

Whatever it is, it's surrounded by her beautiful, rainbow aura … a swirling, iridescent haze with a myriad of lights flickering within it. Her aura flows in a never-ending circle around the ball of light, protecting it from the tendrils of *ick* that relentlessly try to break through. Occasionally, one of those black tendrils manages to get past the aura's defenses and plunges itself into the ball of light. The Sliver greedily slurps up as much of the light as it can before the tiny sparks inside the aura rally together and push it back out.

Ecko 'watches' as Tanda's firestorm turns her insides into a battlefield, lighting her up from within as it attacks the Sliver's taint. The white flames blaze through her, burning away the alien organism that has invaded and attempted to drain her of magic.

The inky tendrils immediately begin to boil and evaporate wherever the fire touches it. Now *it's* screaming too, right along with her, writhing against the pain and the damage that Tanda's pure magic is inflicting upon it. It's clearly in agony but it refuses to relinquish its hold on her. It fights back, striking out at the flames even though pieces of it get singed off, melted on contact.

Ecko feels every bit of the internal battle and she can't tell whose screams are louder, hers or the Sliver's. The two of them howl and shriek in tandem as the war rages on and on and on for an eternity. Eventually though, the Sliver learns that it just cannot win, and it begins a hasty retreat. The inky veins withdraw, pulling itself backwards through her body, back to its own core self. But Tanda's blazing white Soul Fire has it now, and it will not stop until every last bit of black taint is eradicated. Light chases away the darkness, burns it away… even from within.

At last, the tendrils are all burned away and all that remains is a disgusting, black slug-like worm embedded into her back. The parasite thrashes and wriggles about, trying to escape, screaming all the while. It wriggles itself free and slips out of her, leaving a raw, bloody hole in her flesh as big around as a quarter. It tries to get away, but Tanda's ready and waiting for it. She catches it in a jar and quickly screws the lid down tight.

Then she holds her hands up and calls her flames back, but they don't heed her call right away. They hover around the bright ball of light, pushing into Ecko's aura to focus on the three black blemishes that swirl amongst the iridescent rainbow colors. The Soul Fire does its best to burn the small blights away, but these were not caused by the Sliver. They're a part of her, part of her makeup, and it will take more than a Soul Fire to extirpate them. The white flames are forced to give up and leave that particular taint behind, uncleansed. They sweep backwards through her body, surge out of her chest, and flow back into Tanda's awaiting hands.

She doesn't get to see what happens to the Soul Fire once Tanda gets it back because it's suddenly all too much for her to bear. The many ordeals she's had to endure… the uncertainties of being thrust into a new vampire world, being kidnapped by hobglins, the parasitic Sliver draining her, the whole horrid Sorrow Marshes experience, the trauma of almost losing Boodark and then Sephyr, and the constant worry for her safety since, the absolute *agony of* a Soul Fire cleanse, and all the other experiences in between are just too much. *Too much.*

All that's happened to her in such a short amount of time, with little food and minimal downtime has caught up. She needs rest, a total mental shutdown and a hard reboot. It will no longer be denied, nor will it wait for a more convenient time and place. Her mind and body cease all functions, completely and instantly… like a computer that's been forced to shut down. She loses consciousness and falls to the floor in a heap from which she doesn't move for eighteen hours straight.

When she does finally regain consciousness, it happens just as suddenly as when she'd lost it. There's no waking slowly, no blissful, languorous stretching or sleepy yawns… no slow computer boot up. She's wide eyed and alert with the suddenness of a light bulb being switched on. She finds herself incredibly full of energy and brilliant enthusiasm… and a desperately urgent need to empty her bladder. The moment her eyes open, she's sitting up and scrambling her way out from under a mound of unfamiliar blankets. Poor little Boodark gets tumbled out in the process.

"Sorry!" she shouts as she leaps to her feet, a pinched, distressed look on her face.

"Through there, child!" Tanda hollers out as she points to a small alcove that she hadn't noticed before. Situated between the fireplace and that first doorway to the left, she assumes that Tanda's directing her to the bathroom. She hopes so, anyway because that's what she'll be using it for as soon as she gets in there, bathroom or not. As Boodark is fond of saying… It's coming out right now!

Thankfully it *is* a bathroom. Well, it's more like a privy or an outhouse, only it's situated inside the house instead of in a little shed on the outside. There's a small niche off to the side that's set up as a wash station. She bypasses that and runs to the 'toilet'. It's just a long, wooden plank with a round hole cut out of it, but who is she to complain? She's been squatting behind bushes and trees for days, so this is actually a Godsend.

She quickly (and blissfully) takes care of her business and moves to the wash station. There's a wooden bowl, a pitcher of water, and even a small blob of homemade soap that she uses to scrub her hands with. There's no drain system for the bowl/sink, but the very basic and rustic shower in the corner *does* have one, so that's where she dumps the dirty water.

She studies the shower's set up with admiration and sincere longing. There's a huge rain barrel-type container that looks like it's for water storage, and it's actually built *into* the ceiling. She assumes that the top of it is opened up to the outside world so that it can collect rainwater.

There's a handmade hose, one end attached to the bottom of the storage tank and the other held aloft by a hook in the wall. She peers closely at that hose, trying to figure out what it's made out of. It's almost like rubber, but not quite. She shrugs to herself; the substance is unfamiliar to her.

The end that's hanging up has a cup-like shower head with little holes drilled into it. She assumes that when the hose is let down, gravity will do its thing and the water will flow out. Aside from the hose, the whole set-up is carved entirely out of stone. She wouldn't be surprised to learn that even the hose is somehow made from a tree or a plant too. Whoever built this shower (indeed, this entire tree house) had been incredibly resourceful, clever, and talented. It's brilliant and rustic and charming, and oh, so *very* tempting. Her fingers are actually reaching for the hose when a loud and very angry shout startles her.

"Ecko! Get your oversized butt out of there and carry me outside! I've had to poop since LastPitch!"

She throws her hand over her mouth to stifle her giggle. But seriously…poor Boodark. He's been forced to hold it as long as she had. At least she'd been unconscious. He's had to suffer through it. For hours.

She rushes out of the privy, scoops him up, and runs out the door with him held out at arm's length in front of her… just in case he can no longer hold it and his bladder and/or bowels decide to let go. Tanda's laughter rings out and merrily follows along behind them.

Once their most pressing demands are taken care of, they return to find Tanda working on helping them with their next-inline needs … filling their empty, grumbling bellies. She's busily stirring a large pot of stew that's bubbling over the fire, the rich, herby spices wafting throughout the room.

"Come, carry this to the table for me, child. It's much too heavy for me," Tanda calls out. "Mind you, it's hot!" she adds as she hands her some cloth rags to use as potholders.

She does as she's told, carrying it to the table while the older woman shuffles about the kitchen.

"Go on, dish it out. Fill the three bowls for us, but only one ladle-full into each of the three saucers for the Kreeleerians. They won't eat any more than a spoonful. I'll be right there."

Tanda begins to hum softly to herself as she turns a loaf of bread out onto the countertop. The heavenly, mouth-watering aroma of freshly baked bread fills the air as Ecko ladles the thick stew into the bowls and saucers. She can't help but watch every move that their hostess makes as she cuts chunks of bread from the steaming loaf and thick wedges of cheese from a large wheel. Boodark groans from the torture of having to wait while so many wonderful smells tease his twitching little bat nose.

"Can't she move any faster?" he whispers in desperation. She doesn't answer him, but she wholeheartedly agrees as they both watch the bread, cheese, and even rich, creamy globs of butter all get stacked onto a tray.

"*Go!* Help her, big dummy. You move faster! Carry it for her," Boodark urges. She frowns her disapproval at him but does it anyway. "Here, let me help you!" she insists as she rushes over to carry the tray. He's right, she *does* move faster, but it's also the polite thing to do. After all, Tanda has been very kind and accommodating to them both. Not only had she removed the Sliver for her, but she's also sheltered and fed them.

"Thank you, child. I know some are impatient and don't want to wait on an old woman," Tanda retorts with a mischievous glance in Boodark's direction.

Ecko giggles as he guiltily hunkers lower in his chair, his ears flattening against his skull. "Busted," she whispers to him as she sets the tray down. He doesn't care that she's teasing him though; he never even lifts his eyes from the feast that she lays in front of him. She hastily grabs his bowl and pushes it back out of his reach when he immediately tries to bury his face in it.

"It's too hot to eat! Don't you see the steam? And you call *me* the big dummy!"

Tanda chuckles and then calls her pets to come eat before she seats herself. "Sit down, child. Eat. You must be famished by now. *That one* acts like I allowed him to go hungry while you were recovering from your ordeal, but I'll have you know that he ate quite well. I feared his belly would never get full!"

She smiles and nods her agreement. "Yeah, there's not much that will curb his appetite."

Tanda calls for the Kreeleerians again, a bit louder this time before she continues. "I cannot fault his loyalty though. When you fell, he dove out of the chair and ran to your side and wouldn't budge. He curled up beside you and never once moved, snarling and snapping at anyone that drew near you. He refused to leave even long enough to relieve himself."

Boodark scrunches his face into a fierce scowl and snarks at them, "Yeah, I'm a regular good-er do-er. If you two are going to talk about me like I'm not here, at least push my bowl closer first so that I may eat. Some of us are starving, no matter what old ground stompers have to say about it."

Ecko's mouth drops open in shock. "Boodark!" she whisper/shouts in horror.

"What? She doesn't know me! She doesn't know my life. She doesn't *understand* how much food it takes to support this belly!" He is *very* indignant about it as he reaches for his bread.

"It doesn't matter!" she snaps. "That was very rude! Apologize!"

He tears off a chunk of bread, stretches as far as he can reach, and double dunks it in the stew. Then he quickly stuffs it into his mouth. "Huh uh. Can't do it. Ah got ma mouf full," he mumbles around the bulge in his cheeks.

She knows there's no use. He won't budge, so she apologizes for him. But Tanda's quietly laughing at them, her shoulders shaking with mirth. She nonchalantly waves the apology away and repeats, "Eat, child. Worry yourself not. I am not offended. Ruder things than him abound."

Then she raises her voice to a shout. "Loryss, Danika, and Caheera! If you do not wish to eat your supper, I suppose I'll let our hungry little guest have your portion!"

Apparently, they *do* want to eat because the three incredible cat creatures descend the spiral staircase together, but each in their own unique way. The winged one obviously makes use of its feathers and glides down. The mer-cat slithers down the spiral ladder, sliding down the fungi steps like some sort of ancient sea serpent. Only ole Beelzebub the Hellcat descends in the normal fashion: gracefully, one dainty paw after another. He really would be quite beautiful (even in his darkness) if he would just stay silent like a good little kitty.

"Ugh, I see that she still hasn't mastered cleanliness. I can't believe that you expect us to eat in these terrible conditions."

Boodark, bless his heart, comes to her defense like a tiny, avenging hero. A clumsy, most unattractive one, but a hero, nonetheless. "Pay him no mind, Ecko. And don't you dare apologize again," he tells her. "Why *should* you be sorry for not being able to lick your own arse like he does?"

It takes every ounce of willpower she possesses to keep her giggles inside. "Thank you, Boodark" she praises. Then she turns to Beelzebub, lifts her chin up, and calmly throws her own wordpunch. "And I see that *you're* still the rudest thing I've ever had the misfortune of meeting!"

His two cat-mates titter with quiet laughter at his expense, but if they can speak, they decide to stay out of it. He hisses threateningly at them and then turns his burnt amber eyes back on her. "You should be grateful. You should be thanking me. I *did* save your life, after all. You *owe* me."

She can't deny that. He *had* been the one to point out the fact that she had a Sliver attached to her. "Thank you," she tells him, simple as that. She *is* grateful, but that doesn't mean she'll let him be rude to her to his heart's content. Boodark, however, isn't having any of it.

"Ecko owes Talla-hatcha-pa-doochie, or whatever *her* name is," he corrects as he points at Tanda. "*She's* the one that got rid of the Sliver. *She's* the one that saved her life. All you did was point out something that the old woman already knew. We owe you nothing!"

Tanda smiles at him but all she says is,

"Talahatchapadoochie?"

He shrugs his embarrassment away and digs back into his food, ignoring the hisses that are aimed his way. Ecko deliberately ignores the hellcat too as she samples her food. "Miss Tanda, this is delicious! If your rude pet does not appreciate your hard work and your expert culinary skills, I will gladly eat his portion. This stew is too good; it would be a shame to allow it to go to waste. And *after* I am done eating and if it's not too much trouble, would you mind if I use your clever little shower? I promise I'll use the water sparingly. I don't want to use up your resources. I know fresh water is scarce on this world."

Beelzebub snorts into his food. "*Please* don't use it sparingly."

Tanda smacks the table sharply with the flat of her hand, startling everyone…except for Boodark who ignores them all and continues to dunk and slurp, dunk and slurp.

"Loryss, you will stop insulting our guest *this instant!*"

He lifts his head up long enough to send a hiss in 'the guest's' direction. The old*ish* woman lets out a long-suffering sigh and then she apologizes for her own rude companion, much like Ecko had been forced to do just moments ago with *her* rude sidekick.

"Of course, you may use the shower, and don't you worry about using up the water. The SeeAll Tree provides plenty, and I also have a recycler system in place. When you have finished, we two shall finally be able to sit comfortably and get to know one another better."

Ecko smiles and nods at the kindly woman. "I can hardly wait to get out of these clothes and get clean." She turns to Loryss and adds, "Contrary to what you believe, I am normally a very hygienic person. I do not *enjoy* being dirty. Perhaps once I have bathed, we two can start over. Perhaps you will like me better when I'm clean."

Done with his meal, he blithely licks his paws and cleans his face. "I will not," he states as he gracefully rises to his feet and narrows his eyes at her. "But at least you will smell better."

She nods her head in casual, silent acknowledgement of his equally silent declaration of 'there shall be no peace between us'. If war is what the nasty little furball wants, war is what he'll get. She's been through entirely too much to let herself be bullied and insulted by a house pet.

She feels rejuvenated and better than she had in a long time, now that the Sliver is gone. She's more than ready to give as good as she gets for the short amount of time that she'll be here. "Game on, pussycat," she murmurs. "Game on."

Don't mind the Blood, Dear

The Lokskell

The Vika Vakooja skitters along behind its master, faster than it has ever skittered before. It dare not fall behind. Such a discretion would mean unimaginable pain for the entire Vika collective, should the master become displeased with it. It has never personally felt the pain of the mind crush. It has been many years since the last time the master had felt the need to punish them. Many, many years before its own hatching. But the memory of that agony is stored within their collective mental library for all new hatchlings to observe. To bear witness. To learn. To obey. There is not, nor will there ever be, a single Vika in existence, now or in the future, that will ever, *ever* risk another mind crush. The pain that the Shadows can deal them is the ultimate boogeyman of their entire buggy world, and they'll do anything to avoid it. It shudders with renewed fear and skitters ever faster, dodging the bloody footprints that the Master leaves in his wake.

The Lokskell continues to watch the scene unfold in the Vika's mind as he turns down the hall that will lead him to the women. Anticipation of the pleasure he'll soon receive, coupled with the excitement that he feels for this encounter between the blue creature and his daughter speeds his steps. His breath comes faster as his eagerness grows, and he almost enters the first chamber he comes to. The woman within is lovely, but he quickly decides to move on to the next door. What Shayla has to offer will be more specific to his current needs.

He dismisses the guards, unlocks the door, and barges inside. The petite beauty with soft, gentle curves and white-blonde hair cries out in fear, either from the abruptness of his entrance or shock at his fearsome appearance. Perhaps both.

She stares wide-eyed as he unbuttons his blood-drenched shirt and peels it off to expose his firm, chiseled shoulders and muscular chest. He should be extremely handsome, but she cannot find beauty in him, no matter what his appearance may dictate. He's a monster, and the crimson smears that glisten wetly on his torso only emphasize that fact. She watches as his hand reaches for the ties at his waist, shuddering at the thought of what's coming.

"Shayla, my beauty, I have urgent need of your talents… that exquisite mouth, in particular."

She bites her lip to suppress the whimpers she feels rising inside her as she scrambles off the bed. "A bath, Master! I'll draw you a nice, hot bath to soothe you. I'll bathe you. And when you're all clean once more, I'll do that thing that you so love."

She rushes to the claw-footed tub, but he snarls out a warning before she can begin drawing the bath. He steps up behind her, so close that she can feel the heat of him. So close that she can smell the blood-scent mixed with his own particular aroma, spicy, woody man-scent mixed with the sharp sting of sweat and adrenaline. So close, she can almost feel the pounding of his heart.

"No bath, Shayla." He wraps his arms around her and pulls her in close to his body, closer, closer, closer until every inch of her backside is pressed against him. He buries his nose into her hair and breathes in her sweet scent. "Now," he growls into her ear.

"Right. Now."

"But," she whimpers. "The blood!" She looks down at herself and cries out in dismay at the bloodied arms wrapped around her, staining her pink, satin gown an ugly crimson red. She doesn't struggle to escape his embrace, no matter how much she wishes to. Much like the Vika Vakooja that's chittering loudly from its perch on her vanity table, she *knows* better.

The Lokskell becomes distracted with her for a moment as he focuses his attention on the dramatic events coming through the Vika's mind-link connection. He watches as Krispin springs out of hiding to snatch a Darkling out of the air. He sees the look of horror on his daughter's face as he crushes the fragile body in his grasp and casually drops it into the dirt.

He lets his hands wander over Shayla's beautiful body, his fingers toying with her hardened nipples through the sheer satin gown as he continues to watch what is happening on Oblerian. His breath quickens when Krispin launches himself at Ecko, his excitement rising as they fiercely battle it out. When Krispin pins her to the ground and rubs himself against her buttocks, he can't help but mimic the motions. He groans aloud and rubs his throbbing, rock-hard manhood against the woman in his arms as he watches Krispin sink his teeth into his daughter's shoulder. His attention zeroes in on the blood that immediately wells up and spills over, running in crimson rivulets down her arm.

The Lokskell snarls out his anger as Ecko's hideous little companion comes to her defense by pouncing on Krispin's back, just when things are heating up. His own body is now screaming, demanding release. So, while the two creatures are engaged in their little tussle, he uses the distraction to turn Shayla around to face him. His eyes immediately focus on her beautifully sculpted lips, and he sucks in a breath as her small, pink tongue nervously darts out to wet them.

"Don't mind the blood, dear. It looks ravishing on you." His hands move up her body, skimming up over her chin. His fingers gently trace her lips to indicate what it is that he wants from her, what he craves… what he *demands*. "I want to see your mouth reddened with it. I want to see it smeared on your lovely face. I want to watch it drip, crimson from your lips."

Her large, crystal-blue eyes fill with tears, but she dutifully nods and whispers, "Yes, Master." Her delicate hands immediately move to his waistband. Her fingers tug at the ties, and his skin quivers where they brush up against him. She lowers his pants, peeling away the wet fabric when it sticks to his skin… fabric drenched in the lifeblood of his prisoners. Lowers, lowers, lowers until his member, engorged and enormous, springs free, and *it's* covered in blood too, just like the rest of him. Just like she knew it would be.

She shivers in revulsion, but she reaches for him anyway. She runs feather-light fingers over the tip of him before she takes him full into her hands. She toys with it, gripping it and caressing it, more in an attempt to scrub the blood from it than out of any desire to bring him pleasure.

He throws his head back and grits his teeth. His body is at full attention, but his mind is divided between the pleasure at her hands and the ongoing drama on Oblerian as the battle rages on. Krispin seems to have the upper hand at the moment. He's got the ugly little creature pinned to the ground, threatening to crush him beneath his feet. Ecko appears desperate to keep that from happening. There's panic in her eyes as she pleads for the life of the worthless, insignificant little varmint. Foolish girl. She's above begging, she just doesn't know it yet.

"Enough!" the Lokskell shouts as he grabs Shayla's hands and drags her up against him. She gasps as he roughly picks her up, his big hands gripping her thighs, his fingers splayed wide to balance the weight of her. She has no choice but to wrap her legs around his waist to steady herself. "Don't think I don't know what you're doing!" he snarls.

His tirade is interrupted as a snarl rips from Krispin's throat. He watches the blue creature's eyes fill with blind rage as he raises his foot, drawing it up for leverage. He's going to do it!

The Lokskell focuses his attention on his daughter. He wants to see her face when it happens. He wants to see what she'll *do*.

A low growl of desperate need rumbles in his throat as he carries Shayla to the vanity table. The Vika Vakooja chitters and scrambles away just in time to avoid being squashed under her butt when he brusquely lowers her onto it.

"Now, Shayla. No more distractions. Open those sweet lips and give me what I want. Or would you rather I bend you over and fill your ass instead?"

She immediately opens her mouth and sucks him deep into her warmth. She gags at the initial coppery taste of blood, but she doesn't stop. In another life, she had much enjoyed the act of giving oral pleasure, so that's where she sends her mind… back in time to that other life. She blocks out the unappealing taste of blood, and she soon forgets that she has no choice but to please her captor.

She works him just as she would have any other lover from her past. She strokes him with her tongue before she closes her lips around the throbbing head. She uses her hands to work the base of his shaft as she slowly draws him into her mouth, sucking him in deeper and deeper until her lips meet her fingers. She pretends that he is someone else, someone of *her* choosing, and she quickly brings him to the brink of climax. And then she holds him there, toying with him, denying him the release that he's so desperate for.

He allows the defiance only because he loves what she does to him. It's *so* good. None of the women do it better than his Shayla… certainly better than *her*, that Gods-be-damned woman that continuously invades his mind. It's almost magical, the things this woman can do with her mouth. He groans aloud and buries his hands in her hair as the tension builds and builds and builds, within his body as well as the events being played out Oblerian.

Krispin's foot begins its descent, in slow motion, it seems to him. A mere fraction of a second before the killing blow lands, a brilliant white light bursts out of his daughter, and it blasts Krispin right off his feet. It is absolutely glorious.

Indeed, the magnificence of it seems to be just the stimulant he himself needed in order to bypass Shayla's games. He holds her head steady as he thrusts himself into her, plunging, over and over into the deepest recesses of her mouth until he feels himself sliding in and out of her throat.

She issues a strangled, gurgling cry, struggling to draw breath between each frantic thrust of his hips. The fingernails that she digs into his buttocks sends him hurtling over the edge and straight into one of the most intense, mind-shattering climaxes of his entire existence. It goes on and on, waves of ecstasy cresting and ebbing like the tides crashing against the shore. It is perhaps the closest he will ever get to the Heavens.

When it's over, at last, when he comes back to himself and awareness has returned to his mind, he immediately searches the mind of the Vika that's cowering on the edge of the vanity table. Unfortunately, it has nothing to offer him. The images have gone dark as Pitch. The mind-link has been terminated. The Lokskell knows exactly what that means. Vika death. The blast that Ecko emitted had killed the spy bug.

Oh, but how magnificent, how glorious she had been in those last milliseconds before her magic manifested itself! So much power! So much potential!

He glances down at the woman gasping for breath before him. Her body is now painted with nearly as much blood as his. Bloodied handprints decorate her lovely, pale skin. Her white hair is streaked with it. It is, indeed, smeared across her face. Her lips are painted crimson, and they glisten with her saliva and his seed. She's beautiful. And she belongs to him.

"Again," he growls as he lifts her from the table and carries her to the bed. As she leans over him and draws him into her lovely mouth once more, he realizes that he and Krispin have one thing in common, besides their mutual love of woman-flesh. He, too, loves the filth.

She did WHAT in her Cup?

Ecko

Ecko leans back in her chair with a contented sigh and rubs her full belly. Everyone's finally finished eating and she can't help but feel a twinge of guilt about how much she and Boodark the Bottomless Pit had consumed. She'd tried to show restraint, truly she had. But it was beyond her power to manage it. Everything was so scrumptiously tempting, and she'd been malnourished to the point of emaciation.

Boodark hadn't even attempted to hold back, and now the little piggy is in a food coma. He'd eaten so much that he could barely move. He just fell over, curled himself up on top of the backpack/booster seat, and passed right out. His ferocious snores are loud enough to send the two female cats back up the stairs after their fellow Kreeleerian (Brother? Mate?) She still doesn't know which one is Caheera and which one is Danika, but she's not overly concerned about that. She'll figure it out eventually.

When she can bask in the glow of contentment no longer, lest she fall asleep and begin snoring alongside her piggy friend, she gets up and makes herself useful by clearing the table, stacking the dirty dishes and carrying the trays and the considerably lighter soup pot back to the kitchen area. She offers to clean the dishes too, but Tanda shoos her away. "You're a guest. Go, take the shower that you're so desperate for…You keep staring at the bathing room as if your long-lost friend is locked behind that door! Make yourself comfortable so that we can finally have our chat. There are things we need to discuss, important things."

Yes, she knows that already, and she's suddenly anxious to receive whatever answers her hostess can provide. She nods and turns away to do as she's told. She graciously lets Boodark bathe first, but it takes every bit of her willpower to do it. She sets the wash bowl onto the shower floor, adds some of the sweet pea body wash that she'd given to him, and then fills the bowl with warm water so that he can have a bubble bath. Then she carefully peels the bandages off his back. "I don't know…It's hard to tell under the snake poop, but I think it looks better. I'll come back in and wash the wound after you get in the bath and all your naked bits are hidden under the bubbles."

She steps out and waits for him to get undressed and settled into the bowl/tub. Once he's fully submerged himself below the bubbles, she goes back in and gently scrubs the funky black goop from his skin. It is *so* much better that she almost starts to cry. It's still difficult for her to look at, but it's much better than its previously ravaged and infected state.

When the wound is as clean as she can possibly get it, she leaves him to enjoy his bath. Pinched between her thumb and pointer finger is his dirty pants that she's intent on scrubbing when she washes her own clothes. Tanda, bless her, magically produces a tiny outfit from somewhere that he can wear until his own are cleaned and dried, a shirt with holes cut out of the back for wings and a pair of pants just his size. He no longer has wings, but he still has the little nubs of wing tendons that stick out, so the shirt with wing holes will be perfect for him.

Although curious, she doesn't question why the old*ish* woman has clothes that small just lying about. It really isn't any of her business. So, she merely thanks her and sets them inside the privy where Boodark can get to them when he gets out of his bath…*if* he ever gets out. He's taking his sweet time, not that she can blame him. Being filthy really is the worst feeling, and the two of them have been feeling really bad for a really long time. So, she waits. And she waits. And waits.

She opens her mouth, preparing to threaten him with bodily harm, but he comes out of the privy half a second before she lets loose on him. She can't help but smile as he walks out strutting his stuff, thinking he's all that now that he's clean and sweet smelling. And with a new outfit to boot!

She makes certain to compliment him extensively, for he is a vain, but at the same time, very self-conscious creature… but she does it as quickly as she can. She patiently waited for her turn as long as she could stand it, but she can stand it no longer. She shoos Boodark away and closes herself in the bathroom. She dumps his dirty bath water out, then cleans and replaces the wash bowl. A whimper of relief escapes her lips as she peels her filthy, stiff clothes off and steps into the shower. Although she does as promised and uses up as little water as possible, the shower in Tanda's tree house is one of the most blissful experiences of her entire life.

The water, although not quite hot, is actually very warm. She assumes this is because the storage tank is right up against the fireplace, with only a thin wall between. She scrubs herself so intensely that when she finally emerges from the privy, her skin is pink and squeaky clean. Her hair though, is a mass of long, tangled tresses that she's not looking forward to tackling. But at least it's *clean* hair, not the greasy locks of yuck that she'd previously been stuck with. To put off the torture of detangling it just a bit longer, she wraps the whole wet mess up into one of the silky towels that Tanda had provided, bundling it all atop her head. She'll brush Boodark's hair out first, it'll be less painful… for her anyway.

She finds him stretched out on the rug before the fireplace, just staring into the flames. "Where is everyone?" she asks as she carries her bag over and drops down beside him.

"The old woman said something about needing ingredients to make some kind of tea and then she climbed up the stairs. The nasty hissers haven't come back down. As far as I'm concerned, they can just stay up there until we leave. When do you think that will that be? I'm ready whenever you are. Those things seriously shiver me. They don't *scare* me, Ecko" he sneers that last bit at her as if she'd called him a scaredy-cat. "They just shiver me."

After taking her first aid kit out of her bag, she smears a blob of triple antibiotic ointment onto the nasty bite mark on her shoulder and sticks a clean bandage over it. Boodark's eyes light up as she takes her brush out and gestures for him to crawl into her lap. He eagerly rushes over and once he's settled, she gently begins the chore of detangling his scraggly brown and green hair. It's grown even longer now than when they'd first met.

"I'm not sure how long we'll be here. I want to hear what she has to say; I want to know her story. And I have so many questions! I'm sure she has answers to at least *some* of them. I can learn from her the things that my mother never had the opportunity to teach me. I want to stay a while and hear about my world, my people. But I can't do that. I *know* I can't. I need to move on… soon. I'm on borrowed time here. I feel it inside me… Whatever it is that's been calling to me is calling more urgently than ever. The pulse beats harder and louder every day, urging me to hurry. I must get to it, and I must do it *fast*. Something's coming." Her fingers move of their own accord, first gently brushing and then weaving her little friend's hair into plaits as she watches the flames. "And whatever it is, I'm running out of time."

Tanda, who had somehow returned without their knowledge, slams a bowl onto the island's countertop, causing them both to jerk and cry out in fear. "You are quite right, child. The EverGlass calls and you *must* answer."

She turns to meet the oldish woman's eyes and softly murmurs, "Tell me, Miss Tanda. Tell me everything."

She nods but turns away and begins to putter around the kitchen while Boodark huffs loudly in agitation. "How can someone so old move so silently?" he grumbles as he pats his hair to feel the braids.

"Let me see!" he demands. He wants his picture taken. She takes one from the front so he can see how spiffy he looks in his borrowed clothing and then one from behind for a view of his hair. He cringes when he sees his own face, but a true smile of pleasure lights up his eyes as he admires how nice his hair looks.

Tanda makes her way over and hangs a teapot high above the flames, then reaches for a rope that's tied to the left side of the mantle. She tugs on it, and they all raise their eyes up to watch as whatever's attached to the other end gets lowered down from the ceiling. It's a bench swing, and she lowers it until it's in proper seating position. There's another one stored up there as well, tied to the other side of the fireplace, and they watch as Tanda lowers that one too.

"I enjoy sitting in front of the fire, but I found that having any sort of seating in front of a fireplace that I must use so often for my chores is impractical. Chairs get in the way and are not very comfortable anyway, so this is what I eventually came up. I built swings on a pulley system so they can be stored up there out of my way when I'm not using them." She sits down with a sigh that Ecko has heard a thousand times from Charlie. It's the sound of relief that the elderly make when they can rest their old, weary bones.

"It's brilliant," she praises with true admiration in her voice as she gets up off the rug to sit on the opposite-side bench. Boodark elects to stay on the floor. He plops down and scrolls through the photos on her camera while the two women gently rock their swings back and forth.

Tanda silently watches the fire, and she does not disturb her. She feels as though the old*ish* woman is gathering her thoughts, trying to figure out what to say and where to start. She confirms it a moment later when she asks *her* to go first. "I know you have a lot of questions, child, and I will answer all that I can. I ask that you hold onto those questions just a bit longer. You were correct when you said there is urgency and that you must leave soon.

Therefore, we must make the most of these hours that we do have. You will remain here until the next Pale arrives and then you must be on your way. We'll get a couple more meals into you, and you'll be able to have one more Pitch-sleep within the safety of the SeeAll Tree. That doesn't leave us much time, especially when I have so many things to tell you. I beg you, tell me your story first, and then I will tell you mine."

Boodark rolls onto his belly and props his chin in his hands. "Tell her about foodoraters!" he prompts with an anticipatory gleam in his eyes. She smiles and gently tells him that now is not the time to talk about Earth's food related inventions, and she reminds him that there are more important things to be discussed.

So once again she starts from the beginning, telling how she'd grown up in a world with little to no magic, amongst people that she'd been fundamentally different from. "I grew up knowing that my mother and sister were not my own blood relatives; my father had an affair that had resulted in me. From all accounts, he'd just shown up at the door one day with me in his arms, begging my stepmother for forgiveness, but also refusing to explain or defend himself. It broke her heart, but she was a good, kind woman and she eventually forgave him. And she accepted me. I know that looking at me every day had to have hurt her, but she was a good parent to me and cared for me as well as she could."

She gets up and retrieves her backpack as she goes on to tell of her childhood, of how she'd been able to see other worlds through mirrors and that she'd found another girl that looked just like her… Samara, her mirror image. She tells her of all the little terrors that her new 'friend' had inflicted and all the monumental ones. Tanda and Boodark cry with her as she explains how Samara used her Shadow magic to make the dolls come alive and kill her family. *She* cries even harder as Charlie comes into the tale, telling of how he'd rescued her from her burning home and then on to how she'd been sent to the mental hospital because of all the psychological damage she'd sustained. That was the doctor's reasoning for her recount of everything that had happened. Psychological damage. Tanda hangs on to every word as she learns of the years in the mental ward, the doctors acting like she was crazy and defective, and all the drugs and small hells she'd had to live through.

"If I'd been in my right mind, I wouldn't have said anything about dolls and teddy bears coming to life or girls that look like me living on the opposite side of the glass. I wouldn't have told them about the OtherWorlds in the mirrors. I was used to concealing all of my little oddities; hiding was nothing new to me. But I was scared and lost, and I *was* psychologically damaged. Who wouldn't be? But I wasn't so damaged that my mind had created some weird fantasy world as a way of escaping the truth. I knew exactly what had happened. In the end, I'd had to lie… and I *hate* lying. It goes against something deep inside of me, something in my fundamental makeup. But I'd done it anyway. I lied and changed my story to one that the people around me were more comfortable with, one that made more sense to them. I lied and I made myself fill the mold they wanted me to fit into."

She goes on to explain how dear, sweet Charlie had been there for her every step of the way. How he'd even helped her get released from the hospital and then given her a place to live… with him and his new bride, Susan. And then she'd found her father's surprise note in the time capsule and how it had contained the first clue on where she would learn the truth. She tells Tanda of how she'd eventually found all the clues and followed them to Maggie's house where the *truth* was waiting for her.

A sad smile tugs at her lips as she removes items from her bag until she gets to what she's searching for… her mother's box and the rose key necklace. "I learned that my father had lied about everything. I wasn't his child; I'd never been his. He loved me though, so much. And although it almost broke me to learn the things I learned and was forced to accept; in the end he'd done it all for his love of me. He didn't even have any idea who I was! All he knew was that some stranger, some magical being had basically handed him a baby and ordered him to keep it safe. And to never, ever tell the truth about where I'd come from. And he never did… not until after my entire family was dead and I'd spent several years in Hell. He hadn't known any real information anyway. He hadn't been told much. He left me a letter… well he left me several letters and clues to follow so that I could find the things my mother had left for me, things he'd been instructed to hide away until I was old enough to understand."

She unwraps the protective bubble wrap from her mother's box and Tanda gasps as she gets her first look at it. She watches the woman's face closely as she removes the rose key necklace from its protective velvet bag. "You feel it too. Don't you? That thrumming pulse," she asks in a hushed, revering voice.

The old*ish* woman's eyes flood with renewed tears as she nods and whispers, "Irredarrian magicks!" Then she gleefully claps her hands like a small child when Ecko pays the price of a single drop of blood to coax the rosebud key to unfurl its petals into a fully bloomed flower. She explains that only then can it be used to open the treasure box, and that it only responds to *her* blood.

"Well, go on! Open it, child!" Tanda is beyond excited.

Ecko gets up, scoops Boodark up, and then moves to Tanda's bench so that they can all watch as she opens the box. Subconsciously aware of the fact that the Kreeleerians all jump up onto the back of the swing to watch also, she inserts the rose key until the lock clicks open. Her breath sucks in along with everyone else's as the box opens, letting the magic spill out along with its secrets.

They eagerly watch as the holographic image of her mother delivers her message about who she really is, and where she'd come from. And also, about how the girl in the mirror is her twin sister, Samara. When the message is played out and the image of her mother disappears once more, she passes one of her father's letters to Tanda. In the letter, he tells of the dream that her mother, Laelynn had sent to him so that he would better understand the importance of hiding and safeguarding her daughter. The old woman sobs as she reads the horrors that her fellow Irredarrian, her Wandelaar had endured at the hands of the Lokskell.

"I hid myself away until my magic matured, just as my mother told me to do. But we didn't know when that would be. We had no idea when my *true* eighteenth birthday was because my father had never been told that information. He'd *picked* a date and called it my birthday. But I did as my mother instructed and we secluded ourselves out in the deep wilderness, away from other people. I didn't know what to expect, and I certainly didn't want to hurt anyone. But hiding out and waiting for something, waiting for *anything* to happen didn't work out quite as well as I had hoped it would. I was impatient and bored of being caged and held down yet again, so I'd gone into town with Charlie to buy supplies for a hiking trip I was planning on taking. Of course, *that's* when my magic hit me, and when it did, I found I couldn't control it, just as my mother had predicted. Thankfully no one was hurt, no one but me, that is. It was *terrible,* and I wound up in a hospital where the doctors were *very* confused about the things they discovered about me from all the tests they ran. They were asking too many questions, taking too much interest in my oddities. I knew I had to escape, but before I could… well, long story short, I accidently opened a mirror, and my twin was right there waiting. She pulled me through and took my place on Earth. Before I even knew what was happening, she used her own magic to shatter the one and only mirror on this cursed, vampire world… or so Samara said. I believe there's another one, a special, magical mirror… an Irredarrian mirror. I've been fighting my way towards it ever since I first felt it's call. Of course, I have no way of knowing if it's *really* a mirror that I've been chasing, but I feel in my heart that it is so. Whatever it is though, it puts out that same thrumming heartbeat that my mother's box and the rose key does."

She meets Tanda's eyes and quietly adds, "*You* have that same humming sound about you, although it is much more muted than these objects."

Tanda smiles and assures her that she, too, has it. "Irredarr magick… all Irredarrians can feel it. The louder the hum is, the more magical the object is. You, my dear, hum so loudly that I'm forced to put up shields in my mind just to block the intensity of you out. And your instincts are 100% correct. What you've been following is the call of the EverGlass, and it *is* an Irredarrian mirror... *your* mirror and your birthright. It felt you the moment you entered this world, and it's been crying out for you ever since, begging for you to come and take what's rightfully yours. She's been waiting for you for so long, I fear that she's growing impatient, as her cry grows more insistent with each passing Pale. It's how I learned that our new Mirror Walker, our beloved Wandelaar, had finally arrived."

Ecko closes her mother's box and runs her hands over the crystals and other precious stones. "Tell me, Tanda. Tell me everything. I need to hear about my mother. I need to know exactly what happened to her after she sent me away."

But the old*ish* woman sighs and sadly shakes her head. "I cannot, child. We haven't time enough for the telling. I don't know exactly what happened in any case. I never met Laelynn, and too many pieces of *that* puzzle are missing. I *will*, however, tell you a bit about myself, and of course, I'll explain the EverGlass... but then we need to get to the lessons. There are things you must know how to do before you leave here. I've been watching you and I've noticed that your magic is, well, let's just say it doesn't usually go the way that you intend. Am I correct?"

Ecko and Boodark both burst out in laughter at that delicately put admission. "It *never* goes as planned!" she admits when her she regains her composure. She gently smacks Boodark when his fit of laughter continues far longer than necessary. "In all honesty, it never happens when or how *I* want it to. My magic only seems to come out when I'm emotionally overwhelmed, and it *always* has a mind of its own."

Tanda nods thoughtfully as she gets up to take the teapot from the fire and carry it back to the little kitchen island. "I'll be back in two shakes of a Na-Loof tail!" she cheerfully calls out as she walks over to the door, opens it, and steps outside. Curious, Ecko and Boodark watch as she reaches up and picks an eyeball off the tree and carries it back inside where she drops it into a wooden bowl. She drizzles something that resembles honey over the freakily staring optic orb and then proceeds to pulverize it, crushing and grinding it up with a stone pestle. The two horrified guests can't tear their eyes away as she spoons the disgusting, jellied paste into one of the cups.

"She did *what* in her cup?" Ecko whispers in her best hillbilly, Tow Mater voice, then adds, "Is she really going to drink that?"

Boodark's quick to vehemently shake his head. "Nuh-uh. No ma'am. *I'm* not drinking it, Ecko. And you shouldn't either!" he whisper/hisses back, his eyes almost as big around as the eyeball victim that just got used to flavor the crazy old woman's tea.

Tanda pours the tea into all three cups and carries them back to her waiting guests. "Oh, relax, you two. I only added it to mine. You *know* that; you watched me the entire time. There are things that I must see, and the SeeAll fruit allows me to do that. There are always so many things that I have to watch, things that I must *keep an eye on,* if you will!" She cackles madly at her own pun as she tries to hand out the cups that neither one of them reach out to accept.

"I promise, yours is just regular tea. I *only* added the special ingredient to mine," she reassures them as they reluctantly take their cups. Ecko chooses to ignore the mumbled, 'For now,' that the old woman mutters under her breath. She'll just have to keep an eye (ha, ha, gulp) on all food and drink preparations while they're here. She takes a hesitant sip of her tea and nods to Boodark to let him know that it tastes fine to her. As far as she can tell, it's eyeball free, as promised.

Tanda sits back down and takes up the conversation right where they left off, as if the last several minutes hadn't even occurred. As though she's *not* sitting there drinking eyeball juice from a cup. "I imagine the Lokskell's Sliver had much to do with your magic acting erratically," she theorizes as she sips. "It was leeching you, draining your magic and leaving you weakened... physically and magically. Magic regenerates itself, so although it would never have been able to steal it all, it took enough to make what remained behave erratically."

Ecko focuses on drinking her own tea and she keeps her mouth shut. Sure, the Sliver may have hindered and held her back a bit. Certainly, it stunted her magical growth, but not *all* of the blame could be placed on the nasty little soul-leech. She'd already been magically handicapped by a mental monster named Rage, *before* the Sliver ever got to her. But she's keeping her mental monsters to herself. At least for the time being.

Tanda steadily sips her tea as she contemplates what the most important things to discuss are. "So little time," she murmurs. "Well, let's make the most of it, shall we? I suppose I should start with the EverGlass, seeing as how it's the most important thing within your reach at the current moment. The EverGlass is a mirror pendant, much like your mother's rose key. It once lay at the center of a necklace strung with tiny seed pearls. But it's not *just* a charm on a necklace; it's so much more than that! It may look like a trinket, but it also has its own life force. And Khalidah, which means eternal, is her name. I know not where it originally came from; that is a Wandelaar secret. All I know is that the EverGlass gets passed down from retiring Mirror Walkers to their successors, and that it has been so for thousands of years."

"The last one to wear the EverGlass was Lamora Deidra, whom your mother mentioned in her message. She was my best friend, my closest confidant and companion. I loved her like no other and she loved me in return, even though we both knew that nothing could ever come of our love. She was Irredarr's Mirror Walker, and therefore had many responsibilities and duties to fulfill. So, I contented myself with merely being by her side, lending aid where I could and just being a friend whenever her Wandelaar duties overwhelmed her."

"I loved traveling with her, discovering new worlds and meeting all the peoples in their many great diversities. But *this* was to be our home away from home. We set up a little house here and it became our getaway, a lover's secret paradise. I see the disbelief in your eyes, but this world was much different back then. Oblerian was beautiful, once upon a time, and we were happiest when we were here, together. We could never stay long, but it was here for us on those rare occasions that Deidra managed to break away from her duties. And I, too, had duties to perform. I was a record keeper's apprentice, and it was my job to study and record all new discoveries. All my findings got sent back to Irredarr, the information chronicled and archived and then stored away in our history vaults."

"During the times that Deidra's responsibilities took her from my side, I came here to fulfill mine. I'd set out to learn all I could of this world, filling our little home with things I knew she would love as I went about my duties. In fact, the only reason I was with the group on that fatal expedition was because there were several things that I wished to trade with the tribes… with your father's people."

"Now, keep in mind that over the years I've gathered a lot more information than I had access to back then. I won't go into your father's history and background right now. That's a conversation for another day, as is your mother's and even Irredarr's history. All I will say is that your father's world was our most recent discovery. It was still new to us, and as such, was still very much unexplored. The tribes were friendly though and had acceded to our requests to join in and become part of the trade system that we'd worked so hard at setting up between the worlds."

"I met your father, who went by the name of Samael Kalaraja back then, and although it was just a brief greeting, I immediately noticed the way he watched Deidra's every move. I didn't like it, and I could tell that it made her uncomfortable too, so I kept a close eye on him while I was there. The things I learned about him only confirmed my suspicions that he was not what he pretended to be, and that he wanted things from Deidra, things that she would not give to him willingly. Oh, he desired her body, but it was her *power* that he wanted even more than carnal pleasures."

"I warned her, I did my best to get her to leave with me, but she refused. She'd become obsessed with finding a certain magical tree, the Mother Tree, it was called. We quarreled, and in her anger, she decided that she wanted to be alone, away from me and my nagging and my demands on her. Those were the exact words she'd said to me, when all I'd wanted was to get her away from *him*, from the evilness that I knew was infecting his mind. And in *my* anger, I did not refuse to leave."

Tanda's breath hitches in and out she tries to hold back her tears, and Ecko's heart breaks for her. She knows the sound and the feel of suppressed tears all too well… like sharp little pieces of gravel rolling around in one's throat.

"I should have stayed by her side," Tanda whispers. "I should have refused to leave. So many regrets… so many things I should have done differently. So many things I should have said." She lifts her head and meets Ecko's eyes, her own shining with regret and oh, so much pain. "But I didn't say them, and she didn't say them either. We both remained stubbornly silent as she escorted me to the mirror that would send me away from her. Every village, every town we traded with got its own mirror to make traveling easier, and this one was at the center of the village. I remember every detail of that walk to the mirror; I've relieved it at *least* a million times. I will *never* forget how she looked in those last moments by my side, her chin lifted at a stubborn angle even though her eyes welled with tears."

"Standing before the mirror, I turned back to look at her one last time. Her eyes softened and she opened her mouth to say something, but I'll never know what she would have said because that's when Kalaraja made his move. He attacked her internally, *on the inside,* pitting his magic against hers even as he threw her to the ground and physically struck her. I tried to help her, as did several others. Every time I drew near, Deidra would use her magic to push me back, a metaphysical hand in the center of my chest shoving me away to keep me safe. I realized that I wasn't doing anything to help her. I was in fact, hindering her with distractions, forcing her to divide her attention and to use her magic on me as well as her attacker. So, I stopped. I stood there helplessly, dying a thousand tiny deaths as I watched her fight for her very life."

"They battled for a long, long time, each second as painful to me as it was to her. Our people as well as Kalaraja's tried to get him off of her. Eight of them were killed and several more were wounded. The two combatants, both bloodied and filthy, rolled across the ground with no signs of either one letting up... until Kalaraja ripped the EverGlass necklace off of her, scattering the seed pearls in every direction."

"The EverGlass fell to the ground and immediately opened up to the abyss, the static void that exists in between the worlds. Deidra explained it to me once. Terrible, terrible place, the abyss." She falls silent as she stares into the fire for a moment before she shudders and turns back to continue where she'd left off. "When the necklace broke, those tiny white pearls scattered, but they *grew* as they did so. They grew as large as nectar melons. A few of them had bounced and rolled far enough away to avoid it but thankfully, most of them got sucked out into the abyss before the EverGlass closed once more."

"But one, oh, one of those enlarged pearls that remained behind cracked open, and I watched as two incorporeal beings, two *Wyrms* spilled out. The pearl had been an egg, you see, a Wyrm egg, and after the hatching, the empty pearl/egg fused itself back together and turned black as Pitch. It got kicked aside during the struggle and I never saw it again after that, but the Wyrms were where the danger lay anyway."

"The two floated up into the air like ethereal spirits, twining together and writhing against one another as they made their way towards Kalaraja. They poured themselves into him, right in through his mouth. It distracted him long enough for Deidra to break his hold on her. She snatched the EverGlass up out of the dirt and then ran to me, her eyes full of panic and pain and desperation as she pressed it into my hands. She begged me to go, begged me to keep it safe. She said that it was more important than I could ever fathom and that if I loved her, if I *truly* loved her, I would do this one thing that she asked of me. If I loved her, I would honor her last request no matter how much pain it caused me to do so. Then she pressed her lips to mine for the very last time. I tasted her blood and her tears and her anguish as she opened the mirror at my back. And then she pushed me through, and I fell to the floor of the little house we'd shared here on this world. I sat there in shock for several seconds, until I realized that the EverGlass was vibrating inside my hand. I glanced down at it and saw that the glass was reflecting everything that was happening back there on that other world. It was *watching*, waiting to see what would happen, and it was allowing me to watch too."

"While Deidra had been busy sending me away with the EverGlass, the Wyrms had gained Kalaraja's permission to become their host. In exchange, they would grant him unimaginable power. Once the agreement was struck, the Wyrms settled themselves into a Wrymknot over his own soul, binding the three life forces together as one. Deidra knew that she had only seconds in which to stop him, mere seconds before the power of the Wyrms combined with his own magic. For when that happened, he would be such a powerful force that she would *never* be able to beat him. She did the only thing she could under the circumstances. She conjured a storm, much like the one that you created in the Sorrow Marshes. She commanded the winds to lift them up and carry them to the nearest place of strong magic, the closest EverRealm… Sheol castle."

"As the storm subsided and dropped them within the castle walls, Deidra quickly whispered a symbol into her hands. It was unlike any rune I've ever seen and when it was completed, it lit her hands up with a strange, mirror fire. It was somehow reflective and liquid, dripping molten puddles of melted mirrors onto the stone floors. She wrapped one burning hand around Kalaraja's wrist and then slammed the other hand onto one of the castle walls. I watched as she threw her head back and screamed her spell of binding into the air."

"She cursed him, bound him to remain there forever, never to set foot beyond the castle walls again. And it took all her magic to do so. When she pulled her hands away, her silver, mirror handprints were left behind, one on the wall and the other embedded into Kalaraja's flesh. She tried to run then, although I could tell by the look on her face that she knew she wouldn't make it. She opened the closest mirror and ran towards it with everything she had left in her to give."

"But she was just too spent, wounded too badly, and drained from the amount of magic she had to use. Despite all that, she'd almost made it to the awaiting mirror when Kalaraja's brand new Shadow magic burst out of him, along with his screams of rage. The Shadows shot out after her, wrapping themselves around her just as she was stepping into the mirror. Deidra's and Kalaraja's combined magics were too much for the mirror, their magics too conflicting in nature. Kalaraja's Shadows fouled her magic, polluting the mirror and placing further strain upon it. It could not withstand such incredible opposing forces, and it became unbalanced for several moments, opening and closing in quick succession on all the worlds and the spaces in between them."

"Deidra was held immobile, forced to watch as his Shadows got sucked through the mirror, tossed out and spread to all the worlds that the mirror spit them out on. Then the mirror shattered; it exploded and threw them both backwards. A large, befouled shard lodged right into my Deidra's heart. I'll never get the sound of her screams out of my head as she realized that he'd made her beloved mirrors turn against her. I could only watch in horror, crying out my disbelief, my soul-rending despair as my love, my Wandelaar slowly died. Her skin turned to mirror glass, cracked, and then shattered into tiny particles of shimmering dust. I felt that my heart had shattered right along with her. I wish that it had, because the turmoil that came after was just as traumatic as watching my beloved die right before my eyes."

Tanda daintily blows her nose and wipes the tears from her face. "I sat crying on our bedroom floor, clutching her EverGlass to my heart until I felt it begin to move. *She* came alive in my hand, and she bit me to get me to release her." Tanda rubs her thumb over the two silver dots on her left hand, a small, sad smile on her face as she continues. "I wasn't mad, but I *was* hurt by her actions. Deidra had entrusted the EverGlass to me, but *she* did not want me in return. She spoke to me as she sank her fangs into my hand, spoke the words right into my mind. She told me, *"I'm sorry, dear friend of Lamora Deidra. Know that my bite is not intended as a punishment. It is a gift. I share with you the magick of foresight, so that you may prepare for things yet to come. Forgive me for not being there to guide you with your new abilities, but I cannot remain here with you. I must hide myself away until the new Wandelaar comes... as you must also."* An image of the SeeAll Tree filled my mind as she continued. *"You must go there. Make your home in the SeeAll Tree. Hide yourself away. The tree will protect you and preserve you until the time comes. You will be needed... to teach her, to guide her. She will be lost and broken, but powerful beyond anything you have ever known. Prepare her well, for she is the only one that can put an end to the evil that has just been released onto the worlds. Fare thee well, friend of Lamora Deidra... friend of Khalidah."* And then she was gone, and I never saw her again. But I felt her awaken. I heard her call, and I knew that finally, *finally* you had arrived."

Boodark interrupts her then, touching on a subject that had also been bothering her. Ever since she'd first laid eyes on the woman, she just couldn't figure out how old she was. At times, she looks like a woman in her mid-forties, still young and spry. Other times she appears to be an old crone, ancient and worn down by the ravages of time.

She, of course, would have asked about it with a bit more tact and respect than Boodark does. "I want to know what the EverGlass meant when she said that this tree would preserve you. If your story is true, then by my calculations... you're over a thousand years old. I thought it was only the wee folk, the magic fae, that are long lived now. I didn't realize there were any ground stompers left that could exist for so long. I thought they lost that ability long ago."

Tanda shoots him a stern look but all she says is, "Patience, little one. I'm getting there! Let me tell it in my own way. I promise you will have your answers."

Boodark, thoroughly chastised, scrunches down and whispers a quick, "Yes ma'am." She smiles at him to soothe the sting of her scolding and then she continues with her tale.

"Hours after Khalidah abandoned me, I picked myself up off the floor and somehow managed to function enough to get through the rest of the Pale. Then I made it through the next Pale and the one after that, but things got really, really bad after we lost Deidra. All of Irredarr felt it when she died, and we fell into a deep mourning at her passing. We were a people without hope. We'd *never,* in our entire history, lost a Wandelaar in that way…taken from us by a brutal murderer and then left without a successor to take her place. Deidra hadn't yet bore a child to pass her magic to, so the line died when she did."

"My very first experience with the foresight ability that I'd been given was of home, and it came just days after we lost her. All of Irredarr was under a shroud of mourning. I had *never* seen my world so bleak, so colorless and lifeless. It was like a haunted place, with sad, desolate ghosts moving listlessly throughout the streets. And the mirrors, oh, the beautiful, ornate mirrors that we all cherished so much, why, they'd all frosted over so that not even the Mirror Gazers could see into them! Many of my fellow Irredarrians could not bear the heavy weight of despair, and they chose to go into the pod-sleep. It was a time of all-consuming pain, an age of sorrows that lasted a long, long time."

The mer-cat crawls into Tanda's lap, offering her the only comfort she can give in the warmth of her soft little body. Tanda smiles down at the Kreeleerian and strokes its strange scale/fur before she continues. "And if things were bad back at home, it couldn't even compare to the atrocities that were befalling our lost, wayfaring clans-people. I do not know much about Earthians, but from what I've seen, they're not linked as we are. They don't feel things on the same level that we feel them. We Irredarrians are spiritually connected, and we can *feel* when our kith and kin, our fellow Irredarrians are under great distress. We mourned the loss of Deidra as a collective, and as terrible as that was, things only worsened. As your mother said in her message, all of our itinerant explorers had become trapped upon whatever world they happened to be visiting when we lost Deidra. Not only did we have to endure the death of our Mirror Walker, but we had the added uncertainty of how we would survive without another to take her place. We had to endure the reality that we would be separated from our loved ones, those of our kith and kin that were trapped far from home…perhaps forever."

She takes a deep, shuddering breath as she continues her tale. "And then we had to feel the fear that those trapped souls felt as Kalaraja sent his minions out to hunt them down. During that time is when he took up the name of Lokskell, Lord of Shadows, and all learned to flee before his wrath. His lackeys and henchmen inevitably managed to capture some of our people, no matter how far or how fast they ran. We experienced every bit of their pain as he had them tortured and murdered, and all we could do was suffer in silence. We had no way of getting to them. We'd lost our only means of traveling to the OtherWorlds when we lost our Deidra. Unable to endure the collective pain, tired of running and living in fear, the surviving Irredarrians that were stranded on all those other worlds went into the pod sleep. I alone, have stayed awake all these long years. I've had to watch as the Lokskell ruined this world, and so many others like it."

Tanda stands up, gathers their empty teacups, and sets them on the kitchen counter. "We'll continue our talk upstairs. I have chores that need attending, and I promised you a tour." She glances at Boodark and says, "And I'll be sure to provide the answers that you seek. Come now. Follow me."

Ecko gets up to follow but the action unbalances her backpack. It falls over, spilling several items to the floor, and she bends down to clean it all up. In the process of scooping up and shoving things back into the bag, the Night Pearl falls out and rolls across the floor. All three of the cats immediately begin hissing and spitting and yowling before they jump up and scurry away, moving so fast they're nothing but a blur of color. Tanda's face is grave, but all she says is, "They don't like the Night Pearls."

She quickly shoves it back in the bag and cries, "I'm sorry. I didn't know! It's a Wyrm egg, isn't it?"

When Tanda only nods she hurries to add, "I didn't know what it was when Faoira gave it to me. Faoira is the Naiad from the…"

But Tanda interrupts and says that she knows who Faoira is, and that there's no need for her to explain because she'd watched the whole event in one of her visions. Ecko gulps, unsure of what to do or even how to feel about having a Wyrm egg in her possession. "I only realized what it was when you were describing how the pearl grew and then turned black after it had hatched. I didn't know I was carrying something bad around with me! It doesn't *feel* bad!"

The old woman lifts an eyebrow at her. "Why do you

assume that it is bad?"

Finished with repacking the spilled contents of her bag, she stands up and answers. "Well, a Wyrm came out of it and went into the Lokskell… I *refuse* to call him my father, so Lokskell it is. If the Wyrms wanted anything to do with *him*, then they had to have been bad."

Tanda nods at her logic, then turns and again orders her to follow. So, she scoops Boodark up and they all climb the stairs as Tanda gives her a brief Wyrm lesson. "I didn't know it back then, but the Wandelaars were the guardians of the pearls, just as they had always been the protectors of the EverGlass. It was their responsibility to ensure that the Wyrms didn't escape their pearl prisons. I know not where the eggs and the EverGlass came from, nor do I know when it all began, or even *why* it began. Those are Wandelaar secrets that I have never been privy to. All I *do* know is that there are three types of Wyrms: positives entities, negative ones, and the rare neutrals. They are incorporeal, bodiless beings and therefore need a host body if they wish to live materialistic lives. Or they could choose to remain as spirits, roaming free and bodiless for all time. I'm sure some do just that, but if they want a *physical* life, they must first find a host. And as with all life, there are rules for the ones that choose to gain flesh. They can't just hop into *anyone* and take them over. Not only do they have to find someone that's powerful enough to withstand the possession, but they must also first gain permission for the merging of their life forces."

Tanda stops climbing to glance down at her as she adds, "It was a series of one bad stroke of luck after another that resulted in your father becoming the powerful and evil… *thing* that he's become. The necklace breaking, *that* particular pearl, containing not one, but *two* negative Wyrms rolling just far enough to escape the pull of the abyss. The timing of it, hatching right there in the midst of a battle between good and evil. The two Wyrms, who I've since discovered were Wrath and Greed entering him just moments before he would have been defeated." She sighs heavily and resumes climbing. "It is not normal for one egg to bear two Wyrms, and it *certainly* shouldn't have been possible for Kalaraja to live through the merging of them both. But it all happened, impossible though it all should have been. So many times, I've wished it would have been a positive Wyrm that hatched that day, or even a neutral one like my Kreeleerians possess. Perhaps then I would still have my Deidra …"

She falls silent then, but Boodark picks up the conversation. "You mean to tell me those foul cat creatures of yours have worms inside of them? And so does the Lokskell? No wonder I don't trust those furballs!"

Tanda tssks at him. "Wyrms, not worms. And they are not negatives like Kalaraja's; they're neutrals. They're neither good nor bad."

Boodark harrumphs back at her. "That distinction doesn't matter to *me*. A worm is a worm is a worm. They're still weird, and I don't like them one little bit."

"Fair enough," Tanda laughs as they step onto the second level of the treehouse. "I just have to gather some things, and then we'll be going up to the next floor."

Ecko glances up the spiral staircase and wonders just how many more levels there are, because it looks like it goes a long way up.

Tanda brusquely points things out for their 'tour'. In much the same layout as the room below, this one is also a large, open room with a counter and wash station on the far-right wall. Three smaller rooms line the back wall, two with the doors open and the third firmly shut. And that's where the similarities end. While the ground floor is used for the main living area, this floor is apparently used for extra storage space and sleeping quarters. There are shelves and shelves of supplies, clothes and blankets, bowls and buckets, bundles of dried herbs, and jar upon jar of canned goods. That's where Tanda busies herself, selecting things from the shelves and packing them into a large, wicker-type basket. She points to a shelf that holds an assortment of beat up, old milk pails and buckets. "Do you mind carrying two of those buckets for me? Grab the ones that have handles. Those are the easiest to carry."

She selects two that have both handles and lids and Tanda nods in approval before adding a stack of cloth bags to her basket. She notices Boodark's interest in the beds that are pushed back along the wall, close to the staircase. They're not beds, as in bed frames and mattresses. They're just mounds of pillows and blankets… sleeping pallets laid right on the floor.

Tanda explains, "As you can clearly see, this is where I store all of my extra supplies. Sometimes I get guests, usually hungry or wounded creatures, and this is where they sleep." She waves a hand towards the doors on the back wall. "Those are extra bedrooms for when actual people show up and need to stay a while."

Boodark points at the closed door and asks, "What about that one?"

Her basket full, she whirls around and heads for the stairs. "*That* one is private, and it stays locked! Come along!"

They turn and give one another the big 'what was *that* all about' eyes before Ecko scrambles to catch up. Whatever's behind that door, it's clearly none of their business.

They ascend to the next floor, and she immediately feels like she's stepped into a rainforest, an *Earth* rainforest. (She doesn't even want to consider what horrors a rainforest on this world would produce.) The air is warm and moist, the perfect temperature for the plants and small trees that are growing *everywhere*…literally everywhere, many of which are bearing strange fruits and vegetables and berries. The room is filled to capacity with vegetation, the plants growing right out of sections of logs that have been hollowed out into pots and planters. There are even vines trailing up the walls, twirling up the staircase, and crawling across the ceiling. She reaches up to touch one of the dangling… fruits? It's shaped just like a small cucumber but it's yellow as a ripe banana and fuzzy as a peach.

"Come along!" Tanda calls as she sets off, weaving her way through the vegetation like she's walking through a maze. In the center of the room, there's a small stone table set up with a bench on either side of it. Situated in the middle of the table is a very large, glowing crystal that stands taller than Boodark and emits a bright, yellow-tinted light. Tanda sets her basket down beside it and then gratefully lowers herself onto the nearest bench, her chest rising and falling a bit faster than normal from the exertion of climbing all those stairs.

"What is *that*?" Boodark whispers, his awe evident in his voice.

"Sunstone," Tanda gasps and then holds up a finger in the universal signal to wait. She's too winded to speak, so the two of them stand there studying it with rapt fascination while she catches her breath. It's some sort of crystal, quartz-like in appearance, and as its name suggests, it shines bright as a sun. It's odd though; looking into its light doesn't hurt her eyes.

"It's a piece of a sun that exploded long, long ago. Amazingly, the sun didn't die when it shattered. It lives on; it just does so in thousands of pieces. Fragments of it got flung out to several worlds, and I was lucky enough to get my hands on this one after I became trapped here. As you can see, it provides the plants with light and heat… even the moisture in the air."

Boodark murmurs, "I sure wish I'd known about this place when my family …uh…well… uh before I was cursed. You have enough food here to feed a hundred clans of pixies!" He says it lightly, but Ecko can hear the trace of bitterness, the underlying sadness in his voice. He had a family that he'd been responsible for feeding, day in and day out, on a world where food is exceedingly difficult to come by. It had to have been a great burden to bear, a terrible fear that he wouldn't be able to feed his family each Pale. She doesn't blame him for feeling resentful, and she hugs him a little tighter to her chest.

Tanda nods at him, her own eyes sad and full of pain. "Yes, I do have a lot of food. And I share it with all who need it. Just as I will share it with you and your family, now that you know about it."

Boodark looks away from her and holds his tongue, choosing to say nothing, lest his bitterness get the best of him.

"I can see that you don't understand, and how could you? You think that I am greedy, that I keep all this here, hidden away for myself. I will tell you a bit about this EverRealm, this SeeAll Tree now. I will also explain how I am such a well preserved 1,214 years old. Perhaps once you know the truth, you won't be so quick to judge me as harshly as you are doing so right now."

Realizing that they're going to be here for a while, Ecko settles Boodark on the empty bench and then sits beside him, eager to hear what she has to say.

"There are seven EverRealms, special, magical places on this world that also exist simultaneously on other worlds… as far as I know, they exist on *every single* world ever created, in every single timeline. I've learned quite a bit about the EverRealms over the years, and you'll need to learn it all too. But for right now, all you really need to know is that this tree is one of those magical places. It exists in some form or another on every known world. Sheol Castle, the fortress that Deidra bound your father to is another."

"Now, as you know, all *that* happened a thousand years ago… the battle that resulted in Deidra's death and Kalaraja's banishment to the castle. That means your father is over a thousand years old. As am I. The Wyrms inside of Kalaraja keep him from aging, just as they have done for my Kreeleerians. But I don't have a Wyrm to keep me young. It's only the spell of the SeeAll Tree that's kept me alive these many long years. It's also what keeps the plants alive, although it won't allow for new plants to grow from the existing ones. No matter how many times I tried to expand the plant life beyond what you see in this room, the attempts always ended in failure. The seeds just won't grow. Cuttings and grafting won't take. Removing whole plants from the SeeAll Tree and transplanting them elsewhere on Oblerian only results in the deaths of desperately needed, food bearing vegetation."

"And it's the same for me. I am bound to this EverRealm just as surely as the Lokskell is bound to his castle. He literally cannot step foot out of his castle. I may leave any time I choose… if I wish to rapidly age and die within minutes of leaving the SeeAll's influence. Oh, I didn't know any of this in the beginning and it didn't happen right away, of course. It wasn't until several hundreds of years after I made this my home that I figured it all out … figured out that there are rules and stipulations to living in the SeeAll Tree. *Strict* rules. Time spent here is cheating death. I found that out too late, although I wouldn't have changed it. It put me right where I needed to be, *when* I needed to be here… to meet *you.*"

Tanda fiddles with her apron, smoothing it out and brushing imaginary lint off of it. Her shoulders slump and she sighs as she continues her tale. "Once I realized what was happening, I was forced to limit my time away from the SeeAll. It put serious restrictions on the things I could do, the places I could go. It eventually got to the point that when I left, I immediately began to age. The further I got from the SeeAll Tree, the faster it happened."

She glances at Boodark as she gestures out at the vegetation around them. "I would have gladly shared this magic outside of my home if only I had been permitted to do so. I would have planted huge, wonderful gardens out there, reintroduced the plant life to this dying world. Between the SeeAll Tree's spell over the plants and the Lokskell's terrible wasting influence over the world, this is the *only* place safe for them. And for me. So, you see Boodark, all I can do is share what I have with those that I can reach. Those that make it to my door and those that get sent my way by word of mouth from others that I have fed and nursed back to health."

Now that he knows the truth, now that he understands, Boodark's forced to apologize. "You're right. I was quick to jump to conclusions. I judged you harshly, and for that I am truly sorry. You are a good female ground stomper, to think of others and to willingly share what you have. There aren't many others that would do the same, even if they had plenty."

She's still stuck on the fact that Tanda is over a thousand years old. "*That's* why I keep thinking you're older than you look! It's a magic spell!"

Tanda gives her a small, somewhat sad smile. "Yes. I don't really look my age, do I? Unfortunately, I feel every bit of it though."

Boodark suddenly jumps to his feet with a tiny yelp, startling his poor unsuspecting companions half to death. "Are we stuck here now?" He turns huge eyes on her, panic clearly stamped on his face as he frantically begins tugging on her hand. "Come *on*, you big dummy! Move! We have to leave before the spell gets us too! I can't be trapped in this tree for the rest of my life! I already *have* a curse that I need to break! I have my own family trapped in a tree that I need to save. How can I do that if I'm stuck here in *this* tree, and they're stuck in another? Oh, come *on*! *Please*, Ecko!" Tanda has to shout to be heard over *his* shouting. "Calm yourself, Boodark! You are not trapped here! Spending a few Pales in the SeeAll Tree won't do you any harm. You'll not age and turn to dust when you leave here on the Morrow, I promise. That wouldn't happen even should you spend several years here. Hundreds of others before you have come and gone without any aging issues whatsoever."

He slowly loses the wild-eyed, deer in the headlights look. His little body relaxes and then up goes his chin at a stubborn angle.

"Well, that's a relief! I wasn't *scared*, mind you. I just think you should have made all that clear from the start."

She coughs into her hand to hide her giggles while Tanda just smiles and agrees. "You're right, of course. I'm so sorry for the oversight." Then without even the slightest bit of warning, she sticks her pinky finger and her pointer finger into her mouth and produces a piercingly shrill whistle that has both of her guests clapping their hands over their ears to block it out. "Sorry, but that's the only way to call them," she says. "Perhaps that was another thing I should have warned you about!" And then she cackles, sounding exactly like the ancient, thousand-year-old crone that she is.

Boodark opens his mouth to fire one of his snarky comments back at her, but there's no time for a witty response. Thumps and thuds from the level above have them turning their eyes to the ceiling in alarm. Ecko whimpers as the spiral staircase begins to shake as something... *several* somethings scurry down towards them.

Her mind immediately conjures up the memory of the Spidder Frost, reminding her in great detail of the sounds that the thousands upon thousands of spiders made as they landed on her DreamSnare pod shelter... the thudding of their *meaty* bodies landing, the skittering of their legs as the scuttled away. She shivers with renewed horror as she snatches her little orc-bat up in her arms and prepares to make a run for it as the sounds of the stampede draw closer and closer.

The Finer Things in Life

Samara

Several weeks pass in a blur, a snow-white haze filled with pleasure and pain, learning experiences, and a shit-ton of power housing and muscle flexing. Samara spends an inordinate amount of time in Mr. Chadwick's bed where he teaches her about human limitations and safe words and how to not kill what she fucks, though she still hasn't quite gotten that last part down very well. In fact, she's only managed that feat with Mr. Chadwick himself. She breaks everyone else; she doesn't allow them a safe word. Not one that works, anyway. But then, she likes Mr. Chadwick a lot more than any other human that she's ever met. He's a sweet, filthy soul wrapped up in impeccable manners and a deliciously strong, manly body.

Lenny introduces her to every illegal substance known to man, and she quickly learns to steer clear of the ones that bring her down. Who the fuck wants to feel like that all the time? Or *ever?* Slow and low and gloomy. Nope, the stoners and the downers and the mopers can keep all that. More for them. She'll take a fast

"

paced, rocker roller high any day… multiple times a day. Her absolute favorite is still what Lenny calls blow, or snow white, but these days it's a bit more amped up in the form of speedballs. Crystal meth and ecstasy are very close runner up choices, and Samara goes through ungodly amounts of them all.

In the early days of their arrangement, Lenny had been terrified that she would give herself an overdose and end up dead within a month, but she honestly doesn't believe that's even possible. Something about her body's make up… she burns right through the drugs. Or perhaps it's her magic. Honestly, she hasn't got a clue. It's all speculative. All she knows is that she goes through an extraordinary amount of the stuff, and anyone else wouldn't survive it.

During those first weeks, Samara met a lot of people, *tested* a lot of people, and killed a lot of people. Lenny flexed his new muscle by giddily showing her off. Together they let it be known that he was changing the rules, resetting the board for a new kind of game. One where he was king, and she was his queen. All other players were just pawns, disposable and easily replaced. Word spread far and wide, doubts of her abilities were expressed and then promptly laid to rest as she revealed, in gloriously bloody detail, the atrocities that she was capable of. A couple of horrendous, nightmare-inducing scenes and even the staunchest disbelievers were convinced to fall in line and play their parts.

It was a time of great change in the world that Lenny introduced her to. Loyalties were checked, and most were discredited. Boundaries were set, fear was brandished like a weapon against all opposition. Fear earned respect, new loyalties were gained, and an empire was built. And throughout it all, Samara learned and grew and flourished.

She learned patience and self-control… *mostly*. She learned to play the game, draw it out, bide her time until the perfect opportunity to strike arose. She mimicked Mr. Chadwick's behavior and became sophisticated and suave, and she turned herself into something that resembled a real lady… at least outwardly.

With Lenny and Mr. Chadwick's help, Samara turned herself into a queen. She bought herself an insanely large house and filled it with only the finest, most extravagantly lavish and luxurious things… fine crystal, quartz countertops marbled with gold, and hideous, but outrageously expensive art. She purchased more jewelry and clothing than she could ever wear, even if she were to wear each item once and then toss it into the garbage. And the shoes! She filled entire rooms with stilettos and heels, pumps and sandals, boots and ankle booties. Perhaps the reason she'd become so obsessed with footwear was because she'd never owned a pair of shoes before she'd arrived on this obscenely materialistic and superfluous world. Perhaps she's merely making up for lost time or trying to fill an unfillable void inside of her. Or perhaps she just loves the way she looks in a nice pair of heels. Who knows?

True to his word, Lenny introduced her to a wealth of rich, important, and powerful people. Oh, not powerful in the way that *she's* powerful. No, powerful in a human way. She had to learn sophistication, grace, and elegance in order to hobnob with the snobby snobs. There'd been plenty of 'Julia Roberts, Pretty Woman' spoof moments along the way… embarrassing little scenes or *would* have been embarrassing if she'd been a lesser, inferior woman. (She *adores* that movie and has such fond, pleasant memories of the first time Mr. Chadwick played it for her. They'd lain together on his bed, surrounded by sticky sweet treats and watched the entire movie while a swinger couple licked strawberry and chocolate sauces off their bodies. Watching Mr. Chadwick play with that couple after the movie was over had been the single most erotic and wickedly lascivious thing she'd ever seen, and she'd encouraged him to continue his fun long after the life had left their bodies. She'd watched it all, from start to finish and if she had possessed a heart, she surely would have given it to Mr. Chadwick that day. *That's* how impressed, inspired, and awed she'd been.)

But, getting back to the hobnobbing with the snobs and all of her mishaps and blunders… no one ever laughed at her. Well, no one had laughed at her since that one unfortunate dinner party and the nasty, 'I'm better than you and you're nothing but dogshit on the bottom of my shoe' Loretta Myers incident. Not a single person who attended that dinner will ever forget how that old crone had turned her nose up at her, how blatantly rude and unaccepting she'd been. Nor will they ever forget how in the midst of partaking of the palate cleansing, mint sorbet, Loretta Myers had suddenly and tragically decided to remove her own eyes from her head with her dessert spoon. But all's well that ends well. No one ever laughed at her again. Whenever she made a mistake in snobber hobnobber etiquette, Mr. Chadwick or Lenny quietly corrected it while everyone else found other things of interest to look at... *anything* but at her. She was training *them* even as she was learning *their* ways.

In all that time, during all the learning and training, the flexing and fucking and flying high in a perpetual drug-heightened state, Samara toyed with Lenny. She teased him mercilessly, until he was hard and throbbing and begging, and then she'd laugh and back out at the last second. She played with him for weeks, until he was half mad with desire for her before she finally had her way with him.

She found great pleasure in tormenting him, especially at the most inconvenient and inopportune times. She loved to send her Shadows out, to have them sneak beneath the table at his almighty, important business meetings to rub against him, to toy with him until he grew so hard that he just couldn't stand it... hard enough to burst. Then she'd have her Shadows pull his jeans open and take his dick out. They'd grip it tight, tease it, pulse around it like a hot, living thing. They'd lick at him with soft, gentle tongue strokes and then swallow him down and suck him off, right there under the table ... all while he'd been setting up his operations and negotiating his million-dollar deals.

The first time she'd done that to him, he'd been oh, so pissed but completely powerless to put an end to it. Even if he could have found the will to tell her to stop, (Never happen, not in a million years. What man will put a stop to getting his dick sucked... even if it's getting sucked by some sort of Shadow/ghost magic?) Even if he could have uttered the word stop, he'd been in the middle of a meeting, in a room full of the most affluential players of the game. He'd gotten through it… somehow, but he'd been forced to sit there at that table long after all the others had departed. He'd even had to call Mr. Chadwick and have him bring in a change of clothing. He couldn't very well go walking about with the entire front of his trousers soaked and semen stained. Oh, he'd been so furious with her for that. And he'd been so screwed, because just as she'd promised him, he found that he *did* crave her just as desperately as any drug.

And then he did what *all* men seem to do. He became obsessed, possessive, and controlling. He wanted her all to himself and he began to resent her being with other men… especially Mr. Chadwick. Perhaps because the man had become as loyal to her as he was to Lenny himself… if not more so. But more than likely, it was simple jealousy. Samara enjoyed Mr. Chadwick so much more than she did him. Perhaps if he could figure out what the fuck to do with a spaghetti spoon, she'd find more satisfaction in his bed.

At one point during the experiment phase of their partnership, back in that first month or so, Samara had come up out of the fog of pleasures long enough to remember that she'd been on a personal mission before she fell in with Lenny and his magic powders and Mr. Chadwick and his kinky fetishes. She'd been looking for Ecko's old geezers. And then she remembered the file.

She'd taken it from Dr Bradburn's hands and stuffed it down the back of her jeans to keep it safe and free of blood and goop and brain matter. And that's the last time she'd seen it. She must have lost it when she'd stripped out of her clothes in that cheap motel room. It's the only thing that could have happened.

So, she casually asked Lenny about it, watching him closely for any hint of a lie. And he'd looked right in her eyes, and with a straight, completely composed face, informed her that he never saw any file. She'd gone still as a snake in its striking position as she calmly insisted, "It was there, in my dirty clothes when I left to get into the shower."

He'd only shrugged and held his hands out as if he was apologizing. "I paid one of the maids to bring clean blankets for you, to take away the bloodied ones and have them disposed of. Your clothing too. They were disgusting, ruined beyond repair. I'm sorry. I didn't think to have them searched before she carried them out and threw them into the dumpster. Do you mind me asking what was in the file? Is it anything I can help you with?"

He offered his help, and he had seemed oh, so sincere, but her Shadows were churning inside her, roiling in fury. They tasted the lie on his tongue, and they wanted to swallow it up, swallow *him* up amid his screams and pleas for mercy. But no. That's not how she wanted to handle things. She wanted to play the game.

So, she had merely smiled and waved him off. "Oh, you needn't worry yourself with it. It was nothing of any real importance anyway. Just a little something I was looking into, that's all."

And Lenny, ignorant Lenny had been so relieved that he hadn't been caught in his lie that he took her at face value. He never questioned the ease in which she let the entire situation slide away... because it's what he'd *wanted* to believe. He knew that he fucked up, and that if she ever found out his little secret, he would lose the best thing he'd ever had... and probably his life as well.

Samara had walked away, retreating into her own houses where she cranked up the rock and roll to almost deafening decibels and took out her fury on one poor, unsuspecting man after another for three days straight before her temper cooled enough to chance being in Lenny's presence again. During that time, she even refused to see Mr. Chadwick, because she knew herself entirely too well. She would have killed him in her anger, just as she'd done to all those hapless young men that she Shadow-coaxed into her bed. Oh, she would have regretted it afterwards, for she truly does enjoy Mr. Chadwick, but that wouldn't have stopped her while she was lost to her rage.

Once she'd finally exhausted herself, and therefore her fury, she'd kicked everyone out... everyone that had managed to survive her wrath, that is. She sequestered herself away and forced herself, for a short time, to go without stimulants of any kind. No drugs, no sex, no alcoholic beverages, no violence or bloodletting. She needed to think clearly, to plan and strategize. If ever she needed a cool head, that had been the time for it.

In the end, she decided to bide her time, to continue playing the game and then, when the time was right and all the pieces were in the right places, she would make her move and take the upper hand. And she has such a wonderful surprise for Lenny when that day finally arrives. She can hardly wait! In the meantime, though, she'll continue just as she had been. She'll continue to be his weapon, until she decides to turn that weapon around on him. And then she'll take his place as the new leader of his precious empire. There can only be one winner, and her name is Samara.

"You lose, Lenny."

Niggles, Lessons, and SeeAll Sessions

Ecko

Ecko clutches Boodark against her breast as something small and very fast flashes by her on the right, then on the left. Then it's above her, behind her, now back on the left. She whirls around and around, feeling just like Sarah in the Labyrinth when the goblins came to take her little brother away. "I didn't say the words!" she cries out, totally nonsensically to everyone else in the room.

Though she does not understand the meaning behind her words, Tanda immediately recognizes the fear behind them. "Be not afraid, child. They won't hurt you; they're friendly."

Suddenly, a little white and brown creature darts forward and takes a bowl from the basket of supplies that Tanda had brought. It's just a bit larger than Boodark, being closer to sixteen inches tall rather than his own twelve. Not a spider then. Thank you, sweet baby Jesus!

"They're Na-Loofs," Tanda explains. "I saved a family of them from being eaten by a Sluggeelian, oh, three hundred years or so after I moved in here. It was a mama, a papa, and their two offspring. I brought them back here to tend their wounds and they just never left. I guess they decided that this was home."

The little creature looks like some weird cross between a cute, big-eyed monkey and one of those toy Furbies that were so popular when she was a small child. It has long, silky fur, big pointy ears… like a Maine Coon's, and an extra-long, fluffy tail. It chitters up at Tanda and then scampers away, the bowl clutched in its tiny racoon-like paws. "Oh! It has wings!" she exclaims when she gets a glimpse of the brown feathers on its back.

"Yes, they have wings, although the ones I saved all those years ago do not. The Sluggeelian ripped them off, and they never grew back. But they get around just fine, the four wingless ones. And all of the Loof-Lings that have come since have wings." Tanda laughs and adds "Although, I don't think I'll ever know if they can actually fly with those tiny things or if they're just for show."

A snow-white one dashes in and snatches a cloth bag out of the basket. When it turns and makes a run for it, she gets a better look at the wings. "They *are* tiny! Ohmygoodness! They're so cute!" she gushes when she realizes that they're *extremely* disproportionately small to their bodies. "They don't fly at all? I guess their wings are just too small to support them. I wonder why they would even have wings if they can't use them. That's so strange."

Tanda laughs and shakes her head. "Oh, I'm sure their wings would work just fine; they're just too afraid to even try them out!"

Boodark squirms out of the tight grip (*oops*) that she still has on him and insists, "That's ridiculous! They shouldn't be afraid. They were born with wings; they should trust them."

A shy black and brown one hides behind a plant and holds its little paw out towards Tanda. "That's not it, though. It's not that they don't trust their wings. That's not what keeps them firmly on the ground. Or, uh firmly on the tree, that is," Tanda replies with a laugh as it grabs the sack she offers and scampers away. Then she looks at Boodark and grins. "They're afraid of heights!"

He sputters in response. "But that's ridiculous!" he repeats.

"Flyers shouldn't be afraid to fly! That's just all kinds of wrong!" He watches another one dart in, snatch a bowl, and run away with it. "What are they doing with the stuff?" he asks.

But *she's* already figured that part out. She climbs up on the bench, stands upon her tiptoes and gazes all around the room. She bends down and scoops Boodark up so that he can see too. They both watch the little creatures rush about, carefully harvesting the ripe produce from the plants and trees. "They like to help, and to be honest, the older I get, the more I *need* the help. There's ripe produce every single Pale that needs picking. They harvest it and carry it to the bottom floor where I wash and separate it. What I don't use for our daily meals or for preserving and storing for later consumption gets taken outside and left for others to find. This helps all of us. It saves me time and energy, and it also helps them feel like they're paying back a debt that they owe me. In all this time, I've never been able to convince them that they owe me nothing. Kindness doesn't cost a thing and should not be something that one feels indebted to pay back. But it pleases them, and it gives them something to do. And I really can use all the help I can get. There are always so many chores to see to."

Ecko wholeheartedly agrees with her. "It *is* a good set up… everyone helping with chores and pulling their own weight."

Tanda hands the last bowl to a little tan colored Na-Loof with an extra floofy tail. She sighs and admits, "I would feel better about it if they would actually eat any of the produce that they help harvest. But they refuse. I've never seen them eat anything but the SeeAll's eyeballs. Oh, and Vika Vakooja's. They eat every one of those nasty little spies that come near!"

Ecko shudders as she thinks of those roach beetles. "Good!" is all she replies. She can't stand the disgusting things.

She's still standing on the bench watching in complete fascination as the Na-Loofs quickly and efficiently get their tasks done. "There's so many of them! Look Boodark! Look at them all. Aren't they adorable?" She turns to Tanda and asks, "Just how many *are* there?"

She gives an exaggerated, long-suffering sigh but she's smiling when she answers. "There are one hundred and eightyseven Na-Loofs, all descended from my original four, and then an additional female that came to us years later. The SeeAll's spell doesn't seem to affect their breeding abilities. I don't know why they can reproduce but the plants cannot. Not that I'm complaining, mind you. I love having them around… Oh! I take it back. There's one hundred and eighty-*eight* of them now!"

She turns her eyes to follow Tanda's line of sight to the NaLoof that's running towards them, its racoon hands clutching something tiny to its chest. Tanda giggles like a little girl and cries, "Reloo has finally given birth!" She squats down on the floor, ignoring the cracking and popping of her old bones as the Na-Loof reaches her. It points to the empty basket then out at the plants, chittering all the while and Tanda shakes her head. "You are excused from chores for a good long while. Your Loof-ling will be more than enough work for you. You just rest and enjoy your first infant. Now, did you have a boy, as I suspected? Let's see! Show him to me."

Ecko drops down to her knees and watches as the proud new mother chitters excitedly and jumps up and down before holding the baby out for Tanda to inspect.

"A boy!" she exclaims as she gently takes him in hand. "Oh Reloo, what a handsome boy you've had. He looks just like his father. I bet Keet is a puffed up, proud papa."

The Na-Loof chitters again and turns to point out a black one with a white face that's *pretending* to pick berries but is actually watching every move they make around his new baby. Tanda bursts out laughing and gestures him over too. He moves in more cautiously than his mate had, staring at the strangers with worry in his eyes.

Tanda's quick to put him at ease. "This is Ecko. She's the one we've been waiting for." He chitters back at her, his voice just a bit deeper than Reloo's. "Yes," Tanda replies. "She *is* the new protector."

He turns to Ecko, closes his eyes and bows his head at her. And then he just stands there like… waiting. Tanda explains what it is that he wants from her. "He wants to niggle with you. It's a mind sharing experience, and also a trust builder. While your minds are connected, your thoughts will be linked to his. He'll be able to get to know you, and you him. All you have to do is lean in and press your forehead to his if you wish to accept the niggling. If you don't want to, gently run your fingers down his face, from his forehead to his chin. Like this." Tanda demonstrates on her own face.

She nods her understanding and leans forward, pressing her forehead to Keet's tiny one. She takes a deep breath and then closes her eyes. She waits for his thoughts to come to her, but that's not what happens. Not at all. She sees a vision instead. Keet's small gasp of surprise assures her that he's seeing it right along with her.

The scene that unfolds looks like the aftermath of a great battle, with bloody carnage as far as the eye can see. There are bodies, broken and discarded, everywhere… people and creatures and fae folk that she's not familiar with. And then she *does* recognize someone. Keet, his fur matted with dirt and blood, stands guard over several wounded Na-Loofs. The vision shows her running to them, opening what she assumes is the EverGlass mirror, and then sending them to safety… to Irredarr. Several things happen after that, in such quick succession that she can't process it all. And then it's over and the two of them break the link that binds them.

Keet steps back, teary-eyed, and places his fist over his heart. She mimics the action as she tries valiantly to shake off the images of the horrors she'd just witnessed. In a voice choked with emotion she tells him, "I'm very glad to meet you, Keet. And you too, Reloo. I think your new baby is probably the sweetest thing I've ever seen in my whole life. He's just adorable."

Keet *does* puff up then, his chest all poofed out with pride as he takes his new son from Tanda and lifts him up towards her. She holds her hands out, her eyes brimming with incredulous tears as he gently, *trustingly* places the squirming baby into her hands. He very much resembles a pygmy marmoset, one of those adorable, miniature monkeys that only grow as big as a human finger.

"Ooohhh," she breathes. "He's so soft and tiny! Such a little body for such great, big responsibilities that the future has planned for him." The Loof-Ling makes a tiny mewling sound and then opens his enormous blue eyes, instantly capturing her heart. He chitters up at her as she strokes a gentle finger over his silky fur. Tears run down her face as she whispers, "Hello Kurloo. You're destined for great things. Aren't you, little one?" She snuggles him to her face for just a moment and then hands him back to his mother.

Keet surprises her by holding his arms open for his own hug then. She wraps her arms around him and whispers, "I'll get them there. I promise." He pulls back, nods, and then ushers his little family away.

Tanda studies her face closely as she asks, "You shared a vision, did you not?"

She has to clear her throat several times before she can answer. "Yes, but it was unlike any vision I've ever had, not that I have many to compare it to. But it *was* different from the few that I've had. The images flashed by so fast! I couldn't make sense of it all." She quickly tells her the bits and pieces that she can remember, knowing that her words don't make any sense. Nor do they convey the proper amount of horror that she'd witnessed. Sometimes, words just aren't enough.

"Niggle-visions are rare, especially from two individuals who have never niggled before. What you saw may not make sense now, but it will in time." Tanda collects her now empty basket and slowly gets to her feet. "I was not aware that you had the foresight," she remarks with a thoughtful frown on her face. "Perhaps we should have a SeeAll session? Hhmmm, or perhaps not. It may not be such a good idea to… I will need to think on this for a while. Come, there's one last thing to do before we go up to the roof. Don't forget the buckets, dear."

Tanda leads the way to the back of the room, expertly dodging the scampering busy-bee Na-Loofs until they arrive at a small tree that looks remarkably like a peach tree in full blossom. The little creatures have obviously neglected harvesting this one because it's laden with strange fruits, the branches sagging under the heavy weight of them. The large, egg-shaped vegetables look similar to eggplants, but they're not the traditional purple-black color. They're a milky green color that she finds a bit disturbing, if she's being honest.

Tanda pulls one of the wooden hair-sticks out of the messy bun atop her head. It looks lethal, like a long, sharp needle. "Come here, child. Hold a bucket up under this one for me."

So, she sets Boodark onto her shoulder in order to free up her hands as she steps forward to do as she was instructed, situating the bucket below one of the alien eggplants. Tanda reaches out and suddenly jabs her jabby, poker hair-stick into the bottom of the fruit/vegetable thing.

"Oh!" she cries out as a trickle of milk-white fluid pours out of it and into her bucket. The fruit quickly empties, deflating like a balloon that has a slow leak. It doesn't take long, maybe thirty seconds or so for all of the liquid to drain out, leaving nothing but an empty, translucent, green-tinted skin behind. It reminds her of the blister-thorns back in the Sorrow Marshes, and her heart gives a tiny twinge as she's reminded of Sephyr.

She quickly sends up a little prayer for her sweet Darkling friend and then peers down into the bucket in her hands. "It looks like milk!" she exclaims. "What is it?"

Tanda laughs as she points to the next, milk laden fruit, signaling for her to move the bucket below it. "That's because it *is* milk. This is a milkweed tree. It came all the way from Irredarr, as did several of the plants in here. My Deidra loved milk, just adored it, and I wanted nothing more than for her to be happy. I tried to give her everything she ever wanted… at least the little things that I was able to provide. So, I brought this tree, along with many others, to our home and planted them there for her, to make sure she would always have milk and fresh fruits and vegetables. Small comforts, I know, but it showed her how much I loved her."

She jabs the hole into the bottom of the fruit to start the milk flow as she explains. "The milkpods can be picked and eaten as a deliciously sweet treat. But if I pick the pods, then new pods must grow in their place and that takes several days. That's why I choose to *only* collect the milk and leave the pods behind. I need as much of that precious liquid as I can possibly get. There are so many that desperately need the milk that only *I* have the means to provide."

She sighs under the heavy weight of burden as they move on to the next milkpod. "The milkpod's skin is highly regenerative. Within an hour or two, the holes will be repaired and then they'll begin to refill, preparing for the morrow's milk harvest." Tanda bends down to check the moisture of the soil and nods in approval. "This little tree has saved many lives. I don't know what I would do without it, and I wish I had ten more just like it."

The bucket grows heavier and heavier, and when it's three quarters full, they switch to the second pail. "This is the reason I collect the milk myself. The Na-Loofs would be happy to do it for me, but they tend to spill, and every drop is precious. Normally I carry up one bucket and several small jars with lids. I fill the jars and let the Na-Loofs carry those down while I carry the heavy bucket. That way none gets spilled, and I don't have to make two trips. I can only carry one pail at a time."

Tanda reaches up and plucks the last full milkpod from the plant and passes it to her guest. She vehemently tries to refuse such an imperative supplement in Tanda's food supply, but her words get cut off before they can ever leave her mouth.

"I want you to have it," Tanda assures her. "I want you to experience a tiny piece of your homeworld. One pod-full of milk won't make much of a difference in the scheme of things. And besides, it's done now. I already picked it, so you may as well enjoy it."

Touched by her thoughtfulness, Ecko thanks her as she takes it in hand. "You're welcome, child. It works best if you take a bite from the top and then sip some of the milk out. Drink the milk as you work your way down, that way none of it spills out."

She doesn't have the heart to tell her that she really isn't a fan of milk, never has been. She feels a little bit self-conscious with Tanda and Boodark focused so intently on her, but she takes a hesitant bite from the top, quickly sipping a little of the milk like she'd been told to do. She chews slowly, swallows, and then takes another bite.

"Well?" Boodark demands. "How is it? What's it taste

like?"

She smiles, feeling her entire face light up with pleasure. It's probably one of the most delicious things she's ever tasted… even better than chocolate. "Oh my gosh, Boodark! It's wonderful!

You *have* to try it!" She takes a sip of sweet milk and then bites off another, much larger bite. "It tastes like cake fondant, or buttercream icing or …. Oh, I don't know! *Something* to do with cake!" Another bite and sip. "And the milk! Oh, Boodark, it's amazing! It's delicately sweet, with just a hint of a nutty aftertaste." Bite, enthusiastic sip. Her mouth overly full, she murmurs, "Mmmmm. Boodark, you've *got* to try this!"

Boodark smacks her on the back of her head and shouts, "I will if you'll stop acting like a greedy Grunter! Put me down *this instant* and share, you big dummy! I wish to taste it too!"

"Oh! I'm so sorry, Boodark. You're right, of course." She sets him on the floor, takes one last bite, and then passes the treat to him. "Here, you can have the rest. Unless … Do you want some?" she asks her host.

Tanda smiles gently. "No, child. You two enjoy it. I can have one any time I choose."

Boodark sniffs at it, then experimentally dips his tongue into the milk and takes a tiny, sample nibble. And then he's wolfing it down even faster than *she* had. He consumes in under a minute flat and then turns to look longingly at the tree. She laughs and tells him, "Yeah, and *I'm* the Grunter! You don't get another one, you piggy little thing!"

Tanda picks up one of the milk pails and she takes the other and they slowly, carefully head back towards the stairs. They make their way around the room, keeping close to the walls where the path between the plants is the clearest.

She stops in her tracks when she comes to a door… an *unusual* door. It's sort of hazy and out of focus, like it's there, but it's not there too. The word *'Hidden'* whispers through her mind as she studies it. Covered in extravagant runes *that glow*, it also has that humming sound coming from it, that thrumming that she feels whenever there's Irredarrian magic present. But Tanda doesn't mention it, so she keeps her mouth shut too. She just continues to follow where the old woman leads, looking over her shoulder at the door until she's moved beyond sight of it.

"See something?" Tanda asks, her face closed and suspicious.

"Nope," she answers. "Nothing at all." If Tanda had wanted to discuss the hidden room, she would have pointed it out as part of the 'tour'.

They make their way up to the next level, leaving the milk pails beside the staircase to collect on their way back down. Tanda doesn't even stop on the next floor, she just pauses long enough for her guests to get a look at the massive nest in the middle of the otherwise empty room. It's just like a bird's nest, made from sticks, leaves, and bits of fluff, but on a much larger scale. It appears big enough for a family of Foul-Kries to live comfortably in, and she can only hope that's not the case. Tanda has the kindest heart, but surely, she wouldn't allow those horrible creatures into her home.

"The Na-Loofs sleep on this level. They pile up in the nest in a big Loofa pile. It's quite adorable to watch them all get settled in." Tanda tells her. She involuntarily lets out a tiny sigh of relief as they continue moving upwards. She never wants to encounter another Foul-Kry as long as she lives!

At last, they come to a stop, and she glances up to see that the stairs have ended; the way up to the next floor is blocked by a trapdoor. It's odd though. It doesn't push open in typical trapdoor fashion (if such a thing as typical trapdoor functionality exists) It's built into grooves on the ceiling/floor and opens just like a sliding door. So instead of the door opening upwards, it slides sideways along the grooves, more like a panel than a typical door. As they climb through, Tanda explains that the door is more for keeping out the poison rains than anything else.

"The SeeAll keeps itself pretty well hidden from things that wish to do harm, but it doesn't block out the sky waters. It can protect itself from absorbing the poison, but keeping the water from pouring down the stairwell, not so much. There was already a door here when I moved in, the kind that you just push up, but I had to rethink the design. When I brought the Na-Loofs home and realized they were here to stay, I had to come up with something else. They couldn't push it open, so the slide-door is what I came up with. This way they can all come and go as they please. They even shut the door behind them as they go in and out."

They step out onto a flat platform, a sky-deck hidden among the branches. It takes her a moment to look past all the eyeball fruits that pop open to watch them. She shudders and does her best to ignore them, quickly turning away and to inspect the rest of the deck. Like the house, it's sparsely furnished, with only a small table and its four handmade chairs, a hammock made from some sort of netting, and a bench swing that hangs from an overhead branch. It's made exactly like the swings downstairs in front of the fireplace, and it's set up at the edge of the deck where it seems to overlook the entire world.

She makes her way over and slowly lowers herself onto it, her breath drawing in with an amazed but slightly horrified gasp. The view is absolutely spectacular or *would* be if the world she was looking out on was a pleasant one. But this… it's like looking at a post-apocalyptic world. Which she figures, it kind of *is*. Her biological father is a deadly disease, a filthy, black plague that indiscriminately kills anything and everything that he has influence over. And he's slowly been killing this world, leaving only the warped and perverted behind, along with a dwindling few innocents for them to victimize. Still, the view is something else, what with them towering so high above it all.

"Wait," she calls out. "How are we this high up? There were only four floors inside the tree house. The rooms have really tall ceilings, but not tall enough to account for *this*!" She gestures out towards the ground that looks so far away. "This… this is more like being on top of a high-rise building, thousands of feet above the ground. The math doesn't add up!"

Boodark nods. "Hey, that's right! And why have I never seen this tree before? I've flown over the Dead Forest for hundreds of years and I *never* noticed it. Surely a tree so tall would stand out amongst the rest."

Tanda just shrugs her shoulders. "Magic? Illusion? Cloaking spell? I cannot tell you. It's not my doing, not my magick. It's exclusively up to the SeeAll Tree to decide who gets to come and go, or who even gets to look upon it. All I can tell you is that if it doesn't wish to be found, it will *not* be found. Oh, and that it randomly changes whenever it feels like it."

Boodark scratches his head in puzzlement. "Huh? Changes? What do you mean, it *changes*?"

The old woman sits down beside them on the swing and peers out over the expanse of the Dead Forest.

"It means," a snippy, sarcastic voice from above calls down, "exactly what she said. It *changes*." They all glance up to see the three Kreeleerians lying on the tree branches, half hidden amongst the multitudes of eyeballs. She knows *exactly* which one of them had spoken, too. Nasty, *rude* Hellcat.

"Oh great," Boodark sneers as he rolls his eyes. "It's the talking hairball, come to spy on us and butt in with his not-soclever repartee. Please, spare us the torment."

And then the inevitable bickering ensues, but Tanda quickly nips it in the bud by threatening to banish them all to the lower levels if they can't 'shut up and behave'. "Ecko and I have many more things to discuss, important things to figure out, and not enough time to accomplish it! So be silent or be gone with you! *All* of you!"

Danika and Caheera, curled up and half asleep, seem to pay no attention to any of it, but Loryss (aka Beelzebub the Hellcat) harrumphs and turns his face away as if he's offended. Poor Boodark scrunches down and quickly 'yes ma'ams' her. Again.

Tanda nods her satisfaction and goes on to explain. "It does not always remain the same… It *changes*. It means that sometimes, like now, there are four floors inside the tree, and other times there are more. Sometimes there's as many as twenty levels, although there has never been less than the four that's present right now. They come and go with the whims of the SeeAll. My sleeping quarters are usually situated between the ground floor and the storage floor."

She stares incredulously at the old woman for several seconds. "Seriously?"

When Tanda just nods her affirmation, she asks, "Well, where do you sleep if your room just comes and goes whenever it wants to? And what if it decides to disappear while you're inside it? That would be *awful*, to go to sleep and then just disappear!"

Tanda laughs and tells her, "It doesn't work like that. It's more like the main rooms get relocated than actually disappear. And sometimes it *does* happen while I'm asleep in my bed. All it means is that sometimes I have to climb down one level of stairs and other times I must descend down six or seven flights." She says it all so blithely, as if self-relocating rooms are no big deal. Apparently, for her it's not. She's had a thousand years to get used to it, after all.

They sit in companionable silence for several minutes as she continues to stare out into the distance, beyond the edge of the Dead Forest and across the expanse of a huge, open field. "I can feel it, the EverGlass. She calls to me from somewhere out there, somewhere in that field, I think. I'm so close now. I should go; I *need* to get to her."

Tanda gets up and changes her seating from the swing to a chair at the table, gesturing for her to follow. "Patience, child. You will be on your way soon enough. In the meantime, I brought you to the roof for a reason. You need to test yourself, test your abilities. Controlling your magic, making it to obey you should be easier now that the Sliver's no longer draining you."

The older woman must see the hesitation and uncertainty on her face because she rushes to assure her that she doesn't expect miracles from her. "I know this is all new to you and you haven't had many opportunities to experiment, what with you having to face one threat after another. I suspect that you've only managed a spell or two. And that's ok. But when you leave on the Morrow, I want to rest easy knowing that you can at least defend yourself. Come, show me what you *can* do, and we'll go from there."

While it comes as a huge comfort to know that she's not yet expected to be in any of the advanced Hogwarts classes, she's still very much unsettled by Tanda's expectations of her...of *everyone's* expectations of her. She hasn't learned jack diddly poop about her magic, unless making weird things happen when she's on the verge of freaking out counts for anything. She's pretty sure it doesn't though, and her heart starts racing at the thought of trying to find and control something inside of her that's so hugely powerful...with an audience, no less. Her breath speeds up and that hazy film descends over her vision. For the first time in days, she longs for one of her 'chill out' pills because she recognizes the signs of the oncoming panic attack.

Boodark, bless his cursed little heart, recognizes her discomfort too, and he knows that he must do something to distract her. "She knows plenty!" he shouts as he climbs up onto the table. He stands in staunch defense of his giant friend, his feet spread apart and hands on his hips as he stares the old woman down. "She's made it this far, hasn't she? That's got to count for something!"

They all ignore Loryss's snide comment. "And *that* tells me she knows nothing but what it means to survive on dumb, blind luck."

Tanda remains quiet as Boodark spins back around to murmur soft, calming words until her breathing eventually slows and she's able to blink the fog from her eyes. "Well done!" She calls out as she claps her hands. "Well done, *both* of you!"

Loryss makes a rude, disapproving noise as he drops from the branches, landing lightly (as cats do) onto the table to confront her. "Well done? What mean you, well done? The childling did nothing but come within inches of a tantrum that could have potentially destroyed us all."

Boodark's lips curl up in a snarl. He's instantly prepared and *very* willing to argue, but Tanda holds her hand up to silence him. She jabs a finger at the insufferable feline and comes back with, "But she didn't destroy us, did she? She stopped it in time and *that,* in itself, is miraculous. You just don't know; you don't understand. You've never seen a Wandelaar come into her magick. You haven't witnessed the chaos and internal volatility that comes along with it."

Her lips tremble and she has to wipe tears from her eyes before she can continue. "My Deidra was an absolute nightmare for the entire first year after she came into her own magick. The amount of damage she caused…. I'll *never* forget it. Everyone was terrified of her. Our people literally scattered and hid when they saw her coming!"

She chuckles and closes her eyes as if she's reliving it all in her mind. After a moment, she opens them back up and tells them, "New Wandelaars need a Soother, someone to calm them when the storms inside themselves become too much to bear. Someone that will remain by their side no matter how tumultuous or perilous the situation. I was that for Deidra. I was her focal point when things became too overwhelming for her."

She turns her head and smiles gently down at Boodark. "*You are Ecko's Soother. You calm her when the storms rage inside of her. You keep her grounded and focused.* It's remarkable what the two of you have accomplished in such a short amount of time, especially under the circumstances. So yes, I meant just what I said. I'll even repeat it... Well done!" Then she focuses her attention on the Hellcat. "Just learning how to keep the magick from spilling out when she's emotional is a triumph. It's all a delicate balance, and it takes tremendous self-control to learn how to be a Mirror Walker. So, you see? Patience is a requirement. We must move slowly, with baby steps. It would do more harm than good to try and rush things now."

But Loryss obviously disagrees. He glares up at the other two Kreeleerians and mutters, "Baby steps. *Baby steps*, she says." Then he jerks his head back down to confront Tanda once more. "There's no time for baby steps; you *know* this! End times are upon us! She must not be coddled and pampered and sheltered. You must push her, Athtandakapootha. You *know* that you must. If she's to be the one that saves us, she must get it under control and learn it all. *Right now!* Before there's no time left *to* learn it!"

The old woman has had enough of his interference. She slaps her hand down on the table as she gets to her feet. "That is quite enough, Loryss! As the Truth Speaker and also as my friend, I value your opinion and your council. But in this, you are wrong. I've had more experience with Mirror Walkers than anyone here, therefore, we will do this my way. I know very well that time is short, but we'll just have to work with what we've got. We'll have to *make* the time. Pushing her too far, too fast, would be a huge mistake that could cost more than a bit of lost time."

Ecko listens to the two of them with rapidly growing annoyance. They're arguing about her like she's not even sitting right here. Like she's a mindless idiot who's incapable of making decisions on her own. She closes her eyes and searches within herself until she finds that electric fire deep down inside. She calls on it, and she finds that it *is* easier to command now that the Sliver is no longer drawing her magic. She studies it as it moves through her, getting a feel for it as it lights up her hands and clouds her vision. The haze over her pupils is so thick, it reminds her of trying to see through the thick blanket of fog that sometimes covered the Sorrow Marshes.

She focuses her attention on the Kreeleerian pain-in-herbutt, only to suck in her breath in wonder at the beauty of him. With *these* eyes, she can see what she assumes is his aura…what *has* to be his aura. And it's magnificent, shimmering with all the brilliance of a moonshine opal. Who would have guessed that such a nasty, obnoxious creature would have such a spectacular aura, such a beautiful soul? Unless…. Perhaps it's all a big show, his surly, sourpuss (haha) nature. Perhaps it's all an act… but then she hears what he has to say next, and she no longer cares how or why the unpleasant creature has such a contradictory aura. "And furthermore, this little… cursed, wingless thing is *not* suitable to be her Soother. Just look at him. He…"

But she doesn't allow him to finish his sentence. "Hey Loryss. How about we practice right now? I'm game if *you* are. Go ahead. Say one more word about Boodark. We'll learn together *exactly* what all I can do."

He spins around, mouth already opened to fire back a retort. He takes one look at her and then spits hisses as he frantically backpedals. In his haste to get away from her, he ends up falling, yowling in alarm, off the table. And apparently, cats do *not* always land on their feet. At least not Kreeleerian ones.

Boodark bursts out laughing as Loryss scrambles to his feet, turns tail, and darts away, back through the trapdoor and down the stairs. She laughs too, until Rage's voice whispers through her mind. *'Aww how cute. Look who thinks she's all grown up and in control.'*

Her magic falters then and begins to recede. "Not this time," she whispers as she draws it back and holds onto it tighter. She lifts her chin in stubborn defiance and ignores how Rage laughs and laughs.

Three hours later and she's beginning to grow tired of his little taunts and his interminable laughter. Tanda's been helping her figure out how to hold onto her magic, even when it wants to shy away. She's been practicing how to guide it to where it's supposed to go and do what she intends for it to do. As a former Soother, Tanda's also been working with Boodark, giving him pointers on how to help calm her and how to talk her down off of figurative emotional cliffs that could end in disaster. Tanda has even managed to teach her a few 'basic' tricks, as she calls them.

Ecko beams with pride at the tiny ball of flames dancing across the palm of her hand, and she realizes just how much the

Sliver had held her back. Not only can she focus better now that it's gone, but she also suffers no ill effects from using so much magic. No headaches, no fatigue… at least not yet anyway. And she's steadily been using her magic for hours now. She spent a long time just conjuring it and then putting it away, only to call upon it again and again. She's always been a firm believer that repetition is key to success. Practice makes perfect and all that. She didn't even begin to get frustrated until she finally moved on to Tanda's 'basic' spells. It took her so long to conjure a 'simple' fireball that she'd started to believe she wouldn't be able to manage it at all. She'd eventually done it though, and she nearly wept at the sight of it.

Rage, of course, could always be trusted to ruin the moment with his mocking laughter. *'You call that a fireball? Look at what the old woman can conjure up. Now **that's** a worthy ball of flames. No one would ever cower before your puny pebble of fire.'*

Although smaller than her mentor's (much, *much* smaller) it still counts as a fireball! So what if it's not a fearsome, flaming sphere the size of a cantaloupe? As far as she's concerned, her little firegrapes of wrath will be just as effective at getting a good campfire going. "Fire spreads you idiot. I don't need big balls. Little ones will work just as well!"

Rage remains silent. Boodark snorts but he doesn't say anything about her talking to herself. He's grown used to her strange habits and her quirky quirks. She does, however, receive many questioning, sidelong glances from Tanda and the two remaining Kreeleerians, glances that she steadfastly ignores. She snaps her hand closed, effectively snuffing out the tiny fireball that she's proudly and affectionately named Grapefire. Having successfully conjured it dozens of times, she decides that she's ready to move on to something else. "Can you teach me how to do that Soul Fire thing?" she asks.

Tanda smiles at her, pleased with the progress they've made. "I can show you how it's done, but perhaps we should wait on that particular lesson. It's a bit more difficult than conjuring simple fire. We really don't have the time to spare for it right now, but you *will* need to learn it as soon as you come back with the EverGlass. You'll need to be able to use Soul Fire on yourself, just in case more of your father's Slivers, or any other unpleasant little nasties, ever find you. And they will. Make no mistake about that. The Lokskell is *always* watching."

She stands up and stretches, her old bones cracking and popping in protest. "The Pitch is fast approaching, and I want us to share a SeeAll session before it's upon us. We need to discuss the foresight. Do you have visions often? Are you able to determine what they mean? Do you have any idea how accurate they are? I need to hear about everything you've seen. And then I'll prepare our Endmeal. I'm getting hungry!"

Boodark's oversized bat ears perk up at the thought of food. Right on time, his stomach lets out a loud rumble, causing the ladies to laugh out loud. Ecko stands up too, rolling her shoulders to ease the tension in them.

"You've done well," Tanda softly praises her. "You seem to have much more control over your emotions, and therefore your magick, than my Deidra had in the beginning of her time as Wandelaar."

Oh, how Rage laughs then. *'Aren't you going to tell her? No? You don't think she needs to know that you keep your emotions and your memories locked up like animals in steel cages in your mind? How about you let me out? I'll tell her for you.'*

She briskly shakes her head to send his words tumbling out of her mind, but she can't block his maniacal laughter. "Shut up," she whispers. She almost loses control of *everything* when he suddenly lashes out in a neurotic fit of biblical proportions. *'LET. ME. OOOUUTT! Let me out or I swear I will tear you apart from the inside out. I don't care if it kills us both!'*

She winces and ducks her head, trying to hide her pained facial expressions from old eyes that see too much. "Go away!" she whispers beneath her breath. And then he starts scream/chanting his litany, *'Let me out! Let me out! Let me out! Let me out!'* Unable to stand one more second of it, she slams her hand down on the table and shouts, "That's enough! Just *SHUT UP!*"

Rage lets out one last satisfied chuckle before he falls silent once more. He'd gotten exactly what he'd wanted, an explosive reaction from her that's witnessed by all those present.

Boodark, bless him, tries to cover for her when Tanda's eyes fly open wide with shock at her seemingly uncalled for outburst. As she waits for an explanation of what had just happened, Boodark takes it upon himself to come to her rescue. He turns to Ecko and shouts back, "No, I *won't* shut up!" Then he spins back around and shrugs helplessly at Tanda. "You see how she talks to me sometimes?" he asks with feigned innocence. He begins to stammer, the words on his tongue tripping over themselves when the old woman quirks an eyebrow at him. "Ya-Yeah, she m,m,meant me. She was t,t,talking to m,me." He bravely stands his ground although he visibly quakes beneath her scrutiny.

"Hhhmmm," Tanda murmurs, her eyes darting from

Boodark to Ecko and then back again. "I'll let it slide for now, but just know that the two of you aren't fooling anyone. I *will* expect answers eventually." She narrows her eyes at Ecko, her face stern and serious as she adds, "I woke up with whispers in my mind this Pale-Morn. I think perhaps they were meant for you. *Be careful which beast you choose to feed, for that is the one that will grow stronger.*" Then she shakes herself like she's coming out of a trance. "Strange, right?"

Boodark's eyes dart to hers because he, too, would like answers. But all she does is press her lips firmly together and nod her acknowledgement that she hears what Tanda's sayings. She makes no promises on *anything* as she picks Boodark up and follows the old woman down the stairs.

"I'm not eating that. There's no *way* I'm eating that! You can't make me." She shoves the bowl further away from herself and leans back in her chair, her arms stubbornly crossed over her chest. The old woman pushes it right back, grunting her impatience. Loryss snickers from across the room and both women turn towards him as they simultaneously shout, "Shut up, Loryss!"

Boodark has excused himself, mumbling something about having to go outside and poop. He's been gone for several minutes though, so she uses that as an excuse to escape Tanda's glaring eyes. She walks to the opened door and shouts, "Boodark! You still ok out here?"

He saunters out from behind a tree stump, fumbling with the fastenings on his pants. "Yep," he says with a grin that should have warned her that he was about to be gross. "Everything came out as expected!" He giggles as she scrunches her face and tells him that he's disgusting. "Speaking of disgusting," he says, "have you eaten all of your eyeballs like a good little girl?"

She gags as they make their way back inside the SeeAll Tree where Tanda's still sitting at the table with the awaiting bowl of said eyeballs. They're just rolling around like googly eyes inside their purple skins, probably trying to figure out why their view of the world has changed so drastically. She shudders, gags, and then shudders again. Just the sight of them is absolutely puke-worthy… and Tanda expects her to eat one of them? Not. Happening.

"I told you, I'm not eating those things. I don't know how *you* can."

The stubborn old woman jabs a bony finger at her. "I can do it because I must. I can do it because it is worth every bite. I have learned important things with the consumption of the SeeAll fruit. *Critical* information. It's how I was able to watch you and send you all those little messages that you so rudely ignored." She reaches over and snatches an eye out of the bowl. "Here. I'll go first to show you how easy it truly is."

And then that freaky old woman shoves the whole thing into her mouth and starts chewing, her cheeks bulging out like a chipmunk's. Unable to turn away, Ecko and Boodark both watch in horrified fascination as she swallows the whole mess down and then daintily wipes her mouth. She levels an exasperated look at them and insists, "I've learned so many things, things that you can't even *fathom,* all because you refuse to endure a tiny bit of unpleasantness…"

The old woman's words are cut short, and her eyes fly open in alarm when Ecko's *entire body* flares up with that bright blue, fluorescent glow that's normally restricted to her hands. "Unpleasantness? Did you just say that I won't endure a bit of *unpleasantness?* Did you *really* just say that to me?" She desperately tries to calm herself, to make it go back to sleep once more.

"Oh, troll turds and pissing pixy penises! Now you've done it!" Boodark curses.

Dimly, she can hear him telling her that she doesn't want to do this, that the old woman didn't mean it like it sounded. He tells her it's not worth all this and she should just eat the blangdang eyeball already. "I'll eat one if you do. I'll even go first!" He's talking nonsense, hoping that the sound of his voice will penetrate and get through to her. He's trying his best to be a good Soother, but this, *this* just may be beyond anything he can sooth, or she can control.

She wraps her arms over her chest, hunches in on herself, and takes deep, calming breaths. Doing everything in her power to suppress it, she visibly trembles from the sheer amount of effort it takes to hold it all in. Rage howls with laughter at her loss of control, even as he snarls to be let out so that he can show the old woman what unpleasantness *really* means.

That's enough to shock some semblance of reason back into her mind. She knows that she doesn't want to hurt Tanda. She doesn't want to hurt anyone. She has to stop this right now or someone *will* get hurt. Unsure if she'll be able to pull it back and suppress it in time, she spins around, jerks the door open and runs out into the Dead Forest. She can't hurt anyone out there; they're all dead already.

She returns within minutes, back to 'normal' and rather proud of the fact that she hadn't decimated any of the trees, even if those trees *are* already dead. Tanda and Boodark watch her with wide, worried eyes as she walks back in and calmly, quietly closes the door behind her.

Tanda opens her mouth to say something, but she holds her hand up to stop her. She pulls her shoulders back and straightens her spine. And then she marches to the table, snatches an eyeball from the bowl, and shoves it into her mouth whole, just like Tanda had done. If she finds the experience as disgusting as she'd thought it would be, she refuses to let it show. She chews and swallows and then sits down in her chair, and she never once shows a hint as to what she's feeling.

Boodark walks across the table, his shoulders slumped, and his head hung low in dejection to select his own eyeball, deftly impaling the chosen one onto a claw. A deal is a deal, and Boodark the Honest is no liar, but at this precise moment he wishes that he *was*.

It takes significantly more effort for him to consume his gruesome treat. He's so much smaller than the ladies are, so's forced to eat his in several bites, watching the eyeball the whole time as *it* watches *him*. When it's done and the last bite is swallowed, he looks up at Ecko and grins as he smacks his lips together. "I don't know why we put up such a fight. That was actually quite tasty." And then he belies every word he just spoke as his own eyes roll back in his head and he falls down in a dead faint. Poor little guy. She knows exactly how he feels, and she doesn't blame him one little bit for taking a timeout from reality. She only wishes she could do the same.

"Where'd you get the meat?" Boodark asks several hours later as he watches Ecko fill their plates with thick steaks and healthy portions of mixed, chunky-cut veggies. His little bat nose twitches spasmodically as she sets his in front of him. "Please tell me we're having Kreeleerian for Endmeal and not one of those cute, floofy things from upstairs."

He's feeling extra snarky and sullen because the nasty old kitty cat had made fun of him for fainting and sleeping through the entire 'SeeAll session' as Tanda called it. Not only had he missed their shared visions, but he'd also missed out on the chore of scrubbing the swamp filth from their clothes, the lucky brat. Although grateful for the latter, he's steadily bemoaning the former. He's such a nosy little busybody and he just can't stand not being privy to all the gossip and going-ons.

Tanda tsk tsks at him. "We most certainly will *not* be dining on Kreeleerians or Na-Loofs. Not now, nor ever. This actually comes from a large fruit. If it's harvested before it becomes ripe, it very much resembles meat in texture and flavor. It's an excellent substitute. Go on, taste it. Tell me what you think. You too, Ecko."

Boodark takes a bite and doesn't say another word as he begins to scarf. She slices off a piece and holds it up to examine it. "We have something similar on Earth called a Jackfruit. I read that it tastes like pulled pork. I don't know how true that is though. I've never tried it because it doesn't grow where I live… lived." She pops it into her mouth without hesitation because really, how much worse could it be than an eyeball fruit? "Wow! This is really, really good! It *does* taste like steak."

She samples the vegetables and sighs with genuine pleasure. Even though they're unfamiliar, they taste like heaven on her tongue. It feels like it's been months since she's had fresh veggies, indeed fresh anything. And when they've all cleaned their plates (licked clean in Boodark's case) and Tanda brings out little fruit tarts for dessert, she really *does* think she's died and gone to Heaven. This time she joins her piggy little friend in eating so much that *she* almost goes into a food coma.

Tanda laughs at the pair of them struggling desperately to keep their eyes open (just like small children are wont to do after a large meal) but they're epically losing the battle as they keep nodding off. "Go to bed, you two. It's been a long, full Pale and the Morrow will arrive sooner than you will wish it to."

She tries to protest, saying that the least she can do is clean up the meal mess and wash the dishes. But she mumbles it with her eyes closed, making the old woman chuckle again. "Go to bed, child. I've got this under control."

Without another word, she pushes herself to her feet, scoops an already snoring Boodark up, and stumbles to the rug by the fire where she drops down without even covering herself with a blanket. And then it's lights out for the dynamic duo.

We Hates Her/We Wants Her

Krispin

Back in control of Krispin's body once more, it turns them around and heads for home. Trudging through the cold slime of the swamp waters, it contemplates this interesting new development, this shocking but delightful situation. For the first time ever, it is completely ensconced inside the host's mind... without it first having been pickled with rotgut, grog water. It feels good in here, right. This is much more preferable, being in control of a body that's unencumbered by drink, so much easier to operate. It feels like home in here, like this body and the mind within it was

designed specifically to become its host. It will never find another that fits so well, one that already had such depraved and perverted tendencies even before it had begun to influence him.

The only fault that it's found is that this body contains very little magick. Brute strength, speed, and agility aplenty, but very nearly a null in magicks. Also, his stubbornness is vexing. As close in temperament as the two of them are, it should have been a simple feat to convince Krispin to let it in, to allow the merging. But the man's obduracy blinds his eyes and plugs his ears. He cannot accept what his eyes show him. He cannot hear the filthy nothings whispered into his ears. It's been working on him for ages it seems, floating along beside him Pitch and Pale, continuously whispering in his ears... conditioning him, urging him to let it in. To accept it.

So far, all those efforts have been in vain. It still has not been granted permission for the merging. And yet, here it is, somehow installed within the host's mind even though Krispin is sober, completely free of alcoholic influences. It finds that it quite enjoys being inside Krispin's body when he is at his best... even if his mind is a bit rattled by whatever that creature had blasted him with. And oh! What a magnificent creature she had been! Never in its wildest imaginings would it have ever guessed that the breathtaking Samara had a sister. A twin even more powerful than she! A hundred times more powerful! It had tasted the magick on the very air that surrounded her, even before she'd unleashed all that impressive magickal might.

Thankfully, it had decided to keep its distance while Krispin tried (and failed miserably) to subdue the female. It had held back, hovering amongst the trees and the moss and the bracken of the swamp line, far enough away that her wave of power hadn't reached it. But it had felt the shockwaves on the air, tasted the magick in the slipstream. And in that very moment, it decided that it now wants the lovely Ecko instead. Oh, it still wants Samara, but it no longer wishes for her to be host to its own mate. It will take Samara for other purposes. It will fuck her and then it will eat her, just as it had done to its own pearl egg-mate twin, way back when they were still in the incubation process. Or perhaps it will take her and make her part of their lady collection. Or... Oh! This is delicious! Perhaps it won't even bother merging with this stubborn blue beast, after all. Perhaps it will just take both females, Ecko and Samara. One for its mate and one for its own host. Once the two of them undergo the merging with the sisters, they could even keep Krispin around for playtime fun. He does have a beautiful, luscious body, after all. Strong, durable, and always hard, always ready to act on his own wicked desires. It feels itself beginning to respond, Krispin's dick growing rock hard to the images of the two Wyrms merging with the sister twins and all the debauchery that would come after... when the sisters come together as sister-lovermates.

When Krispin regains consciousness, he's no longer lying upon his back at the edge of the swamp. He's upright, walking through the Sorrow Marshes on his own two feet. It's happening again. His body is moving on its own, without him being aware of it... without him telling it to! He tries to think back, tries to remember.

"Ecko!" he snarls. He'd thought that he was dead. *Truly* dead. Samara's disgusting sister had blasted him with a wave of magic so powerful that he can only wonder why he's *not* dead.

"Want her."

Krispin whirls around, turning in a complete circle before immediately and instinctively crouching down in a defensive position. "Who said that? Who's there?" he growls.

"Hmmmm. Can you hear me?"

"Where are you?" Krispin shouts as he looks up, searching the bare tree limbs towering above his head.

"You do hear me, you really do! This is new; this is progress! We are both in this body, both at full awareness simultaneously, and yet we have not done the merging. How? How is this possible?"

"Who are you?" Krispin shouts. "*Where* are you? How are you speaking in my head? GET OUT!"

"Calm yourself host, and I will gladly introduce myself, although some part of you already knows me. Come, let us continue on our way as we converse. Let us get back to our lovely ladies. We mustn't keep them waiting."

Krispin's eyes narrow dangerously as realization and sudden clarification sets in. "It was *yooouu!* All this time it's been *you* killing those women, doing those… things to them!"

"Yes!" it cries out amid its giggles. "Yes, it was me! Or us, I should say. My consciousness and your body. Although, as I've already stated, some part of you was aware of the shenanigans… aware and agreeable to the things we did together, the fun we shared. If you hadn't wanted it, I could not have forced you, drunk or not. It was your body that we used, after all. I had to have your permission, at least on some small, molecular level."

"Gah! Get out of my head!" Krispin roars. "Get out, get out, get out!"

"Oh, do calm down. Don't get us all worked up and excited with no way to unwind ourselves! There's nothing left for us to play with in this dreadful bog."

"What the fuck are you talking about? Why are you in my head? Explain yourself!"

"Certainly. I'm a Wyrm."

"A worm? I have *worms* in my head?"

It laughs at his outrage and obvious disgust. "No, fool. Not worms… I am a Wyrm, an ancient race of incorporeal, highly intelligent and perspicacious beings, descended from the dragons of old."

An image of some sort of ethereal dragon/serpent creature materializes in Krispin's mind, showing him just what the Wyrm looks like. It seems to be made of wisps of smoke, its body incorporeal and translucent.

"You see? I am a spiritual being, and if I wish to live on the physical, materialistic plane… and I do so love my physical pleasures, then I must take on a host body. Not just any host; it must be strong, so very strong. Powerful enough to survive the merging."

The image shifts and zooms in on a tangled knot of ropey tendons, veins, and arteries that pulse and throb right at its center. It looks to be a bit more solid than the rest of the creature, more substantial somehow.

"When we undergo the merging, our souls will align. My Wyrmknot will unravel and then wrap around your spirit to form a new knot, and then the two of them will fuse together. We will still be individuals, but we will also be one."

"Merging?" Krispin snarls. "Merging? There will be no merging!"

"Oh, there will be. I'm just not sure who I wish to merge with anymore. You, or your mate, Samara."

"What the fuck do you know about Samara!"

"I know plenty. Enough to know that she has more magick in her scrumptious little toes than you do in your entire body. Enough to know that she would survive the merging with my own incredibly powerful mate. Oh yes, I've been watching the two of you for quite some time. I had to be certain. You see, I've been searching for a host for a long, long time. Not just for myself, but one for my mate as well. I thought I'd found the perfect matches for us when I came across you and Samara. You were to become my host and she was to be host to my mate. It had to be that way, for our females are much more powerful than we are. If my mate tried to merge with you, it would just burn your soul up, and you would be lost to us. But Samara, oh, now she is a worthy vessel for my mate."

Krispin goes dangerously still, like a predator stills just before the killing strike. "Is that what happened to her? Did your mate…. infect her? Is that why she's left me? Tell me, *Wyrm*, before I rip you right out of my skull and crush your knot into a bloody pulp!"

Delighted giggles ripple through his mind as the thing laughs at him.

"Not at all, Krispin! Not at all. I have no idea where your mate is, just as I have no clue as to where my own mate is. Seems I've misplaced her. Again. She ran from me much the same as Samara has run from you."

Deep, rumbling snarls and growls erupt for Krispin's mouth. "I'll get her back!"

"Yes, you will. And I will help you, just as you will help me retrieve my own headstrong, wayward female."

Krispin neither agrees, nor does he disagree. He's quiet, thinking things through as he wades through the sludge-water… He suddenly stops walking, lifts his head up, and sniffs the air. "This is wrong! Where are you taking me?" he shouts.

"I told you. We're going back to our ladies. Don't you miss our beauties?"

"Yes. No. Yes. I don't know! I don't care about them right now!" He spins around to retrace his steps, to go back to the edge of the swamp where he'd had his encounter with Samara's filthy slut sister. Where she'd swatted him down like he was nothing more than a shit-fly bug.

He's seething, snarls of rage rumbling around in his chest as he thinks of her, of what he'll do when he gets his hands on her again. "I don't care about dead whores! I have to catch back up to Ecko. I have to punish her. I have to hurt her. I have to fuck her. I have to sink my teeth into her and fuck her and bleed her and fuck her! I will torture her for *ages* before I grant her permission to die!" He's shouting from the force of his fury, trembling as the rage turns to lust within him. He's so hot and hard, so fucking furious! He's desperate for relief. He needs to pound into something, either with his fists or with his dick. He doesn't care which. Either. Both. He needs to find an outlet. He needs release. He stomps onward. He *needs* to find Ecko right now and fill her dirty little…

Krispin's body suddenly locks up, freezing him in place. "What the fuck is going on?" he roars.

"You cannot hurt her, at least not yet and especially not in the way that you will try to go about it. Brute force and a hot head will not win us the female. I am thinking. Evaluating. Calculating. Planning out our best course of action on how we will take this sister of Samara's, this magnificent Ecko. I am also going over our options on what we shall do with her once we do have her in our clutches. She is incredibly gifted. It will be difficult to restrain her, to hold on to her. We must proceed with great care, or we risk losing her. We risk losing our very lives going up against one such as her. Carefully, cautiously my rambunctious friend/host. Let us return to our ladies. We will learn all we can of the sister, search for weaknesses. Let us play with our dolls, find release within them while we work out our plan of action."

Krispin's body pivots and moves in the direction that the Wyrm wishes him to go in. He moves forward several paces before he takes back the control, slamming his feet down and turning around once more.

Over the next several minutes, the two opposing entities that reside within the same body have a brief but intense battle of wills. Krispin takes a few steps in the direction that will bring him closer to Ecko, and the Wyrm inevitably stops him, spins him around, and forward-marches his stiff, protesting legs in the direction of home and dead whore dolls. If anyone were to come upon him at this moment, they would think him mad and deranged. He's not so sure they wouldn't be right.

Somehow, he gains exclusive control of his arms, and he reaches out and grabs onto the nearest tree to stop his forward momentum. Meanwhile, the Wyrm holds onto its control of his lower extremities and continues its commands to move their body forward. He must look ridiculous with his arms wrapped tight around the tree whilst his legs steadily churn in a forward march.

"This is ridiculous. You must yield! You must listen to reason. You are not a dumb beast. You must know that we will not survive a hasty, rushed attack on this creature! She is not like our other females. You will die!"

"I do not fear death! I welcome it. It is preferable to a life without my mate. Ecko is to blame for everything. She took her from me, and I *will* have my revenge on her." His anger lends him strength and he, at last, regains control of his limbs. He stomps through the marsh… in the direction that *he* wishes to go in, punching out at GloomDooms as he passes by them. Loving when the atrophied limbs shatter and the frozen, petrified heads roll off the stumps of their body's. Relishing the sound of the resulting splash they make as they splat down into the muddy water. He's mentally gloating, proud that he'd won the battle…

"But not the war."

… when he suddenly stops in his tracks. Is that…?

Laughter, delighted euphoric laughter.

There's a body stuffed into a hole in one of the half rotten swamp trees. A naked, contorted body with its legs and one arm sticking out of the crevice, making it appear as if the tree is alive and having itself a snack. He glances around the swamp in confusion as suspicion sets in his mind. "Did you do this?" he asks.

More laughter. "Yes! Yes, we did! We found her as we were stumbling around in endless circles, just as we were beginning to succumb to the spirit of the marshes. Our desire for her is what snapped us out of the spirit's influence and saved us from its clutches. We dared not take too long playing with her, for the longer we remain in this cursed bog, the more we chance becoming a permanent occupant. I have no wish to remain here forever, and I know that you do not wish it any more than I. So, we played with her for just a tiny, short while. Such a sad thing, to not have enough time to properly adore one such as her. When we were finished, we stuffed her in there, we hid her away just in case someone else came along and saw her and decided that they too wanted to play with our doll. Then we became so distracted by thoughts of the Ecko female and our struggle against one another that we forgot all about the lovely little thing!"

"I don't remember any of that."

But then the Wyrm shows it to him. It replays the scene inside his mind, showing him exactly what he/it had done to the unfortunate woman. And now that he's seen it, he finds that he *does* remember. He recalls the taste of the swamp's mud on her lips, recalls watching the life leave her face as she stared off into the shadows of the marsh. She hadn't cared that he/it had done those things to her, hadn't struggled or cried. She'd never made a single sound.

"Her mind was already gone anyway, not nearly as much fun as we have with the ones that are in complete control of their mental facilities."

Krispin reaches out and grasps onto a tiny, delicate foot and pulls the female out of the tree, his brow furrowed as she plops down into the mud with a loud squelching sound.

"But look at her; just look at her! Don't you see the beauty in what we do when we work together? Isn't she a most excellent specimen? We can take her back with us, make her one of our own. Good work, host! You've led us back here for a reason. You want to make her into our new dolly!"

His eyes rove over her body. She *is* lovely, he can't deny that. Filthy, but still incredibly desirable. Her skin is palest white, her frozen lips tinted blue… He leans in and presses his mouth to those soft, cool lips, sighing in pleasure as he slips his tongue inside to taste her.

"Yeesss, we want her. Yes, we do!"

He pulls back and looks down at her. "What should I do?" he asks her. "Should I listen to it? Do I go home and let it work out a plan to capture the slut sister? Do I carry you home with us and introduce you to the others? Or do I say fuck the Wyrm, leave you here to rot, and go after her… find her and fuck her and punish her instead?"

He lifts her up into his arms, cradling her close as he leans in to listen to her whispered reply.

"You want out of the Sorrow Marshes? You wish to go home with us? Is that it?"

"She does, oh she wants it so bad! Can't you feel her desire for us?"

He leans down and presses a gentle kiss to her temple, right at the corner of her eye, his tongue darting out to taste the tiny trickle of blood that had leaked out and dried there. "I'll save you, lover," he whispers as he turns and heads back to his/their doll collection. "I'll take you far away from here."

"Yes, Krispin! Yes! Hurry!" Their cock has never been so hard before.

"Show me," Krispin growls. "Show me again what we did to her. Show me what we did to them all... every second that you were inside of me. I want to remember everything. And then you can fill me in on *exactly* what it will mean if I allow the merging. Oh, and know that I have no intention of letting Ecko live long enough to become host to your mate. She will pay for her sins against me. She will suffer for all that Samara suffered. We hate her for *that* most of all."

"But we wants her!"

"We hates her."

"We wants her!"

"Yes, we do," Krispin agrees. "We do wants her. But we hates her."

"Agreed. We can hate her and want her at the same time. And we can argue it all out later... We will negotiate, compromise, work out a peace between us and then figure out what to do to her once we have her tied up in our lair. But you do know... we can fuck the things that we hate. We can fuck all the things. And we do soo want to fuck the Ecko creature, even though we hates her."

"Agreed," Krispin snarls as he runs with his new lover/doll tenderly cradled in his arms, his long, powerful legs eating up the miles between the Sorrow Marshes and his home.

A.C. Mooney

The Field of Screams and Broken Dreams

Ecko

Boodark peppers her with rapid-fire question after question as she removes their dried garments from Tanda's clothesline. "Come on, Ecko, talk to me! What happened? What did you see?"

She hands him the tiny pair of pants that she'd made for him, smiling a little at the memory of how happy he'd been to get new clothing. "Well, I saw Sephyr," she nonchalantly tells him and presses her lips together to keep herself from laughing at his excited yelp.

"You saw the Darkling? She's alive? Is she ok? Did those wackadoo, hissing anomalies honor their promises and get her back to her clan? *Talk* female!"

For a brief moment, she contemplates teasing him further, but she just can't do it. She knows how much he'd come to love their tiny friend and that he's been just as worried about her as she has. "Yeah, they got her back home a lot faster than it took us to get out of the swamp. She's doing good, I think. They're keeping her asleep most of the time though, which makes sense. It keeps her from being in pain while her body heals. I think she'll be better in no time. Her mate is taking good care of her."

It's not *exactly* true, but it isn't enough of a lie to stop her from telling it. Bracken *is* taking good care of her, and she *will* get better, but she's going to have a lot of painful days between now and 100% healed. She doesn't say any of that to Boodark though. Why make him worry more than he already is? And besides, he already knows just how broken she was. He knows that it'll be a long road to full recovery.

Tears fill her eyes when the tears fill *his* eyes and roll down his wrinkled, leather face. She doesn't say a word though as he spins around and marches off to hide his emotions. He wants so badly to appear tough at all times.

Giving him the space that he needs to get himself back under control, she carries the clothes inside to fold and replace back into her backpack. Now all she has to do is find room for them. Thinking back to last night, she grins as she reorganizes her recently restocked supplies. After their SeeAll session, and after making certain that Tanda hadn't wanted her help with preparing dinner, she'd dropped down to the rug before the fireplace and dumped her belongings out of her bag. After setting her water bottles aside so that she could refill them, she began the chore of inventorying her pitifully low food supply.

As if she read her mind, Tanda had called out, "Don't worry, child. I have supplies for you, more than you'll be able to carry, I'm sure. I'll not send you out there without food." The stubborn woman had then given her a stern glare as she warned, "Don't even try to argue about this. I have more than enough to share, you know that. Besides, don't you have enough to worry about without trying to figure out where your next meal is coming from?"

She knew that the old woman was right, but she hadn't been happy about it. She couldn't refuse the help though; she was in no position to do so. She'd been so stressed about Boodark going hungry on those last few days of their journey. It'll be nice to take food off her worry list, at least for a while. Boodark the Ravenous is *always* hungry.

This morning, Tanda had made good on her word by providing them with enough provisions to see them through at least another week… even taking into consideration Boodark's voracious appetite. She hadn't stopped with food either. The kindhearted woman had also provided them with medical supplies. Herbal remedies, tonics, salves, and spiddersilk gauze bandages now take up even more of the limited space in her bag.

She crams her clothing in wherever they'll fit and forces the bulging backpack closed. Then she straps the bag to her back, the heavy weight of it more of a comfort to her than a burden. Outside this magic tree, a harsh world awaits, with Dangers Untold and Hardships Unnumbered, and she is thankful for anything that will make her journey through it easier. There's nothing left to do now but say goodbye… and break the news to someone who's bound to get angrier than one of Texas's insanely hostile red wasps.

She had prepared herself for Boodark's explosive anger, foul curse words, and a fierce fight of epic proportions. What she hadn't prepared herself for was his broken-hearted tears and soulwrenching sobs.

"Don't cry, Boodark! Please don't cry. You know it's for the best. Tanda will take good care of you, and you'll have all the food you can eat." Nothing she says phases him. He merely continues lying face down in the dirt, wailing in distress.

"Ugh, put it out of our misery!" Loryss yells over the incessant bleating.

"I won't be gone long, Boodark!" She's crying now too. She'd known that trying to leave him behind would be difficult, but this is breaking her heart.

He lifts his head up and looks at her, tears literally pouring from his enormous green eyes. "You would leave me behind? I knew it! I knew that I was nothing but a burden to you. Stupid Boodark, stupid! To think that anyone could ever care for you!"

She kneels down in the dirt beside him and insists, "That is not true, and you know it! Look at me, Boodark. I can't protect you… I can't even protect myself! I almost died when that blue creature was crushing you under his foot. I can't lose you. I can't!"

She stands back up and wipes the tears off her face. She strengthens her resolve and firms up her voice. "You'll be able to protect yourself once your wings grow back. Until then, you need to stay here where you'll be safe. I love you, Boodark the Cherished, and I won't risk your life. Not for anything. I'll be back as soon as possible."

She turns to leave but spins back around when something hits her square in the middle of her back. Her mouth drops open in shock as she's immediately pelted in the belly with an eyeball fruit.

She watches in disbelief as it bounces off her and rolls away.

Ah, here it is, the angry theatrics. "Stop it, Boodark!" she shouts as he throws another one so hard that it splats onto her shirt, the abused fruit crying eyeball juice all over her.

"Who's going to protect *you,* you big dummy? I as much saved you from that blue man as you did me. In fact, I saved you first! Without me saving you, you couldn't have saved me, and then neither one of us would be saved! We'd *both* be dead!" He lobs another missile at her as he forces the words out from between his gritted teeth. "We save each other; that's what we do! And I am *not* helpless!"

She ducks and dodges five more flying eyeballs before she shouts, "Alright, alright! You win. You *did* save me first. I didn't mean to imply that you're helpless, I know that you can take care of yourself. I just…"

One last eye-bomb smacks into her, stopping her explanation. "I don't want to hear it, Ecko. Just march your big butt back inside and get my beddy-bye basket!"

She turns to go back inside and the moment she's out of his sight, she lets the grin form on her lips. She'd seriously been dreading making her way without him.

Tanda laughs and steps out to intercept her. She'd obviously been prepared for this very outcome because she holds Boodark's belongings in her hands. "You didn't really think that would work, did you?" she asks, her lips twitching with suppressed laughter.

So, she shrugs her backpack off and forces his things into the already overfilled bag, the two outfits Tanda had generously given to him, his sweet pea body wash, and the last granola bar that she'd been leaving for him. She re-shoulders the backpack, loops the beddy-bye basket's handle over her neck, and then reaches down to lift him up. She can't resist giving him a little apology hug before she settles him into his basket. She turns to thank Tanda for everything and to say her goodbyes, but the old woman stops her by informing her that she, along with several Na-Loofs, would be traveling with them for a short way.

"But I thought you couldn't leave? Won't you get old… umm old*er*?" she asks.

Tanda lifts up the large basket that she's filled with food and milk to distribute throughout the Dead Forest. "I may wander as high as the SeeAll branches reach and as far as its roots stretch. As long as I remain within its boundaries, I remain under its protections. Beyond its reach is when I begin to age. We'll walk with you as far as we can." Then she lets out that piercing whistle to call the Na-Loofs and sets off at a brisk pace, trusting that all who wish to come along will fall in behind her.

The SeeAll Tree's roots must extend in a radius of epic, mind-boggling proportions because Tanda is able to accompany them for about a mile… which makes sense when taking into consideration how massive the tree is. It would need a root system large enough to support its gargantuan stature. As they walk, Tanda passes items out for the Na-Loofs to distribute, bowls of milk and water and small satchels filled with fruits, vegetables, and nuts. They dart about, delivering the items and bringing back the emptied bowls that they had left the previous Pale.

Boodark's had time to think about how he'd almost been left behind, and now he's questioning the why's of her decision to go on alone. "Did you see something?" he suddenly asks as he glances up at her. "In your eyeball visions," he adds when she merely looks at him in confusion. "Did you see something bad happen in your visions? I'm not going to cause you to get hurt, right?"

Ah, now he's second guessing his decision to throw a fit in order to force her to bring him along. He doesn't want to put her in harm's way anymore than *she* wants *him* in danger. Sweet little guy.

"No. After you fainted, all I saw was Sephyr, which I already told you about, and some jumbled mess about flowers and webs and poison. Oh, and a spider. Tanda and I discussed it. She said that she's certain that it pertains to the EverGlass, but neither one of us could figure out what the vision meant."

He huffs angrily. "Couldn't you have just looked for answers in your Night Pearl? And why does everyone keep saying I fainted? I did *not* faint! I was merely overtired from the ordeal of keeping *you* calm all Pale. It's not easy being your Soother, you know!"

Tanda and Ecko both quickly look in opposite directions. They know that if their eyes meet, they'll burst into laughter and neither one of them wants to hurt his feelings. "You're right,

Boodark." she tells him as she stares off into the trees. "I'm sure that *is* hard on you. Forgive me for implying otherwise."

A tiny choking sound comes from the old woman's direction but when he jerks his head around to look, her face is calm and serene, without a smirk in sight.

"You females are too soft. You should tell it like it is, the sensitive one be damned," Loryss calls down from the branches of a nearby tree.

"What are *you* doing here?" Boodark snarls. "Go back home, house pet. No one wants you here."

The Hellcat yawns, giving the impression of being bored and unconcerned with Boodark's inferior opinion. "I thought it prudent that a male with… a stronger constitution than you yourself possess accompany the women. Just in case."

Boodark sucks in an outraged breath. "I'll have you know; I possess a warrior's mighty constitution! I'm fierce and brave and… I'm *savage*! You're nothing but a mewling house cat, an old lady's pet, no offense Miss Tanda! I bet you wouldn't have survived one single Pale in the Sorrow Marshes! What are you going to do? Hiss at the danger? Yeah, that'll keep the females safe for sure!"

Tanda stops walking and turns to face them. "Stop it, you two. Loryss, why must you antagonize him?"

The cat creature lithely jumps to the ground and replies in a haughty voice, "I am the Truth Speaker. I speak the truth. It's what I do."

Caheera and Danika hop down beside their male companion. "Some truths don't need to be said aloud, brother. You merely enjoy the reaction," says the blue/purple one that looks like it belongs in the ocean.

Loryss hisses and swipes a paw at her. "Bite your tongue, Caheera! 'Tis none of your concern!" Well, that answers two of her questions. The females *can* speak, and Caheera is the mermaid wannabe. Which means that the white, feathered one is Danika.

Tanda loudly and exaggeratedly clears her throat before the argument can escalate further. "This is as far as we go, I'm afraid. Just a few hours more and you'll leave the Dead Forest and enter the Field of Screams and Broken Dreams. It is, unfortunately, just as unpleasant as it sounds. Don't let anything you hear get to you. Don't even listen to it."

She studies them both in all seriousness, first Boodark and then her. "Take care of one another. Get there, get the EverGlass, and get back to the SeeAll just as fast as you can. My visions have been unclear as of late, but they've all taken on a foreboding that I cannot lightly dismiss. I feel the Lokskell's eyes are upon us... I fear that he will make a move against you. I'm sorry Ecko. I would go with you if only I could."

"That's why we came along." Caheera says as she moves in closer. When all eyes turn to her, she adds, "Danika says that we need to gift the new Wandelaar with some added protections."

She glances around at her feline companions and then cheerily adds, "Right! I guess I'll go first." Then she lowers her head, bites down on one of the scales over her heart, and begins to tug at it. "Er, gah, ra, ooff, aahhh" Unintelligible, nonsensical sounds ensue for a moment, but then she gives a sharp yowl of pain as the scale finally pulls free of her skin. "For you," Caheera proudly mumbles around the purple/blue iridescent disk in her mouth.

She leans down, holds her hand out, and accepts the offering (strange though it may be.) She's a bit flustered over what she's just witnessed, and even more so when she sees that the Kreeleerian is bleeding ever so slightly from the new bald spot on her chest. Before she can remark on it, Danika performs her own extraction to donate to the cause. Instead of a scale, a white feather from her left wing is plucked and offered.

Boodark gives Loryss the stink eye as he waits for whatever oddity *he'll* contribute. "Great!" He grumbles as the Hellcat nonchalantly makes his way over to them. "Here he comes with his 'I'm better than you and my butt don't smell like poo' attitude. Is this *really* necessary?"

Loryss sits back on his haunches, hacks a couple times, and then coughs up a slender, two-inch-long bone. It looks very similar to a fish bone, sharply pointed on one end and with a small, perpendicular ridge of thicker bone on the other end. She wants to refuse the gift in the worst way. What could she possibly do with a scale, a feather, and a disgusting bone? A puked-up bone, at that. But she doesn't refuse it, and she doesn't let on that she finds it absolutely revolting to pick up his gift of regurgitated garbage.

Loryss looks suspiciously disappointed when he doesn't get a reaction from her, but Boodark, good old Boodark can always be trusted in delicate situations. He's steadily going on and on about how stupid, not to mention how unsanitary, the male cat's gift is.

"Stop, Boodark. A gift is a gift and should be appreciated, whether you find value in it or not." When his mouth pops open to let loose his ire upon *her*, she quickly adds, "Not only should you appreciate a gift, but you should also *always* try to reciprocate in kind. I'm sure you'll find something of equal… uh, value to bring back for Loryss."

His eyes twinkle and he grins mischievously the moment that her meaning dawns on him. "You're absolutely right! Thank you, Loryss," he croons, but everyone present can clearly see that his mind's on what he'll be bringing back as a thank you gift. She grins briefly at his antics and then thanks the Kreeleerians herself as she opens up a pocket on her backpack to store the peculiar presents in.

Danika, who has not said a single word up until now, pads over to stop her. "Keep them close, at the ready." she says sotto voce. Her voice sends chills tickling up and down her spine, and she has no choice but to look into the black galaxy eyes that peer intently up at her. *"You shall need every advantage available to you. Dismiss these gifts not, for they may save your lives. You will know precisely when each one is needed. Now, come closer. See clearly what I show you. You need to memorize this symbol. It is the activation instructions that will trigger the magick in the objects that we've given to you. You will need to trace this rune onto your palm, just as Athtandakapootha did when she used the bubble-speak to warn you of the Sliver."*

Ecko squats down and scratches out the simple rune in the dirt. *"That's it. Practice drawing it in the dirt, for you must not get it wrong, but know that you must only trace it onto your skin when you are certain that you're ready for it. Once the rune is completed on your palm, your magic will seek to do your bidding. Meaning, it will immediately move to fulfill the activation, for that is what you will be commanding it to do. That is when you will take the appropriate gift in hand and place it directly onto the rune. Arise now, Adrina, and say your goodbyes without further delay. Danger approaches."*

Ecko blinks as her eye refocus. Drawn into the dirt all around where she's squatting is the Activate rune, although she only recalls having practiced it once. Boodark's calling her name, and by the slightly panicked sound of his voice, it's obvious that he's been doing so for some time. She stands up and glances around, taking notice of how everyone is staring at her…even the Na-Loofs. "What? Why's everyone looking at me?" she asks with a nervous flutter in her belly.

Boodark, naturally, is the one that snarkily answers her. "Well, you and the winged wonder over there were giving each other the stare down when you suddenly dropped down and started playing in the dirt. It was weird, even by your standards!"

Tanda picks up her basket of empty bowls and tells him, "They were mind speaking. That is Danika's preferred way of communicating."

Ecko turns back to stare at Danika, trying to ease her confusion. "All that happened in my mind?" she asks and the Kreeleerian dips her head in affirmation. "Trippy," she mutters under her breath. Instead of sealing the gifts up in a pocket on her bag, she tucks them into Boodark's beddy-bye basket… up under his t-shirt blanket.

Tanda laughs as she agrees, "It *is* unsettling at first, but you will get used to it. Now, we must say goodbye and be on our separate ways. The sooner your task is completed, the sooner you can get back to the SeeAll Tree. And we *will* be discussing what Boodark meant when he asked why you didn't consult the Night pearl for answers. I was not aware that the Pearls serve as oracle. We will have to explore this…. But for now, just stay safe, you two." She reluctantly turns to make her way back home.

"Ahem, excuse me, Miss Tanda, ma'am?" Boodark quietly interposes. "Would you happen to know in which direction the Tangled Wood lies, and perhaps how far it is from here?" He glances around at the dead trees and adds, "Everything looks the same from down here at ground stomper level."

The old woman's eyes grow mournful as she points to the left. "The Field of Broken Dreams lies that way." Then she turns and gestures towards the right. "The Tangled Woods are about a Pale's walk in that direction."

Boodark's ears droop in disappointment as he mutters, "That's what I thought. Thank you." He situates himself more comfortably in his basket. "Let's get going. Ecko. The sooner we find this EverGlass, the sooner we can move on to other things."

Boodark's been squirming around for the past twenty minutes, as if he can't get comfortable. "Do you think that eyeball I ate can still see? Is it looking at the inside of my belly right now?"

She raises her eyebrows at him and demands, "What kind of question is that? Of course, it can't see anything. It's probably completely digested by now."

He squirms again and the lightbulb comes on in her mind. "You have to go to the bathroom, don't you?" she asks.

He looks up at her and nods, his brows drawn up in a worried frown. His voice lowers to a whisper, "Do you think it'll look at me bum when I poop it back out?"

Absolutely disgusted, she lifts him out of his basket and sets him on the ground. "Get out of here, you nasty little freak. Hurry up and take care of your business." She lowers herself to the ground and leans against a boulder, resting her legs and her back while she waits.

He reappears a few minutes later and throws a victorious fist up in the air. "Let me assure you, that is one eyeball that won't be seeing anything else… ever again!"

She rolls her own eyes as she picks him back up. "You're so gross," is all she has to say, but she grins anyway because he's laughing like a juvenile. "Sooo," she hesitantly begins after a few minutes of silence has passed. "Why did you ask Tanda about the Tangled Woods? Is that… Is that where your family is?"

Boodark nods his head, his eyes lowered as he fiddles with his t-shirt blanket. "Yes," he whispers. "Our home lies deep in the Tangled Wood. I thought… well, I had hoped that we could take a roundabout route so that I could check on things, but it's just too far out of the way." He jerks his head up and his eyes are bright with frustrated tears. "If I just had my damn wings, I could go and be back within a matter of a couple hours! Oohh, when I catch up to those fooking Madar-gens, I'm going to rip their wings off and shove them…"

She interrupts his tirade with a shocked gasp at the foul language. Not that she isn't used to it. It's the *way* he's doing it. Oh, he spews curses aplenty, but his expletives aren't *real* swear words so she never pays them any mind. She just can't take phrases like *Oh, troll turds! Flaming fairy farts! and Elfslugs and Earwax!* seriously. She just can't. But *this* kind of swearing…he's very upset, and he's *scared*. And it tears at her heart.

"I'm sorry, Ecko. I'm just so frustrated. Ground stomping takes so *long*! I don't know how you can stand to travel this way."

As if I have any other choice, she thinks as she steps around a dead beetle bug the size of a small dog. Glancing ahead, she sees that more and more deceased insects are scattered along the trail. Apparently, the way out is littered with the dead, just as the way in had been. She shudders as she remembers the sound of the bug shells crunching under her feet as she walked.

"I'll take you," she tells him. "When this is done, once we've retrieved the EverGlass, I'll carry you home so that you can do whatever it is that you need to do."

Tears of relief instantly begin coursing down his face. He's all choked up with emotion and unable to speak, so he simply nods and looks away from her as he wipes his runny nose on the back of his hand.

She fills in the silence while he gets himself back under control. "I know that we haven't really had time to talk about them since your drunken… admission? Confession? Well, whatever it was, it wasn't the whole story, not by half. It was bits and pieces of drunk-talk, so I still don't know what happened. Do you even remember that conversation?"

He shakes his head. "No, not really. I remember speaking of them, but not what was said."

That's what she thought. "I figured as much. I had every intention of questioning you the next Pale, but you were hurting so badly that I knew that conversation would have to wait. And then Sephyr came along, and it was one thing after another and I'm sorry for that. I just want you to know that I think about it all the time; I haven't forgotten about them. We just haven't found the right opportunity to have this talk. But we're alone now. For once, nothing is chasing us and I'm ready to listen, if you're ready to finally talk about it."

Her little friend sighs with a deep, soul-weary heaviness. "I still don't want to tell you, but not because I don't trust you. You *know* that I do. It just hurts so bad," he whispers as his voice catches on his suppressed tears.

"That's ok," she assures him, her hand comfortingly stroking his hair as her feet crunch through the bug corpses. "But don't you think talking about it will help? I mean, thousands of therapists can't be wrong."

He has no idea what a therapist is, and his face reflects his confusion.

"Never mind," she mutters. "Are they alive? At least tell me that much. I mean, will we be going on a rescue mission, or will we be attending a funeral wake? I just don't know what I'm dealing with here. You were pretty out of it and said some very contradictory things. You said you damned them. You said you trapped them and then you said you killed them. If they've passed on, you need to grieve…"

Boodark's shout silences her. "They're not dead! Don't you *dare* say they're dead!" Then in a much quieter, sorrowful voice he adds, "They just *can't* be." His breath hitches once, in and back out again. "Truth is, I don't know if they're alive. I have hope, but no proof. I cursed them, you see? Just as I cursed myself."

He sort of folds in on himself then as his shoulders slump further. "I stole something from Ametrine, the witch of the Black

Forest. I want you to know that I am no thieffer! I don't make it a habit of taking things that don't belong to me. But I did what I had to do. I'm not going to go into the why's of it… the backstory of my life leading to that point will have to wait until later. Just know that I had a very good reason for what I did."

He whimpers as his clawless hand strokes the golden band around his arm. "I can still see my Secret, the tears in her eyes as she begged me not to do it. But I felt I had no other choice. I was desperate, and so I did it. I thought I'd gotten away with it too, but it was all a trick. Ametrine knew I was there the whole time. She *allowed* me to steal it. She followed me home and *that's* when she cast her wicked witch's spell. She turned me into this disgusting, hideous monster and then forced me to watch as she flooded my home with thick, sticky sap. That sap hardened into amber and froze my family in place within seconds. That's the only thing I can be thankful for, that it all happened so fast. I don't think they were even aware that anything was amiss. They were given no time to be afraid, no time to suffer…. unlike me. Ametrine *wanted* me to suffer. She wanted me to hurt. I was the one that needed punishing after all, and she found the perfect way to do it."

She impulsively bends down and scoops up a handful of bug shells to offer him. He takes one and bites its head off, crunching away like he's eating chips. Comfort food… it's all she can offer him other than meaningful but completely useless words.

"I tried and tried to break through that amber that my family's trapped in. I tried until my hands bled and my claws got ripped off. It's unlike anything I've ever encountered, more like a crystal than amber. When that clearly wouldn't work, I went after Ametrine. I tried so many times to get at her. In the beginning, I wanted nothing more than to tear her apart with my bare hands until she released them, but I could never even get close to her. She is in league with the Lokskell… with your father, and as such, they have many eyes in the Black Forest. I have tried everything I can think of. I've even begged her to release my family… many times. I told her that I would gladly remain in this form. I would even go away, never try to see my family again if she would but spare them punishment for a crime that they did not commit. I even offered up my own life in forfeit. She has only ever taunted me and laughed in my face in for my efforts."

Ecko stops walking and looks down at him, so overcome with emotion that she can do nothing else but listen to his words. "I don't even know if they are alive in there!" he wails. "It's been so long. Two years, Ecko! Two years, they've been imprisoned, and I'm no closer to freeing them now than I was on that first Pale. I'm afraid to hope. Can they possibly still be alive after all this time? Are they aware? Are they scared?" His voice breaks as he continues. "I try to comfort myself by imagining that they're merely in a deep, enchanted sleep. Maybe, just maybe they're completely unaware of the perdition I've sentenced them to. But the truth is, I just don't know, do I? I don't know anything."

And then he's sobbing, and she's sobbing, and she lifts him out of the basket and squishes him to her chest. He buries his face in her shirt and just lets loose, and that's all they do for several minutes. They cry together, sobbing and wailing out their shared misery. When they're finally cried out, she lifts him up to face level so that he has no other choice but to meet her eyes. And with tears and snot covering both of their faces, she vows to find a way to help him save his loved ones. "We will save them. Do you hear me? I am making this promise to you right here and right now. We will get them back. I don't care if I have to stick that witch's broom where the sun doesn't shine, I will find a way to break the curse!"

Although clearly confused by the broom comment,

Boodark can hear the sincerity in her promise. He knows that she'll do everything she possibly can to see that she honors her oath. He has no words to express his gratitude and the hope that she's given him. His throat is too raw to speak, too sore from the sheer amount of emotions that have just spewed out of it. His voice is hoarse and scratchy as he whispers a simple thank you, but he tries to put all that he can't say into his eyes as he looks deeply into hers. She nods her understanding before gently setting him back in his basket. No other words are needed anyway.

Ecko turns to look behind her for the tenth time in as many minutes. She's got an uneasy feeling and she's convinced that they're no longer alone, nor are they safe. Someone or *something* is watching her, skulking along behind her. It probs at her mind, trying to force its way inside, past her protective barriers… security walls that she never even knew she had until they came under attack. She feels the burning itch on her skin where unseen eyes linger. Whatever it is, it's content to remain concealed behind the death and decay that surround her.

Boodark suddenly snorts in his sleep, startling a frightened squeak out of her. The poor little guy had fallen into an emotionally exhausted slumber soon after their talk, leaving her to walk along in silence, her mind going over all that she'd learned. She feels so bad for him, losing his family like he had. She knows exactly what that feels like, and she wouldn't wish it on anyone.

A soft rustle to the left whispers through the silence and she freezes in her tracks. She turns to look… nothing. Well, nothing that she can see anyway. She's certain that something's out there though. She can *feel* it, but she walks on anyway. Continuing in this fashion for several more minutes, she alternately stops to listen, turns to look all around, and then inevitably moves on when her eyes detect nothing out of the ordinary.

But something nags at her mind, a memory… something to do with Sephyr. She stands still with her eyes closed, searching the files inside her mind for the elusive information. The evocation of her time with the spirited little fairy brings a bittersweet smile to her lips. How she misses that Darkling!

Her thoughts, at last, settle on the moment that Sephyr was presenting her with the Mushroom clan's 'hurry up and be gone from our territory' gifts. "The hagstone! Yes!" She pumps a gleeful fist into the air when she realizes that she knows exactly what to do. She shrugs off her backpack and quickly begins rifling through it.

Her motions must jar Boodark and disturb his sleep because he sucks in a huge snort, pops up like a sprung jack-in-the-box, and looks wildly about. "Hu? Wha… what? What's going on?"

She merely grunts as she delves deeper into the bag, searching for the cut-down water bottle that she'd store the Darkling gifts in. "I know I put it here, close to the…ah ha!" she exclaims in triumph as her hand closes around it and lifts it out.

"Talk to me, Ecko," Boodark demands, and so she quickly explains.

"Something's following us. I can't see it, but I know that it's out there. I can feel it." She removes the hagstone, being *very* careful not to jostle the snail shells. It would be just like her to accidentally unstopper one and release a MerryFairy giggle or a Banshee cry onto herself. Hagstone in hand, she repacks the remaining gifts and re-shoulders her bag.

"Ah, bouncin' boggart balls! I knew this wouldn't be no simple snatch and dash! What do we do? What do we *do*?" Boodark the Nervous frets, teetering on the edge of full-blown panic. "Oh! I have a *great* idea! We can just stab its eyes out with that dumb cat's puke-bone!" He turns his head and dramatically widens his eyes at her. "*Well*? What are you waiting for? Get your magic ready, you big dummy! Conjure your fireball! Prepare for waaarrrr!" And then he follows it up by raising his claws up in the air and letting loose his battle cry.

Oh yeah, he's panicking, all right… no longer teetering on the edge. He dove off headfirst. She ignores his mad rantings and raises the hagstone to her eyes so that she can peer through the hole.

"What are you *doing?* This is no time to admire your rock collection," he fairly shouts at her.

She shushes him as she slowly scans her surroundings through the stone, searching for anything out of the ordinary. "Slivers," she whispers. "Several of them," she adds as she pans around in a 360 circle, sweeping every bit of the forest with her witch's view. "Slivers and Vika Vakooja's, they're all around us. And shadows…like the ones that Samara commands."

She passes the hagstone to Boodark so that he can look too. "Shades," he mutters. "They're called Night Shades, and they belong to the Lokskell. He's *very* determined to keep you in his sights. I wonder why they're not attacking."

She thinks about that for a minute and then answers, "Maybe they've been instructed to only follow us, to see where we're going."

Boodark tries to hand the stone back, but she shakes her head. "Keep it. Be my eyes so that I can keep my hands free just in case they *do* decide to attack. Maybe my fire will hold them back long enough for us to get away."

He nods and brings it back up to his eye. As she starts walking again, she adds, "I have a bad feeling about this. Something tells me that these are just the watchers, the spies. For some reason, I feel like there's a bigger threat on the way. Something with a tangible, physical body. Something formidable… with teeth."

She stands at the edge of the Dead Forest looking out onto the ruin of what was once a thriving grassland. It saddens her, watching the dried, brown heather as it rustles slightly in a barelythere breeze. Somewhere out there in that vast expanse of ruined flatland, the EverGlass awaits. The call, louder than ever before, is almost a physical thing, a *desperate* thing resonating inside her very soul. She *must* find it. She must silence its cries or risk going stark raving mad... for real this time versus Dr Bradburn's previously faulty evaluation of her mental facilities. *That's* how distressing the cry has become. The closer she gets, the louder and more incessant it becomes.

One more step will carry her into the Field of Screams and Broken Dreams and one step closer to the X on her mental map. But she can't seem to make herself take that step. She can't force herself forward. There's something very, very bad about this place. Some sort of psychic residue clings to the land, and whatever it is, it's tormented. There's a war going on inside her as she stands on the dividing line that separates one dismal landscape from the other. The EverGlass desperately urges her forward while the residual energy repels her back.

Boodark tells her that it's just like when she first saw the Sorrow Marshes. "Remember how much you dreaded the idea of entering the swamp? It's just nerves, that's all. Buck up, girl. It's going to be fine. You'll see."

She slowly shakes her head as she scans the field as far as her eyesight will allow. "No, Boodark. This is something completely different. Entering the Sorrow Marshes *was* bad, but that was mostly due to my own dread, my own fears. I didn't want to go into the swamp because of my own phobias. I hate swampy, stagnant waters where all kinds of dead things and monsters and ghosts can lurk. Dead things in dark, dank, standing water...it's one of my most irrational, yet powerful fears. But this... this is something else. This *belongs* to someone else... several someone's." Her breath hitches in and out as she adds, "Something terrible happened here."

Boodark shivers violently at the sudden chills that goosebump his leathery skin. "Ah, *come on*! Don't tell me there's spooks out there. I *hate* spooks!" He rants for a minute or so, going on and on about how 'spooks are dead, and they need to accept that and just get over it already and move on to wherever it is that spooks are supposed to go and leave the rest of the lifers to live in harmony without them lingering where they no longer belong.

"Scary, inconsiderate things, spooks are… always creeping around, leaving their spooky ghost turds where anyone can just come along and step in them. We wouldn't even *know* that we stepped in ghost shite! *It's invisible!*" She would laugh at his dramatic and impassioned tirade if she weren't so terrified of what she knows she must do.

"Hey!" Boodark suddenly shouts, startling a tiny yelp out of her. "Sorry, but I just had a great idea. Maybe spooks can be seen through the stone! If so, perhaps I can steer you clear of ghost poop piles!"

Slightly irritated with him for almost scaring her into an early heart attack (or making her create her own poop pile in her pants) she tells him that she couldn't care less about ghost poo, and she admonishes him to not shout out like that unless something was coming after them.

"Sorry," he sullenly repeats as he moves to bring the hagstone up to his eye.

"Don't," she whispers in earnest. "Don't look through the stone. I don't want to see what lies out there. I don't want to know." And drawing on every tiny spec of courage she possesses, she lifts her foot and steps over the invisible line.

Unbeknownst to the travelers, that's just what the watchers had been waiting for, and they immediately send out an alert to the creatures that are closing in on them.

"I don't like it here," Boodark whimpers just minutes into their trek through the field. He sounds slightly confounded by that fact, as if she hadn't already warned him that this place was going to suck. *So bad.* But nothing's happening, nothing to explain why he feels so uneasy. It's quiet all but for the sighing of the wind and the gentle sounds that the dry, brown heather makes as it whistles through it. It should have been a peaceful place, tranquil and soothing, but it is anything but pleasant. "There *must* be spooks here, as you suspected. There just has to be! Are you sure you don't want to look…"?

But she quickly silences him, settling her finger against her lips to warn him to be quiet for a moment. Eyes gone wide with distress, he watches her face as she turns in a circle, scanning the field for dangers. Just then, a piercing, blood-curdling scream rends the air… right beside where they're currently standing. Well, to clarify, right beside the spot that they just vacated.

She can run like the wind when she needs to, she just can't do it for long, a testament to the fact that she's already huffing and puffing from the exertion. Needing to catch her breath, she drops down to hide amongst the heather. "What," she manages to gasp out, "was *that*?"

Boodark just stares up at her with huge, watery eyes and trembling lips. When a tormented moan sounds right in their ears, his eyes overflow and he begins to wail. "I wanna go back! Take me back!"

She covers his mouth with her hand as she peeks out through the withered stems and spent blossoms. "I don't see anything!" she hisses, her voice a quiet, harsh whisper. "Give me the hagstone and I'll take a look. I need to know what we're dealing with." Although she dreads it with her entire being, she reaches down and holds her hand out, her eyes never stopping the search for bogies.

"Uhh, ab-b-bout that," Boodark stammers. "I d-d-dropped it. I didn't mean to!" he wails. "It just flew out of my hand when someone decided to sound like they were being murdered right beside us. I was startled, ok? I admit it. Also… I may or may not need to change into my extra trousers."

She just blinks down at him in disbelief. "You dropped it?" she blurts but then feels bad when he winces in guilt. Attempting to comfort him, she adds, "Well, I guess it's not like we could have done anything about whatever the stone would have revealed anyway. It's ok Boodark. Easy come, easy go, I suppose."

His eyes brighten when he realizes that she's not angry. "Easy come, easy go…I like that. I'll have to remember it. Now can we please fast-stomp ourselves away from here?" he blurts out just as another shriek rings out behind them.

"Sure thing!" She squeals as she scrambles back up and takes off again. Every minute or so, some new sound spurs her on. She has no desire to meet the beings that are currently bemoaning their tortured existence with wails and moans and hair-raising screeches. Sooner than she likes to admit though, she's out of breath again and no longer able to keep up the grueling pace of running for her life from unseen spooks. She comes to a stop and bends at the waist, her hand resting on her knees as she sucks in precious oxygen.

"Girl, we're gonna have to work on your escaping techniques… maybe teach you some sort of breathing exercises. Oh! Maybe Tanda knows a spell for…" His words are cut off by the next tormented moan. He cringes and whimpers as she straightens back up and glances around. She's still out of breath and not ready to run again, not nearly ready.

"Maybe if we ignore them, they'll go away. It doesn't seem like they're able to do much more than make noise," she observes. But she can't suppress her tiny yelp as the next scream rings out.

"Perfect! That's a *great* idea," Boodark snaps. "Let's just ignore them as they try their blangdang hardest to make me shite my pants!"

She starts walking again, slowly, hesitantly… tiptoeing as if that will really do her any good. "Besides," she continues. "Didn't Tanda tell us to ignore whatever we hear?"

He snorts in response. Loudly and rudely. "Easy for *her* to say. She's back at the SeeAll Tree where she's in no danger of pooping herself!"

"Do you see that?" she asks as she points straight ahead. They've managed to travel another twenty minutes or so without incident. Oh, the screams never cease, but like she'd predicted, that's all that they do. That's not to say that the two of them aren't terrified the entire time. Brave soldiers they are *not*, but they continued onwards, nonetheless. They have no other choice. "It looks like someone's coming this way," she says as she squints her eyes to bring the far-off but moving closer blob into focus.

"That's because someone *is* coming this way… Looks like a Grunter."

She continues walking and pretty soon she can make out his features. Short and stumpy, it appears to be half man and half pig, its face all melted wax-like. "It almost looks like an orc," she mumbles to no one in particular.

"Uh, Ecko? I think we have a problem." She turns to look where Boodark's pointing.

"I see them," she says as she studies the two new weirdos that are also heading towards them, one on the left and the other closing in from the right. They're still too far away for her to make them out properly, but she doesn't need to see them to know that her father has sent them.

"They're trying to box us in," she murmurs. She's afraid to look back behind them, but she has to know. She whirls around and sees… nothing. But she *feels* it, the Lokskell's slimy attentions focused upon her. His spies are still out there… following, watching. She turns back to watch the three goons close in as Boodark pleads for her to turn tail and make a run for it.

"We're outnumbered! We gotta go back!"

But she continues walking forward. "We can't go back. You don't feel what I feel back there, just waiting for us to be so foolish as to try and retreat. That way is blocked… it's like his spies have become an invisible wall. I don't think we'd be able to get through it either. Trust me, forward is the only option." He groans aloud as she adds, "Besides, we're *so* close… the EverGlass is so *loud* now. Keep your eyes peeled for anything unusual. It *has* to be around here somewhere."

Boodark snorts at that. "I would, truly I would, but I can't seem to keep my eyes off those three big scaries heading our way. What's your plan?"

She studies the two newcomers as they draw ever closer. "Plan? What plan?" She knows what the thing on the right is. She was with Urza and Blaxx long enough to recognize a hobglin when she sees one. But the other unfortunate creature is something new.

It's a man… sort of. Like a centaur, its top half is just like a man's. A massively built man, at that. But his bottom half, *oh*, his bottom half is just horridly *wrong*. It's a slug's body… there's no other way of explaining it. It's a slimy, gelatinous slug body of frightfully immense proportions. She can't seem to tear her eyes away from the monstrosity as they all come to a stop with about thirty yards separating them from her. She doesn't even look away from him when the hobglin calls out to her.

"The Shadow Lord wants a word with you, little girl. If you come along peacefully, we won't hurt you… I promise."

All three of them chuckle at that, but she's still staring at slug-man.

"If you run, we will catch you and make you bleed *so bad,*" the hobglin threatens in his pinched, nasally voice. Then he snarl/growls as he adds, "Please run. I, for one, wish to taste your blood upon my lips. I want revenge, little one, and I shall have it one way or another. You killed my brother! Blaxx was always a fool, but fool or no, he was hobglin-kin. So, what's it going to be? Hmmm? Where is your big decision? Will you willingly come along to speak to the Lokskell, and bleed just a *tiny* bit along the way? Or will you flee and bleed buckets before you speak with him?"

Boodark groans, "You just make friends everywhere you go, don't you?"

She reaches up and thumps him as she hisses, "Shut up, Boodark!" But she doesn't respond in any way to their threats.

What's there to say, anyway? She will *not* be going quietly, that's for sure.

Her eyes dart between each opponent as she calculates the distance between them, even while she desperately tries to home in on the exact location of the EverGlass. She knows that she should make a run for it… towards the left, between the Grunter and the slug-man. She's certain that's the direction that the EverGlass is calling from. But she *really* doesn't want to go that way. She would *so* much prefer to dash between the Grunter and the hobglin. They feel like less of a threat to her, not as depraved or lecherous as the slug-man.

Time and time again her eyes stop to linger on him, and it's not just because he's absolutely grotesque. It's more than that. She instinctively knows that she must avoid him at all costs. He's *bad* and he makes her feel violated just by having his eyes touch on her body.

"Oh, she'll run, boys," he suddenly growls out in a deep, gravelly rumble. He grins at her then, but her eyes are drawn downwards, down, down, down his man torso. Down his slug… anatomy? … to where a large slit is opening up like a vertical smile. She watches, horrified to the depths of her soul as a massive tentacle-like appendage pushes out of it and stretches towards her.

"Penis protruding!" Boodark screams with equal parts panic and disgust. And you know what? Slug man had been absolutely, 100% correct. She's running, boys.

She turns tail and darts away, back towards the invisible wall, but only as a delay tactic. They don't even bother to chase after her, which tells her all she needs to know. She *can't* get past her father's invisible wall of spies, and they know it too. Sooner or later, she'll have to turn back towards them or risk running right into a wall of icky things that she can't even see.

Just then, a sudden image of Danika's feather flashes through her mind. The Kreeleerian had said she'd know when to use her gift… Perhaps this is her sign. But use it how? And for what?

Only one way to find out, she tells herself as she spins back around and charges back towards the goons. She gets one brief glance at their startled faces before Boodark starts whimpering and *they* begin to laugh at her. They can't believe that she's running *towards* them.

"Give me the feather," she quietly calls out to her terrified little friend.

"Hu?" That's all the response that his poor, confused mind manages to form for his mouth to articulate.

"The feather, from the Kreeleerian. Give it to me!" she repeats. "And don't drop it!" she adds. While he's frantically digging it out from beneath his blanket, she quickly but *very* carefully uses her finger to sketch the Activate rune onto her palm. She has to get it exactly right, just the way Danika taught her, or it won't work … whatever *it* is. She can see no trace of the symbol once it's drawn, but it's there. She can feel it waiting, itching and tingling below her skin.

Boodark holds up the feather and yells, "Ah ha!" Then he immediately frowns and adds, "This is *dumb*! What are we gonna do with a feather? Tickle them to death? And *why* are we running towards the enemy? Are you daft, girl? Why don't you blast them with fireballs? That makes more sense than charging them with a blangdang *feather!*"

She sucks in a desperate breath as she admonishes him, "No fire. We would be trapped just as much as them. Look around you. This whole field would go up in flames. Don't worry, Boodark. This will work."

She snatches the feather as he cries out, "*What's* gonna work?"

Her dumb brain takes a tiny detour from the current events as it starts playing the Wonder Pets theme song. '*What's gonna work? Teamwork!*' But what comes out of her mouth is a shouted, "I don't know!"

She slaps the feather onto the rune on her palm and immediately feels her magic react to the Kreeleerian's. The symbol lights up with that familiar, electric blue that she's grown used to. It burns and yet somehow doesn't hurt at all as it initiates the feather's intended purpose.

They both watch as the feather lifts up from her hand to float in the air while a strand of her sizzling, electric magic keeps it safely tethered to her. Then it begins to quiver and shake, faster and faster and faster until it becomes nothing more than a blur of motion. Meanwhile, the three goons continue to stand there, grinning and laughing as she draws nearer. Slug-man's pukeworthy tentacle penis pokes itself back out and stretches towards her in anticipation.

Knowing that they'll expect her to run away from the unspeakably horrendous slug-penis, she runs *towards* it instead. She glances back up at the feather just in time to watch it vibrate itself apart. It just… explodes into a thousand tiny, fluttery feather fragments. But they don't stay tiny for long; they grow… *fast*! One second, they're nothing but bits of fluff and the next they're huge, fully formed feathers.

Her feet continue pounding the ground, moving on autopilot even as her mouth drops open in shock. She watches with rapt amazement as the feathers come together to form the largest, most spectacular pair of wings she's even seen. Even Boodark cries out in wonder at the incredible display. As they stretch out above her, she can feel that her magic is linked to them. She instinctively knows what to do, as if the wings are just another extension of herself…. like they've always been a part of her. And they are so easy to command, just as easy as commanding her legs and arms to obey her brain's instructions.

Using her purely psychic connection, she lifts the wings and stretches them as wide as they'll go. The three goons are no longer laughing as they take in the full, twelve-foot wingspan. They've apparently reevaluated their stance and decided that darting forward to catch her is now their best course of action, because here they come…. barreling right at her. They'll be upon her within seconds.

"Go, big dummy! *Fly!*" Boodark shouts.

"Up," she whispers inwardly as well as out loud. Just in time, the wings give a mighty flap that lifts them twenty feet in the air, high enough that even the insanely tall slug-man can't reach her. Boodark howls like a loon, laughing hysterically as the three idiots crash into one another… *hard*. The crack of their bodies colliding reverberates out across the entire field. Cursing and screaming, they go down in a pile of twisted limbs while she focuses on their getaway.

The bad guys aren't down nearly long enough, and they're soon chasing along behind them as they soar over the swaying heather.

"Umm, is that supposed to happen?" Boodark shouts to be heard over the sound of the wind in their ears. She jerks her eyes up to where he's pointing and her heart almost plummets to the ground. The wings are losing feathers. They're falling out at an alarming rate, just coming loose and being swept away by the wind of their own making. She glances back down at her burning palm… the rune is disappearing! It's burning itself up, leaving no trace behind. It's more than halfway gone already!

'Focus!' she chides herself. She's disoriented, no longer sure where the EverGlass's cry is coming from. She closes her eyes, scrunching her face up as she concentrates with every brain cell she possesses. "Oh no! We've passed it!" she cries out as her eyes spring open. Veering sharply to the right, she turns back towards the call, sacrificing several more feathers with the sudden shift and change in pressure.

"Look!" Boodark shouts as he points a claw at a strange, wooden door, freestanding out in the middle of the field. It stands directly between her and her three would-be kidnapper/torturers.

"That was NOT there a moment ago," he insists. "I don't like it, Ecko. Not one bit!"

And yet, that's exactly where she needs to be. The EverGlass calls more insistently than ever, and it's coming from behind that strange, absurd door. She drops down lower to the ground and aims straight for it. The only problem is, it looks like she'll reach it at the same time that her father's henchmen will.

The feathers are coming loose in giant batches, streaming out behind her like a kite tail as she leans forward and flaps her borrowed wings harder, desperately trying to lend a burst of speed to her forward momentum. No longer able to function properly, the shredded wings begin to falter. The ground closes in… fast. "Houston, we have a problem!" she hollers into the wind.

"What does that even *mean*?" Boodark yells right back.

"It means we're gonna crash!" she answers as she wraps her arms protectively around him. "Brace for impact!" she screams while at the same time *he's* screaming, "Oh, shiiiiitteee!" And then they're rolling, skidding across the ground, the dead, crumbling heather getting uprooted and flung up into the air in the process.

She wastes no time… not even to access herself for damage. She's back up on her feet, running flat out those last several feet to the door. She slaps her palm against it and screams,

"OPEN SAYS ME!"

She'll never know why it obeyed her command, whether it was because the very last bit of rune on her palm was still active or simply because of who she is. Whatever the case, the door swings open at her touch, and she tumbles through… straight into a completely different landscape.

A Message for Father

Samara

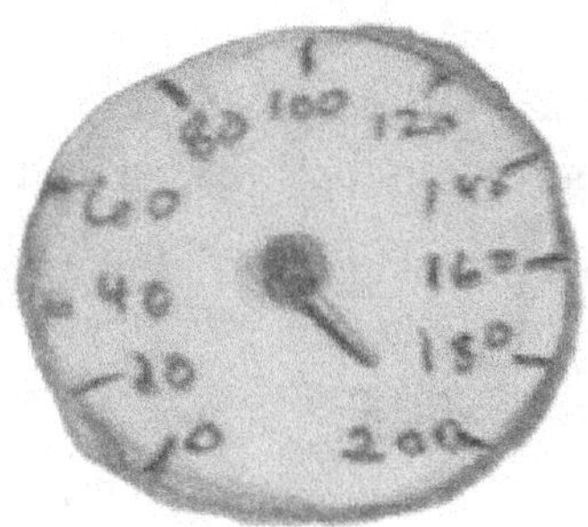

Lenny gets into the back seat of her car, slamming the door behind him in his irritation. "This better be important, Samara. I've already told you; this just isn't a good time. I'm waiting on the call from Miquel on the merger deal and you know that I have that meeting with …"

Samara turns cold, calculating eyes on him, and his words freeze up in his throat even as his mouth goes dry. Something's wrong, he can feel it in the air around him… a blanket of doom wrapping tight around him like a mummy's bindings.

"Shut up, Lenny," she orders in a voice that raises the fine hairs on his body in warning. He checks his breathing as she leans forward to talk to Mr. Chadwick, "Did you get my chocolate cake?"

The man smiles as he takes a white box from the passenger seat and passes it back to her. "Of course. I would never forget a lady's chocolate." It's what he always tells her, without fail. "Your bourbon's in the cooler also. Would you like me to come around and pour you a glass?"

She waves a dismissive hand at him. "I'm perfectly capable of pouring my own drinks, Mr. Chadwick. What I need for you to do is drive. Take us to the Roanoke address."

Lenny spits and sputters beside her. "Roanoke? What the *fuck* is in Roanoke?" he demands as the car pulls away from the driveway.

Samara pays him no attention as she takes her first bite of the sinfully decadent confection that she's become so addicted to.

"Are you listening to me? I don't have time to go to Roanoke today! That's three hours away!"

She begins to speak, never once diverting her attention from devouring her treat. "Have I ever told you how much I despise liars? Oh, silly me! Of course, I did. I made that very clear on the day we met. If I'm not mistaken, I made it a part of our deal that you would never lie to me. Is that not so?"

He opens his mouth to reply but chokes his words back when she whips her head around so fast to glare at him that she could have given the girl in The Exorcist a run for her money. He takes the hint and shuts the fuck up.

"Yes, you do remember. *But* I bet you didn't know that I can almost always tell when I'm being lied to. Of course, you didn't know. I never told you that, and for very good reason. My Night Shades go crazy, absolutely bugfuck, bat shit crazy when they sense a lie directed at me. They seethe and writhe and roil around inside of me, burning me up like fucking lava. It's how I immediately determine who you can trust and who you need to get rid of, even before I send my Shadows into them. It's like having my very own, built-in lie detector system inside of me. And they're never wrong."

Lenny shifts in his seat, suddenly uncomfortable and finding it difficult to keep his breathing slow and steady. He tries to reply but has to stop and clear his throat several times before he can speak properly. "I didn't know that," he finally manages to croak. "But I can see where it would come in handy. I know that we, as in myself and *our* empire, have certainly benefited greatly because of your many talents."

Samara nods and murmurs, "Yes, you certainly *have* benefited immensely just by having me at your side. Tell me, Lenny. Do you remember me asking you about a certain folder, a file that mysteriously went missing?" She calmly places a thick manila folder onto the seat and watches him go stiff as a board and deathly silent. He swallows the sudden lump in his throat as his eyes travel from her to the ordinary, seemingly innocuous folder laying there between them, bold as a line drawn in the sand.

He holds a hand up and stutters, "Now, Samara. Hear me out…"

But she talks right over him. "That day at the sleazy little motel room that you took me to…"

"I can explain!"

"Do you remember what I told you then?"

"If you will just listen!"

"I. Fucking. Hate. Being. Lied. To."

"It was an accident!"

"An accident? Oh yes. Just like the man that came home to find his wife fucking his best friend. She must have tripped, fell, and landed on his dick. Right? That kind of accident?"

"What? No! I just meant that I didn't mean…"

"You broke our accord, *Lenny*. I warned you never to lie to me.

"I did it for you! So, I could find her for you. Your sister, right? Your twin? Adrina, wasn't it?"

The fork with the chocolate cake pauses halfway up to her mouth as she goes still, her eyes filling up with roiling, black storm clouds. He gulps and a little squirt of piss wets the front of his fiftythousand-dollar Kiton K50 dress pants when she turns them on him. "You really shouldn't meddle in things that don't concern you."

Lenny's almost sobbing now. "I only wanted to help!" he insists. "I couldn't find her. I went to her old address, but there was no longer a house… it burned down years ago in a fire."

"You shouldn't have gone there, Lenny. You should have minded your own business. You don't even have anything to show for it. You have no new information to offer. You're not telling me anything I wasn't already aware of. I already knew that my sister wasn't there. I *caused* the fire that burned her house down and killed her precious family. I'm the reason she was locked up in the crazy house!"

Lenny gulps. "I didn't find *her*, but I did find something else! She was released early, into the care of an old couple. Uh, uh, uhhh, a Charlie something or other guy. I don't remember his full name, but I can tell you where he lives! I can tell you…"

"Well of course you'll tell me where he lives! You'll tell me everything I wish to know; of that I have no doubt." She takes another bite of cake as she waves her other hand towards him, her Shadows pouring out to fill the air around them.

"Oh, God! *Please!* I've been good to you! Haven't I been good to you? Haven't I made you a queen, just like I promised I would? Don't throw it all away now, not over one minor discretion, one tiny mistake that I made in the very beginning of our relationship. We've come too far for that!"

"No secrets, no lies, and sex with me whenever I chose. Those were my stipulations and you willingly agreed to them. Did you not?"

"Yes! Yes, I agreed! B,b,but the deed had already been done by that point! Yes, I saw the file fall when you stripped off your clothes. Yes, I took it while you were in the shower and hid it from you. But that was before we came to an understanding… before I knew what your stipulations would be. It was my one and only falsehood. I've been completely honest from that moment on!"

"Really? Then you didn't lie when I came to you days later and asked if you'd seen it? You didn't look me in the eye and tell me that you never saw any file?" She watches the blood drain from his face, leaving him pale as a spook. "You're fucked, Lenny. If you believe in God, now's the time to get right with him. I suggest you pray anyway, whether you believe or not because truly, only God can save you now. Maybe. I'm not sure that even He would want to go up against my vengeance."

And then all Lenny can do is whimper as the Shadows begin their assault on him. They attack him with gentle caresses and soft tongue strokes in all the right places. "Samara…please…" He tries to beg but the Shadows move so seductively against him that he's powerless to hold on to a single coherent thought. She has them toy with him mercilessly while she eats her cake until, with a blissful sigh of pleasure, she takes the last bite and passes the empty box back to Mr. Chadwick for later disposal. Then she turns to watch as her Shadows open Lenny's pants, letting his cock spring free. He groans aloud as he throws his head back, his eyes rolling up from the pleasure. He's so close… *so close*. His pulse pounds at his temple, the chords of his neck bulge as the breath tears in and out of his lungs. And then the Shadows stop. They cease all ministrations, just long enough to force his body to cool, to deny him the release that he craves.

"Fuck!" he shouts as he punches the seat in frustration. Her mouth twitches… just a bit before she can control herself. She gives him a moment to catch his breath and then sends the Shadows back in for round two. "Oh God! Please Samara, just *please*!"

And just like that, the rage that she's been suppressing *for weeks* rears its head and tries to consume her. She has to fight for control, squash the urge to slaughter him, here and now and be done with it. *Play the game* she mentally murmurs in an attempt to calm herself. She raises her eyes up and meets Mr. Chadwick's gaze in the rear-view mirror. Somehow those amused eyes, slightly crinkled at the corners, do what she's failing so miserably at. They soothe the rage, calm the storm within her… just enough to play out the rest of the game.

She holds up her pointer finger and spins it in circles, making air swirl motions, and her Shadows rush to obey the mental commands they'd been given. They wrap themselves around Lenny's junk, at the base and lower to encompass his sack in a vaporous cock and ball ring clutch. When her hand forms a fist up in the air and squeezes, they tighten oh so slowly, almost imperceptibly at first. But soon enough, they've got him held in the tightest grip he's ever experienced, and he's no longer having fun. None at all.

"That looks so painful," she croons as she reaches over to thump the head of his swollen, blood-engorged member. The grip on him is so excruciatingly tight that the blood has become trapped, forcing him to maintain a permanent erection. His fluids have no leeway in which to flow. The blood can't circulate, nor can his seed escape in that hot rush of release that he's so desperate for.

She has her Shadows hold him there, just like that as she moves on to the next item on her to-do list… painting her toenails. They're a shameful mess! She had an appointment with her beauty technician *and* her masseuse today, but she'd been forced to cancel in order to make this little trip. She gets the toes on her right foot done, the nails painted a soft, pearly pink that completely misrepresents her nature but looks oh, so cute on her.

"God Samara, ease up! Let's talk about this!" Tears leak from Lenny's eyes as he grits the words out. He's in a world of agony that he can't escape. He wants to cum so bad. He hurts so bad. He wants to make her let go of his dick. He wants to trap *her*, make *her* helpless as he pounds himself into her, hurt and punish *her* just as she's doing to him. And he's mad, even in the midst of his fear and his suffering. He swore long ago that he would never allow another to use him, to punish him like this…make him feel weak and helpless. Not ever again. But he *is* weak and helpless against her magic, and there's nothing he can do to change that. He can't stop her, and he can't overpower her, so all that's left is begging and sobbing and praying.

"You know what your first mistake was, Lenny?" she asks but continues without waiting for a reply. "Your first mistake was taking something that belonged to me, something that didn't even concern you or our relationship with one another. Your second was lying about it, even after I made myself crystal clear about how I feel about liars. And the third was being so stupid that you held on to the evidence of your betrayal, as if was a souvenir. A little keepsake to remind you of your one, tiny victory against me. That was a dumb move, Lenny. You should have destroyed that file immediately. By keeping it, you only ensured that this day would inevitably come about, and I would have you by the balls.

Literally."

Finished with painting her toenails, Samara sets up a couple of little white lines and exuberantly powders her nose. Then she shuffles through her music list until she finds something that she's in the mood to hear, something that will cover the sound of Lenny's crying and grunting pig noises.

She reaches over again and runs her fingers over his purple, blood deprived cock. "Be quiet now, Lenny" she tells him. "You be oh, so quiet now… until I give you permission to speak. If you open your mouth a single time before then, I will cut off your dick and gag you with it. Do you understand? I wouldn't try to answer aloud if I were you. Just nod… silently. Do you? Understand, that is."

Lenny clamps his mouth shut and grits his teeth to silence his cries as he miserably nods his head.

"Good!" Samara praises as she makes a show of checking the time. "You only have two hours and twenty-six more minutes… give or take, until we arrive at our destination. I hope you make it that long; I really do. I have such a wonderful surprise waiting for you. I wouldn't want you to miss out on it." And then she hits the play button and cranks the volume up on Coma White, one of her favorite Marilyn Manson songs. Yeah, this song sounds just about right for her overall mood today. Manson usually has the right of things, with a firm grip on reality and absolutely no fear of speaking the harsh and ugly truths that most humans try to avoid.

Samara rocks out to her favorites playlist while Lenny passes in and out of consciousness throughout the entire trip. He's definitely not a fan of her particular tastes and he has no tolerance for pain. None whatsoever. That's why he enjoys plain vanilla sex, boring people sex. She doesn't like vanilla, not in her mouth and not in her bed. She doesn't even enjoy vanilla scented candles or vanilla flavored body oils. She's all luscious chocolates, dark and sinful and delicious.

She glances over at him… unconscious again. They're only minutes from their destination now though. Time to wake him up and get him moving. She calls her Shadows back, and his eyes immediately pop open and his screams of pain pour, one after another, from his mouth as the clamp around his cock is finally, *finally* released and the blood is able to flow once more. She grins as he howls; she knows how much pain he's in. It's *always* painful when the blood begins circulating again after it's been cut off for such a long amount of time. She can only imagine how much more excruciating it feels to him right now … all that blood flowing back into the most sensitive parts of his body. Yeah, she lets him scream it all out. What she doesn't allow is for him to pass back out and escape a single second of it. What would be the fun in that?

Mr. Chadwick pulls into a shopping center full of sad, rundown buildings where sad, wretched people come to buy subpar merchandise at discount prices. He stops the car in front of a couple of vacant shops, in exactly the same spot that he always parks in and then he waits for further instructions. Samara stares out her window, as *she* always does, out into a dark and filthy alley situated between the two abandoned buildings. She waits for Lenny to get himself back under control, but he seems to be having a time of it. "Are you nearly done with the theatrics?" she asks him without ever looking his way.

He somehow manages to suck it up, silencing his gasps and groans and cries, but he's in hell. He knows he is. His balls throb painfully. His dick feels like it's been crushed. The muscles in his belly ache from straining, and his groin feels like it's been pummeled like a punching bag. Everything from the bottom of his ribcage to his thighs is screaming in pain. Even his asshole hurts. He reaches for the bag of cocaine, but Samara stops him before he can partake. "No. No drugs. I want you sober."

He whimpers but drops the baggie back down in obedience. He'll not chance another dick-squeeze session… he wouldn't survive it.

"Get out," she tells him, and Mr. Chadwick jumps out and rushes around the car to open her door and help her out… just like she's a queen while Lenny moves as slowly and carefully as a snail that's slithering between salt pile obstacles. Not only is he in a tremendous amount of discomfort, but he's also scared out of his mind right now. He has no clue why he's been brought here, but he knows it won't be pleasant. He doesn't even know if he'll make it to see another day. He very well may die and be left here in this wretched, filthy parking lot. He toys with the idea of jumping into the driver's seat and speeding away but immediately abandons the idea. Samara's Shadows would catch him and make him suffer even more than he will already suffer. He saw the same thing happen once to a rival that thought he could get away with stealing a mere hundred thousand dollars' worth of product. He still has nightmares from what she did to that man. He shudders as he regretfully passes the driver's door and continues slowly making his way around the car to her side. He leans back against the car when he gets there, his breath ragged and sweating profusely from the pain that moving has caused him. Walking bent down almost in half, hunched over like an old, hunchback crone hadn't helped ease his suffering a bit either.

Samara nods her head towards the space between the buildings. "Tell me, what do you see there?"

He's worried, so very worried about where this is all going but he obediently raises his eyes and looks to the short, narrow passageway. His eyes quickly shy away, and he turns to look at her instead. "Nothing," he croaks. He clears his throat and tries again.

"I don't see anything. Just a dirty alley in some Godforsaken shithole. What's this all about, Samara?"

She turns to Mr. Chadwick, who's standing on the opposite side of her. "And you? What do *you* see?" He turns his attention from her to the place in question. "I see what I always see, every time you ask… the same thing Mr. Lennard sees. An empty alley, but it's…shivery this time. Almost like this isn't real, like the alley doesn't truly exist. At least not on this plane of existence. Reminds me of a mirage in the desert. It's incredibly difficult to keep my attention focused on it. My eyes want to turn away. It feels as if they might bleed if I keep it up for long. Or perhaps that my mind will crack." He turns back to look at her instead.

Lenny squints, trying to see what the other man saw… trying to see the shivery. He, too, discovers that his eyes won't stay focused on the seemingly empty space. "What the hell?" he whispers as his eyes shy away time and time again. "What *is* this place?" he murmurs, but he's not entirely sure that he wants to know.

"It's an EverRealm," Samara answers. "One of seven incredibly magical places that exist simultaneously on every world… in all times and in every single dimension. They are complicated, mysterious things, and every one of them is different. Sometimes they are cloaked, such as this one is. Sometimes they only reveal themselves to the gifted and the powerful, people who have magic inside of them. Other times they're visible to all. Sometimes people deliberately seek them out and other times they're stumbled upon by accident. But once found, all are welcomed within, whether intentionally discovered or by accident. It's also been said that their appearances differ from world to world."

She pauses to wave a hand out at the emptiness. "Want to know what *I* see?" she asks the men. One nods and the other just stares at her in misery and pain and fear. "I see a castle, dark and ominous and foreboding. Sheol Castle…*my father's castle*. I'm not human, as I'm sure you've both already guessed. I wasn't born on this world. I'm from a world called Oblerian, a horrid, filthy place.

Not a dog-eat-dog world, as you humans are fond of saying. It's infinitely harsher, deadlier… an *everything*-eat-*everything* world that you, with your silly little pampered and sheltered lives wouldn't survive a day on. I spent my entire life as a prisoner on that world, suppressed and controlled and tortured by my father. Not by him personally. No, he has thousands upon thousands of men at his disposal that follow his every command. The Lokskell is a man so powerful that entire *worlds* fear and obey him. A man who, in fact, never even set foot on Oblerian during the whole of my existence there. He lives on a completely different world. *That's* how powerful he is. He doesn't even have to step outside of his castle to have his every command carried out. Not that he can… step out of it, that is. For all his power, for all his incredible and fearsome might, he's trapped there and has been for a long, long time. There was a woman, you see?"

She throws her head back and laughs at that. "Isn't there *always*? Anyway, this woman had a great magic inside of her. My father saw that power and he coveted it. And much like you, Lenny, though he craved her body, it was the magic that he truly desired, and he sought to steal it from her. They fought a fierce battle and even though he managed to kill her, he found that he was not able to take that magic from her. Just before the woman died, she banished him to Sheol Castle and then quickly spelled it before the life left her body. She magicked the windows and the doors, the walls and ceilings and the floors too, so that every living being within its walls became trapped inside for all time."

"My father spent the next thousand years searching for ways to get out. He did unspeakable things, things that make what *I* do seem like child's play. I won't bore you with all the details, but that's how I came along. I was an inconvenient little side effect of his attempts at gaining his freedom. Just before I was born, my mother, who'd been his prisoner for years, escaped him. She bore my twin sister and I on the run, and then she separated us. She sent my sister here and left me to rot on Oblerian. The bitch abandoned us to save herself, but no matter. *She* has nothing to do with the point of this story. Back to my father… and this is where things get complicated."

"Since Sheol Castle is an EverRealm, it exists not just on *his* world, but on all other worlds as well. Which also means that it exists somewhere on Oblerian too. Do you see where this is going? If I disobeyed him, if I were ever to displease him beyond his patience and tolerance, he had the power to have me tossed into the Sheol Castle EverRealm on *my* world, and therefore land in his world where he would then have access to me in person. I would rather have a Sluggeelian butt fuck me, lay its disgusting slugbaby egg deep inside my colon, and have the nasty thing hatch and feed on my guts until it grows big enough to survive on its own and thereby make its own exit by eating a hole right through my belly. And just so you know, Sluggeelians are as disgusting as they sound. Massive… sometimes ten to twelve feet tall, bright orange, slimy-skinned slugmen. Truly hideous and repulsive creatures, in appearance and essence. There are no Sluggeelian females. They're all male on the outside, but they have female organs on the inside that enable them to reproduce. And since they are all men, they're all rump lovers. I'm not sure if that's because they're just gay or if it has something to do with the fact that their offspring can only grow within a colon. Apparently, a woman's womb will kill the repulsive sprogs every time."

"Sluggeelians are a brutal race that enjoys rape above all else. If the victim survives the assault, and not many of them do, they inevitably die from the birthing of the slugbaby that they unwillingly become host to. The reason I say that most of their victims couldn't possibly survive the mating… I once saw a Sluggeelian with a dick as long and thick as your leg, Lenny. Oh, I know you think I've gotten off track with this lecture on Sluggeelian anatomy and their behaviors and characteristics, but I can assure you that there *is* a point to it all. I'll get to it shortly, and faster than you'll want me to!"

"Now, since I've never actually *seen* my father's castle (and I thank all the UnderGods that ever existed for that) I can only go by what I've pieced together. Years of suffering my father's tormenting and bragging and threatening painted a pretty detailed image in my mind. From what I understand, there's a great big room in the castle's keep, and it's filled with windows… hundreds of windows of all shapes and sizes. Every one of those windows look out onto a different place, giving him a view of every single world that the castle exists on. And no, the windows won't open or break, no matter what is done to them. Not even a thousand years of abuse against them has ever led to a single crack in the glass. I'm not sure if that's because of the woman's curse or if it's just another aspect of that particular EverRealm. I wonder how much time my father has spent staring out those windows."

A sharp wind suddenly sweeps through and swirls around them, bringing with it a feeling of nostalgia and dread. Samara imagines that she can smell her world on that breeze and although it brings fear and loathing with it, there's also the tiniest sharp stab in her chest when the image of a beautiful blue man-beast fills her mind. A man beast that her father had tortured and killed because he'd dared to fuck her… dared to fuck something that her father believed was *his* exclusive property.

Krispin, the wind sighs in her ear and she takes a step back, her butt thumping into the car behind her, snapping her out of whatever mind funk *that* had been. Whatever spell had been swirling around her dissipates as the precipitous, spontaneous wind blows itself out. She shoves the hair out of her eyes and looks into the empty alley/shivery/castle/EverRealm. Then she looks up and up and up, her eyes following the outline of a castle front that only she can see. "So, if my father just happened to be standing at the window that looked out on Earth, at this precise moment, he would see us standing here talking about him. What do you think the odds are on that, Lenny? You're big on laying odds and taking bets. How much do you want to bet that my father somehow sensed me standing out here and is even now watching us?"

But Lenny, poor terrified Lenny, can't think of wagers right now. His mind is spinning around and around with the words she'd said. *'Getting back out, now that is usually a bit trickier. Most never find their way out… tossed into the EverRealm on my world, land in his world where he would then have access to me in person.... I once saw a Sluggeelian with a dick as long and thick as your leg, Lenny... trapped in that castle for a thousand years.'* Her words echo loudly in his head, and he can't escape them. He's got a really, *really* bad feeling in the pit of his belly and it's all he can do to clench his ass tight enough to not shit himself.

"I hope he *is* standing there at that window. I hope he can see me now. I want him to see just how beautiful and amazing I've become... how rich and powerful. But more than anything... above all else, I want him to see how fucking *free* I am. Free from him, free from Oblerian, free to do whatever I wish to do while he remains a prisoner in his castle for all time."

She smiles a little wickedly, victoriously as the two men process all she's told them. Mr. Chadwick is even more in awe of her magnificence, and he gazes upon her face in pure, rapturous admiration. Lenny frowns at the empty space, still trying to see what she sees while he also tries to work it all out in his head. There's a voice suddenly screaming inside his brain, screaming for him to run, run, run away. Shadows be damned, run anyway. Die *trying* instead of merely standing there accepting his fate.

But fear is a funny thing. It gives warning signs when danger is near. The little hairs on the body stand up in goosebumps, the heart pounds, the breath speeds up, hands tremble, fluttery things come to life in the belly, and little voices in the mind scream words like *RUN! FLEE! ESCAPE!* But then it will throw the body into complete lockdown mode, freeze the bones and nail the feet to the floor.

Lenny can't run, he can't even move. But his mouth apparently has no such limitations. Nor does it do anything to sharpen his wits because he stupidly demands, "Why are we here, Samara? Why have you brought me here?"

She turns to face him, her eyes widening at his daring, not realizing that his words were merely a reflexive reaction, not bravery. No, not bravery. She beams up at him then, a broad, terrifying smile that he would swear was full of sharp, jagged teeth.

Like shark teeth hiding behind pretty, blood-red painted lips. "I'm so glad you asked!" she gushes in an ecstatic and overly joyful voice. "You must be punished for your crimes, Lenny. You *know* this."

He gulps in a breath to renew his begging. "Now, wait a second…"

She shakes her head and speaks over his protests. "I warned you. I *told* you that you would regret crossing me. You should have listened. You should have taken me seriously, Lenny."

His lips tremble just a bit. "But I *told* you why…"

She grins again, softly this time. "I don't care *why*. There is no reason good enough to justify the crime."

He glances around the area, his eyes darting about in search of help that he'll never find. "B,b,but the business… the men. Who will run things if I'm not there? Do you really think the men will follow you?"

She takes her phone out of her pocket and presses # 3 for speed dial. She puts the call on speaker when the man on the other end picks up. "Yes ma'am?" he asks, simple and to the point.

"Victor! Is it done yet?" she asks, just as direct and to the point as he'd been.

"Almost ma'am. Miguel's delivery boys are just now arriving with the product. We'll inspect it, make sure it's up to your standards before paying them off and sending them on their way."

Samara twirls a strand of her hair around her fingers, and she stares right into Lenny's eyes as she asks, "And the other thing?"

They listen to Victor clear his throat on the other end. "Already taken care of, ma'am. The team of interior decorators you hired have been in, made the changes, and have already left again. Everything should meet your satisfaction upon your return this evening."

She watches every emotion as they pass over Lenny's face. Surprise, disbelief, annoyance, outrage. "Just to be thorough, tell me exactly what changes were made," she demands.

"Well, let's see. The changes you wanted completed today were in the master bedroom, the dining hall, and the office. The workers removed all the furniture and ripped all the carpets out, replacing it all with what they've assured me was your choice of furnishings. They also took down the painting of Mr. Lenny in the dining hall and replaced it with the one you had made of yourself. And might I say, it is absolutely exquisite."

And finally, *there's* the anger that Samara had been waiting for. She watches as it fills Lenny's eyes and flushes his face red, relishing every second of it. "Thank you, Victor. And since you've been such a tremendous help to me, I've decided to make you my # 1 lieutenant. I'll see to it that your paygrade increases to fit your new position." She disconnects the call while Victor gushes his appreciation and spews his thanks. She's made her point crystal clear to Lenny, which was the whole reason for that conversation with one of his men... *her* men now.

"You see, Lenny. I already have the men's loyalties. *You* saw to that. You wanted them to fear your beautiful, deadly weapon. You wanted to use me to force their obedience. Well, yay for you, Lenny! You got everything you wished for. The men *already* follow me. And it was you that set it all into motion!"

She can't help but laugh in the face of his anger, his useless, impotent rage. She steps in close to him and softly runs her fingers across his cheek. "So, you see, I don't *need* you, Lenny. I never did. Oh, you may have taught me about the finer things in life, the very best this world has to offer, but all that's done now. I want you to know that I would have kept my word to you. I would have upheld my end of the bargain indefinitely. I would have let you continue with your delusions of control." She suddenly lashes out at him, slamming her hands against his chest and screaming, "I would have left our arrangement alone but for your betrayal, your filthy fucking *lies*!"

He begins to cry again, sobbing and blubbering, "I'm sorry! I'm so sorry!"

She takes a deep breath to calm herself, lest she punch a hole straight into his chest and rip his heart out. She doesn't want that. She doesn't want him to die so easily. "Sshh, sshh now. No more apologizing. No more begging. No more excuses. You did what you did and all that's left is the consequences, which, might I add, are going to seriously suck for you." She glances back at the alley/castle. "What do you think the odds are that I ended up in this state, mere hours away from an EverRealm? *This* EverRealm in particular."

Blubber blubber, sob sob. That's all the answer she gets. "No matter. I guess it is what it is, and I am actually grateful that I was drawn to this place. At least I know to stay away from this city… until I come across the next liar that truly deserves the fate that you are about to be delivered into."

Lenny drops to his knees, hysterical beyond coherent speech. She reaches down and strokes his hair, her voice soothing as she expounds on the things to come in his very near future. "There's one thing you should be aware of, Lenny, before I send you in there. As terrifying as I can be, as cruel and ruthless and bloodthirsty as I am… let me assure you that I am an amateur compared to my father. He's not called Lokskell (the Death Bringer) and the Shadow Lord for nothing. He taught me how to be the way I am. My magic, my Shadows… it all came from him, and I promise you that if I can do it, he can do it bigger and better. He's had a thousand years to practice, after all." She digs her fingers into Lenny's hair and yanks his head back so that she can see his face. "Now get up off of your knees and take off your shirt."

He jumps to his feet and begins fumbling with the buttons, his fingers trembling so violently that he can barely manage the task. "W,w,why? What are you gonna do to me?" he stutters as the tears pour down his cheeks.

"Hurry now," she snaps. "You're wasting my time. I have places that I need to be."

He peels the shirt off his shoulders and balls it up in his hands, holding it protectively against his belly. He quakes, actually quakes in terror as she sends her Shadows out. She holds her finger up and uses it like an ink pen, writing letters in the air. The Shadows, as always, rush to obey her commands. They mimic the movements of her finger-pen and carve the letters that she airwrites deep into the flesh of his chest. All he can do is scream aloud his agony while she writes a brief message to her father.

A GIFT FOR YOU FATHER

FUCK YOU ALWAYS

FROM YOUR DAUGHTER

SAMARA

Once the message is carved upon his chest and the blood's pouring down to soak and stain his trousers, her Shadows seep into the wounds, burning and searing, the flesh bubbling up as they mix with his blood and settle inside of him in a new, Shadow-ink tattoo.

"Look Lenny!" she taunts. "My Shadows found a way to get inside of you after all! And now they'll always be a part of you. Something to remember me by, although I'm sure you won't need the reminder. I can almost guarantee that you'll be screaming my name daily, cursing me for the rest of your miserable life. And I do hope my father lets you continue to breathe for a *very* long time."

The Shadows wrap around him and begin to drag him towards the alley/shivery space/castle, but she holds up a hand to halt them when he beseeches her. "Please Samara, I beg you. Don't do this! Is there…is there a Sluggeelian in there? There is, isn't there?"

She grins wickedly back at him. "Well, of course there is! Several of them, in fact. Sluggeelians are among my father's most favorite henchmen. They're usually his weapon of choice when he requires a death that he doesn't wish to take an active part in but still wishes to deliver the maximum amount of pain and damage. More bang for his buck, you could say! Good luck to you, Lenny!" And she waves her hand once more, giving her Shadows permission to continue dragging him the rest of the short distance to the EverRealm. He uselessly kicks and screams and sobs every step of the way, struggling in vain against her power. She waves a sad little goodbye as they shove him through Sheol Castle's everopen, ever-welcoming front gate.

"Goodbye Lenny," she whispers as he disappears.

Samara turns to gauge Mr. Chadwick's reaction at the murder of his boss but for once, he's not looking her. He's too busy staring up at the empty space in awe.

"You saw it," she murmurs in a quiet voice.

He nods his affirmation. "For a brief moment, right as he went through." His eyes lower to hers and instead of the anger or even the horror that she always expects to see, he smiles the sweetest smile at her… the fucking maniac. He never ceases to amaze her, this gentle freak of a man with his quiet acceptance of everything she does, everything she is.

There's a sudden pang somewhere inside of her chest. "You realize, of course, that one day I'll have to kill you," she tells him.

He nods, his smile slipping as his expression grows serious.

"Of course, my lady."

She frowns and adds, "I allow myself no weaknesses."

"Naturally. I would expect nothing less from a queen."

"Not today, but someday I'll have to do it."

"It's ok, my lady. I understand. And I'm grateful."

"Grateful? What the hell for?"

"I have no wish to go back to living my life in a world without you. When you tire of this old fool, I will welcome death with a smile on my lips… grateful for this time with you."

"Fuck," she whispers. Then she spins around and smashes her fists into the side of her 3.3 million-dollar Bugatti. "Fuck, Fuck, Fuck!" she screams as she takes out her frustrations on the car instead of on him. She screams and punches until the bones in her hands give. Then she quiets herself. Turns. Calmly tells him, "I'll have to do it… sooner now than I'd thought."

He nods again, just as calmly, just as accepting. "I know. But not today."

Now it's *her* turn to smile. "No, not today."

He winks at her and then grins in that shy, devilish way that lets her know he's thinking of all the naughty things they both love to do to one another. "Very good, my lady," he murmurs and sparks a slow fire to burning in her belly.

"Come on, Mr. Chadwick. Get us out of here."

He opens the passenger door for her, instinctively knowing that she'll want to be in the front seat with the windows down and the rock and roll blaring. "Where to now, m'lady?" he asks as he walks around and slips into the driver's seat.

"Why, to your playroom, of course. As fast as you can get us there."

He starts the car and gives her one last lust filled glance. "Oh, *yes ma'am,*" he whispers as he puts the car into gear and they take off, going from 0 to 60 in less than 3 seconds flat. He groans softly in frustration because even though the Bugatti can move at 200+ mph, it still won't get them back home, get her back into his bed fast enough to suit him.

The Tunnels to Hell

Ecko

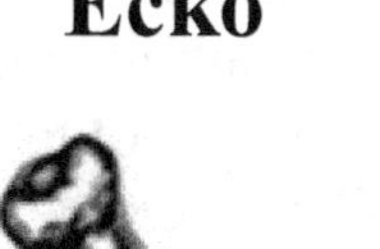

Upon landing, Ecko immediately struggles into an upright position, groaning in pain from her violent collision with the ground. She throws a quick glance over her bruised shoulder to see how close the three stooges are to the door. Only there *is* no door. It's gone, vanished as mysteriously as it had appeared. She pries her arms apart and lifts Boodark up out of his basket to ensure that she hadn't squished him. His eyes are enormous green pools as she hurriedly checks him over for injuries. Once assured of his relative wellbeing, she gently places him on the ground, lets out an exasperated groan, and allows herself to fall backwards. She's just going to lie there and take herself a little respite. If ever anyone deserved a time out, it was the two of them!

The smell is the first thing that they notice… besides the fact that they're no longer in the Field of Screams and Broken Dreams. The intoxicating whiff of a floral paradise assails their senses,

321

drawing a perplexed frown to their faces. The scent confuses; it does not match up with the image that their minds insist that their eyes should be seeing.

Their sniffers are telling them that they should be surrounded by flowers in the middle of a springtime meadow, breathing in the sweet fragrance of blossoms in full bloom. But that's not the sight that meets their peepers. The two of them are lying on their backs, looking up at a canopy of bare tree branches. It's dark here, eerie… and definitely *not* what their noses insist that they're smelling.

They sit up to better study their surroundings. They appear to be inside a tree tunnel, and *not* a beautiful, flowery one. It's a tunnel-path made up of trees that are either dead or sleeping their winter sleep. They're packed in so close together that there's no break between them, no space large enough for even tiny Boodark to slip between them. The branches above their heads are a tangled mess that's almost as impenetrable as their trunks, with the slightest, random gaps that allow patches of weak light to filter in. It's every bit as dark and imposing as the Fire Gang's Firey Forest in the Labyrinth, every bit as spooky as the Haunted Forest in the Wizard of Oz. But this isn't a movie, no matter how much she wishes otherwise.

"Ah, elfslugs and earwax! Where are we now?" Boodark whines.

She looks down at him, and smiling gently, she begins pulling bits of heather from his tangled hair. "Well, I can tell you that we're not in Kansas anymore, Toto."

He blinks up at her in confusion before shaking his head. "You say the strangest things."

She giggles and pokes him. "Really? Your favorite swear words are elfslugs and earwax, but *I* say the strangest things?"

He staunchly defends his choice of profanity, insisting that it's a perfectly good expletive. "Sometimes the already made curse words are insufficient for certain situations. Sometimes I'm forced to make up my own, ok?"

She throws back her head and laughs up at the branches.

"How can you laugh at a time like this? We almost died back there!" he shouts. "What's so funny anyway?"

She picks him up and squashes him to her chest in a tight bearhug. "That's why I'm laughing… because I *can* laugh."

He struggles against her and grunts, "Hu? That makes no sense. You're squishing me!"

She loosens her hold but refuses to let go as she explains. "I'm laughing because I'm still alive *to* laugh. We made it! We escaped my father's henchmen. We survived me impersonating a bird…despite my never having taken a single flying lesson, and now we get to move on to a new adventure! Like this one," she cheerfully adds with a wave of her hand out at the creepy tree tunnel.

"Yeah well, forgive me if I don't share your enthusiasm," he grumps back. "I'm still trying to recover from the last ordeal. I don't know how you can so easily dismiss the horror of such a close encounter with a Sluggeelian's slimy penis." He shudders violently and adds, "Remind me to explain their mating rituals to you some time. *Then* you'll understand why it's going to be a while longer before I can relax."

Her smile melts away as quickly as an ice cream cone in the Texas summer heat… She gags, frowns fiercely at him, and then promptly gags again as she sets him back down beside her. "You just had to remind me," she complains.

Desperate to get the disturbing images out of her head, she focuses on her raging thirst and reaches into her backpack for a water bottle. Upon further consideration, she decides that she's hungry as well. It must be nearing lunch time by now. "Well, since we're already down here on the ground, let's have a little picnic, shall we? You hungry?"

If anything can make him feel better, it'll be food. She has to grin at his overly enthusiastic nod. "I don't even know why I asked," she laughs as she rummages around in the bag for food.

She removes two small jars of diced veggies and a piece of flat bread wrapped in a large, banana-like leaf…very Lord of the Rings, lembas bread-style.

In the process of setting them both up for their meal, she notices an unfamiliar bundle. Whatever it is, Tanda must have slipped it into her bag, because she immediately recognizes the soft spiddersilk towel. She carefully unwraps the bundle and almost cries aloud at what she finds. Tanda, bless her beautiful, ancient heart, had picked two of her precious milkpods and stowed them away as a wonderful surprise. "Is this enough to make you happy once more?" she asks as she shows him what she's discovered.

Boodark *does* cry at the sight of them, but he giggles like an excited child through the tears.

"We'll eat our lunch and then split one for dessert," she tells him as she sets one aside and rewraps the remaining one. "That way we have one to enjoy with the Endmeal too. How does that sound?"

He eagerly nods his head as he scarfs his food down just as fast as he can, his eyes never once lifting from the enticing treat. She laughs but has no room to talk as she's rapidly shoveling food into her own mouth too. They finish eating their meal in record time and then move on to what they really wanted all along.

Sighing in blissful pleasure with every bite and sip, they devour the milkpod in a shockingly short amount of time.

"What *are* you doing?" Boodark asks, his puzzled voice loud in her ear. He's perched up on her shoulder as she walks along the tunnel. He'd wanted to stretch his legs a bit, but he also knew that he'd walk much too slowly, so he'd asked if he could ride on her shoulder… just for a little while. She doesn't mind. She knows that he's just tired of being confined to his basket.

"*Hello*. Ecko, I asked what you were doing. What are you looking for? And where in the fickle feckle heckle is that smell coming from?"

Bewildered but curious, he's been watching her drag her hands along the tree trunk wall, poking her fingers into every nook, dip, and crevice that she comes across. "Oh, I'm looking for secret openings," she casually replies.

They've been walking for over half an hour down this spooktacular tunnel without a single change or break in the scenery. "What?" she snaps at his scoffing snort. She turns her head to glare at him. "Don't you dare call me a big dummy. It could happen!" He rolls his eyes and snickers at her instead.

"Do you remember when we talked about movies?" she asks him. He nods and then proceeds to gush about the 'moving pictures.' His eyes light up with excitement as he thinks back on their conversations, how she'd promised to find a way for him to watch one… provided that she gets herself out of the mess that she's currently in, that is.

"Well," she says once he's exhausted his extremely limited knowledge of such things. "My favorite movie of all time is called Labyrinth. The main character is a girl named Sara, and she goes into the labyrinth to save her baby brother from the Hobglin King… I mean, the *Goblin* King. I always say that wrong! Anyway, once she was inside, she realized that she hadn't *really* made it into the Labyrinth. She was trapped in a long, never-ending passageway, with no turns or openings… no way to get out." She gestures out at their own never-ending path.

"What did she do?" He demands to know what happened.

"Well, she walked and walked and then she ran and ran, but it never turned into the labyrinth."

Boodark kicks his legs in frustration. "Did she die in there? Did she have a magic bag of food with her?" He sucks in a deep, horrified gasp and then whispers, "Did she *starve* to death?"

She turns to face him, her eyebrows raised incredulously. "What? No! She didn't die. Why would it be my favorite movie if she died…especially right in the beginning? No, what happens is, she eventually meets a worm that tells her about the secret openings in the walls that would take her into the labyrinth… he insisted that there was one just across from them on the other side of the passageway. She didn't believe him because she couldn't see any openings and she argued that it was just wall… no way through. *'Try walking through it, you'll see what I mean. Things are not always what they seem in this place, so you can't take anything for granted'* That's what he told her. So, she tried it and sure enough, there *was* an opening. But I think you're right, Boodark. There aren't any secret openings here."

She sighs in disappointment as she turns to look back behind them, just to see if anything had changed since the last time she checked. Nope. It's still the same endless passageway, identical to what lies in front of them. What's even more disconcerting is the fact that the EverGlass has gone silent. She hasn't heard it even once since she came tumbling through the door, therefore she can no longer use its call as a homing beacon to guide her. They'd only chosen to walk this way because it's the position that they'd been in when they crashed through the door. They figured their best bet would be to continue on in the direction they were already facing.

But perhaps they chose wrong. (Too late now!) Perhaps they should have turned and walked the other way. She's thinking about turning back and trying the other direction, contemplating how bad it would suck to do so and then find out that they'd been right the first time. No, she'll stick to the course they'd decided on. For now, anyway.

"Well, what happened to her?" Boodark demands.

She blinks at him in confusion for a moment before she understands. "Oh, Sara went on and made her way through the labyrinth, through many dangers until she finally defeated the Hobglin King and rescued her brother. Then she took him back home, safe and sound."

Boodark pumps his fist into the air in triumph. "Yes! A happy ending!"

She nods and adds, "Yes, it was a happy ending, but it was a bit sad too. I always felt a little bad for the Hobglin…*Goblin* King.

I think he was lonely. Plus, Sara had to say goodbye to all the new friends she'd met along the way. Sir Didymus, the stuffed animal in my bag…he's a character from that movie. He's one of Sara's friends that helped her make it to the Hobglin City. I fell in love with him the very first time I watched it. I was five years old at the time." She stops walking and glances thoughtfully up at one of the gaps in the overhead branches. "Hey, Boodark, do you think…"

He doesn't even wait for her to finish the sentence. "Say no more. Lift me up." She lifts him up and sets him high up in the branches. "Be careful!" she calls as she watches him monkey crawl along them until he reaches the opening. But no matter which way he tries, he can't even get his head to fit through so that he can take a peek beyond the tunnel's borders. So much for openings, secret or otherwise.

"I think I see something up ahead! Boodark, you have better eyesight than I do. Does it look different to you?" He stands up on her shoulder and uses his hand to shade his eyes as if he's blocking out a bright light, which makes no sense seeing how dark it is. "Red. It looks red," he tells her as he sits back down. She only nods. That's what she thought too. It's another ten minutes or so before they're close enough to see that the tunnel is about to change… drastically. The walls will no longer be tree trunks, the canopy above their heads will no longer be branches that stretch across the passageway.

This, she realizes as she gapes at the scenery in awe, is where that amazing smell is coming from. Their tunnel prison has come vibrantly alive with bright green vine walls and cascading clusters of wisteria blossoms. A wisteria tunnel, just like the one in Japan that's on her bucket list of things to see… only these aren't soft shades of purple and lavender. They're cluster upon cluster of crimson-red and onyx-black blossoms, cascading down the walls and dripping from the ceiling in a thick, fragrant curtain.

"Ooohhh, isn't it lovely?" she breathes as she stops just beyond the seam where the two tunnels come together.

Boodark, on the other hand, has tensed up and gone on high alert. Something's nagging at him, some long forgotten memory that's just out of reach. But whatever it is, it has his guard up. He doesn't trust those flowers, no matter how sweet they smell. "I don't like it, Ecko" he mutters uncomfortably.

"Well, I love wisteria," she tells him in a dreamy voice as she ignores his warning. She reaches out and gently cups a brilliant cluster in her hand, moving in so that she can sniff its sweet perfume. She smiles and adds, "They're my favorite flo…" just as Boodark shouts "No!" straight into her ear. "That's not *wisteria*; it's *Hysteria* vines! They're deadly!"

But his memory had been jogged too late, therefore his warning comes too late to spare her. She cries out and jerks her hand back when each bloom in the cluster drips a single bead of… something onto her hand. Something that burns like acid! She lifts her hand up to inspect the damage and sees little curls of smoke drifting up from seven reddened blemishes on her skin.

"Ow," she cries and then watches in horror as the teeniest, tiniest vines poke up out of the wounds and begin to grow… right out of her hand. "Meteor poop!" she yelps when all she can picture is the episode in Stephen King's Creepshow where the alien plant grows all over poor Jordy Verrill.

In absolute panic, she violently waves her hand around as if she believes that she can shake the growths off. She soon finds that she cannot, and her panic quickly escalates. But then she feels her magic rush through her, concentrating on that one hand and lighting it up with glowing blue energy. The miniature vines thrash about for a mere second or two before they wither, turn grey, and then fall off of her skin, leaving nothing but small, painful blisters behind. "Ow," she repeats in a hurt, betrayed voice as she tries to figure out what just happened.

"I'm sorry!" Boodark blurts. "I knew not to trust them, but I couldn't figure out why. It's because I've never actually seen Hysteria plants before; I've only *heard* about them. If everything I heard is true, and I have no reason to doubt it… not after what just happened, then we are in serious trouble, my friend. I hate to say it, but I think it's best that we turn around and go back the way we came and just hope that the EverGlass lies in that other direction."

She hears what he's saying. She can even acknowledge the wisdom in his words, but she has to ask, "Do you *truly* believe it lies back there, in the other direction? Truly and honestly?"

His mouth opens and he sucks in a breath… then he lets it gush right back out. His shoulders slump in dejection as he answers honestly. "No. It almost certainly will be at the end of this doomtrail."

She nods because that's the very same conclusion she'd come to. "We need a plan," she advises. His ears suddenly perk up and his eyes light with excitement, making her wonder just what he's up to now. She doesn't have to wait long for an answer either. "I have an idea!" he chirps in an eager voice. "We should take a break… sit down and think it over with a little snackysnack."

She snorts out a laugh; she can't help it. "You just want to eat the other milkpod!" she tells him.

"Well, don't you?" he asks in all seriousness.

She stops giggling because she *does* want to. "We just ate an hour ago! Besides, wouldn't it be better to save it? It'll give us something to look forward to once we're past all this."

He grunts and blows a strand of hair out of his eyes. "That's one way to look at it, I suppose. Another is that if we don't make it past the death tunnel, at least we can take comfort knowing that we didn't let it go to waste. We can die happily with the sweet taste of EverLand nectar on our tongues instead of the bitter flavor of disappointment and regret for wasted opportunities."

She raises her eyebrows at him. "Wow. Just… wow. That was quite the motivational speech… very convincing."

He grins cheekily at her. "I know, right? Did it work?"

His smile gets wiped away with her short, to the point, no nonsense response of "No." She hides her own smile when he mumbles a disappointed, "Drat," under his breath. "We do need a plan though." She agrees with that much. "Tell me everything you've heard about Hysteria plants."

"They're very invasive," he begins. "And by invasive, I don't mean that they will simply take over a small section of land. Invasive as in they take over *everything*. As you've already learned, it will grow on whatever it can, but it's also smart. See how the ground is clear of vines? That's because it has already spread as much as possible in this confined area. It knows that to spread further would be to bring about its own demise. It would choke itself out… not enough food, not enough light, or whatever it needs to sustain it. Spreading further would kill the whole system. You still with me?"

When she nods, he goes on with his explanations. "The blossoms drip a single drop of poison, each one containing a single seed. The poison eats a hole in whatever surface it lands on, and the seed drops in and takes root. Be glad that your magic was strong enough to stop the growth and kill it off. There's a reason they're called Hysteria vines, because that's exactly what they do… cause hysteria."

He pauses and glances down at the ground until he spots a small rock. "Ah ha!" he cries. "See that rock? Throw it in there and watch how the flowers react."

She does what he suggests and tosses it… perhaps ten feet in. The clusters that it passes under all begin to vibrate, and then the dripping begins. But she notices that the ones closest to them don't release their poison at all. They just shiver.

"The ones in the front let the rest of the plant know that something's coming. They don't want to start dripping too soon and warn their victims away. They'll wait until we move in far enough that we can't back out quickly or easily."

They watch as the once smooth stone becomes riddled with holes until it resembles a lava rock, pitted and pock marked. When the seeds begin to sprout, it only takes seconds before the entire rock, what's left of it, is completely wrapped up in a tangle of writhing vines.

Boodark turns back to look at her as he continues his lesson. "By the time the unsuspecting traveler gets as far as that rock, he will be covered in dozens of wounds. He'll most likely stop to inspect them, just like you did. Only he would be standing out *there*, receiving more and more poison drips. By that time, the traveler will surely be in a panic. In other words, hysteria. The victim will then try to run, but he won't get far, as the seeds and vines grow incredibly fast. I've heard it's a terrible way to die."

She can only imagine it would be. "One more thing," he tells her.

"Oh great," she grumbles, and he nods in commiseration. "Not only does the plant sense movements, but it reacts to it in sort of a time-lapse ripple, as well."

"I don't understand."

He frowns as he thinks about how to explain it. "Remember how the flowers shake and vibrate to alert the rest of the plant? Well, why didn't *all* the flowers…all the way down the tunnel… just dump their poison right then and there?"

Her eyebrows rise up further as she sees what he's getting at. "It works like a ripple. Aside from the ones in the front, the *guards*, the rest of the flowers will only react if they each sense movement themselves. Didn't you notice how the clusters beyond where the rock landed never even reacted?"

She *hadn't* noticed, but now that he's mentioned it, she's curious. She looks around until she finds another rock to throw. She wants to watch it again, now that she knows what she's looking at. She tosses it in and it's just like he said. It *is* smart, and it *does* work like a ripple effect. She wonders just how many rocks she'd have to throw in before the blossoms run out of poison… *if* they would *ever* run out. For all she knows they have an endless supply of toxic flower pee. Not that she has enough rocks to throw anyway. There are literally millions, *billions* of red and black blooms just waiting to pee on her and spread their seeds.

Brow furrowed and teeth nibbling at her bottom lip, she concentrates on the problem at hand, resolutely searching for a solution… one that involves them *not* becoming vegetable matter. Her magic could possibly save them from that fate, but that's a whole lot of trust to put in something that has proven to be faulty many, *many* times already. Plus, she really doesn't want to be covered in blisters, even if her magic is able to remove all the vines from her skin. The nine wounds on her hand throb painfully still, and she doesn't even want to imagine how excruciating it would be to have them all over her body.

That's not to mention the fact that they probably wouldn't make it very far before becoming completely saturated in poison. The Hysteria tunnel stretches farther than her eyes can see, and it's filled, entirely covered, in the crimson and obsidian blossoms. There are no breaks or baren patches that she can see, so there will be no stopping to rest or regroup once they get started. And for all she knows, it stretches as far as the tree tunnel had… for *miles*.

She's wracking her brain, having no luck coming up with any sort of viable plan when it happens again. An image of Caheera spitting the shimmery scale into her hand flashes through her mind. Just like with Danika's feather, basic instructions (in picture form) also come along with the mental images. The information rushes through her mind so fast that it feels like it's a file downloading at high speed directly into her brain. Then it's over and she knows exactly what she has to do.

Wasting no time, she shrugs off her backpack and takes her previously useless sunglasses out of the side pocket that they've been stashed in. As she wraps her tarp around her bag, she briefly explains the plan to Boodark, although she's careful to leave out some pertinent details that she knows he's not gonna be thrilled with. "I'm just adding another layer of protection over my belongings," she tells him. "Just as a precaution in case some of the poison gets through the armor."

Then she bends down and tightens her shoelaces, tying them into double knots before she straightens back up and tucks her shirt into her jeans.

"What in the butt-cheek flappin' fannyfarts are you talking about? And what *are* you doing?" he asks in a confused and bewildered tone of voice.

She rummages around in his beddy-bye basket until she locates the scale, continuously babbling as if she doesn't even hear him. She's mostly speaking to herself anyway, talking herself through the upcoming events. "Have to remember we'll be under a strict time restraint, a short one. We'll have only minutes, so we gotta move fast…stop for nothing. There's no telling how far this Hysteria tunnel extends. I can only hope that it's not as long as the tree tunnel was."

Boodark leans in close to her ear and shouts her name to get her to stop rambling on and on. "Oh yeah, *that* got your attention," he snarks when she winces in pain. "You're going to have to talk to me like I don't know what's going on…. Because I don't know what's going on!"

She slips her sunglasses on, turns to face him, and calmly states, "Weren't you listening? We're going to make a run for it."

He doesn't say anything at all for a moment… he *can't*. He's actually, for once in his life, speechless.

"It'll work!" she insists. "This is what Caheera's scale is for."

He remains shocked and mute as he watches her sketch the rune into her palm. Holding the scale above the rune in preparation, she pauses long enough to level a serious look on him. "Remember, we'll only have a few minutes so don't struggle, ok? Don't make it harder than it has to be." Then she slaps the scale down onto her palm to activate the magic.

"What are you… Hey!" he shouts as she snatches him from his parrot perch on her shoulder and promptly stuffs him down the front of her shirt. Just in time too. The scale flips over in her hand and as it does, a second scale unfolds out of it. They both flip over in opposite directions and then there are four of them lying on her palm. They flip and multiply, flip and multiply in every direction until her entire arm is covered in a layer of scales, one overlapping the next in a full armored sleeve. And it keeps going and growing, spreading like wildfire to quickly cover her chest (and a wildly thrashing Boodark) and then on across her right arm. It flows downwards, over her belly and wraps around her back and buttocks, then down to cover her legs and feet, while at the same time it climbs up her neck, over her head and covers her face. No part of her is left exposed except her mouth, the underside of her nose and her eyes, which she has protected as best she can behind her sunglasses.

In less than a minute, her entire body has been encased inside a shimmering, iridescent scale-plated bodysuit. She wastes no time admiring it though. She snatches her backpack, hugs it against her chest (triple layer of protection for Boodark, as the poison will have to go through the tarp, the contents of her backpack, and then the scales before it can harm him) and takes off running before the suit of armor is even 100% completed. She has a few seconds before the flowers start dripping their poison anyway, and she knows that she'll need every second of protection she can get.

The Hysteria immediately reacts to her presence, and all too soon, the first drops of poison are splatting against her armor. They don't seem to do much damage against the hard scales at first; they just cause a slight discoloration to the iridescent blue/purple sheen.

Good, oh good! she thinks as her legs pump and her arms clutch her bag tighter. Poor Boodark is squished between her boobs and he's squirming around, struggling with all his tiny might to push them apart so that he can climb up out of there. She listens to his muffled curses and complaints, and she knows without a doubt that he'll have some choice words for her… if they survive.

The Hysteria reacts like a wave in the ocean as she passes… wave after wave of clusters come alive to drip their poison and sow their seeds. She runs as if her life depends on it… because it does, and even more than that… so does Boodark's.

She looks up as she runs, watching the ripple effect she's causing amongst the blossoms, but she quickly abandons that and turns her face down when several drops land on the sunglasses, resulting in smoking, melty spots on the lenses. She keeps her head tucked down as she barrels on… She does *not* want vines growing out of her eye sockets. (Insert the terrible images of the last time she saw Karen… with the severed doll hands reaching out of her eyes.) Slam the door shut on that nightmare-inducing memory.

Lock it back up in its proper compartment. Add more chains and then padlock it so securely that it can never escape again.

When she first starts hearing it, she believes the hissing sound is merely the wind whistling past, as if the speed in which she's moving is fast enough to create a wind, but she soon realizes that's not the case when she sees the smoke rising up off her armor. The hissing is the poison burning through her protective gear! The scales are being eaten away, growing thinner and lighter in color with every drip that lands on them. And honestly, what the blossoms are doing can no longer be called *dripping*. She's moving so fast, the Hysteria keeping up with her every step, so the poison is now *raining* down on her, pouring down like a thunderstorm… a flowerstorm.

The blood pounds in her ears, her breath tears in and out of her lungs as she watches her feet fly over the ground. And thank you, sweet baby Jesus that she *is* watching where she's running, because that's the only reason that she notices the thick vine pull away from the wall and suddenly snake across the ground. Attempting to trip her up or to ensnare her, she doesn't know which. It doesn't really matter though, as either one would have been disastrous, had it succeeded. But she leaps over that thing like a horse jumping over obstacles in a hurdle race… just as she feels the first sting on her forearm.

She glances down and sees that she's lost a scale, either to poison or to the magic running out of time. She looks down at herself and half panics when she sees just how thin her armor has become, so thin that several of the scales seem like nothing more than paper-thin, crystal-clear disks of glass… fragile and brittle.

Seriously beginning to question her chances of success, she nevertheless puts on as much speed as she can force her body into. The scales are falling off now and dissolving away beneath the blossom's toxic onslaught. She grits her teeth against the stinging pain and chances a peek ahead of her. Is that… Is that the end of the tunnel? Far off still, but within sight?

Yes! Her heart races with excitement (as well as exertion) as she realizes just how close she is to escaping. But can she make it that far? That's the question, because unfortunately, the all too smart Hysteria vines realize the exact same thing… that she's nearing the finish line and that she might actually make it out alive. It takes immediate action and sends vine after vine out after her, and she has to use all her concentration on avoiding them.

By now there are several tiny vines growing out of her skin, mostly on her arms and back. And one right on her freaking face, growing out of her right temple. It begins to wave about in front of her eyes as it grows longer and longer. It's distracting her, blinding her to the dangers that steadily keep emerging to trip her up. She reaches up and pinches it between her thumb and pointer finger, then ruthlessly yanks it out. She cries out at the pain as it pulls away. She sees that the impossibly long, bloody root is covered with spiky barbs, designed to cling inside the flesh to make removal difficult and exceedingly painful.

She tosses the hateful little thing away and then promptly realizes that she's just screwed up. She should have just left the nasty thing hanging out of her face, because she'd been so distracted by it that she'd somehow missed the vine that she'd just stepped on. Her ankle twists sharply and sends her crashing down to the ground, just as the last of the rune disappears from her palm and the few remaining scales fall away. Tears stream down her face as she grits her teeth and struggles back to her feet.

She hobbles on, sting after sting biting into her skin. She calls on her magic, desperately begging it to listen and to behave because she's not going to make it otherwise. Thankfully, it comes as soon as she calls, instantly lighting her skin up in blue… as if it had just been waiting for permission to act. Hundreds of little vines writhe in agony as death claims them while she limps the last several yards to the end of the Hysteria tunnel… and collapses right into the new funnel tunnel made of spider webs.

Boodark, gasping and desperate for air, his green face flushed a horrible, mottled green-red color and his hair a tangled, disheveled mess, uses his claws to slash his way out of her shirt.

It's ruined anyway, as are her jeans. They're both indecently riddled with holes, revealing a shocking amount of her poor, blistered skin.

He bursts up off her chest, snarling and cursing while she just lays there staring up at the webbed ceiling as she sucks up precious air. "Ugh! Gah! Ack! Don't you EVER do that again! What's the *matter* with you? You can't just go stuffing good folks between your boobs, which by the way, are *way* bigger than they look from the outside of your clothes. Also, way sweatier."

He gags a couple times, dry heaving at the thought of being the filling stuffed inside a sweaty boob sandwich. He stomps off, grumbling and cursing with fouler language than she's ever heard come out of his mouth. "The *nerve* of it! I mean *really*. What was she thinking, shoving me inside her shirt? Giant, sweaty boobs are sooo being added to the list of things I hate!"

He goes on and on and on until she's caught her breath and has plain and simple had it with his ungrateful tirade. With a whimper of pain (that he never even hears over his indignation) she sits up and glances down at herself to assess the damage. It looks bad, *really* bad, and it feels even worse… but thankfully none of it seems to be life threatening.

"And furthermore," Boodark continues. "We are *supposed* to be a team! If you had just *told* me what you were planning, we could have worked it out together, *with no sweaty, giant boobs involved!* But no. You just couldn't do that could you? You just *haaad* to…"

That's it. That's it, that's *it!* She's had just about enough. "Shut up, Boodark! Just shut *up!*" He shuts up, and he whirls around with a shocked and outraged expression on his ugly little face.

"If you would stop spewing your self-righteous verbal vomit at me for one second and just listen, I could explain. Better yet, why don't you just take a good look? Really *look* at me." She gestures down at her body, drawing his attention to the tattered remains of her clothing and the blisters that cover her from her head to her feet like a lethal case of the chicken pox, many of which have burst open to ooze blood and clear fluids down her skin. His eyes find and track the trail of blood that trickles from the spot where she'd pulled the vine out of her face.

His mouth starts to tremble and his eyes instantly well up with tears. "Oh. *Oh,* Ecko. Oh, I'm so sorry. You're right and I'm so, *so* sorry. I guess I was just panicking. And grossed out. And I couldn't breathe. And I was panicking. And, and, and..." He throws himself face down on the ground and starts wailing at the top of his lungs in misery, his little shoulders shaking from the force of his sobs.

Her own shoulders slump and she sighs wearily, all the violent winds stolen from her anger-sails in the face of his distress. She booty-scootches over to where he lies and strokes his tangled, messy hair. "It's alright, Boodark. Don't cry. I'm sorry I yelled at you." Instead of comforting him, her words seem to do just the opposite, as he cries harder, practically howling out his grief.

"Look, I'm sorry, ok? I'm sorry I subjected you to my huge, sweaty boobs. I promise you, I didn't enjoy it any more than you did. It was extremely unpleasant, feeling you squirming around in there. I'm sorry I didn't tell you the whole plan. I'm sorry..."

He jumps up and turns his big green eyes, streaming with tears, on her. "Stop!" he wails. "Just *stop!* Why are you saying you're sorry for saving my life? For saving me from suffering all *that,*" he cries as he gestures to her wounds. "You saved me from dying a horrible death and becoming a plant forever, and all I can do is yell at you for it! I'm an arse, a stupid, ungrateful shitecovered, worm-infested arse! You should punch me. Go ahead!" he cries as he bravely lifts his chin and pokes his belly out at her. "Do it, Ecko. Punch me in the belly. Better yet, pummel my face. I deserve it, and it's ugly anyway."

She smiles at what he thinks would be a fair retaliation on her part. "I'm not going to do that. You *know* I won't. But if you want to do penance, you can help me clean the wounds that I can't reach. Deal?"

He lays his hand over hers and gives her a tremulous halfsmile. "Deal," he whispers.

Two bottles of water, all the cotton gauze and alcohol wipes from her first aid kit, and a full hour later, they're finally done cleaning and patching her up. Now she's sitting on the ground in clean, hole-free undies, the area around her littered with wet, bloody pieces of gauze and strips of Tanda's spiddersilk towel that they'd ripped up and used to wash her wounds with. Of course, they'd been forced to consume the milkpod that was wrapped *inside* the towel first. Hey, they were 100% prepared to do whatever they had to do to clean those wounds, and they *needed* that towel to do it. Simplest solution... eat the milkpod. That's their story anyway and they're sticking to it.

Thinking about it now though, she wishes that they'd saved it so that they could enjoy it later, *after* all this nonsense was past them. Sighing out her disappointment, she says as much to her little friend while he begins gathering up their trash.... He's spent several Pales observing this ground stomper and her strange ways, so he knows that she won't just leave it lying there.

"We probably should have saved it for later," she laments as she carefully tugs a fresh t-shirt over her head. When he merely grunts back, she asks, "No regrets?"

He sweeps the last of the garbage into a pile then turns to face her, hands on his hips and a small frown on his face. "Just one," he answers. "I've been thinking about it, and I truly believe that you got one more bite than I did."

Her mouth drops open in disbelief and he cuts her arguments off before they can even form. "Now, hear me out. You took the first bite, am I right?" At her nod, he continues his irrational rationalization. "Well, you also took the *last* bite. By my calculations, I should have gotten the last piece. You, my friend, are a greedy Grunter!"

She sputters for a second but quickly recovers. "It evened out; you know it did! You *know* what you did!"

He turns shocked and dramatically innocent eyes on her, but she ignores them. He's not fooling anyone with those adorable cartoon eyes of his. "Don't you give me that innocent act! I *saw* you. You took a bite and then snuck in a second one when you thought I was distracted. Greedy Grunter, indeed."

Boodark lifts his chin up and insists, "I don't know what you're talking about. *If* that really happened, I don't remember it. And I certainly didn't *mean* to do it. Now what do you want me to do with this mess?" He kicks at a scrap of gauze to draw her attention away from the conversation. Brat. He knows exactly what he did.

She grins as she tells him to just wrap it all up in the leftover scraps from her jeans. She had ripped the rest of her clothing into strips to bind her injured ankle with, although she hasn't wrapped it up yet. She's been dreading doing it, so she left it for the last chore.

"I guess I can't put it off any longer," she complains as she pulls on a clean pair of jeans, being ever so careful as to not bump her ankle. Once she's wiggled into them, she starts wrapping it with the strips of cloth. She has to bite her lip to stifle her cries as she binds it up tight. It's swollen to double its normal size and she's terrified that it won't hold up under her weight when she stands up. And she doesn't even attempt to put her shoes on. Not. Happening. So, she ties the laces together and then ties them onto her backpack. She crams everything else back into her bag and stalls just one more minute. The two of them have studiously ignored their surroundings for the entire past hour, refusing to talk about it.

Heck, refusing to even *look* at it. But it must be done. They can't ignore it forever, more's the pity.

"So Boodark, what are your thoughts on *this* tunnel? Do you know what this is?"

He slowly shakes his head as he raises his eyes to inspect the burrow-type passageway that they've landed themselves in. "I don't. It *has* to be a spidder web, but this is something I've never seen nor heard of. It's not normal spidder-butt webbing, that's for sure. I've *never* heard of shiny, silver webs. These are so shiny that we can see our own reflections!"

She'd definitely noticed that. It looks like someone had taken a razor blade to a (somehow pliable) mirror and sliced it into hair-thin ribbons that they then proceeded to spin round and round into this funnel tunnel. It's extremely disconcerting to see themselves reflected back in tiny, broken strips. She shivers and quickly looks away, then she slips her backpack onto her back and starts talking in an attempt to dispel her immense unease.

"On Earth, there are some species of spiders that make a web like this. Well, similar in shape anyway. They're called funnel spiders because that's what their webs resemble… just like this one. They spin their web tunnel and then hide inside a little den at the back end of it. When their prey wanders into the mouth of the tunnel, they jump out, snatch them up, and drag them back into their lair. I know I don't have to tell you what happens *then*. Thankfully, they're only about this big though," she says as she holds her fingers about an inch or so apart. The words that Sephyr had said on the night of the SpidderFrost comes back to haunt her now. '*Some spidders tiny. Ground stomper eyes not even see them. Some big as you, Change Bringer.*' How that little Darkling had laughed when she'd seen her horror.

"I miss Sephyr," she murmurs now. Boodark snorts. "Pffft, I don't." he says. Then glances up at her with sad eyes that make a liar out of him as he adds, "But I do hope the mouthy little bug is ok." Yeah, he misses her just as much as she does. Perhaps more.

She stalls a moment longer… just long enough to work up enough courage to climb to her feet and continue the journey. "I'd hate to meet up with the spider that made this web. It *has* to be massive," she observes.

Boodark turns to look back at the Hysteria tunnel, shudders and then spins back to face the web tunnel. "Perhaps it's a silkworm. I've heard that they can grow quite large. Maybe not *this* large, but…"

His words trail off and she picks up the conversation. "I only have one question," she retorts. "Are silkworms happy, little plant eaters or are they meat eaters?"

Her hopes plummet when he answers. "They're meat

eaters."

Of course, they are. They look at one another with wide, worried eyes and simultaneously whisper in twinsy, horrified voices, "*We're* meat!"

She lightly pokes him in the belly and chides, "Yeah, thanks for that Boodark, but somehow the thought of a giant, meateating worm doesn't make me feel much better than giant, blood sucking spidders."

He nods solemnly and mumbles, "I accept that."

She quickly swallows down two more Tylenol capsules and shoves the remaining single-dose sample packets into her pocket. She's keeping them within her reach because she knows that this is really, *really* going to hurt. "Climb into your basket Boodark, and let's do this thing."

Once she's got him secured around her neck, she slowly, carefully climbs to her feet and tests her tender ankle. It's painful and she'll have to hobble, but it holds her up. So long as she puts most of her weight on her other leg, she'll be able to walk… at least for a while. What she needs is to find herself a crutch. Why are there never any good Gandalf sticks around when she needs one? For a world that's full of magical creatures and supernatural plants, sorcery and witchery and all manner of hoodoo voodoo, it is *sorely* lacking in magical items to aid weary travelers on their quests.

Stupid vampire world.

"I sure hope this is a short tunnel," Boodark remarks. "I'm not sure how long you're going to be able to walk on that foot." He glances up at her, noting how pinched her face is as she tries to hide her pain. "I would carry you if I could," he whispers earnestly. Sweet boy.

"I know you would," she assures him. "And just so you know, this will probably be the shortest but hardest tunnel to get through yet." She explains her reasoning when he asks how she could possibly know that. "Just think about it. The tree tunnel was easy, but it took hours to get through. Nothing tried to hurt or stop us. It just took forever. Then there was the Hysteria tunnel, and *that* was absolutely horrid. It was a challenge to get through, that's for sure. But it was only about a third of the distance as the tunnel before it. It still felt like forever getting through it though. Thank you sweet, baby Jesus that Caheera gave us that scale, or we wouldn't have made it at all."

Boodark snorts and lifts his little bat nose up in the air. "I guess a Kreeleerian scale wasn't such a stupid gift after all. And the feather sure came in handy too. But I still refuse to believe that the rude one's puked-up bone is going to save the Pale!"

She smiles down at him as she reaches up to swipe the flyaway curls that have escaped her ponytail off of her sweaty face. It's not particularly hot but limping and hobbling is wearing her out. Gesturing at the webby walls, she continues on with her observations. "Now *this* tunnel, it could be half the length as the Hysteria tunnel, but it will most likely be just as dangerous… if not more so. I'll get us out though; don't you worry. Even if I have to crawl, we're making it out of here. I just hope there are no sneaky, creepy surprises at the end of the line. I wouldn't even be able to outrun a one-legged spider right now." Then she giggles as her mind draws up *that* picture for her amusement. Intent on telling him to just imagine what a one-legged spider chasing after them would look like, she looks at him and grins. But he's got a very serious, *very* worried look on his face … almost a scared look.

"What is it?" she whispers. He holds a claw to his mouth, telling her to be quiet as he cocks his head from side to side, his oversized bat ears perked straight up on high alert. She can't help herself; she's just got to do it. There's *literally* no holding it back. "What do your elf eyes see, Legolas?" Titter, titter. "I mean, what do your bat ears hear, Boodark?" Snort, snort.

"Shut *up*, girl and let me listen!"

Oh. This is serious time. She stands still and strains her ears, listening for… whatever *he's* listening for. After a full minute of shifting her weight around to ease the burden of standing still and hearing absolutely zilch, she's decided enough is enough. She can't stand here all day. "I don't hear anything Boo…"

But then she *does* hear something, and it causes all the tiny hairs on her body to stand on end. A barely-there rustling, a soft swooshing shift of displaced air. Something's back there. She's had it all wrong. The monster isn't waiting up ahead for them. It's creeping up behind them, herding them in.

The softly sighing sounds fall away as fast as they'd come, and everything goes silent and still as a tomb once more. They stare at one another with frightened owl eyes, just waiting for something terrible to happen… but nothing does. She's entirely too afraid to turn around and look, so she just starts walking again. She's going to pretend there's nothing wrong and just keep going; she's good at ignoring unpleasant things that she doesn't want to deal with…. Until they jump up and bite her on the butt like a butt-pinching sea monstrosity. Hopefully not literally.

She shuffles forward slowly, cautiously as if moving at a snail's pace will render her movements invisible to monster eyes. After a dozen or so hesitant steps, they begin to hear it again, that swooshing, whispering sigh. Boodark whimpers as she freezes in place where they once again listen and wait. And again, the noise stops seconds after they do. She is suddenly terrified, and a chill goes through her… like there's spider legs tickling down her spine.

She can't look, she just can't. If she turns and sees a monster, she'll just have to die of fright and get eaten. She can't run. There's no way she can run. "Maybe it'll go away if we just ignore it," she whispers as she creeps forward again. But there it is again, after she's gone only a few feet. How are they supposed to ignore something that's shadowing them with every step she takes? She can't keep this up, freezing in place every time she gets started walking. It's like the world's most twisted and dramatic game of red light, green light, one that could potentially end with real-life consequences. Horrible consequences. She trembles violently as she stays locked in place.

She can't look. She has to look. But she *can't!* So, all of a sudden, she whirls around to confront her creepy stalker.

Boodark throws his hands over his eyes even as she's turning. "No Ecko, no! I don't wanna see it!" But he cautiously lowers his hands and peeks out when nothing happens, other than her sucking in a surprised gasp, that is. "Oh, fornicating Fext folks and obscene Ogre orgies!" he cries out.

She doesn't even acknowledge his odd choice in curse words. She's too busy trying to not have a heart attack. What they discover isn't a monster but is equally terrifying in its own way. The tunnel is almost silently collapsing behind them, effectively cutting off their only escape from whatever may be lying up ahead. They're left with no chance of turning back... not that going back was much of an option, but now it's *no* option.

"Does this happen with your funnel tunnel spidders back on

Earth?" Boodark asks, his voice trembling and squeaky with fright.

She solemnly shakes her head. "I don't think this happens with *any* of Earth's spiders, or any other creature for that matter. What about here? Have you ever heard of *anything* like this?" He grimly shakes his head too. "Yeah, I didn't think so" she groans. "I'm starting to think that the humans got it all wrong. The Path to Hell isn't a highway. It's a tunnel."

The two of them study the wall made of silky, silver strings. "I wonder if it will collapse right on top of us if we stay still. Or does it react to motion like the Hysteria did?" She starts walking backwards (not the easiest task with a twisted ankle) but after fourteen painful shuffling steps, they get front row tickets to watch The Collapse of the Web Tunnel in real-time… up close and personal.

"That's *very* disturbing," Boodark mumbles.

She doesn't voice it aloud, but she couldn't agree more. "I guess all we can do is keep going and hope that we continue to stay ahead of it. I don't think it will catch up to us."

He lifts his arms up and says, "Let me back on your shoulder. I'll sit facing backwards and keep my eyes on it…. Not that it will do us much good, but at least we'll know that we're about to get webbed and then we can panic accordingly."

They only make it another twenty minutes or so before she has him turning back to face forward so that he can see what she's seeing. Or what she *thinks* she's seeing. "Do you notice anything strange? Look closely."

His anime eyes roving up and down the walls and across the ceiling. He frowns fiercely as he goes over it all a second time. "Is it getting smaller in here? Is the tunnel *shrinking*?" he asks.

She sighs and glumly mutters, "It is. I was almost sure of it. Soon my head will be brushing against the ceiling, and those walls are *definitely* closing in on us."

Her little bat friend seems unconcerned, or at least optimistic. "Well," he says, "There's still plenty of room for us to get through."

Yeah, there's plenty of room for *him* to get through. He's only a foot or so tall. But she keeps her snarky comments to herself. She's beginning to panic; she knows the signs and it's not his fault. So, she keeps her mouth firmly shut as she continues on in an upright, ground stomping fashion. But after a while, she drops her backpack and carefully lowers herself to the ground. She needs a break already. Not only does her ankle throb mercilessly, but her head has begun to scrape the ceiling. She's been walking with her head lowered for the last several yards to accommodate it, but that won't give her enough leeway anymore.

Even Boodark's forced to revise his wording. He's clearly beginning to worry, but still trying to think positively… looking for that silver lining and all that. "There will be plenty of room if you crawl upon your hands and knees. *And* it will get you off that ankle for a while."

She nods as she opens a water bottle, pours some into his cup, and then chugs down the rest of it. She'd already come to that conclusion, but she'd been trying her darndest not to think about it. She rummages around in her bag and removes one last item… her *'just for emergencies'* Ativan pills, the ones she'd been prescribed for her sudden, uncontrollable panic attacks. She stuffs the pill bottle in her jeans pocket, so they'll be close at hand…. just in case she decides to have a freak out. "I sure wish we hadn't already eaten that last milkpod. It would be a wonderful morale booster right about now."

She sighs dispiritedly and levels a serious, solemn look on her friend. "I guess I never told you that I don't do well in small, confined places. Like, at all. My doctor said that's why I hate the dark so much too. All that blackness closing in on me, suffocating me… it's just like being in a dark, locked box with no way out." Her breath hitches at the thought of it and Rage laughs inside her head.

'Oh really? Welcome to my world' Rage sarcastically whispers but she just ignores him. "This may get bad, Boodark. Really bad."

He reaches out and pats her knee. "Don't worry, Ecko. We'll get through this nonsense just like we've gotten through everything else. *I'll* get you through it."

She nods and slips her backpack back on. "You're right. We got this. I think you'll have to ride on my back now, but the first time I hear *'Giddyup'* or *'mush, doggy'* you will magically and instantaneously become a ground stomper." To his credit, he manages to restrain himself and even keep the grin off his face… for as long as she can see him anyway. There's no telling how big his smile is once he's back there.

The way forward beyond that point shrinks faster and faster and faster… at least in her mind if not in actuality. Boodark only gets a short horsey ride before he's forced to climb back down and start walking beside her. At least his short little legs can keep up with her now.

Soon, there's no room left for her to crawl on her hands and knees, and her mental breathing exercises are no longer doing anything to keep her calm either. When she realizes that she's sobbing, she hangs her head for a moment before reaching down and removing the bottle of pills from her pocket. Then she lays down flat on her belly, sets the pills on the ground in front of her face, and just stares at them with silent tears coursing down her face. She knows that she needs to take one (or three) but doing so feels like giving up. She's gone so long, been through so many stressful situations without the help of any of the pharmaceuticals that her doctor had insisted that she needed. This feels like, *tastes* like failure, harsh and bitter on her tongue, just like the little white pill that she places under her tongue to dissolve. Angry at herself, she shoves the bottle back in her pocket and lays her head back down to wait for her heart to stop racing. When it slows to a more survivable rhythm, she begins to army crawl forward. There is no more room for baby-crawling on hands and knees.

Boodark walks backwards, facing her as he steadily calls out praises and encouragement. She soon wears herself out, from too many things to count. The long trip, hobbling on an injured foot, her anxiety, the harsh workout of the army crawling. But mostly it's from the emotional wreckage and the Ativan… on top of the Tylenol that she'd already taken. She stops moving, stops dragging herself forward for just a minute or two. Her vision swims and her ears ring, and then she's out like a blown-out candle.

She wakes slowly, her head foggy and stuffed with cotton (spiddersilk?) and her mouth dry as the Sahara. She cries out because she doesn't know where she's at and the sight of those tooclose walls have her on the verge of full-blown panic, a freakout of epic proportions. But then Boodark's up in her face, his ugly little features all pinched up with worry for her.

"You're awake! Finally!" he yells. "I was so scared! You just… passed out and you wouldn't wake up. Don't you *ever* do that to me again! Do you hear me?"

She winces as his shouted words stab her eardrums. "I hear you. The whole world can probably hear you!"

His shoulders slump with relief as he lowers his voice. "I thought we'd be stuck in here forever." And then he smiles and perks up. "But guess what? We're almost there! We're almost to the end! I went on ahead to check out the situation. Another ten minutes or so and we'll be at the end of the line!"

His smile falters when he sees that she isn't as happy as she should be.

"You *left* me? While I was asleep, you just left me here? Alone?"

His mouth trembles and his eyes water at her crestfallen look, at her obvious feelings of abandonment. "I didn't *want* to! And it was only for a few minutes. I didn't know what else to do! You were asleep for hours and you *wouldn't wake up!* I was going to start dragging you, but I needed to know what *exactly* I would be dragging you to. I couldn't very well haul your unconscious body straight into a spidder's clutches, could I? NO! If we die here, at least we'll both do so fighting… *not* while you're sleeping and vulnerable and have no chance at all."

Her breath catches on something in her throat as she whispers, "I don't want to die here."

He stomps up to her and angrily gets all up in her face. "You will not die! Stop thinking that way. I refuse to let this be the end of us. When we go out, it's going to be gloriously heroic, and the entire world will know our names! Not lying in a funnel tunnel upon our bellies. You got it? Good. Now get that bag off your back.

I'm going to have to drag it. The way forward is about to get tighter, but you can fit without the bag."

She gulps back her fear and does as she's told. When he actually starts pulling the bag down the path she calls out, "You were going to try to drag me?"

He grunts as he heave-ho's. "No try about it. I *was* going to drag you. I keep telling you, I may be smaller than you, but I'm strong. At *least* as strong as a feeble female like you. I *did* manage to fly your giant arse up out of the scream patch, did I not?"

Her mouth instantly drops open in disbelief. "That was *you?* What? *How?* And why didn't you tell me sooner? I can't believe that something as small as you could lift a full-grown person!"

Boodark grumbles at her lack of faith in his incredible abilities. "Well now you know, and you can stop doubting me. Appearances are deceiving. I'm a lot stronger than I appear. Now can we *go*? I'm really tired of this shagging tunnel!"

"You're just gonna have to be a ground-humper worm. There's no help for it. You'll have to hump your way through from here on out."

She blows a strand of hair out of her face and glares at him as her breath tears in and out of her lungs. She desperately wants another pill, but she knows she would never be able to get to them, which is a good thing because she really doesn't want to go down that path again. She doesn't want to be dependent on drugs to help her get through each day. Doesn't stop her longing for one though.

"Excuse me?" she gasps in a bewildered voice. "What are you even talking about right now?"

"A ground-humper wiggle worm moves like this!" He holds his pointer finger up and inches it across her backpack in a demonstration of how an inchworm would crawl. "Ground hump.

You have to. It's the only way. The walls are too close now; you won't be able to stick your elbows out for leverage. Your hips will have to do the work. But look!" He flattens himself and her backpack up against one side of the tunnel so that she can see past him. And she catches sight of her own startled, red, and sweaty face.

"It's a mirror! Is it the EverGlass?" She excitedly wiggles forward.

"Uuhh, not quite. It's just the end of the tunnel, a wall made of those silver webs… same as what's behind you. All around you actually."

She turns her head and watches herself in the reflective web as she ground humps the last remaining feet to the end of the line. The thick, impenetrable web-wall closely resembles a mirror, but her face reflected back is shattered, torn into a billion hair-thin strands… As though she's seeing herself through the eyes of some strange alien bug. Spidder eyes, perhaps.

The EverGlass

Ecko

"Welp, we made it." Boodark sounds confused as he directs the beam from one of her mini flashlights around the small, tight space they're in. "But I sure don't understand it. What are we supposed to do now?"

She doesn't answer him. She can't. She's too busy trying to convince her mind that she's somewhere, *anywhere* else right now. The walls have narrowed in on her until there are only inches of wiggle room left. The way behind her has stopped collapsing, but it came so close that she can stretch her legs and touch the new barrier with her toes. The webby ceiling is so low that her head brushes up against it every time she moves. It feels just like being locked inside a casket and buried alive.

"I can't breathe," she rasps in a harsh whisper. She turns wide, desperate eyes on her friend and repeats, "I can't breathe, Boodark!"

Now *he's* panicking, throwing his hand up to smack himself on the forehead while crying out, "What do I do? What do I do?" But then he takes a deep breath and mumbles to himself, "Be her Soother. You're her Soother, now *soothe*!" He squeezes past the backpack and gets up in her face, forcing her to look into his eyes. "It's ok, Ecko. It's all gonna be ok. Just try to remain calm. I'll see if I can cut through the webs. Ok?"

Although she's looking right at him, she doesn't seem to hear a word he's saying. "So much for soothing," he mutters as he turns and makes his way back to the tunnel's end. He raises his hand, the one that still sports long, dagger claws, and viciously swipes it across the end-wall. And he promptly breaks all five of *those* claws completely off in the process. They just slice right off and go flying like tiny pieces of shrapnel. Stunned, he stares down at his hand. He looks at the wall, then back down to his newly declawed hand. He turns to her with an incredulous expression, and that's the exact moment that she reaches her breaking point.

"We're trapped," she whispers. She stares at the single, severed claw that had landed right in front of her face for all of thirty seconds before she starts screaming and thrashing. "Let me out! Let me out! LET. ME. *OUT!*" She frantically bangs her fists against the walls until the skin on her knuckles splits open. She kicks out at the collapsed wall until her feet are bruised, not caring that she's injuring her sprained ankle further. She wiggles forward until she can scratch at the end-wall with her own nails, digging at it until they bleed. She flounders and flails about like a fish pulled out of the water on a fisherman's hook. And all the while she's howling, "Let me out! Let me *ouuuttt!*"

It hurts Boodark's heart to see her like this. He *has* to get her out of here. He frantically searches all around him, taking note of every detail, trying to figure out what they're missing, because surely the EverGlass hadn't led them to a literal dead end. Their prison is made of flimsy, fragile spidder webs, but there are so many of the silken strands packed in so tightly together that they've formed solid and impenetrable walls. He studies the end-wall closely, noting that his claws hadn't even managed to cut through a single, fragile (or supposedly fragile) strand.

He reaches out and separates a single thread from the others and tugs on it… and tugs on it some more. It's flexible and pliable, but it's *strong*. It refuses to break even when he lifts his other hand up to grasp it and tries with all his strength to pull it apart. He even tries to gnaw through it with his teeth.

No wonder his claws broke off! He can't even sever a single, silken filament. He certainly can't get through an entire wall of them. "It's a magic web; it *has* to be," he murmurs to himself. He would say it to *her* but he's desperately trying to ignore her 'Let me outs!' because her cries are filling him with so much anguish that he can't think straight. "If the web is magic, then it will probably take magic to get through it. But she has a hard time accessing her abilities at the best of times… when her emotions are in check. Speaking of which… why hasn't her emotions overwhelmed her already? Why hasn't her magic come out and…"

His dialog with himself comes to an abrupt end as he turns and sees that her eyes are beginning to change. "Oh, no you don't!" he shouts and jumps in front of her. He holds her face in his hands and tells her, "Look at me! Look at me, Ecko."

When her storm-cloud eyes actually land on his, he has hope that he can stop this before either one of them gets hurt. "You have to calm down or you'll destroy us both. Do you understand? I know that there's a way out of this. It's like a puzzle, just like in your Labyrinth movie. We just have to stay level-headed long enough to figure it out, that's all." Her eyes clear the slightest bit, as if a gentle, soothing wind has come along to blow the storm clouds away as he continues to soothe her. He presses his forehead to hers and softly croons, "That's it. Breathe with me. Focus on my voice and just breathe through the fear. You've got this… *We've* got this."

"I'm so sorry, Boodark!" she chokes out. Her throat hurts and her voice is hoarse and scratchy from all of her senseless screaming.

He pulls back to study her features. Although her eyes still have a few clouds roiling around in them, she appears to be much calmer now. "I'm going to get some water for you out of your back pouch. I know your throat must hurt." He turns away and adds, "Don't worry. I won't go far!" Cheeky little booger. He *can't* go far.

It takes him forever, but he eventually manages to root out a water bottle and roll it over to her. She greedily guzzles it down, trying to put out the fire in her throat. But she does have enough wits about her to save the last quarter of it for him. He hasn't done any screaming, but he's got to be thirsty too. She lays her profusely sweating face down onto the cool stone floor beneath her while he drinks his share.

"Oh, that's good," he mumbles and then lets out a huge belch. Once he has the bottle tucked back into her bag, he walks back over and sits down next to her face. He glances down at his hands, both of them clawless now. "So, when I tried to cut through those spidder web strands, I couldn't even break *one* of them. They *must* be magic. So, I was thinking that you'll either have to try to break them with your magic or hope that *this* is what the rude Kreeleerian's gift is intended for."

And just like that, the answer appears in her mind, and it *is* what Loryss's gift was meant for! The blueprints are all right there in her head, just waiting for her to act on them. "Boodark, you're a genius!"

Obviously offended, he frowns at her with a wounded expression on his face. "I am not! There's no need for name calling! I'm just trying to help." The indignant little orc-bat crosses his arms over his spindly chest and turns his head away in a wounded huff.

She can't help but grin as she explains that's not a bad thing. "Don't be mad, Boodark. It's a good thing. It means that you are super smart."

He turns back and eyeballs her suspiciously, but he relaxes when he senses no trickery. "Well, yes," he agrees. "I *am* a genius then. We both already knew *that*." Once again, he digs around in her bag to find his beddy-bye basket, then produces the Kreeleerian's nasty bone.

She wastes no time in sketching the rune onto her palm. She wants out of this tunnel… yesterday. She knows (mostly) what's about to happen, so she advises Boodark to get out of the way. "Come back here, Boodark… just to be safe. Climb up on my back for now."

She slaps the bone down onto the symbol on her palm the very instant that he's out of the danger zone. The rune lights up blue and her hand begins tingling and burning with that painless, heatless fire. It shoots from her palm, straight into that sharp little bone.

Now *it's* lit up in electric blue, and suddenly, it's no longer two inches long. It's *twenty* inches long. It's grown, expanded into a double-sided, razor-sharp dagger. The bone handle fits perfectly in her hand. It feels good there. It feels *right*. But now is not the time for admiration. Now's the time for action.

"Come on, come on," she urges as she watches her magic flow into the intricately carved swirls and symbols that are etched into the dagger. They glow brilliant blue against bone white, turning the short sword into a thing of beauty. Not that she cares a flying furry rat's bootie about how beautiful it is. All she cares about is that it's sharp enough to cut through alien spidder butt webs that seem to be strong as bands of steel.

She inchworms forward (inchworms… because she refuses to refer to it as 'ground humping') until she's almost up against the end wall. There's very little room to work in, crammed up against her backpack as she is. She won't be able to get a good swing in, as there's no room for her to draw her arm back. So, she slashes the dagger across the web wall with as much force as she can put behind it in such tight quarters. The webs instantly sever beneath the blade as easily as spider webs are *supposed* to break, but she's dismayed to discover that she's only managed to cut through a thin top layer. She's going to have to slice and dice like a wild thing if she's to have any chance of getting through the thickness of this wall before the magic runs out.

So, that's exactly what she does. She hacks away at it, and severed silvery strands fly everywhere from her crazed, frenzied motions. All those years of practicing with fake swords, fighting off legions of monsters and defending her treehouse castle with her dad have actually come in handy. She knows how to haphazardly slash a sword through the air and cut down anything that gets in her way. The only problem is… it's just not doing enough damage. Not fast enough anyway. As the rune burns away, small chips and cracks begin to appear on the blade. Still, she hacks on, faster and harder than ever. She can't afford to baby the weakening blade, and tiny bits of bone soon begin to chip off. She watches the rune on her palm as she continues fighting her spidder web foe until only a speck of the symbol remains… meaning she only has seconds left before time's up and the magic is done.

Left with no other recourse, she puts every ounce of strength into a final, mighty thrust, and she plunges the dagger right into the middle of the webby end-wall. Then, with the last few seconds left to her, she uses the blade like a saw to hack out a hole that's big enough for her to slither through…. hopefully. That's the plan anyway, and it had better work too, because it's all she's got. She feels the last bit of her magic fade and what's left of the dagger crumbles to dust in her hand.

"Arrgggg!" she cries out with equal parts triumph and frustration driving her. Her tired, limp-noodle arm drops, and she lowers her head to the ground as she takes a moment to catch her breath. But nope! No can do. There's apparently no time to rest, because the web tunnel disagrees with the way it's been treated. *Violently.* It's shaking and rumbling as if they're in the midst of an earthquake (vampire world-quake) The webbed walls and ceiling are vibrating madly, and they're *shrinking again*, closing in all around them.

"The back wall is collapsing again, and it's not waiting for us to move out of its way anymore!" Boodark shouts.

She hastily shoves her backpack out the hole even as she screams at him. "Find something to hold on to! We're getting out of here… right now!" And with no more warning than that, she hurls herself out after her bag. The top half of her body bursts through the opening with ease… and there she dangles.

She's hanging half in and half out of a tunnel that's apparently positioned up higher than the outside ground… like an aqueduct pipe that pours rainwater out into a river. And Boodark, bless his clever little soul, *did* manage to find something to grab hold of. Her hair!

So current situation: She's hanging face down, every bit of her that's outside the tunnel is hanging upside down like a bat. Boodark, eyes tightly shut and whimpering in fear, has his hands firmly embedded into her hair. He dangles down, swinging from his double handfuls of her sweat-frizzed curls.

"Ow, Boodark. Let go," she demands as tears of pain prick her eyes.

"Let go? *Let go?* I don't have any wings at the moment! I'm not letting go!"

With an unlady-like snort she sarcastically replies, "I don't think you'll break any bones if you fall two feet. Open your eyes and look down. See for yourself."

He warily cracks an eye open. "Oh," he sheepishly murmurs and then thankfully lets go of her hair. He drops down and safely lands on his feet.

"Great, you survived. Now help me get out of here. I'm stuck."

He looks up at her and his eyes widen… along with his smile. With a hooting, howling laugh at her expense, he cries out, "I *told* you your butt's too big!" And then the little brat actually has the nerve to turn her camera on and snap several photos, capturing her shame. He howls like a loon the entire time too.

"I'm serious, Boodark. Get me loose… before the web

finishes collapsing, and I get stuck here like this forever!"

That sobers him up. He'd totally forgotten about the dangers; he'd been too busy poking fun. He quickly sets her camera aside with a rueful shoulder shrug. "Oh, yeah. Sorry. You're right, of course." He removes his beddy-bye basket from her bag and tosses it up to her. "Catch! Now hold onto the basket but give me back the rope handle. Will it reach? Stretch as far as you can…Got it! Hold tight!" Then he starts a game of tug of war with her, and she can only pray that he comes out the winner. He walks backwards, tugging with all his tiny might until his face turns red. "Come on, girl. Work with me! Wiggle that big ole butt! Ground hump, shimmy and shake it. Show me some hip action!"

She wiggles like mad, frantic now because she can feel the web walls pressing up against her legs. "Hurry Boodark!" she cries, and he can hear the desperation in her voice. He turns his back to her, pulls the rope over himself, positioning it over his belly. Then he walks forward like he's a harnessed horse pulling a wagon.

With both of them grunting and groaning and straining, she finally bursts through and spills to the ground amidst millions of broken spidder web strands… like she'd just gone through some sort of strange birthing. Or better yet, just hatched out of a spidder egg.

Poor Boodark goes tumbling from the suddenness of no longer having any resistance against his pull. The two of them lie there and stare at one another for a few moments, their chests heaving from their labored breathing as they revel in the fact that they've both made it. They're alive, unstuck, and unmolested by giant spidders, and they just want to take a moment to be grateful.

"I don't know how you managed that!" she gasps out between breaths. "I'm about a hundred times your size!" But once that moment of gratitude has passed, she glares at him and snaps, "And my butt is *not* big. The only reason it got stuck was because the walls kept shrinking. Even *your* tiny bum would have eventually gotten wedged in there."

He giggles and immediately sasses back "Sure, Ecko. Keep telling yourself that if it makes you feel better."

"What *is* this place?" Boodark whispers, completely bewildered and yet entranced at the sight above them. The sky(?) is nothing but a solid mass of roiling, churning clouds. *If* it's even sky up there. She can see no trace of blue or even the grey that she's come to expect of Oblerian skies. It's just thick, fluffy clouds that ceaselessly boil against one another. She's not even sure if she wants to know yet. She certainly doesn't want to move just yet. She's thoroughly enjoying the feel of grass beneath her… actual *grass*!

"I don't know" she answers. "I'm too afraid to get up and look around."

He nods at her. "Same here, but we gotta do it. On three?"

She agrees and he begins the countdown. "One, two… three!" He makes as if he's sitting up, but he just *pretends* to do it, grinning when she falls for his little trick.

But she doesn't even acknowledge his bit of tomfoolery. "Oh. Oh, Boodark. Get up! You want to see *this*."

He sits up beside her and his mouth immediately drops open. They're now facing the spot that they'd tumbled out of the web tunnel, but there's no longer any trace of it. What *is* there is a massive, violet purple waterfall. A massive *reverse* waterfall that somehow flows *up* instead of down. It comes straight up out of the ground with no warning. There's no pool, no lagoon or river or any other source of water to support it. It just *is*, and it flows silently, with glittering amethyst sparkles, all the way up to the *sky? ceiling?* where it froths and foams out into those boiling clouds.

She turns in a slow circle, gazing in wonder at this new world around her. She feels something bumping against her hand and Boodark whispers, "Pictures, Ecko. Take pictures with your viewer, or no one will *ever* believe it! Oh, how I wish my Secret could see this!"

Purely by remote, she takes the camera and starts clicking away at every wonder that her eyes behold. They're in some sort of round cavern... an *outdoor* cavern, if that makes any sense. It looks like they're outside, in a circular patch of lush meadowland. There's grass beneath their feet... blue/green, *teal* colored grass! There's no sun or even a trace of sky visible, but it's as bright as day... as brilliantly lit up as an *Earth* day! The walls are entirely made up of those purple, backwards flowing streams of water... they're completely surrounded by them. The camera steadily snickclicks in her hands.

"What *is* this place?" Boodark repeats. "Are we inside or outside? I can't tell! And why can't we hear anything? Those waterfalls or...errr, those water-ups should be really loud in our ears."

She lowers the camera, smiles brilliantly at him, and says, "But I *do* hear something. The EverGlass... she's here!"

She eagerly scans the clearing, searching, searching. She doesn't see it right away, which doesn't necessarily alarm her. It's a big meadow, perhaps the size of a football field (if a football field were round). And the EverGlass *must* be small... Deidra wore it as a pendant on a necklace. It could be out there just lying in the grass, for all she knows. But it's here... somewhere. She can feel it tugging at her.

"Come on, Boodark! Help me look!" And off she runs, excited beyond all control at how close she is... she *knows* she's so very close.

"Wait!" he yells as he uselessly points at her bag. "What about your things?"

But she's only interested in *one* thing. "Just leave it," she calls back. "It's safe here." She doesn't understand how she knows that, but it's true. This is the safest she's been since she got dragged onto this world, and possibly the safest she's ever been in her entire life.

"Wait!" he tries again, but she's darting here and there and everywhere, looking for an elusive mirror that only she can hear. Well, that's not quite true. Tanda claimed she could hear it too. But *he* certainly can't. He's *never* heard it, never felt its pull. In fact, he has no proof that it even exists. He can only take her word for it. Not that he doesn't trust her. He does. With everything in him, he trusts her. But perhaps she's been tricked. She *is* a bit naive… especially to the dangers of Oblerian.

"Wait! What if it's a trap?" He runs after her, his poor, little legs pumping madly as he attempts to catch up to her. He realizes that he has zero chance of success, not with her mad zigzagging. She runs one way then suddenly changes direction and dashes off somewhere else. But time after time, she ends up in the middle of the field, a lost, confused look on her face as she searches the ground around her. He gives up on chasing her and decides to just stand still and watch her wear herself out.

Soon enough, she stops running and makes her way back to him, dispirited and out of breath. "I don't understand, Boodark. It's here; I *know* it's here. I just can't find it."

He looks up at her and he just doesn't have the heart to suggest that maybe what she's looking for isn't here, that perhaps it's not even real. But he doesn't have to say a word anyway. She knows what he's thinking. "Don't even say it!" she snaps. "It's real. It's here. And I'm *not* crazy!"

He just nods to acknowledge that he knows she's not crazy. "Well, maybe it's another puzzle then. I mean, why not, right? Perhaps this is just another test to get through before it will reveal itself to you. What we need to do is *calmly* think it through. Let's go get your back pouch. We'll sit and rest a bit, drink some water. I'm thirsty. Aren't you thirsty? Perhaps while we're there we may even decide to eat our Endmeal. It *is* Endmeal time, you know. I can tell by the rumble in my tummy… It's never wrong."

She snorts and rolls her eyes at him. "That means absolutely nothing. You always have a rumbly in your tumbly. It can't *always* be mealtime." She sighs and glances around the field one last time before reluctantly agreeing. "But you're right. Maybe we do need to think this through some more. And I *am* hungry, so maybe your belly is actually right about it being dinner time."

She grins when his eyes light up at the realization that his ploy for getting food out of her actually worked. "Come on, little piggy. Let's go eat. Maybe a full belly will clear my head and help me figure this whole thing out."

He pumps a victorious fist into the air and shouts, "Yes! That's what I'm talking about! But umm… will you carry me? My legs are tired from chasing after you and I'm *so* weak from hunger. I'm just not sure I can make it that far."

She rolls her eyes again but obligingly lifts him up. "You're such a drama queen. You're not *that* tired. You just want to hurry and get to the food as quickly as possible."

He smirks and doesn't even try to deny it. "What's a llama queen?" he asks instead.

"Can you believe this place?" she asks as she nibbles on a piece of flatbread. "It doesn't even seem real."

He never looks up from his food as he answers her. "Om rom lara nog ling."

"I can't understand a thing you're saying, Yama Lama Ding Dong boy. Just finish eating and we'll talk later."

He lifts his head out of his bowl, his little bat nose all covered in creamy, buttery sauce. He smacks his lips a couple times and then clarifies, "I said, Yes, this place is amazing."

She raises an eyebrow at him questioningly. "Really? *That's* what you said? It sounded nothing like that." He nods and sticks his head back in his bowl even though he's already finished all his food. He has to lick every trace of sauce away. "You're gonna lick a hole right through that bowl!"

He sets it aside with a small, disappointed sigh and watches her as she breaks off a chunk of bread and dunks it into her bowl to soak up some sauce. "This is how civilized people eat," she tells him as she neatly, *cleanly* pops it into her mouth.

"I'm not a people," he counters.

"Nor are you civilized." She takes one last bite and then passes the remainder of her food to her forever-hungry friend. His ecstatic grin flashes across his face, and then he buries his head in *that* bowl. She leans back and turns to watch those magnificent waterfalls, all the while smiling in amusement at his disgusting slurping sounds. "I still don't understand it, Boodark. I know it's here; I can feel it out there. I feel it everywhere… all around this glen." She waves her hand out towards the middle of the field and adds, "Especially out there, at the center." She stares out at the empty space and murmurs, "The only thing that makes sense is that it's hiding… But that *doesn't* make sense too. She's been calling to me the whole time I've been here. If she *wants* me to find her, then why hide from me now?"

Finally done eating (because all the food's gone, *not* because he wants to be done) Boodark burps loudly and rubs his belly. "Perhaps you need to do your own calling."

Her brow crinkles as she thinks about it, and he rushes on. "Now hear me out. Maybe the EverGlass is just waiting for *you* to call to *it*. You know, with your magic… like calls to like, and all that. *Prove* that you're the new Wandelaar. It wants you, you *know* that, but maybe it's waiting for proof that you want it too."

She sits quietly for a moment or two, just thinking about what he said. "That sounds… exactly right. It *feels* right." She looks at him in amazement, as if she's just now seeing his many talents and attributes. "Wow Boodark. You really *are* a genius!" His ears immediately perk up happily at the praise. "Ok, so how does one call a mirror?" she wonders aloud.

"How would I know? I'm genius, but I'm not *that* genius! You're the Mirror Walker. Wake your magic up, see if something comes to you then." He yawns, turns, and lays down in the soft grass, curling himself up into a ball. "I need a nap. Wake me when you have it all figured out." And he's asleep just like that, his loud snores ringing out across the clearing.

"Well, Ecko, looks like you're on your own with this one," she mutters to herself. Shaking her head in amusement at the little, *noisy* ball of trouble that's sleeping beside her, she pulls his t-shirt blanket from his beddy-bye basket and gently covers him with it.

"What to do? What to do?" she mumbles. "Guess I better stop talking to myself, first off. And then see just how willing the magic will be to cooperate with me.... Shut up, Ecko and just *do* it already!" She closes her eyes and goes searching inside herself, and she's surprised to find that her magic is already awake and waiting, eager for action. The radiance of it fills her from head to toe the moment that she reaches for it. It's just suddenly *on*, like a switched-on light bulb filling a room with light. Tanda had been right. The more she practices, the faster it responds to her. The more she works with it, the more in tune she becomes with it... and it to her. They just need to get to know one another better, that's all.

She takes a moment to enjoy it, to just feel it inside of her and get to know it. It's strange. This is all so new to her and yet, it's as familiar as every other aspect of herself. Like she's known it all along, just as she knows her own face and hands, just as she knows her own heartbeat.

She sighs and sways gently as the magic sweeps through her, skipping through her mind and dancing along her skin. Her consciousness follows behind it, going wherever it leads, just happy and content to be so connected with it. It steers her straight to that door inside of her mind... the one that she knows nothing about... not where it came from or what it hides or even when it got there. She certainly hadn't put it there. It's completely different than all the other locked prison cells and boxes and cages that *she* had erected.

At least… she doesn't *think* she put it there. But really, who's to say *what* she'd done during some of those traumatic events in her life. There are entire months missing from her memory of when she'd first been admitted into the hospital. Drug induced or a side effect from the trauma, she doesn't know which, but it's time that she lost and has never gotten back. Perhaps her memories are locked behind that door. If that's the case, does she really want to know? Does she really even want them back?

She studies the door now and realizes that there's light coming out from beneath it, as if a brightly lit room lies beyond it. Will it be unlocked? Will she discover more secrets about herself if she steps over the threshold? What could possibly be in….

"Where did *that* come from?" Boodark's voice shakes her concentration, and she hears the telltale snick of a lock engaging as the room behind the door plunges back into darkness. The magic backs away, away, away, until the door fades and disappears completely. She sighs, half in disappointment and half in relief. She'd been so close to learning what secrets it hid.

She cracks her eyes open, and there in the middle of the meadow, stands an ancient stone dolmen with what appears to be a very large and intricate, silvery spider web stretched beneath it.

"That was *not* there when I fell asleep!" He turns wide, green eyes on her and blurts, "What happened? Is it the EverGlass? Did you call it? *What did you do?*"

She never takes her eyes off of that web as she answers him. "It's the EverGlass… Khalidah. *Finally.*"

She's completely unaware that she's getting up and walking to the simple stone structure. One minute she's sitting with Boodark at the edge of the glen, and the next she's standing right before it, peering up into the chamber formed by the strategically stacked stones. The web that fills the chamber is like no spider web she's ever seen before. It's all stringy swirls and curls, loops and curlicues. It looks more like a delicate swatch of lace than a spider's home. She runs her fingers gently over the whorls, tracing the patterns and following the lines to the center of the web where an exquisite snowflake pattern has been weaved into the mix. Waterfall droplets of amethyst and violet glisten here and there on the fine, gossamer strands, like colorful diamonds glistening on a woman's lace corset.

Sensing more than seeing the movements up above her, she turns her attention to the darkened, shadowy crevice that lies in the space between the capstone and the sidestones. And there she is… peering back at her in all her magnificent glory. Khalidah, the EverGlass.

Slowly she crawls out, a mirror spider the size of a lemon, with reflective, silvery patches on her tear-shaped abdomen. The cephalothorax, the actual upper body that the legs protrude from is a deep cobalt blue, but the scales that adorn her abdomen look like tiny shards of mirrors that have been glued on, and they reflect brilliant colors of red, yellow, green, gold, and cream. She climbs down her web, the mirror patches glinting in the light like sequins.

The two travelers admire her beauty as they watch her draw closer, and so they witness the exact moment that she changes. One second, they're peering up at a spider and the next they're looking at a tiny woman with the palest blue/white skin. Her miniscule body is all woman until just below her shapely buttocks where she has not two human legs, but six long spider legs. Legs covered in fine, silken hairs all moving to carry her closer and closer.

The two females stare at one another as she draws ever nearer, both studying and scrutinizing the other. Ecko can't help but admire her beauty. Although she has no hair, her head is smooth and perfectly rounded; and in her case, hair would have taken away from rather than enhanced anyway. Her face is all delicate features and flawless elegance, with dark eyes and pale lips. Dainty shoulders and small breasts give way to a slender belly and dramatically curved feminine hips. She's beautiful and alien and ancient, just as her name suggests.

"Khalidah, the Eternal One," Ecko whispers with the utmost reverence.

The petite, otherworldly being comes to a stop when she reaches the snowflake pattern in the center of the web, and she opens her arms in welcome. Her lips never move as she greets her new Wandelaar with an eerily haunting voice, but she hears her just the same.

"Well thee met, young one. I have waited many long years for you, Adrina Ecko Zyanya. Forgive me that I do not ease you into our pairing. With each passing moon phase, the scales tip further out of balance, allowing the darkness to spread. We simply haven't the time for pleasantries and gentle introductions. There is much that we need to do."

Ecko lifts her hand, almost in a daze, and Khalidah gingerly steps down from her web and right onto her open palm.

"*Forgive,*" she whispers again, just before she changes back to her spider form and plunges her needle-sharp fangs into her wrist… just below the luminescent glow of her sucky-puss scar.

Ecko freezes up and her eyes immediately blank out and go mirror-side. And she begins to cry… glittering silver tears that are as solid and hard as pearls.

Boodark, who's been perched atop her shoulder, quietly observing it all, now starts hollering his fool head off. Khalidah partway changes back into her woman shape. She's in a strange, halfway existence of both of her forms…. spider with fangs buried deep in Ecko's wrist, and a woman who turns her head sideways at an incredible angle that shouldn't have been possible, like two different realities superimposed, one atop the other. She meets his frantic eyes with her own serene regard and soothes, "Be not afraid, friend of Ecko. She is seeing. Learning. Growing…. Wait. Give her time. Be oh, so still and oh, so patient."

Then she turns her woman head away and it merges back with her spider head. She removes her fangs and scurries up Ecko's arm, over her shoulder and to the middle of her breastbone… just up under her chin. She reaches out and collects the silver, pearlized tears as they roll off her face. One after another, she gathers them up and quickly spins each one up into an intricate web-chain necklace.

All Boodark *can* do is wait… wait and watch and hope that this spidder-lady's not doing anything tricksy. Because if she is… well, he's never eaten a shiny mirror spidder before, but he can bet that she's tasty. Perhaps like the rainbow-colored Skittles that Ecko let him have out of her last MRE meal. Dee-liss-ious.

Ecko is indeed seeing and learning. She sees flashes of… everything. Just *everything.* The past, the present, and infinite, possible futures, things that haven't come to pass yet. Things that need to be done, things that need to be stopped, and things that need to be changed. She sees into the OtherLands (so many of them!) and all the beings that inhabit those worlds. Monumentally important events and small, seemingly insignificant affairs. A mouse in its den. A small black and brown creature with soft, sad ears, crying her ceaseless tears at the edge of an ocean. A gargantuan serpentine dragon-creature (The AllMother) asleep on a faraway world, and the places where all of her thousands upon thousands of younglings reside. Another spider, twin to Khalidah, and yet opposite in every way… dark and bad and destructive with colors of deepest purple, black, red, and gold. Boodark's Secret and a wingless she-pixie and the tiniest fairy with dandelion fluff hair. Jaida, aka Mean Green… the green will-o'-the-wisp and her surprisingly large following of like-minded, angry, Ecko-hating creatures. Red wisp, who hides and watches everything. Her father, the Lokskell. Her *mother,* locked away in a dark, filthy chamber. A pixie mine, a horrible place where pixies are enslaved and forced to mine the Night Flowers for their nectar. A war-devastated, apocalyptic world where it never stops raining… full of lost, hungry, and ragged children. The Soul Eater and the Bone Maker and the Ruined Beauty. A giant of a man, familiar but faceless, purposely striding through a fantasy forest with beautiful foliage that shimmers with more color than her mind can process.

Purpose. Destiny. Fate. Kismet. She sees it spread out before her like a web that stretches across all time and space. It's awe-inspiring and humbling and utterly terrifying as she learns *exactly* how much is expected of her. And words like Wandelaar and Mirror Walker… they're suddenly more than just words.

She *sees* for hours, *learns* for days, for years even. Time has no meaning, no relevance. On and on and on the details pour into her head, so much information… too much. Too much!

Thankfully, her mind takes over and spares her from overload. It works on autopilot, like a machine… sorting it all out in terms of relevance and time frames, and then it files it all away accordingly. And all the while, playing in the background like a silent film are the memoirs of all the relationships between the EverGlass and the many Wandelaars that came before.

Ecko experiences Khalidah's jubilation at each new birth, her joy and hope at pairing with each new Mirror Walker. She feels every bit of the loss and bittersweet sorrow as each woman grows old and severs the connection, undergoing the unpairing for their new, young heiresses to take up the mantle and carry the weight of the EverGlass.

And then the utter devastation at the loss of Deidra hits her like a fist punched straight through her heart. For a moment, she can't breathe. She can't get her breath back until her mind gently reminds her heart that this pain isn't hers. It belongs to Khalidah. And then it passes, but the memory of it will forever be imprinted on her heart. And so will the knowledge that Khalidah had loved her mistresses, each and every one of them. She still does to this day, unconditionally and eternally, until the very end of time.

She comes back to herself slowly, as if waking from a dream that's lasted far too long. She feels older somehow, like she's aged significantly in the time that it's taken for her to 'see' and 'learn' everything. Her eyes automatically search out her batty friend, and his weight on her shoulder is a comfort to her as she assures herself that he's fine.

"Your friend is unharmed," Khalidah assures in her otherworldly voice, drawing Ecko's attention downwards to where she's spinning the last of her pearl-tears up. She watches in fascination as the tiny, busy hands weave extra silken links into the web-chain to make it just the right length. At any other point in her life, up until this very moment, in fact, glancing down and discovering a spider upon her breast would have resulted in a whole lot of screaming and crazy dancing, all while slapping at herself like a lunatic. But not now… not with *this* spider. She'd already been aware of her, had *felt* Khalidah there before she'd even spoken. The two of them are connected now, paired… as it always had been and always will be, from times of old with the very first Mirror Walker, until the last of her kind ceases to draw breath.

If the day ever comes when there are to be no more Wandelaars, then truly, all hope will be lost. At that point, the outcome of the scale's balance will be irreversible, and everything light and good and virtuous will be gone. Khalidah has been there with the Wandelaars throughout it all, and she will remain until either darkness has won and all hope is gone or until it has been conquered and completely eradicated, at which time she will no longer be needed.

"How long?" Ecko croaks, her throat raw from all the tears she had shed. "How long was I out of it?" Khalidah glances at her but never ceases her weaving as she whispers, "Minutes, only minutes."

Boodark nods in accord. "No more than three minutes," he agrees.

She glances all about the glen, half expecting it to have changed drastically. "It felt like years," she murmurs, and the spider bobs her head in total understanding. "Much to see. Much to learn."

She tries to think about it now, tries to reflect on all the things she'd been shown, only to discover that she can't quite remember everything. There are things missing, a whole *wealth* of information that she can almost remember…. *important* things that need to be addressed. She frowns in confusion as she searches her mind for the missing information, but Khalidah hurries to reassure her that all is well.

"It is all there, stored away in your mind until you have need of it. It will come to you in bits and pieces when the timing is right… when the information is relevant and applicable. Too much, too fast would break the mind, damage it beyond repair."

Boodark, impatient as ever, demands, "Well, what *do* you remember? What did she show you?"

She turns her head to look at him, her eyes alight with a myriad of swirling rainbow colors, colors that dance to the tune of her emotions. "Your Secret is alive!" she tells him. "She's alive, Boodark and we're going to get her back!"

And he promptly bursts into tears because he feels the truth of her words resonating within his very soul. She reaches around to gather him up in her arms and hugs his trembling body tight against her, careful of the spider upon her breast. "We'll get them back," she tells him once more before pressing on. "I know that I told you that our very next mission would be saving your family, and I meant it. But I have something that must be done first, a lifesaving side mission. It won't take long, one Pale at the most. It's urgent, life or death urgent, or else I would wait. Do you understand? Please say that you forgive me for my little discrepancy. I don't ever want to break a promise to you. I hope you know that I don't do it lightly now."

He wipes his runny nose with the back of his hand and stares up at her, his green eyes swimming with tears. "It's ok, Ecko. If it's life or death, then of course you must do it. You're not breaking your promise, we're just taking a little detour on the way. I can wait." He firmly nods his head and sniffles back his tears. "I've waited this long, haven't I? I know that I'll be getting them back and that's enough for me right now. Just knowing for sure that they're alive means everything to me." And then, unable to contain his happiness, he grins up at her, his ugly little face all aglow with joy.

She laughs and settles him back onto her shoulder just as Khalidah adds one last link to the necklace and connects the ends of the web-chain together. She changes into her woman form and holds the necklace up, offering it to her new mistress. "They're not the Night Pearls that your predecessors wore and long protected, but they're lovely just the same," she says in that mysterious, ethereal voice of hers.

Ecko takes it in hand and runs her fingers lightly over the silver, iridescent tear/pearls... her tears. "It's beautiful," she whispers in admiration. "You spin the most incredible webs. So strong too... just like the ones in the tunnel." Looking down at the web-chain necklace in her hand, she suddenly understands that it was Khalidah who had built the tunnel. "It was you," she says, and the spider bobs her head.

"You who? Do what? Huh?" Boodark asks in confusion.

"It was her. *She* spun all those webs and created the web tunnel!"

His eyes pop open wide as he splutters, "But...*how?* She's so little! How did she manage to..."?

They both turn their attention to the incredible being who is so much more than just a spider when she begins to speak. "It took me a hundred years to create the tunnel, a hundred years of work, all in the span of a single Pale."

Boodark leans in close to Ecko's ears and whispers, "I don't understand. What does that even mean? A hundred years, all in a single Pale?"

She shrugs. "Time is irrelevant here in the EverFalls. It passes differently here than it does out there. It passes differently in all the EverRealms."

Boodark's eyes dart to the upwards-flowing waterfalls. "Oh!" he exclaims. "I suppose I should have known that this is one of the EverRealms! It all makes sense now."

"It's time," Khalidah says. "Time to leave all this behind. Time to go forth and do all the things that you are meant to do."

Ecko lovingly places the necklace around her neck and Khalidah settles herself at the center of it, gripping it with her hands and every one of her leg's tarsal claws. "Go now. Drink of the Falls. Heal yourself, for you will need to be whole and hale for what is to come. When it is done and you've said your goodbyes to the EverFalls, you must enter the dolmen right here, break through the webs and you shall emerge on the other side. And remember that I am here with you. I'll always be right here if you need me, just a thought away."

Then she wraps her arms and legs around the strands of their combined creation and changes once more, taking on her third and final form. A multifaceted, tear-shaped pendant, glittering with all the brilliant colors that her spider body possessed, it throws rainbows out in every direction like a reflective, glass prism. Silver mirror glass underlies the colors, buried deeply within as if the back of the pendant is made from a piece of solid mirror. Khalidah's arms and spider legs curl up and become the circular jump rings that bind it to the web-chain.

"The EverGlass," she breathes in wonder. "Oh, isn't it magnificent?" She lifts it up, wanting to get a better look… wanting to see if she could get a glimpse of the OtherLands in those mirror-depths when Khalidah's voice suddenly ghosts through her mind.

"Do not go looking for things in which you are not yet ready to see. You must first be in a position to act upon what you learn. Do you understand? You *must* get back to the SeeAll Tree before you look closer. It is there, with the help of the old soother Athtandakapootha Delainnianth Carpathilla… friend of Lamora Deidra, that you will do what needs to be done next. Hurry now, young one. Hurry. Time is short."

Her haunting voice fades away but leaves behind a sense of urgency in Ecko's heart. And suddenly she finds herself standing before the Falls, drinking the water from her cupped hands.

Miraculously, all of her aches and pains, from her severely wounded ankle to the smallest of bruises, cease to plague her. Every hurt is instantly healed by the magical waters of the EverFalls. She stretches her ankle, this way and that, reveling in the fact that she feels no more pain.

"That's incredible!" she exclaims with sincere gratitude, and she spares just a moment to wish that she could bottle some of the water up and carry it away with her for the people that she's destined to lose along the hard roads ahead. But she knows that it wouldn't do her any good. The waters won't work outside of the EverRealm. And not only that, the incredible restorative magic may be able to heal wounds and hurts, but it can't stop Death when he comes calling. One may avoid Death for a small while, put it off, hide from it… even bribe it for a time. But Death will not be denied. Sooner or later, he will claim what he's due. And *everyone* owes.

She takes one last wistful look around the EverFalls as she straps her backpack on and loops Boodark's beddy-bye basket around her neck. He climbs down from her shoulder and settles himself in as she tucks the EverGlass into her shirt to hide it from view. There are those that will stop at nothing to get their greedy hands on her mirror, so the longer she can hide the fact that she's found and claimed it, the better off she'll be.

"You ready for this, Boodark?" she asks as she stands in front of the dolmen, peering doubtfully into the dark recesses of the shallow cavern. His longing sigh and wistful glance back at the magical Falls makes her grin.

"Yeah, I'm ready" he grumps. "Unless you want to carry me over there for one last try. What do you say? Think it'll work this time?"

She pinches the smile off of her lips before he can see it. "You already tried it, like fifteen times. If it was going to work, it would have already done so. I told you. It's *healing* waters, not curse-breaking waters."

He dejectedly slumps down in his basket and sulks. "I *know* what you told me. I heard you the fifteen times you said it. But I *am* hurt." He jabs his thumb towards his face. "I keep telling you… *this* hurts! *Ugly* hurts!" he wails.

"Your face does *not* hurt. And even if it did, the water won't fix it." Her eyes soften as her heart clenches in sympathy for him. She knows him all too well; she understands where all this is coming from. Being this close to getting his mate back has him suddenly terrified that she won't want him anymore, now that he's no longer who and what he once was. "I love you, Boodark," she tells him. "And if I can love you just as you are, then surely your Secret will too. Love doesn't care about looks. Besides, aren't the two of you married? Didn't you exchange wedding vows? You know, didn't you promise to love one another through richer and poorer, through sickness and in health, through beauty and through ugly… to have and to hold for as long as you both shall live? 'Till death do you part?"

Clearly suspicious, he narrows his eyes at her. "We said some words, but none like those." Then, almost under his breath he mutters, "Too bad. I wish we had!" But then he thinks about it for a moment and takes it back. "No, I would not hold her to such vows. She should not have to look upon this face every Pale for the rest of her life. *I* don't even want to see it. But none of that even matters. Whatever happens to me after my family is freed, whatever my fate may be, I will accept it and I will be grateful. That's not to say that I won't wish for impossible things, but I will gladly accept what comes after. It will be enough just to see them awakened and freed." He quickly looks away and whispers to himself, "It'll have to be."

She lightly pokes him and tries to reassure him. "Don't worry, Boodark. She'll be so happy to see you that she won't care about anything else. You'll see."

He nods but he won't look at her, and she can tell that he doesn't mean it. "I suppose I'm ready to go then. Let's get out of here, shall we?" He points into the dolmen and asks, "Are we *sure* that's the way out? It doesn't appear to lead anywhere."

She shrugs her shoulders. "Khalidah just said to walk through here, break through the web, and we would come out the other side. Other side of what? I don't know, but here goes nothing." Boodark ducks down under his blanket so that just his eyes are peeping out.

"Lucky dog," she grumbles and steps forward with her hands held up to protect her face as she walks right into the web. "Break it? What does she mean *break* it? I completely forgot that her webs are like steel. This isn't working!" She grunts as with each step she takes only results in the web just stretching.

"Hey! That's right!" Boodark's snoot pokes out far enough for him to agree with her belated assessment. "It took a stupid cat's magical puke bone to cut through them before! What makes her think we can just stroll right through them now? Is she crazy or is she just…"? His words get cut off as one last step has the entire web not breaking but pulling free of its anchor points on the stones. It wraps around her, the filmy, gossamer strands flowing over her, clinging to her until her body is draped in the most elegantly beautiful ball gown she'd even seen.

"I made it for you," Khalidah says, the words projected straight into her mind. "It was always meant for you. It just didn't know you yet. It didn't know the shape of you."

Ecko runs her hands over her body, loving the silky, satiny feel of it. "Now that the magic has gotten to know you," Khalidah continues, "it will always fit you perfectly and it will be whatever sort of garment you need it to be. Just picture what you want in your mind and the webs will do the rest."

She can't help but try it out. She closes her eyes and imagines herself in a swanky, sleek jumpsuit. The webs immediately begin to move, floating around her and rearranging themselves to mimic, down to the last detail, the silken garments that her imagination had conjured up. Then she imagines herself in a dancing dress with a form-fitting top and a puffy, lacy skirt that's perfect for twirling the night away in.

"That's incredible!" she exclaims, clapping her hands like a delighted child. "Thank you, Khalidah. It's a truly magnificent gift, and I absolutely adore it."

Boodark pops up out of his blanket with a disgruntled snort. (Somehow the web had known that he and his beddy-bye basket, not to mention her bulky backpack, were not parts of *her* and had formed the clothing beneath the obstructions.) "You females! Always so worried about what to wear. Can we go already? We have places to be, things to do, families to save…"

Her smile falters and falls away and she nods solemnly. "You're right, Boodark," she mumbles as she disappointedly pulls the web-garment down and steps out of it. "I shouldn't be taking even a single moment for myself to enjoy a beautiful, magical dress. I don't deserve this… not when so many others are suffering and need my help." She quickly swipes a tear away and Boodark's shoulders immediately slump in regret at his hastily spoken words.

"Forgive me, Ecko. I didn't mean it that way. Of course, you deserve pretty gowns. You deserve them *all*. I'm just anxious and hungry and cranky, that's all. You know I get stupid when I'm hungry."

She nods and sniffles as she begins to neatly fold the webcloth so she that can put it away. "You're not wrong though. Now is not the time for pretty things." He opens his mouth as if to argue but she stops him. "No, Boodark. Just no. We need to focus on what's important right now, and that's our loved ones. We both have families that need saving. So, let's go save them."

She folds the web-dress, and folds it, and folds it some more until it's compacted down to the size of a matchbook. "A ball gown, travel sized for your convenience," she mutters to herself as she gently secures it in her bag for safe keeping. It really had been the most beautiful dress she'd ever seen, and it had been made of gossamer strands of webs, spun up by a spider that turned into a woman, then turned into a mirror. A mirror surrounded by her own silver tears on a web-chain necklace that she now wears around her neck. She snorts at the absurdity of it all. Could her life get any more bizarre, she wonders as she steps into the darkness of the dolmen.

And the answer to that is yes, she realizes, as from one step to the next, the world changes around her. Again.

Two is Better than One

Krispin

On and on he runs with the lovely lady cradled in his arms. He does not stop. He never even slows down to rest. He finds that he doesn't need to.

There's no time for rest. We need to hurry, hurry, hurry, back to our dolls, the Wyrm urges in his mind.

"We do not need to sleep?"

I am delighted to hear you say that word, host. 'We' implies willingness and acceptance.

"I have not yet decided!" he snarls.

No, you have not. That is true. But you will. Two is better than one. You already know this. The two of us joining together as one will be beneficial to us both.

"Just answer the question!

The Wyrm heaves a long-suffering sigh. *I do not need sleep. You do. Together, WE will need sleep, but not nearly as much as you require on your own. That is the true meaning of our merging. That is what it is all about. It is a partnership. A sharing of our individual strengths and weaknesses. I am, even now, sharing my vitality with you, even though you still stubbornly deny us the merging.*

"You just want me to hurry so you can play your filthy games with our dolls."

Of course! I do not deny it. Will you lie, even to yourself, that you do not desire the same thing? Tell me true. Do you not wish to play with the beauty in our arms? Do you not want to introduce her to the others? She will be such a wonderous contribution to our collection. How could we not want her?

Krispin glances down at her, lying there so snug against his chest, so peaceful and serene and lovely. He does want her. He wants everything that the Wyrm is suggesting. He wants to touch her, explore her, violate her.

Yeesss. We will love her so good.

"No."

Oh, yes, we will.

"No. I love only one female. I love *Samara*. I will not deny that I crave these other females. I will not deny myself sweet release within their luscious bodies. But my heart belongs to

Samara. I will never stop trying to get her back. I *will* get her back."

WE will get her back. Together. And then we will retrieve my own mate, the female of my heart's desire.

"And what of Ecko? What of Samara's dirty, slut sister?

Oh, we will have her too. How we will acquire her and what role she will fill remains to be seen. I do not know the answers yet, but we will figure them out, together, host. Together.

"But she *will* suffer. She must pay for her transgressions."

Oh yes, the Ecko creature will be punished. But first, we must figure out how to capture such a magnificent female. And we will. Oh yes, we will. And then we will make her beg.

They make it back to the shabby, dilapidated town in half the time it had taken to get to the Sorrow Marshes. Pitch arrives just in time to welcome them home, shrouding the world in black velvet. Like a chameleon, Krispin's skin darkens to deep smokegrey, allowing him to blend in with his surroundings. He can do nothing, however, to conceal the pale-white beauty that he carries in his arms.

"Just a few more minutes, precious one," Krispin murmurs as he cradles her closer.

Hurry, Krispin! Let us run just as fast as we can!

They are both excited, eager to reach the lair now that they are so close. He lengthens his strides, moving so fast that he appears as nothing more than a black smudge in the surrounding darkness.

Wait! This is not the way to the lair! Where are you taking us, host?

"We have to go to the house first."

Nooo! We need our females! We need them so bad! There is no time to waste!

"I know that!" he snarls back through his clenched teeth. He is so hard, throbbing with every beat of his heart. "I know that we need them! But I must check first, just to be sure."

Your mate is NOT there! You heard what the Ecko creature said. Samara has left us. She is no longer on Oblerian!

"The slut could have lied. She is very tricksy. I hope she *did* lie. And if she lied, perhaps my Samara is still here. Perhaps she is trying to get back to me. I *have* to check. I must know, one way or the other!

Fine! I see that I will not be able to sway you in this, but it is a useless endeavor and a waste of time. We could have our dick buried to the hilt in a matter of minutes, if you would only… STOP!

Krispin stops running and immediately shrinks back into the concealing shadows of the closest building. His pupils dilate, expanding so that they can pick out traces of hidden dangers. His nostrils flare wide to catch the scent of a predator.

It is a trap! They have the house surrounded.

A fierce growl rumbles its way up from his chest and spills out through his teeth in a low, snarling thunder-roll as his eyes detect the slight movements made by many hidden bodies. "It's the Lokskell's men. He wishes to finish what he could not manage before."

We must leave here. There are too many of them. I detect numerous lifeforces. We can come back later. We'll return when they have grown tired of waiting and desist in their efforts.

"But she could be in there!"

She's not. You know that she's not! They would have already moved on her if she was anywhere in the vicinity. As much as the Lokskell wishes you dead, he wants his daughter returned to him even more. She's NOT in there, Krispin.

He debates with himself for a moment more, watching the men as they shift around in their boredom from sitting still for so long with nothing to entertain themselves with.

It would be foolish to proceed with your plan. Do not get us captured, host. We have precious cargo to see to. What will become of her if we get taken? What will become of them all? They need us.

"You're right." He cradles the woman ever closer as he slowly backs away from the ambush. "The women need us."

Yes! Oh, yes, they do!

He watches closely for any hint of discovery as he carefully retreats, walking backwards for several minutes until he's no longer within earshot or eyesight of his enemies. Then he turns, and blending almost seamlessly into the darkness, he quickly makes his way back to the outskirts of town. He'll go around, avoid the town and the danger therein altogether.

See? It's just as I told you. Two is better than one. We worked as a unit to detect and avoid that ambush. We will be even greater once we undergo the merging. Stronger. Smarter. And so much more powerful than you can imagine. But for now, just get us to the lair. Let us play with our dollies. We can discuss the merging further, once our needs have been seen to.

"Agreed," Krispin says as he tears through the Pitch like a NightMare on the hunt that's just scented its prey. "We will discuss it all… after."

Harsh Truths and Lessons Learned

Ecko

Ecko is no longer standing beneath the stones of the dolmen. Instead, she's standing in a familiar field of dry, withered heather. As a horrific scream of agony comes from out of nowhere, she realizes that she's back in the Field of Screams and Broken Dreams. If she has to venture a guess, she's pretty sure they've managed to pop back into the exact same spot that they'd disappeared from, and that very little time has passed on this side of the EverFalls.

Right now, she's standing directly behind her father's three goons who are currently scratching their heads and sporting *'Which way did he go, George'* looks on their dim-witted faces.

"Ah troll turds and harpy pies!" Boodark yells when he notices them. "Oh, frozen dingleberries," he adds with a whimper when they whirl around at the sound of his voice. Their eyes widen in shock at the sudden reappearance of their quarry… behind where they'd lost sight of them. "How'd you do that?" hog-head demands, and slug-man just grins his disgustingly lecherous grin. She gets one brief look at *exactly* how happy he is to see her before she spins around and makes a run for it.

"Sorry!" Boodark shouts. "We're in a bit of a hurry right now, but we'll tell you all about it later! Bye, bye now!"

She's running flat out, the screams and shrieks of the field's ghosts surrounding them like landmines detonating and bombs falling all around them. Boodark squeals just as loudly as the spooks do with every new sound-bomb he hears. And although she runs as if her life depends on it (and it does) like always, she eventually begins to tire and slow. The thugs are gaining on them, drawing closer and closer when she suddenly trips and goes sprawling. Poor Boodark tumbles out of his basket before she can catch him.

"Oh no!" she shouts in dismay. "Boodark? Are you ok?"

He hops back up to his feet and triumphantly raises his fist in the air, waving their lost hagstone at her. "Hey! Look what I found!"

But she doesn't care that he's recovered the stone. What she cares about is that he's about to get pounced on. "Behind you, Boodark!"

His eyes fly open wide at her warning, and he screeches, "Oh shite!" as he dives to the side and rolls away like a doodlebug. Seconds too late, the hobglin curses as he lands in the space that Boodark had just vacated. She wastes no time in scooping her friend up in her arms, and then she's off again, feet flying through the withered heather… until she comes to an abrupt halt and whirls back around to face her pursuers.

"What are you *doing*?" Boodark wails at her. "Why'd we stop? We do *not* want that slug-man to catch to us…. like he's about to do! Run girl, run!"

But she doesn't run. She can't run. "Slivers!'' she gasps. "The wall of Slivers and NightShades is back there, right behind us. We can't get through that way."

His eyes dart around the field as he desperately searches for another escape route. The only two ways out are through that wall or through the Lokskell's henchmen. "Better get your magic out then," he mutters as the bad guys come in closer, effectively boxing them in. "Ah, troll toes! Why couldn't there have been one more dumb Kreeleerian? We need one more trick! Stupid, good for nothing fur-balls…" He goes on and on, cursing the cat creatures for not predicting this and preparing a way out for them.

"Hush now, Boodark," Ecko murmurs as she places him back into his basket. She needs her hands free for when she starts swinging, because she will *not* be going down without a fight.

She stands there, wondering what they're waiting for when she feels it behind her, slithering up her body to swirl around her. Her father's Shadow magic, filthy and foul beyond anything she's ever felt, crawls all over her, searching for a way in. When it realizes that it will not be getting inside her (not today, Satan) it quickly flows away from her and pours itself into the hobglin, in through his nose and mouth… even into his ears. When it's done, he slowly cracks his neck, as if the thing that just entered him is getting a feel for his new hobglin host's body.

His eyes immediately seek her out and he grins wickedly at her. "Hello, Daughter," he greets her, his voice much deeper than anything the hobglin could ever produce with his nasally vocals. "I had hoped to make your acquaintance face to face, but seeing as how you continue to refuse my invitations, it seems that this is the only way left to me. Tell me, Adrina. Why do you run from me? Why do you resist me? I only want to know you. You are my daughter, after all."

She narrows her eyes at him, trying her best to ignore the almost hypnotic pull of his surprisingly melodic voice.

"We could be good together, you and I. Just think of it, your considerable powers combined with my own. Aren't you curious to discover just how great you could become? How great *we* could be? Come to me, daughter. Resist me no more. Just come to me. Let me in and we can rule the worlds together, with you right by my side, just as I always intended."

She raises her chin up in defiance and vows, "Never. I will *never* join you. I don't even want to know you…. not after the things you've done."

The Sluggeelian slimes his way a little closer and he never takes his eyes off of her as he addresses his master. "Why don't you just take her, my lord? Fill her with your Shadows and force her to your side." He reaches down and lewdly fondles himself as he adds, "Or better yet, let *me* have her. I'll have her *begging* to be brought to you in no time at all."

Her father looks at her with pride as he says, "Surely you don't think I haven't already tried that? My daughter is powerful beyond *your* comprehension. Even while she lay unconscious upon the ground after that miserable, blue Krispin creature's failed attempts, she somehow managed to block my advances. I couldn't get in even when she was lost in the Sorrow Marshes, when her mind was not her own. She is strong, too strong for the likes of you."

The Sluggeelian sneers at her. "She doesn't look so strong to me. She looks puny and scared."

The Lokskell turns to face him, and the look in his eyes is all it takes for slug-man to change his tune. Now *he's* the one that looks scared, cringing back and cowering in fear at the anger that's glaringly evident on the Lokskell's borrowed face. Slug-man immediately falls to his knees, bows his head, and begs, "Forgive me, my lord. I misspoke."

But the Lokskell is not of a forgiving nature, and the slugman has only seconds in which to regret his life choices as he sees his own doom reflected back from those cold eyes. The Lokskell spins his hobglin body around and slams his palm into the slugman's midriff, right at the spot where his man body merges into his slug body. The foul black Shadows pour out of the Lokskell/hobglin's hand and slither around him like ghostly serpents.

Ecko and Boodark watch, absolutely 110% horrified as his slug half melts… just like he'd slime/slithered through a pile of spilled salt. He just dissolves, melts into a gooey puddle of ooze, his top half staring down at his liquified parts in terror. Agonized screams pour from his mouth, one after another, adding his voice to the rest of the field's screams.

Her father waves his hand at him and calmly orders, "Be silent." And silent he becomes as several Slivers come forward and cram themselves into his gaping mouth, causing him to choke. They don't let him die though. They allow him just enough air so that he can live with the agony that questioning the Lokskell has earned him.

Boodark, although thoroughly traumatized, can't help but blurt out, "That's what you get for brandishing your gargantuan penis at innocent girls like it's a weapon to be used on them! Shame on you! Girls are for protecting, not hurting!"

Her father turns his attention back to her. "So sorry about that. You'd think they would learn not to interrupt me, to not question my methods. But back to us… what is your decision, Daughter? Will you come to me? Join me, let me rule you… and I will give you everything your heart desires." He holds out his hand, waiting to see if she'll place hers into it.

She raises her eyebrows in disbelief and takes a single step back. "Yeah, I don't think so, Hobglin King. I mean, *Goblin* King. I wouldn't join you even if my life force was tied to yours and being close to you was the only thing that could keep me alive. You are a terrible, *terrible* man and you disgust me."

His borrowed face twists into a fearsome mask of rage. "I promise you will regret it if you walk away from me now," he growls. "This is your one and only chance to come along nicely, peacefully and pain-free. We can be allies, you and I. Don't learn the hard way what it means to be my enemy…. as your bitch of a mother did. Laelynn found out just how foolish it was to go up against me. Do not repeat the pattern. Don't make her same mistakes."

She feels her magic flair to life with the force of her fury behind it. Her hair floats up with static electricity and then begins whipping about her head as power courses through her. In her own calm, deadly voice she tells him, "You leave my mother out of this. You're not even worthy to have her name upon your lips!"

He throws his head back and laughs in pure delight at her anger. "Oh, I love the fire! Your mother had it too… for a while. Until I put it out. And you're right. I *have* done some terrible things. I treated your mother badly. I tortured her for *years* after she took you from me. I tortured her until I broke her mind. I had too. All I wanted was you, and she stole you away from me. She had to be punished, can't you see that?"

Time slows down to a crawl as her eyes begin to cloud over. Boodark can feel the magic humming along her skin now and with a gulp and a whispered, "Oh shite," he burrows beneath his blanket and prays to every god of old that he'd ever heard of to deliver him safely from the coming storm.

"What about *before* she took me away?" she asks. "What about all the things you did to her to force her to bear your children? The six agonizing years she had to endure being raped repeatedly by you? You didn't just take her body; no that wasn't enough. You raped her mind as well. You realized that you couldn't force her to bear your child until you first convinced her that you were someone else. And so, you broke her, and then you tricked her. You used her love for another to create a fantasy world, one where her mate had come for her and rescued her. You made her believe that *you* were her lover, Aruune. I saw it, the things you did to her, and I *hate* you for it. I will always hate you. I have to live with the knowledge that I'm a product of your rape of my mother, an abomination, a freak of mixed magics that should *never* have been. Just as you will have to live with the fact that I will never be what you wanted me to be. I may have your DNA, but I am my mother's daughter."

Her father walks closer, staring intently into her eyes. "You are an extraordinary little thing, aren't you? You have an incredible amount of power within you; I've never felt anything like it. You are young, new to the magic that courses through you, and yet you have remarkable control over it! I can see how much effort it's taking for you to keep it all in check. Oh, but you want to hurt me so badly, don't you? I can't help but wonder, what will you do when you've been pushed too far? What will happen when you reach your breaking point? You are, indeed, very much your mother's daughter, but you can't hide from me. I *see* you, little one; and I'm in there too. There is a deep well of darkness inside you too, living side by side with Laelynn's light. What will happen when you finally allow the two of them to meet? Will they merge and become one fearsome, phenomenal entity? Or will they war within you and tear you apart? I can't wait to find out just how much destruction you will cause when you can no longer keep the gifts that you inherited from me pushed down and locked away."

He stops in front of her and murmurs, almost to himself, "Perhaps I can coax it out, draw the darkness up out of hiding." He reaches out and strokes her face in a distorted facsimile of a loving father, his voice soft and gentle as he croons, "Your mother was my favorite whore, and I used her well and often. In the end, she died cursing your name. Don't make me do the same to you. Don't make her fate become yours. Come to me of your own free will and I…"

She slaps his hand away from her face and steps back. "You lie! My mother is alive. I saw her!"

Surprise and shock flash over his features before he can school them into a nonchalant expression of boredom. "I can assure you that she is not," he coolly counters.

But she just nods her head and speaks over his lies. "She is. She's locked away in your castle. You torment her *still* to this day. Deny it all you like, but I know this. I've seen it. She's there, so yes, I *am* coming. Trust me on that. But I'm coming for *her*, not to join you… *Never* to join you. And I'll do it on my own terms and in my own time. There can never be peace between you and I. Not after the things you've done."

Her father's borrowed face contorts in anger, and he lashes out, his words cutting her like a knife. "You're right, you know. Your mother does lie in a chamber within my castle, but she lies as a rotting bag of bones. Nothing more. I just couldn't bear to dispose of them, but you're welcome to come and collect them. In the meantime, while I eagerly await your arrival, I'll go and prepare her for you. Perhaps I'll dress her in my favorite of her dresses, the red silk one. She always did look lovely in that one. It will surely bring back some memories of our times together."

He watches her face closely for a reaction to his goading and he's not disappointed. His knowing smile alerts her mind to the fact that he's trying to provoke her, to force her into losing control, but her heart doesn't care what his reasoning is. Her magic is pounding through her now. And Rage… Oh, Rage is in torment, howling and hurling himself against his prison walls so hard that they rattle against the foundation.

Her eyes go mirror-side, twin pools of hot, molten, silver glass. Her father's own eyes widen as her hands light up with snapping blue electricity. He takes a single step back before he can stop himself. Perhaps it's the hobglin, hiding somewhere in there and acting on pure self-preservation. She doesn't know or even care… she loses her last vestiges of self-restraint when he suddenly narrows his eyes and bestows a filthy smile on her. "Maybe when I'm done here, I'll go to her chambers and pay her a visit. But it's *you* I'll be thinking of while I fuck her rotting corpse."

Ecko's world goes black as Pitch as she raises her hands and lets him have it. Her magic slams into the hobglin and it blasts her father's Shadows right out of his borrowed body. They quickly retreat, flowing back to rejoin the Sliver/Shadow wall… but he won't escape that easily. She mentally follows close behind, her magic chasing him down like a pissed off, avenging angel. It overtakes him and washes over his foulness, causing his Slivers to shriek in agony as they scatter in every direction, desperate to escape her wrath. They flee from her light, but light is meant to eradicate the darkness, and that's just what it does now. They screech and squeal as their incorporeal bodies shrivel and curl up, becoming tangible upon their deaths. They fall out of the air to the ground, very much resembling a child's hardened, dried up and blackened playdough worms. They crunch and disintegrate beneath her feet as her magic goes after them all, hunting each one down before they can escape.

She does not stop. She refuses to let up until every one of the Slivers has been wiped out, the Shadows have been dissipated, and the spooks have scattered to the winds. She gives the Field of Screams and Broken Dreams one last inspection, assuring herself that she's gotten them all before she turns her attention to the three goons. Make that *two* goons. The Grunter apparently isn't as dumb as he appeared because he's made a run for it. Fear must have lent his feet wings too, because he's managed to make it all the way across the expanse of the field, so far away that he's almost out of sight already. The hobglin lies unconscious on the ground, the steady rise and fall of his chest letting her know that he still draws breath. Beyond that though, she hasn't a clue as to the damage she'd done to him.

The Sluggeelian though, his eyes beseech her as he begs for mercy. For just a moment, she entertains the idea of leaving him there like that. Surely, he deserves to suffer, as he had every intention of making *her* suffer.

'I can't wait to find out just how much destruction you will cause when you can no longer keep the gifts that you inherited from me pushed down and locked away.' Her father's words ghost through her mind, haunting her with the realization that if she ever slips, even the slightest bit, it could start an avalanche that sends her straight down the pathway to hell.

"Feed the light, starve the darkness," she whispers to herself. Then she reaches out, places her hand upon the Sluggeelian's brow and sends a bolt of her magic straight into his brain.

"Thank you," he breathes with relief and gratitude as brilliant shafts of light burst from every orifice in his head. He dies with a smile on his face while tears trickle down hers. It's a mercy killing, but that doesn't make her feel good about it. Dead is dead, no matter how or why it comes about.

The walk back to Tanda's is as silent as it is uneventful. The Field of Screams and Broken Dreams has gone quiet. The spooks no longer cry out at them as they walk along… perhaps they're afraid of *her* now.

Boodark is almost frantic with worry because she's not talking. No amount of trying has successfully drawn her back out of her mind where she's retreated. He doesn't know what to do. He doesn't know what to say. Everything he's tried has been met with blank stares and dismal silence. He knows that she's heartbroken over the things that her father said about her mother. But she's *alive*! She must be so thrilled about that. He almost says so, but he catches himself just in time. Yes, her mother is alive, but she's been held captive and tortured for years and years.

He sniffles as tears drip down his wrinkled, leathery face. Ecko's mind must be in such turmoil right now. She probably doesn't even know what to feel. Hope? Anger? Sadness? Regret? He also understands that she's upset over what she'd been forced to do, putting the Sluggeelian out of his misery. It was the kindest thing she could have done, but to say so would be unwelcome and redundant. She already knows it was the best thing… the *only* thing she could have done. That's why she'd done it. She just needs time to come to grips with everything, that's all. It's what he keeps telling himself as he keeps his eyes locked on her face while they follow the trail through the Dead Forest.

The only real conversation that they engage in during the entire trek back comes about only because he notices a seldomseen splash of bright color. "Oh look, Ecko!" he suddenly, excitedly calls out as he points into the trees on the right side of the path. She stops walking and her eyes follow the line of his clawless pointer finger to what looks like a single orange flower, growing right up out of a grey-white rock.

"Pretty," she automatically murmurs, but listlessly and unenthusiastically.

"Will you carry me closer so I can get a better look at it? I think it's a…" He squints his eyes as she steps off the path, into the copse of dead trees and the equally dead underbrush. "It *is!* It's a star-petaled MorteFleur!" he exclaims.

She draws close enough to see that it's not a white-grey rock at all. It's actually the skull of some unfortunate, long-dead creature, and the flower is growing right up out of its empty eye socket. She also realizes that what caught Boodark's eye isn't even a flower… not really. It's more of a mushroom, the tangerineorange cap unfurled in sections and layers that resemble petals. There's even a small yellow blob of what appears to be some sort of sticky pollen at the center.

"Oh, what a wonderful find!" the delighted orc-bat crows as he claps his hands with glee. "The MorteFleur is very rare and has many legends and myths surrounding it. It's considered good luck to come across one. Although …" A thoughtful expression settles over his face and then he grins up at her. "You know what? I think I'll bring it back for Loryss as a thank you gift for his pukebone. Will you pick it for me?"

She reaches for it but then hesitates. "Are you sure? I mean, if it's so rare, should we really ruin it by picking it?"

"They only last one full Pale/Pitch cycle anyway. Better that someone gets some enjoyment out of it before it dies and is gone forever, don't you agree? Besides, if he eats the stem after the fungus petals fall off, he'll be granted a brief bout of pure joy. If *anyone* needs a joy infused attitude adjustment, it's that sourpuss Kreeleerian! You *know* I'm right. He is downright unpleasant to be around. This'll do him a world of good. And besides, it is said to contain a great deal of nutrients that will make his hair soft and silky and shiny. He'll like that. He *is* a hair covered furball, after all."

So, she shrugs as she bends down and plucks the

MorteFleur fungus flower, pulling it up by its short, shallow roots.

"Perfect!" Boodark praises as she hands it to him and then steps back onto the path to continue on her way with no more said about it.

They make it back to Tanda's house in half the time it took for them to leave it… probably because there are no pesky but lifesaving Kreeleerians to slow them down on the return trip. The Pitch's warning begins its rumble just as the towering SeeAll Tree comes into view. Boodark's glad to see it, and he'll be eternally grateful that they won't have to run from Deaders in the dark.

The old woman is standing in the open doorway waiting for their arrival, her face pinched and lined with worry. Ecko gives her a feeble, wobbly smile as she steps inside, murmuring something about needing a shower. She removes her backpack and the basket from around her neck, sets Boodark down, and quietly tells him that she'll be ok. Then she locks herself in the privy and hides for the next two hours.

Tanda glances down at Boodark and whispers, "What happened out there, Boodark? I tried to look; I tried to steer my visions in that direction, but I lost sight of you in the Scream Field. All I could see after that was a long, dark tunnel."

Boodark snorts and settles himself in front of the fireplace. "I better let her tell it to you. I'm not sure how much she wants to share. And besides, there are things that only she knows anyway. Things that she was shown."

Tanda considers the wisdom of his words as she begins the meal prep process, setting out pots and pans and rinsing a bowlful of vegetables. "Perhaps you're right," she agrees. "Perhaps, talking it all out may help her anyway… with whatever it is she needs to get through." She falls silent then, occupying herself with preparing the food, leaving Boodark to sit before the fire where he stares into the flames and anxiously waits for his friend to emerge from her self-isolation.

Loryss saunters in, takes one look at him, and turns his nose up in the air. "Oh great. You survived," he bemoans in a monotone voice. "Wait! I'll try that again. What I meant was, 'Great! I'm so *glad* you survived!' Athtandakapootha scolded me after you were gone. She said I needed to make more of an effort to welcome the two of you. So there. I'm glad you didn't die a horrible death, even though the look on your face suggests that *someone* has died."

Boodark never even looks away from the fire as he replies. "Don't start with me. I have entirely too many things to worry about at the moment. I can't be bothered with verbal sparring with annoying furballs. Go pester someone else."

Loryss curls up on the rug… leaving plenty of space between the two of them. He breathes a long-suffering sigh as he settles in to stare at the flames too. "I would, but alas, there *is* no one else to pester. You're it. Lucky you."

Boodark snorts but otherwise ignores him, his thoughts quickly moving on to everything *but* dumb kitties that don't know when to leave things alone.

"She'll be alright. You'll see," Tanda calls from the kitchen area. He nods to acknowledge that he hears her words. It seems like even the old lady has taken up his mantra of *She'll be fine.* Surely if they say it enough, it will make it so.

When she finally emerges, everyone studiously keeps their eyes averted from her. Each one pretends to be fully immersed in something other than her. Tanda focuses on filling a basket with fresh, hot biscuits and carrying it to the table. Boodark watches the fire with the deep concentration of someone that's in a meditative trance. Loryss licks himself… loudly and obnoxiously until Boodark can't stand the ssthlump ssthlump sounds any longer.

"Gah!" he shouts as he jumps to his feet and scowls at the Kreeleerian. "Go clean your beans somewhere else, you disgusting creature. No one wants to hear that, and I can assure you that no one wants to *see* it either!"

Ecko giggles and everyone stops what they're doing, their eyes all darting to her face. "What?" she demands, flustered by the weight of their stares. "You guys can stop worrying. Really, I'm fine. I just needed some time to get my head right. There was a lot that I needed to come to grips with." She moves as close as she can to the fire to ward off the chill in the air and begins working on drying her hair.

"*Well,*" Loryss demands. "Aren't you going to tell us what happened? Aren't you going to thank me for my gift? It did come in handy, did it not?" He swipes his paw at Boodark and adds, "*That* one wouldn't tell us a thing!"

She smiles down at Boodark with gratitude and his worried eyes immediately clear as if she'd just lifted a huge weight off of him. Overcome with emotion and a sudden rush of love for him, she lifts him up and kisses his leathery cheek. His face flames red, turning his green skin a very interesting moldy-cinnamon color.

"Oh look," Loryss teases. "He's just received his first kiss." Boodark turns and glares at him, sucks in a deep breath, and then lets him have it. "I'll have you know; I've had so many females that…"

And just like that, the two of them are back at each other's throats. Everyone relaxes and returns to normal, now that they know she's not going to have a meltdown.

"Food's ready!" Tanda calls out in a voice loud enough to shut the two obnoxious ones up.

Ecko settles Boodark onto his backpack booster seat and then helps the old woman carry everything to the table. "It all looks amazing, Tanda. Thank you," she praises as they gather round and take their places at the table.

While everyone fills their plates, she thinks back on all that had transpired since they'd parted ways… which, unbelievably, had been this morning! It seems like it's been days since they left here. A lot can happen in a day when it has twenty-three hours in it. And then being in the tunnels and the EverFalls, where time hadn't existed, has her internal clock even more thrown off. They'd spent at least a day in those tunnels, and yet, no time had passed outside of them. It's all so strange and it hurts her brain to think about it.

So, she *doesn't* think about it, and instead launches into her account of everything that her and her little companion had faced. She makes sure to properly thank each of the Kreeleerians for their gifts as she gets to their part in her story.

Tanda's eyes light up and she sighs with longing when she gets to the part where they reached the EverFalls. "Oh, how I wish I could have gone with you! I've always wanted to see that EverRealm!"

Ecko and Boodark grin conspiratorially at one another as she gets her camera out and shows Tanda how to scroll through the photos.

"Whoa! Forget about that one. And those too!" she jokes as she quickly scrolls past the ones of her hanging upside down from the web tunnel. The old woman tries to cover her smile with her hand while Boodark cracks up. But then she forgets all about laughing when she sees the beauty of the EverFalls.

"The photos are lovely, but they don't do it justice. It was so much… *more* in person," she explains as Tanda breathes a sigh of pleasure at the sight.

"Yes, yes. We get the point. It was beautiful. What happened next?" Loryss, ever the rude one demands.

"Well," she says as she returns to her seat. "Then I ran around in circles like a crazy person, searching for a mirror in the grass." She continues recounting her tale, up until the part where they got back to the Field of Screams and Broken Dreams and faced off with her father in his borrowed body… at which point Tanda interrupts her again.

"I saw nothing of your father in *any* of my visions!" she cries out with a bewildered frown on her face. "What about you, Danika?" she asks of the Kreeleerian with the gift of foresight.

Danika thoughtfully regards Ecko for a moment, then turns her galaxy eyes full of stars on the old lady. "No," she purrs in her soft, quiet voice. "Things are being hidden from our eyes. Something blocks the Lokskell. Something shields his actions from our sight."

Ecko's entire body tenses up as she turns very serious eyes on Tanda and asks, "Is that why you didn't tell me that my mother is alive? Did you *truly* not know?"

The spoon drops from the old woman's hand and clatters onto her plate as her eyes go wide with shock. "Laelynn lives?" she whispers. "After all this time… as his prisoner? Oh. *Oh, Ecko*. No wonder you were in such a state when you returned to us. Your poor mother. I mean, I *am* thrilled that she's alive, but… all this time…"

Tanda's voice trails off and she just nods her agreement because there's absolutely no way she can speak around the lump that's lodged itself in her throat. "Killing the slug-man was bad too," she whispers when she manages to swallow it down. She shivers with revulsion as the image of him pointing his huge, disgusting 'thingy' at her and fondling it invades her mind and causes her to gag, just as it had every single time it popped in there. "He was a revolting, depraved creature and he probably deserved everything that befell him, but I just couldn't leave him like that. It was *awful*."

Tanda smiles gently as she reaches across the table to briefly clutch her hand, "And there's your proof. If you ever needed reassurance that you are good and kind and unselfish, that was it. You may share the same blood as your father, and it may also be true that you inherited some of his darkness, but you *are* your mother's daughter. You will never enjoy the suffering of others, no matter their crimes and no matter how much they may deserve it. I know that you feel terrible for having to put the Sluggeelian out of his misery. I know you wish that you could have healed him. But what you must remember is that you can't fix everything. You won't be able to save everyone, and you will have to find a way to live with that. It's hard on you, I know that. You feel things like no other, so intensely because of who and what you are. It will take time to put everything into perspective and get it all under control. I think you're doing remarkably well with handling everything that's been thrown at you."

She ducks her head and mumbles, "I don't feel like I'm handling anything well. I feel like a hot mess, all the time. But that's basically what Khalidah told me, too. She said that some broken things can be mended, others cannot. I won't be able to fix everything, nor am I expected to. I just have to do the best that I can, every single day, and accept that it will have to be enough."

Tanda smiles softly. "So, you found her. May I see it… the EverGlass?"

She immediately lifts the web-chain out of her shirt and hands it to her, watching as the old woman's eyes fill with tears. "Oh! It's just as beautiful as the last time I saw it!"

Khalidah's woman form appears for just a moment, a ghostly, incorporeal image superimposed over the EverGlass. "Hello, old friend," Khalidah says in her otherworldly voice. "It has been a long time since last we met. It brings me great joy to see you again, after all these many years. It gladdens my heart that you will be here to help Adrina along her way. She has many heavy burdens to bear, many difficulties to face, and many hurts to endure. She will need all the help she can get, as she *must* learn everything in such a short amount of time. She'll need loyal friends for the troubled times ahead."

Tanda replies to Khalidah, but she looks straight into Ecko's eyes and speaks the words like a promise. "I will do all that I can to help her."

Khalidah dips her head in acknowledgement as she croons, "I know that you will, loyal friend. Lamora Deidra would have been pleased to learn that you honor her by aiding Irredarr's new

Wandelaar along her journey. And with that being said, Deidra has a message for you. She left it in my keeping with instructions to pass it along when the timing was right. I feel that now is that time. Fare the well, sweet friend. Until next time."

The image of Khalidah's pale blue/white woman's body fades away, leaving only the EverGlass in the old woman's hand. And then the image of the woman that she's loved for over a thousand years… a love so strong that even death could not end it, appears inside the mirror. She's standing on a beach with flowers in her hair, and her cerulean eyes hold more sparkle than the crystal rose-pink waters behind her.

Tanda begins to sob as the brief video/message plays. *'Hello, my love. Today is our vow-day, and we've just finished promising to love one another for the rest of our lives. Forgive me for sneaking away, but I wanted to take a moment to record this message for you, just in case anything should ever happen, and you need the reminder that I love you more than there are stars in the sky, more than all the grains of sand… here, on this beach that we've chosen to spend our vow-night on. I know how hard loving me is, with all the rules and duties… all the secrets. You'll never know just how much it means that you choose me anyway, regardless of all that you will have to endure. I love you, Athtandakapootha Delainnianth Carpathilla, and my heart chooses you. It will always choose you, even when my body cannot. Oh!'* The video shakes and the angle changes to show another woman approaching. *'Look at how beautiful you are. Do you see yourself the same way that I see you? Can you?'* The video shakes again and focuses back on her. *'This image, just as you are right now, is how I will forever think of you. From here until my last breath, I will remember the wind in your hair, the smile on your face, and the love in your eyes'.* Deidra giggles then and lowers her voice. *'I have to go now! I think you're starting to get suspicious.'* She blows a quick kiss, and the video comes to an end, frozen right on her airborne kiss.

Tanda wipes her eyes as she begins to speak. "This was the day we spoke our vows to one another. We had to sneak off and do it in secret, as it is forbidden for a Wandelaar to pledge herself to another female. Oh, don't get me wrong. We were free to love one another. We were even free to be together. We just weren't allowed to be a mated pair."

Seeing the confusion on Ecko's face, she goes on to clarify. "As Wandelaar, my Deidra was expected to carry on the line… she had to produce the next Mirror Walker. And seeing as how I lacked the parts needed to create children with her, that meant that she would have to mate with a male. She could love whomever she chose, so long as she did her duty first. The only problem with that was that *duty* would not end for years and years to come. She would first have to bear her heiress. The child would then have to be raised to adulthood and trained in the ways that all Wandelaars are trained. Deirdra's duty would not have been considered fulfilled until the day she gave up her magic and passed it on to the young, new heiress. That was the way it had always been. That's how the council of elders ensured the survival of our Mirror Walkers. I didn't realize that it was cruel, not until I, myself, fell in love with a Mirror Walker, that is. I didn't understand how hard all of it was for them. How unfair."

She pauses to wipe her eyes again and then delicately blows her nose. "Deidra had just chosen the man that she would join with… the man that would father the next Wandelaar when she suggested that we exchange vows in secret. She knew how hard it would be on me, knowing that she was to lie in the arms of another. She wanted me to know that she loved me above all others, and that if she had a choice, she would choose me and *only* me. I was selfish, I know that now. I knew it then too, but it didn't stop me from agreeing. We stole away and spoke our vows of everlasting love to one another in secret. And they were binding vows, in our hearts if not in the eyes of the council of elders."

Tanda goes quiet with a soft smile teasing her lips, lost somewhere in her memories.

"Well?" Boodark demands.

She blinks several times as she gets snapped out of the past. "Well, what?"

He grunts out his frustration. "Well, did she do it? Did she honor her vows to you, or did she honor her duty? Did she lay with a male?"

Ecko gasps in shock at his blatant audacity. "Boodark! That is none of our business!" she scolds. But Tanda just laughs. "Deidra did what she had to do…. eventually. It took her forever, but she finally chose the man that she would lie with; Maurone, his name was. Only problem was, he just couldn't seem to pin her down to get the deed done! She kept coming up with ways to avoid it. She became quite inventive too!" She can't help but laugh at the memories. "Once she even drank bean oil to make herself sick. She ended up vomiting all over him when he tried to move in to kiss her!"

Ecko smiles at how the memory lights up the old woman's eyes as she tells of her lover's shenanigans.

"Oh, she eventually lay with him… and she found that it wasn't as terrible as her mind convinced her it would be. She knew all along that it had to be done; we both knew it. And we chose to speak our vows to one another anyway. That's how much we loved one another. Yes, she knew her duties well, and she had every intention of fulfilling them. She just did them *her* way, and in her own time. I had never met anyone so honor-bound to do the right thing but still remain so defiant and unpredictable to the end. Oh, she kept us all on our toes, my love did."

She glances down at the EverGlass still clutched in her hand. "One more time?" she begs. "Please, may I see her just once more?"

As Khalidah restarts the message, Ecko quietly excuses herself to give her some privacy. She takes a flashlight from her bag, lifts Boodark up, and carries him outside to take care of any business that he may need to see to before bedtime. Then she lowers herself to the ground and leans back against the SeeAll Tree to wait for him, and a thousand eyeballs pop open to watch her every move.

After a few minutes, Boodark makes his way over to her, uneasily staring up at the slowly blinking eyeballs that stare right back at him. "I don't think I'll ever get used to that," he mumbles with a shudder as he plops down beside her. "So, when do we set out on this side mission of yours?"

She fidgets uncomfortably for a minute, and he *immediately* understands just what that means. He's already stubbornly shaking his head when she informs him that she'll be tackling this next mission on her own. "Well, *I* will be setting out first thing in the morning… uh, when the Pale arrives. *You* will be sitting this one out, Boodark. I'm sorry, but that's just how it has to be."

He snorts, sneers, and objects, in precisely that order. "You really should know me better than that by now. Where you go, I go too." Then the little brat throws her words back at her. "I'm sorry, but *that's* just how it has to be. Now shut up and go tell that annoying Kreeleerian creature that I have a gift out here for him. I want to get this over with so that I can go back inside and get some sleep. I feel like we're going to need all the rest we can get. And don't even *think* about trying to sneak out on me. You'll be sleeping right beside me this Pitch, up close and personal like!"

She just grunts as she gets up off the ground and steps back inside to summon Loryss the hellcat. "No, I don't know why he wants to give it to you out there in the dark. And no, I will *not* tell you what it is," she argues as she waits for the stubborn cat to decide if it wants to accept Boodark's offering. "All I'll say is that it's a good gift and that I am proud of him for forgiving you and putting aside his revenge vendetta. I was certain that he would have to retaliate for the grossness of *your* gift, but I guess he realizes that even though it was exceedingly nasty, it *did* save our lives. We both owe you our thanks."

A barely heard snorty choke-y sound from Boodark drifts in through the open doorway as the cat haughtily lifts his nose in the air and then gracefully jumps to the floor. "Well, of *course* you do," he sneers as he struts past her. She merely rolls her eyes as she follows him out.

Boodark is standing just beyond the circle of light that pours out of the door, keeping himself mostly hidden in the darkness.

"Well, ugly one, where is this gift?" Loryss demands.

She can barely see his finger as Boodark lifts his hand and points out onto the path. "It's right over there, rude one," he snaps back.

She shines her flashlight out and it illuminates a clothwrapped bundle lying on the ground. She briefly wonders why he wrapped a flower up. She also wonders why the bundle is so large and oddly lumpy.

"Why is it way out there?" Loryss questions with eyes narrowing suspiciously on her little friend. "What are you up to?" It's at this point that she realizes that Boodark is indeed 'up to something.' She presses her lips tightly together as she watches him shrug his shoulders and chuckle nervously.

Boodark hastily blurts out his excuses. "It was hard for me to carry. It's almost as big as I am, ya know? I got tired of dragging it around. And I also wanted to keep it hidden. I didn't want the she-cats to see it. I didn't want them to be jealous and try to take it from you. But if you don't want it, I'll just go ahead and call Danika and Caheera right now. I'm sure *they'll* appreciate it."

The Kreeleerian hisses and snarls, "It's *my* gift. You brought it for *me*. Leave my sister-mates out of it!" Up goes both of his tails as he saunters out, following the beam of light from the flashlight. He never hears the little orc-bat's anxious, urging whispers of, "Go on, *go on!*" *She* can barely hear him and she's standing right beside him. They watch together as Loryss stretches out a paw and swipes the cloth off in one quick movement.

Everything happens so fast that her mind has trouble processing it all. The MorteFleur is exposed in the flashlight's beam for one brief moment, allowing her to see that its yellow center has formed some sort of sticky pollen bubble. A huge malformed, lumpy cyst that's swelled up so large that the 'petals' can no longer even be seen.

"What the…" she starts to ask but never has a chance to finish the thought. One second the Kreeleerian male is standing there, all sleek black fur and beautiful, and then there's a loud pop and he's no longer a black cat at all. He's a sickly yellow, sticky mess. His head turns towards them in slow motion, absolute unadulterated murder in his eyes as the most horrific smell she's ever had the misfortune to encounter fills the air.

"Pick me up," Boodark whispers in an urgent and highly distressed voice.

Loryss snarls at them, one long, low growl as he stalks closer. "A MorteFleur. You gave me a dying MorteFleur." He says it in the calmest voice that somehow seems even more menacing because of the lack of emotion behind the words. "You. Gave me. A dying. MorteFleur. *You* gave me…"

Boodark squeals and begins hopping up and down against her leg like an excited, yapping chihuahua. "Pick me up, Ecko! Pick me up! Pick me *up*!" He's frantically wailing now as Loryss crouches low to the ground, readying himself for the killing pounce.

"Oh, no you don't!" she cries out as she scoops her naughty little friend up in her arm… just as the Kreeleerian makes his move.

"You put him back down this instant!" The furious cat snarls at her as she raises the hem of her shirt up to cover her nose. "Come back down here and fight like a man!" he screeches.

Out of the danger zone and tucked safely in her arms, Boodark instantly and miraculously becomes fearless once more… again much like a little chihuahua. "Um, no. I'm not coming down there. I don't want you to get your stink on me! Ugh, you really are foul. Back up, pussycat. I can't breathe!" He dramatically coughs and chokes as *she* tries to back up and get out of the nauseating death cloud that's clinging to the pissed hellcat. And all the while, Loryss is glaring up at her like it's *her* fault.

"I didn't know!" she protests through the fabric of her shirt… that's doing absolutely *nothing* to block out the stench. "I didn't know it would do that! It just looked like a pretty flower to me!" Her back thumps up against the doorframe and there's nowhere else to go.

"What did you expect a death flower to do? Grant wishes?" he snarls back as he continues to stalk his prey.

"Well, I certainly didn't know it was going to puff up and then turn into the world's most revolting stink bomb, that's for sure!" she argues.

Boodark giggles down at him. "You should see yourself right now. You look absolutely disgusting… and you smell even worse! And *that's* what you get for making Ecko feel bad about not being clean enough to suit you… after she'd just spent several Pales wandering around in the Sorrow Marshes! Shame on you for making her feel unwelcome!"

She has to lift up her foot to block the attack as the incensed cat launches himself up with his sharp, Freddy Krueger claws exposed. "Just go take a bath!" she shrieks, causing the bad little orc-bat to giggle and the Kreeleerian to snarl even more.

"He can't! It doesn't wash off!"

Oh, this is bad. Oh, this is *so* bad. "What do you *mean* it doesn't wash off? He can't stay like that forever! He's foul! You *know* that we're going to be staying here for a little while. Do you really want to smell *that* every day?" She scoots a tiny bit to the right in order to reach the doorway, and then she's backing into the tree house.

"Oh, stop worrying. It'll be gone by Pale-rise. He can't *wash* it off, but it will dry up into tiny flakes and float up off of him all on its own. He'll be fine."

She yelps and jumps back another step as the Kreeleerian lunges at her again.

"Stop right there, Loryss!" Tanda hollers from across the room. "Don't you step one foot inside this house. You'll be sleeping outside this Pitch."

Caheera giggles at the sight of him and adds, "Danika warned you not to poke fun at the guests. You should have listened, brother. You know she's always right."

He points a claw at her and snarls, "You mind your own business, *sister*." Then he turns his glare back on the objects of his wrath. "And you two… just know that *you* did this. *You've* chosen violence. I cannot, I *will not* let this go unavenged."

Her eyes widen in disbelief as she sputters, "But I didn't do it! I didn't know what would happen!"

He narrows mean, hateful eyes at her. 'I don't care. *You* brought the ugly one here, *you* protect him from my wrath. I hold you just as responsible for this insult, this travesty… this unmitigated blasphemy! *This* is what I get in return for my own life-saving gift to *you?* I won't forget this. I will *never* forget! And you, ugly one… know that your Pales are numbered. Revenge *will* be mine!" And with that warning, he spins around and disappears out into the Pitch.

"What have you done, Boodark?" she admonishes as she glares down at him. "I thought you said that the MorteFleur would bring him joy!"

He winces and peeks up at her with a guilty expression. "I didn't lie! It *will* bring him joy… *if* he chooses to eat the stem after all the petals fall off. And it *will* do wonders for his fur, just like I said it would. I just omitted the part about the stink that has to come first, that's all."

She shakes her head at him. "What am I going to do with you?"

He merely shrugs back and mutters, "He started it." And how can she argue with that? The hellcat *did* start it.

"You get in, get it done, and get back out. Do *not* stop for anything! I don't care how tempted you may be."

Ecko sighs dramatically as she pulls her curls up into a tight ponytail. "I know, Tanda."

The anxious old woman rings her hands as she frets. "Oh, maybe I should go with you! What if something goes wrong? What if…"

She turns and places her hands on old, fragile shoulders that try to carry too much weight upon them. "We've been over and over this. You can't go. You can't even walk beyond the SeeAll's boundaries. How do you think you'll survive jumping to another world? No, you have to stay here. I'll be fine. I won't stop for anything, and I'll be right back. In and out, you'll see. You won't even have time to miss me."

Tanda's chin wobbles as she fights back tears. "I doubt that. I already miss you, child. But there's not much I can do about it, is there?"

She smiles gently and shakes her head. "No. I'm afraid not. What I just can't seem to wrap my mind around is the fact that I've spent all this time trying to find a way off of this world, and now that I *have* a way and I finally get to leave… I'm just going to turn around and come right back! Back to this soul sucking, vampire world… *willingly!*" She glances down to where Boodark is clinging like a spider monkey to her arm.

"Don't you *dare* give me that look!" he scolds. "Do you think this is comfortable for me? No. It. Is. Not. This is your own fault, and you know it. *Remember* this the next time you think you can just go off and leave me behind."

She bends down to slip her shoes on but finds it extremely awkward with his arms and legs wrapped around her like a vise. "Can you loosen up, just a bit? I already said that I wouldn't go without you!"

He grips even harder. "Good! That's good. And this is my way of making sure that you don't!"

She manages to get one shoe tied, then bends to get the other one as she asks him, "You don't trust me?" To which he vehemently shakes his head. "Negative… at least not in this. I know you would do anything to keep me safe, so you definitely aren't above lying to see that I stay that way."

She *had* been thinking sneaky thoughts about slipping away… just to keep him safe, so she can't even pretend to be offended by his distrust. "Fair enough," she murmurs as she straightens back up. "But this is your last chance to change your mind. You know how terrible I am at magic. You could very well get trapped over there."

His eyes are wild for a minute as he frantically rethinks what he could potentially be getting himself into. Seeing his indecision, she presses the issue in one last desperate attempt to get him to stay behind. "What of your family? What will happen to them if you're not here to save them?"

He firms his trembling lips and raises his chin up a notch. "It matters not. If you don't come back, I'll have no chance of saving them anyway. Say what you will, but I'm going and you're just wasting everyone's time with arguing."

She nods. It's the answer that she expected but she had to try anyway. "Alright. Let's do this then. Climb up on my shoulder and hang onto my hair. Do *not* let go for anything. Do you understand?"

He nods and quickly does as he's told. He digs his fingers into her curls, wrapping them around his hands several times for a more secure grip.

"I mean this Boodark. Don't let go. I don't care what you may see, what you may hear, or what may happen."

He gives her hair a tiny tug as he squeaks, "Sure," in a suddenly frightened voice. She then throws a terrible, monstrous threat at him, just to get her point across. "If I even *think* that you're about to let go, I'll snatch you up and stuff you down my shirt and between my boobs faster than I can say 'one Boodark-boobie sandwich, coming right up'. You feel me?"

He makes a retching noise in her ear but nods, nonetheless.

"Good." she snaps. "You remember that, or you'll be feeling more of me than either one of us will like! Now be quiet and let me concentrate!"

He clings ever tighter, slams his eyes shut, and ducks his head down as he yells, "Yes ma'am!"

With the web-chain still safely in place around her neck

(because how terrible would it be if she dropped it or had it snatched from her hands the moment that she stepped through to the other side?) she lifts the EverGlass up to eye level. She's not looking into it just yet though. Her eyes are shut tight and she's looking inwards instead, into her mind.

She focuses all her thoughts on one specific scene that Khalidah had shown her at the EverFalls. She watches it play out and then she watches it again, taking note of every single detail. The location. The faces. Was it day or night? Was it raining outside? When she feels like she's memorized the scene and has it locked firmly in her mind, *that's* when she calls on her magic. She takes a moment to have a little talk with it first, basically threatening to never let it out to play… ever again, if it failed her now. Then she takes a deep breath, opens her eyes, and looks deep within the EverGlass, past the myriad of colors and all the way to the mirror at the back.

Random scenes appear and then just as quickly disappear. Faces of strangers and unfamiliar places flash past. Creatures from the OtherLands scroll by. It's a jumble of remarkable beings and unbelievable images, little snippets of lives on all the OtherWorlds… all zooming past at such an incredibly fast pace that she's surprised she can make sense of it. Her eyes oscillate at high speed to keep track of it all until…

"Stop!" she shouts as the image she's been searching for appears. But the EverGlass had already stopped before the words were even formed on her lips. It heard her *mentally* give the command and had acted on it before she even opened her mouth.

She stares into that *other* room, her heart pounding in fear and excitement and longing and eagerness… but mostly fear. She can't afford to mess up now, and if she's learned anything about herself and her magic in all that's happened thus far, it's that she has a *lot* to learn in order to be the Ecko that everyone seems to think she needs to be. She won't say that she's a complete screw up, but things *never* go as smoothly as she plans them… and that's being kind to herself.

"In and out, Ecko. Get in, get out. You got this!" It's the best pep talk she can come up with, and it will have to be enough because time's up. She focuses every ounce of will she possesses on that *other* place inside the mirror, lightly presses her fingers to the surface of the EverGlass, and *wills* herself to be there… in that *other*, far away room.

There's the strangest feeling of suction, a *pull* on her soul as she gets sucked into a black hole. And then she's in a tunnel… a *wormhole,* speeding past colors and sparks of light that remind her of her galaxy smoke/magic. She doesn't have time to feel anything but surprise and the briefest wonder because when she blinks, it's all over and she's standing in that *other* room.

Again, there's a retching noise in her ear and Boodark croaks out, "Oh, I don't feel so good. I think I'm gonna barf!" But she doesn't acknowledge his complaint. She can't. Every bit of her attention is zeroed in on the three people that occupy this *other* room… all three of them staring back at her with shocked expressions on their faces.

Her eyes move over the sobbing, cowering woman, then over the old man that has situated himself protectively in front of her. His eyes immediately light up and he gasps aloud when he sees her standing there in his living room. "Ecko!" Charlie cries out in joy as he turns and wraps his arms around his wife.

She searches his face and when she sees the swollen, black eye and the trickle of blood at the corner of his mouth, her mind immediately goes red as his blood. Her magic *zaps* through her, crackles along her skin and settles into her hands, and it's no longer a pleasant little tingle. It *sizzles* in anticipation as she turns her furious gaze on her twin, standing there with her fist raised up, preparing for her next strike upon Charlie's already battered face.

Boodark whispers into her ear, "Be calm, Ecko! This isn't the time for a showdown. In and out, remember?"

The red-hot fury recedes the tiniest fraction, just enough for her to *think* before she acts. She nods to indicate that his words were heard and appreciated.

Samara's eyes fly open wide with shock at her sudden appearance, causing her to lower her upraised fist as she stumbles backwards. Her eyes immediately drop to the electric, blue energy that's crackling on her sister's palms, and a brief flash of fear dances over her features before she can mask it with her typical nastiness. Her lips twist in an unpleasant smile as she crows, "Sister! I should have known that you'd find a way back to your old geezers. However did you manage it? And just in time to watch them die, too! How exciting!"

She looks Ecko up and down... contempt, disgust, and amazement all warring for first place on her face. "We really *have* switched roles, have we not? Now *you're* the filthy, dirty waif while I'm the pampered, privileged princess. Although I must say, you *never* looked as good as all this!" She gestures at herself, preening as she shows off her fancy clothes, her artfully applied make-up, and her stylish hairdo.

Charlie, never one to back down or wisely hold his tongue, jumps to her defense. "I hate to break it to you, young lady, but your fancy clothes don't cover up your rotten heart. Your perfume does nothing to mask the scent of your fear, just as your make-up can't hide the angry little girl that you try so hard to conceal."

Ecko shakes her head at the foolish, brave Charlie... poking sticks at the pissed off rattlesnake. She rushes to distract her sister, to divert her anger from Charlie and back to herself. "It's true,

Sister. You smell like ignorance; you reek of anger and fear…. even under the sweet stench of your perfume."

The ploy works like a charm. Samara's eyes leave Charlie and dart back to her, right where she wants them to stay.

"Oh, you can't even speak to me of stenches," Samara retorts. "You, who haven't had a proper bath in months. I know, because you're living what was once my life, on my diseased world. I *smelled* you when you popped into the room, even before I saw you. And *what* is that disgusting thing clinging to your head? It's absolutely hideous."

Boodark gulps when he realizes that he's been spotted, that *he's* the hideous creature that she's talking about.

"He's beautiful," Ecko insists. "Only shallow, ignorant people take one look at someone's appearance and immediately judge them for it. Boodark will always have a beauty that you will never possess, no matter what form he's in… cursed or not."

She takes another tiny sidestep. She's steadily been moving, slowly closing the distance between herself and her loved ones. She needs them close enough for the snatch and grab, closely followed by the disappearing act that she's planning on attempting.

Her twin sneers in that condescending way that she's so good at, and she notices for the first time how dilated her twin's pupils are. Almost completely obscured by the huge black circles, only a thin outline of her green irises can be seen around them.

"Are you *high*?" she asks incredulously. "You are, aren't you? Oh, that's rich! You are a lot of things, Samara, but I never took you for stupid."

She watches her sister's eyes go black with rage as she screams, "Don't call me stupid! Don't you *ever* call me stupid!"

Ecko frantically motions Charlie over, then she holds her magic-ready hands up in front of her… just in case as her two old friends scramble to her side. Samara realizes what's going on and she throws her hands up, screaming out her anger as her Shadow/Smoke billows out.

"She's got fart smoke, Ecko! Fart smoke incoming!" Boodark screams so loudly that it rattles her eardrums. "In and out, Ecko! *In and out!* You were supposed to get in and get right back out… without pissing off the yokels and getting us doused in fart smoke!"

She reaches for the EverGlass with one hand while holding the other one at the ready as she shouts out instructions. "Hold on to me, all of you. Hold on *tight*! Don't let go for anything!"

She glances down into the mirror, scared half to death that she won't be able to concentrate enough through her fear to get them all out of there and to safety. She steers her thoughts to Tanda, waiting for her back at the SeeAll Tree.

Just like before, random images and scenes appear and fly past in quick succession. She tries to focus all her will into making that specific location pop up in the glass, but it feels like it's taking so long, and she begins to panic. "Come on, come *on*!" she urges as her eyes dart back and forth between what's happening in the EverGlass and what's happening right before her in real time.

"I'm too young to die!" Boodark wails as he ducks back behind her head in an attempt to hide from her sister's rapidly approaching foulness. "I have a mate! I have younglings that need their Papa! Get us out of here, Ecko!"

There! The EverGlass pulls up and locks down on the image of the SeeAll Tree quicker than her mind can actively process it. "Shut up, Boodark!" she screams as she presses her fingers to the mirror. As she feels that first pulling/sucking sensation on her soul, her eyes automatically (and without her permission) dart down to the two familiar boxes lying atop the coffee table. Without a second thought about it, she reaches down and snatches the pizzas up a split second before her and her little group of cling-ons get sucked into the wormhole. Her howls of laughter are just as loud as her sister's howls of fury. She hopes with everything inside her that Samara can hear her victorious laughter as she carries her loved ones to safety, far out of her reach.

The Lokskell: Epilogue

Immediately following the encounter with Ecko in the Field of Screams and Broken Dreams…

He grabs onto his head and howls in agony as he falls to his knees on the cold stone floor of the castle's keep. The few slaves and servants that are present flee in fear, and his Vika Vakooja bugspies scatter like their roach cousins. Not a single soul dares to remain close enough to witness his pain and suffering. And oh, how it *hurts*. It hurts so bad. His Slivers are part of him, and he felt every one of their deaths as his daughter meticulously and ruthlessly annihilated them.

She killed them, he muses in shocked outrage. No one has *ever* killed his Slivers before, never neutralized his Shadow-smoke. He hadn't even known it could be done. He doesn't know if he should be impressed or pissed. At the moment, he's just in pain…. He's never felt anything like it in all the long years of his existence. It felt just like someone had reached inside of him, plucked out pieces of his soul, and then lit them on fire while they were still connected to him so that he was forced to feel every excruciating second of it.

He lies on the floor for hours, just breathing through the agony, growing angrier and angrier with each passing minute that he's incapacitated. He feels so much rage… he *is* rage. He is rage and pain and vengeance, but oh, how he wants her! All that *power!* He. Must. Have. Her.

Eventually, he manages to sit up, grimacing as he coughs up a mouthful of blood. He spits it onto the floor and grins as he gets to his feet, and then slowly makes his way to Laelynn's chambers. If he can't get to the daughter, he'll just have to take it out on the mother. And when he's done, when he's worn his anger out upon her flesh, he'll figure out what needs to be done about his spectacular, defiant daughter. She's mind-bogglingly powerful, as she'd just proven with her display of anger at his treatment of her mother. He'll need to think about how best to handle her. And he'll need to prepare for when she finally does come for her mother. Because she *is* coming for her. He knows that beyond a shadow of a doubt. He grins again, the blood in his teeth glinting crimson in the light of the torches in the wall sconces. He can't *wait* to see her again. In fact, he's already thinking of all the things he wants to do to her when next they meet.

He waves aside the guards at the door and enters the room. "Laelynn! How're you doing, old girl? You will *never* guess who I just met!" he calls out with a cheery voice that belies the pain he's still suffering. The petite woman with the floor-length, golden-red hair is facing away from him, busily dipping her fingers into a bowl of black, self-made paint that she'd created from watered down ashes from her fireplace. She never acknowledges him as he shuts and locks the door behind him. He stands there in the entryway for several minutes, silently watching as she adds one more object to the soot-and-ashes mural that covers her prison walls. She lifts her blackened hand and adds a line here, a smudge there until she's satisfied with the image that she's drawn. Only then does she set the bowl aside, turning just enough so that he can see her profile. He automatically and unwillingly sucks in his breath at her beauty, just as he does every single time he lays eyes on her. He watches with his breath locked inside his chest as she turns to face him… but not to greet him. No, never that.

Even with her unfocused, empty eyes and the streaks of black soot smudged on her face, she's the loveliest thing he's ever seen. And just like it does every time, his body instantly reacts to her presence. He *wants* her. He *always* wants her. And it fills him with as much rage as it does with lust. He walks forward and takes Laelynn into his arms, never even glancing at what she's drawn upon the wall. He *never* looks. He's always dismissed it all as the mad scribblings of a broken mind. If he but stood back and looked, *really* looked at her picture-words drawn out on the walls, perhaps he'd be able to read the story.

Perhaps he would realize that the EverGlass that he so covets is no longer hidden, that it's back where it belongs… in the hands of the new Wandelaar. Perhaps he would see that a new necklace to unite the EverGlass and the heiress Mirror Walker has been made, forged from Khalidah's steely silk threads and beaded with her daughter's own pearl-tears. Perhaps he would have seen it all… but all he sees is *her*.

Epilogue: Samara

Howling with the most intense rage of her entire fury-laden life, Samara tears through the old geezer's home like a wounded, enraged bull. Room by room she lays waste to every piece of furniture, shreds every stitch of fabric, and shatters every bit of glass… all while screaming and cursing her sister's name. When there's nothing left but tatters and rubble, she moves back into the living room where Ecko had snuck in like a coward and snatched the two old farts right out of her grasp.

She's so angry she's growling, literally growling and snarling with impotent rage as she stares at the spot that her sister had disappeared from. There's a burning, roiling ball of hot hatred building inside her chest. It's *growing,* swelling inside her like air inflating a balloon. Every part of her feels swollen with outrage. Her fingers are claws of wrath, her arms and legs are savagery wrapped up in alabaster silk skin. Her feet are stomping, pounding instruments of raging madness. Every strand of hair on her head is pissed off, snapping about her face like riled snakes. Every bit of her feels volatile and combustible. She's never felt anything like this. She can't think. She can only feel. And she feels *too much.* The fury is too intense, too consuming… even for *her* to bear. Something has to give. It's got to go somewhere. She can't function like this. It builds, and it builds, and it builds… until finally it's too big for her to contain inside her small body. She throws her head back and the rage bursts out of her mouth in an immense, foul black cloud. It pours out of her *forever,* so much of it that it fills the entire house. And when the house isn't enough to contain it, it begins to flow out the windows where it immediately floats away on a breeze to do its own thing, free from its master.

When finally, every bit of it has been purged from her system, she has one brief moment of clarity. One single moment to choose. She can let it all go, let her anger and her overwhelming resentment go. She can be free of her fury. But who would she be without her hatred and loathing and animosity? Who is she without her venom? How could Samara be Samara without her hostility and outrage and her self-righteous vengeance?

Oh, hell no. She immediately raises her hands and sucks it all back up, every bit of her Shadows that she can recall. The majority of them willingly flow back into her and quickly fill her up until every bit of her is taken up with them and there's no room left for any more… as if they've somehow grown larger or perhaps even multiplied. *And they're in her head now,* the one place they've never had access to before. She finds that her head is now stuffed full of her own Shadows, almost like a backwash of blood into a hypodermic needle. And these are changed things, somehow. They feel dirtier… *sneakier* somehow. Like they know a secret that she's not privy to. The bits of Shadows that won't fit inside of her settle around her like a shroud of doom that clings to her skin, following wherever she leads. Almost like a foul stench.

Without any cognitive thought, she turns and makes her way to the shattered front door, kicking aside the debris in her path as she goes. Mr. Chadwick holds the car door open for her, revealing the bound and wildly struggling pizza delivery boy held captive within.

A terrible grin twists her lips as she remembers that she'd arrived here at the old geezers home just in time to watch them pay for their food and send the hapless young man on his merry way. Turns out, it wasn't so merry for him after all… definitely not worth it, even with the generous tip they'd given him.

She'd sent her Shadows out to intercept him before he could drive away. They quickly bound and gagged him, and Mr. Chadwick had tossed him into the back seat where they waited for their mistress to get done with her errand and come back to them.

Now, she grins with pure delight as she climbs into the car, settling in beside the desperately sobbing delivery man. A dark haze suddenly descends over her mind and doesn't let up. Her head has become a mindless, killing void. And when she comes back to herself, *three days later,* she no longer knows if she controls the Shadows or if it is *her* that's controlled by *them.*

Mr. Chadwick had frowned uneasily as he closed the car door behind his mistress and her new whipping boy. It wasn't that the screams began even before he made it back around to the driver's seat once more. No, that was nothing out of the norm. Samara *does* adore her new toys, after all. He couldn't explain it even to himself, but he instinctively knew that something had changed. His mistress was… different somehow.

So, he watched her. As the next three days passed, he dutifully took care of her. He watched over her, fed her, and bathed her while she took out her frustrations on the young man… long after he could no longer feel the punishment. He watched as she finally came back to herself, came back to him. She hadn't known where she was, or what she'd been doing. The last thing she remembered was standing in the old couple's house after she destroyed it… feeling the rage swell within her. That's it. That was all she remembered. He'd had to fill in the blanks for her.

And now he's been sent back to the scene of the crime, delivering what's left of the pizza man's body to the old folk's Samara-ravaged home. He frets and worries about her as he strews the body parts about the crime scene just as he'd been instructed to do. He places the severed head onto the heap of broken table parts, turning it just so in order for the sunlight streaming through the shattered window to reflect off of the shards of mirrors jammed into the emptied eye sockets.

He steps back and surveys the scene with a critical eye. Perfect. Message delivered. "Rest in pieces, kid," he murmurs in his soft, gentle voice as he turns and hurries away. He's anxious to get back to her, now that she's almost *her* again. Because he knows without a doubt that these past three days, she'd not been the Samara that he's come to know and adore. Something infinitely more sinister and horrifying now lurks behind her eyes, hides behind her smile. It's almost like something is wearing her face like a mask… and that mask is ever so slowly slipping.

Epilogue: Ecko

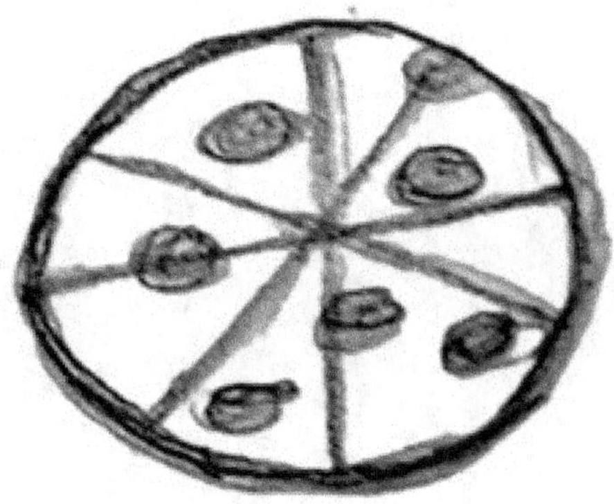

Tanda lets out an undignified squeal and drops the bread dough that she'd been kneading as a sudden *loud* commotion demands her attention. For a moment, all she can do is stand there behind the kitchen island... wide eyed, nut-floured hand pressed to her bosom in alarm as she stares incredulously at the pile of twisted limbs that has just materialized on the floor of the entryway. She watches as an arm emerges and thrusts itself up out of the mix, the hand holding aloft a couple of thin, square containers. A muffled but urgent voice cries out amidst pained grunts and groans. "Save the pizza!"

The old woman hesitantly steps around the kitchen counter, her eyes darting over the heap. She's desperately trying to make sense of the writhing pile when a familiar little bat-like creature tumbles out and rolls across the floor. She immediately sucks in a breath of relief. "Ecko! You made it back!"

The arm waves the boxes in the air as the directive is repeated. "Save the pizza! *Please!*"

Tanda rushes forward and takes the strange squares from the hand and sets them aside on the table. A tiny groan draws her attention back to the creature that had rolled free of the pile of squirming bodies. "Boodark? Are you ok?" she asks but he suddenly throws a hand over his mouth, scuttles around the jumble of limbs and rushes out the door.

Ecko disentangles herself and sits up, her disheveled and tangled curls standing up in every direction. "Tanda?" she asks in a quavering, wondering voice. "We made it? We *actually* made it back?" She glances down and her eyes immediately fill with tears as they land on two beloved sets of eyes that are equally focused on *her* and already pouring tears.

"I did it," she murmurs to herself. Then she repeats it louder, "I really did it! Oh Charlie! I've been so scared without you!" And then she dives into his arms. Susan rolls in to hug her too, turning her into an Ecko-sandwich squished between them. The three of them lay there on the floor and just cry for a moment, overcome as they are with so many emotions at being reunited once more.

"Great!" A familiar… and *rude* voice rings out. "She's brought more of them back with her. Is it her plan to have us overrun? Well, at least these two appear cleaner than herself and the ugly one. Perhaps *they* won't stink up the place too badly."

She sits back up and glares at the Kreeleerian and snaps, "Oh, do be quiet, Loryss!" Then she climbs to her feet and helps first Susan and then Charlie up off the hard floor. Boodark saunters back in, automatically running his hands over his green and black hair in a futile attempt at smoothing the halfway unplaited braid. "We have *got* to work on your landing skills, girl!"

She's so deliriously happy in this moment and she rushes forward to lift him up and hug him to her… squashing him against her chest. She has the overwhelming urge to keep him close as the introductions are made, perhaps subconsciously letting Charlie and Susan know that even though he's an eyesore to look upon, he nevertheless means all the world to her.

Once everyone knows everyone else's name, Tanda ushers the newbies to the table. "You two sit and rest. Try to recover from that umm, heartfelt but turbulent rescue mission!" Then she turns to Ecko. "Come, child. Help me carry the food that I've prepared to the table. We can all get to know one another while we eat. We'll enjoy a nice, hot meal before we get down to the business of discussing what comes next."

So, grinning like a fool, she carries the heavy tray laden with food that is unfamiliar but will certainly be delicious, as is everything that the old woman had ever served her. Well, everything except the eyeball tea, that is. *That* was a horrific experience that she *never* wants to repeat.

"Oh yeah! I brought pizza!" she exclaims as she lays out the food and settles Boodark into his backpack booster-chair. She quickly fills his plate with a healthy portion of everything that their MiddlinMeal spread has to offer, but she watches his face as he leans in and suspiciously sniffs the strange triangle of ooey-gooey cheesy goodness.

His brilliant smile and the way his enormous cartoon eyes light up at his first hesitant bite make the risk that she'd taken by looking away from her evil twin long enough to snatch up the pies 100% worth it. Her little friend deserves every bit of happiness she can bring him… even if it's just in the form of lukewarm pizza.

Playlist for Lost Ecko

I do not own the rights to any of the listed music. This is just my personal playlist that I wanted to share with the readers.

·Prologue: Ecko Lost
Stay with Me~ Blue October
Head above Water~ Avril Lavigne
·Prologue: Samara Girls Just Want to Have Fun
Girls just want to have fun~ Cyndi Lauper
I want to do bad things with you~ Jace Everett
·Prologue: The Lokskell and Krispin
Sanctify Me~ In This Moment
·Roots of Sadness
Stand in the Rain~ Superchick
·Find a Happy Thought
So Far~ Olafur Arnalds
When your feet don't touch the ground~ Ellie Goulding
·Welcome to the Looney Bin
Monsters~ Ruelle
·The Horrible Wonders of the Sorrow Marshes
As the World Falls Down~ David Bowie (Labyrinth)
·Sex, Drugs, and Rock & Roll
Evil Boy~ Die Antwoord
Adrenalize Me~ In This Moment
Bad Girl~ Avril Lavigne & Marilyn Manson

Never Say Goodbye
Only Lost is Found~ Blue October Picking up pieces~ Blue October
·Pleasurable Pastimes
Shadow Realm~ Seraphim Shock
·Hissing Things, Blue Things, Strange Things, Rude Things

Truly Brave~ Sara Bareilles & Cyndi Lauper
·**Don't Mind the Blood, Dear**
The Purge~ In This Moment Sweet Dreams~ Marilyn Manson
·**She did WHAT in Her Cup?** Rival~ Ruelle

·**The Finer Things in Life**
Bad Guy~ Billie Eilish
I F**ked My Way to the Top~ Lana Del Rey

Niggles, Lessons, and SeeAll Visions
Illusions~ VNV Nation
·**We Hates Her/We Wants Her**
Hush~ Aviva
Sex Toy~ Seraphim Shock
Scream~ Avenged Sevenfold
·**Field of Screams and Broken Dreams**
Rabbit Hole~ Aviva
·**A Message for Father**
Richard Ramirez~ SKYND

·**The Tunnels to Hell**
Lullabye~ The Cure
·**The EverGlass**
Matches~ Letts
·**Two is Better than One**
Feeding the dark~ Evanescence
·**Harsh Truths and Lessons Learned**
Breathe No More~ Evanescence
·**Epilogue: The Lokskell**
Come to Daddy~ Aphex Twin
I Want You (She's so heavy) ~ The Beatles
·**Epilogue: Samara**
Monster~ Beth Crowley
Gasoline~ Halsey

·**Epilogue: Ecko**
Warrior~ Avril Lavigne